"Come on. Get wet with me."

Now, there was a tempting thought. Without thinking twice, Trent kicked off his shoes and socks, dropping them in the sand. He pulled up the legs of his jeans, and together he and Chloe stepped ankle-deep into the water.

"I'd love to go swimming," Chloe mused aloud.

"Feel free," Trent offered. "I'll even keep watch if you want to skinny-dip."

"Keep watch*ing*, you mean," she countered.

"That, too," he admitted with an unrepentant shrug. "Seriously, if you want to get in, go ahead. Nobody's around, it's one in the morning...and your little red ensemble could be mistaken for a bikini anyway."

"Ensemble? Oh, so you saw the bra, too?"

He grinned wickedly.

"I have absolutely no secrets left," she said with a disgruntled sigh. She kicked water at him, soaking the bottom part of his jeans.

Trent chuckled and splashed her back. Then, growing serious, he stepped closer until their bodies were separated by only an inch of moonlight. "Honey, seeing what you're wearing beneath your clothes is only making me more interested in seeing what's underneath it all...."

Dear Reader,

Imagine two gorgeous, hunky men—one safe (or so you think) and one outrageously daring and provocative. Now imagine not realizing that they're two different people...and getting involved with a twin you never knew existed! That's exactly what happens to Chloe Weston in *Two To Tangle*.

Chloe is a hardworking, *very* creative woman who is determined to find a nice guy. No daredevils need apply. So when she finds herself involved in a passionate weekend with Troy Langtree, a conservative, respectable retail store manager, she thinks she's found her man. Only, Troy is really *Trent*, Troy's twin brother. And Trent is anything but conservative.

But boy, is he hot!

Writing Chloe and Trent's story was a pure joy. I loved going all out with the humor and sensuality in this book, and I think I've found my favorite cast of secondary characters so far. I hope you enjoy it as much as I did. If so, let me know. You can write to me at P.O. Box 410787, Melbourne, FL 32941-0787, or e-mail me at lkelly@lesliekelly.com.

Happy reading,

Leslie Kelly

Books by Leslie Kelly

HARLEQUIN TEMPTATION
747—NIGHT WHISPERS
810—SUITE SEDUCTION
841—RELENTLESS
872—INTO THE FIRE

TWO TO TANGLE
Leslie Kelly

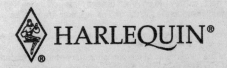

HARLEQUIN®

TORONTO • NEW YORK • LONDON
AMSTERDAM • PARIS • SYDNEY • HAMBURG
STOCKHOLM • ATHENS • TOKYO • MILAN • MADRID
PRAGUE • WARSAW • BUDAPEST • AUCKLAND

To my editor, Brenda Chin.
Thank you for telling me how much you loved
this idea from the very beginning. It gave me the
incentive and the determination to make sure
the story became all it could be.

And to my girls, Caitlin, Lauren and Megan.
I'm so glad you each have sisters.

ISBN 0-373-25982-4

TWO TO TANGLE

Copyright © 2002 by Leslie Kelly.

All rights reserved. Except for use in any review, the reproduction or
utilization of this work in whole or in part in any form by any electronic,
mechanical or other means, now known or hereafter invented, including
xerography, photocopying and recording, or in any information storage
or retrieval system, is forbidden without the written permission of the
publisher, Harlequin Enterprises Limited, 225 Duncan Mill Road,
Don Mills, Ontario, Canada M3B 3K9.

All characters in this book have no existence outside the imagination of
the author and have no relation whatsoever to anyone bearing the same
name or names. They are not even distantly inspired by any individual
known or unknown to the author, and all incidents are pure invention.

This edition published by arrangement with Harlequin Books S.A.

® and TM are trademarks of the publisher. Trademarks indicated with
® are registered in the United States Patent and Trademark Office, the
Canadian Trade Marks Office and in other countries.

Visit us at www.eHarlequin.com

Printed in U.S.A.

1

"OKAY, LOVERBOY, I'm ready. I've been thinking about this all week. Now we're alone. It's time to get you out of all these uptight clothes and into something a little more comfortable."

Not expecting a reply, and, of course, not receiving one, Chloe Weston reached for the buckle of an expensive black leather belt and deftly unfastened it. A quick flick of her fingers undid the button at the waist of a pair of men's designer trousers. Finding the tab of the zipper, she lowered it gingerly. The metallic hiss of the zipper's teeth broke the heavy silence of the room, followed by a wisp of fabric as the size thirty-two, charcoal-gray pants fell.

Dropping to her knees, she reached for the elastic waistband of a pair of fitted, white boxer briefs. She tugged them down in one stroke, then sat back and stared. After several long moments, she sighed.

"It's Friday night. I'm a reasonably attractive, single, twenty-something woman and I've just taken off a man's clothes." Rubbing a weary hand over her brow, she muttered, "Too bad you're as anatomically correct as a Ken doll."

The mannequin didn't respond. Nor did its female counterpart, which stood behind Chloe in the darkened front display window of Langtree's Department Store.

What a way to spend a Friday night. Alone in a deserted, exclusive store in Boca Raton, Florida. Surrounded by designer clothes, ridiculously expensive leather goods, gaudy, pretentious jewelry...with a bunch of plastic mannequins for company.

Shrugging, Chloe referred to her notes to consider the positions of the mannequins for the next week's display. Fridays were changeover nights for the store's main front windows. A big deal, especially lately, since the store manager had finally started giving her some leeway to be more daring with the displays. Before tonight, she'd slipped her own creative touches only in the store's rear windows near the service department, never the huge ones bracketing the main entrance.

Though she'd worked for Langtree's for only six weeks, Chloe knew her creations had already drawn some attention. No, the managing director of the store, Troy Langtree, hadn't been too happy when she'd gotten a little carried away with a spring bathing suit display, and left the itty-bitty top of a string bikini dangling from the plastic fingers of a randy-looking male mannequin. But the public had loved it. So much so that Langtree had finally agreed to listen to her ideas for the store's main entrance area.

As she reached for the zipper of the cocktail dress still adorning the female mannequin, Chloe heard the rumbling of an engine. She peeked through the dark drapes covering the window, watching as a large, black pickup truck came to a stop directly outside at the curb in front of the store. Glancing at her watch and noting it was after midnight, she bit her lip. The night security guard had to be wandering around somewhere. But he could be just about anyplace in the three-story building. With her luck—and with his reputation—he was probably snoozing on a Serta mattress in the bedding department upstairs. That left her alone to deal with the gang of robbers who'd be throwing a bench through this very window at any moment now so they could raid the nearby jewelry cases.

Crouching lower, Chloe watched as one man—not a gang—emerged from the truck. Then, when the driver passed beneath a streetlamp, she got a good look at his face and his thick chestnut-brown hair. She breathed a sigh of relief. "Troy Langtree."

The man was probably coming to check up on her, still fretting over what she might do to his precious windows. "Why do the gorgeous ones have to be so anal?" Chloe mused aloud with a sigh. He was handsome, no question, but about as loose and laid-back as Al Gore at a press briefing.

Troy had caught her eye more than once since she'd started working for his family-owned department store. He was, after all, single, successful, and a complete hunk. In some respects Troy was everything Chloe wanted in a man. The grapevine said he didn't carouse or womanize, worked hard, was intelligent and stable. Just the opposite of the few men Chloe had ever dated—and also the opposite of her own father, two stepfathers, and her mother's succession of boyfriends.

Exactly what she was looking for.

Or so she'd thought at first. But Chloe could not stand a man who didn't smile, who found no joy in *anything*. There was such a thing as being too mature and settled. From what she'd heard, his only passion was running—the man reportedly lived on the beach and liked to run for miles every morning. Which probably explained his physique, not to mention his tan.

They somehow didn't go with the image of the three-piece-suit office mole he appeared to be the rest of the time.

.What it came down to was that Troy Langtree, while attractive, appeared to be completely lacking in a simple appreciation of life. And no matter how much Chloe longed for a nice guy—an established, professional, hard-working nice guy—he had to at least know how to laugh.

Watching curiously, Chloe noted Troy was not dressed in his usual conservative, navy-blue suit. In fact, he wore—of all things—jeans. Very tight, worn jeans that hugged some fine, firm male thighs, not to mention outlined a particularly great butt that Chloe had never even noticed before.

As Troy moved out of the pool of light cast by the overhead streetlamp, a flash of summer heat lightning silently lit the sky. Chloe saw a dark frown on his handsome face and thought she saw him mutter a curse word. When he crouched down next to his truck and poked at a tire, she understood why. "He's got a flat."

Chloe watched as Troy retrieved a jack and a spare tire from the back of the truck, then lay down on the ground to jack up the truck. Funny, she would have pegged him for a card-carrying AAA member. She found herself somewhat impressed that the prep-school king knew how to change a tire.

He got the flat tire off within a matter of minutes. Chloe, still hidden behind the heavy drapes blocking the view inside the store window, fought her basic urge to go help. Exiting the store would involve a call to the security guard, who'd have to turn off the alarm system and unlock the doors to let her out. By the time she found the lazy guard, Troy would probably already be finished anyway.

Chloe saw a few drops of rain hit the top of the window and slide down it, creating curvy lines on the thick glass. Troy didn't appear to notice. "Better hurry up, buddy," she whispered, her own breath creating a misty circle on the sliver of window exposed between the tiny gap in the drapes.

Troy tossed the flat tire up onto the sidewalk, and Chloe paused to appreciate the thick breadth of his arms in his tight T-shirt. "Okay, so the stiff works out," she admitted aloud. He'd have to. His upper arms looked about the same circumference as her thighs. Her mouth went dry.

Troy wiped his hands on his jeans, leaving a streak of greasy black dirt on one hip, but apparently not even noticing. He went back to work but then suddenly stopped and held up one hand. Watching him wince, then suck his pinky into his mouth, she knew he must have hurt himself.

The sight of Troy Langtree's beautifully curved lips wrapped around his own fingertip made time stop for at least five seconds, long enough for her to gulp and picture those fine lips wrapped around some part of *her* anatomy.

He remained oblivious to her presence as she continued to peer hungrily at him from behind the shrouded window. Retrieving a spare tire, he put it on the truck as the misting rain increased its tempo and began coming down in earnest. Troy had just tightened the last nut when the light rain became a typical Florida summer deluge. She half expected him to dive into the truck for cover, or run to the front of the store for protection beneath the awning.

He did neither. Instead, as she watched, her heart stuck somewhere in her throat, he stood, lifted his face to the sky, and began to laugh. His cotton T-shirt soaked up the water as voraciously as a dry sponge, and she watched it grow darker and tighter against his body. It soon clung to him like a second skin, hugging and outlining a chest that went on for days.

Just when she thought she couldn't possibly take another moment of this voyeurism and decided to turn away, Chloe saw Troy reach for the bottom hem of his shirt. She stayed still, nose on glass, eyes wide and unblinking, wondering if he was really about to do what he appeared to be doing.

With his face still lifted skyward, Troy tugged the shirt up. *He's taking it off!* It took forever, it seemed, for the wet cotton fabric to separate itself from his skin. Chloe didn't move a muscle as she watched, breathless and more than a little excited. Then Troy pulled the shirt off all the way, tossed it into the back of his truck, and stood barechested in the rain.

"Whoa, mama," Chloe managed to whisper. His bare, thick chest rippled and flexed with muscle, moving with fluid grace and strength. Chloe's fingers pressed against the window, the coolness of glass feeling nothing like she imagined all that hot male flesh would feel.

She whimpered as Troy slowly raised both his thick, strong arms, extending them straight out to his sides. He looked graceful and powerful all at the same time. Obviously still savoring the rain pelting his face, he slowly turned in a circle toward her, as if wanting to soak up the water or simply dance in appreciation of the elements.

She drew back instinctively, even though she knew

there was no way he could see her wide eyes and drooling mouth between the few inches of parted drapes in the darkened store window. Especially not with the rain and the tinted glass.

No, he couldn't see her. But she could definitely see him. Chloe found herself very thankful for the street-lamp on the sidewalk near where he stood which illuminated him from head to toe. Leaning close again, she saw heavy drops of rain land on his shoulders and ride those long, lean sinews of muscle down his body. Water pooled at the waistband of his tight jeans and darkened the fabric to an even deeper blue.

Troy didn't appear to care. He seemed almost pagan in his sensual appreciation of the elements. Pagan. Powerful. Perfectly, mouth-wateringly, male.

A man fully in tune with his senses. A man savoring the cool relief of a summer night's rain against his overheated skin. A man laughing at the elements.

Definitely a man she wanted to get to know better.

BY THE END OF TWO WEEKS, Chloe was convinced Troy Langtree was a vampire who only came alive after sundown. She hadn't seen a single hint of that spectacular, earthy male since the night she'd watched him change his tire then soak up the rain. Heaven knew she'd searched for him, during meetings or when they'd casually bump into one another in the store. But all she'd seen was the tight-lipped, buttoned-down Troy Langtree who'd hired her. Not the jeans-wearing tire changer. Certainly not the pagan rain worshipper.

"You're sure you don't need me to come along and keep you company in that big, fancy hotel?"

Chloe shook off the memory of Troy Langtree, shirtless and wet, and turned her attention to her friend and co-worker. Lowering her pen to the surface of her desk, she said, "Sorry, Jess, I wish you could. But I'm surprised Langtree even approved the travel expense for me to attend this conference. I don't think he'd spring for you, even if you're the best darned perfume sprayer in the state."

Jess Carruthers, the perfume sprayer in question, wiped off the surface of a stool in the corner of Chloe's office and gingerly sat down on it.

"Office" was probably too generous a word. Actually, Chloe worked in an old stockroom in the darkest recesses of Langtree's. The twelve-by-twenty room still occasionally doubled as a holding area for shipments during the holiday season. It housed boxes, crates, old sales circulars, racks of clothes Chloe planned to use for the displays, even ancient, musty plans for the two renovation jobs the store had undergone in the past few decades. Not to mention limbs, heads and other plastic mannequin body parts splayed about like evidence of a mass murderer's rampage.

"How you can stand being locked away in here all evening is beyond me." Jess wrinkled her nose and coughed into her fist.

"I like it. Besides, I'd rather deal with dust motes than go home every night smelling of thirty designer perfumes."

Jess rolled her eyes. "Tell me about it. My poor dog doesn't know who's going to walk in the door every night under all those Estée Lauder and Tommy Hilfiger smells. Still, don't you get lonely tucked away back here?"

"Nope," Chloe replied. "It's a great place to work. Few interruptions. No distractions." *No hunky, nearly*

*naked guys standing right outside the window keeping me
from getting my display done until 3:00 a.m.*

Truthfully, Chloe felt right at home in her office. She
liked cubbyholes. Liked little places she could call her
own and in which she could hide away—to draw, to
create, to plan. Sam Brighton, the marketing director of
the store, who was also Chloe's supervisor, had
seemed almost sheepish when showing her to her
workspace the first day on the job two months before.
But Chloe had immediately loved the dark, cluttered
room. It had a lot of history to soak up, a lot of silence
in which to work. And blessed, delightful privacy—
something Chloe had often found to be in short supply
in her life.

"If I knew you'd get to go to conventions at places
like the Dolphin Island Resort and Country Club I'd
stay in the store all night putting clothes on plastic people," Jess said with a heartfelt sigh.

"There's more to it than that." Chloe thought of the
hours and hours she spent scouring the store, looking
for the perfect dress, the ideal string of beads, the just-
right accessory. Not to mention the time at home,
thinking, planning, mentally searching for the never-
before-attempted display that would pack the store
and get her noticed. "The actual window dressing is
the cake part of the job."

"I know," Jess said sheepishly. "I wasn't putting you
down. I think you do an amazing job."

"I guess all those years of working in retail have finally paid off," Chloe admitted with a grin. "Not to
mention dressing my Barbie dolls!"

"I was always more into the great big Barbie head
with the phony wipe-off makeup and the hair that

never curled so I usually cut it off a week after getting her," Jess said with a shrug.

Chloe snorted a laugh. "Looks like we wound up with our dream jobs."

"Not exactly. I'm not doing hair and makeup at Universal Studios in Hollywood."

"And I'm sure not dressing in designer gowns for my big modeling career in Paris."

"A five-foot-three supermodel. There's something you don't see every day."

Chloe shrugged. "Who said a six-year-old's dreams had to be realistic? Anyway, I am not complaining. This is a pretty good job. It beats slinging hamburgers at some fast-food chain."

Jess nodded. "Absolutely. And I'm glad you get to go to this conference, even if it has the gossipers working overtime."

Chloe shrugged, knowing more than a few eyebrows had probably shot up in the executive offices when it was announced that she, a new and lowly window and display dresser, was getting an all-expense paid trip to the south Florida retailers and merchandisers meeting at a pricey Fort Lauderdale-area resort. "I think Sam pulled some strings to get me the travel expense money because he knows it'll help me at school. I mean, it was turned down at first. I was as surprised as anyone when I heard Troy had changed his mind and told Sam to send me!"

"I guess the newspaper photo didn't hurt," Jess said, grinning. "I was there, remember? I saw the crowds five people deep coming to see your window when it showed up in the *Boca Gazette*—including old lady Langtree, right? Hey, maybe she's the fairy godmother who got the expense approved."

Chloe smiled, remembering the delight and surprise she'd felt when she'd spotted a photograph of one of her display windows gracing the "What's Happening This Weekend" section of the local paper. The caption had read, "Langtree's front windows provide a fun and sassy glimpse at the summer ahead!"

That was the window she'd been working on when she'd seen Troy Langtree changing his tire. Somehow, after he'd pulled away that night, never even coming into the store, all her creative juices had really started flowing. She'd abandoned her original design. Raiding the sportswear, housewares, men's, ladies' and electronics departments, she'd created a window display with a cutely dressed, intrigued female peeking at a hunky, bare-chested male mannequin dancing in a streamer-and-fan-created rainstorm.

Some of the older crowd imagined she'd been inspired by Gene Kelly tap dancing in the rain. Truthfully, the only inspiration she'd needed was Troy Langtree, shirtless, wet and dazzling.

Troy hadn't even commented on the content of the window. She didn't think he'd ever made the connection, never suspected she'd seen him that night. But he'd certainly noticed the publicity, not to mention the crowds. As had his grandmother, who'd requested a private meeting with Chloe the day the picture came out. Troy had approved her travel expenditure to the conference two days later.

She hadn't heard yet what Troy thought of her latest display, the one still in the front windows. Somehow, after searching in vain for the man who existed beneath the conservative suits and bored expression, she had again gotten a little carried away the previous Friday night. Using the same male and female mannequins from the rainstorm scene, she'd managed to create a woman's daydream. The female stood face-to-face with the boring but smartly dressed male while fantasizing about his half-undressed body double, who stood draped in dreamy folds of gauze in a back corner of the window.

One of her better efforts, she believed.

"Maybe you're right," Chloe finally said. "Mrs. Langtree was awfully friendly when we met, especially for someone I'd heard was a white-haired piranha."

Jess shivered. "Better you than me. She scares me. I'd rather fly beneath the radar."

"And I window-decorated myself right into the line of fire."

"Just don't tick her off."

Chloe shrugged, still unsure why the elderly matriarch of the Langtree family had been so interested in meeting Chloe after the picture was in the paper. Or why she'd stared at her so intently and asked questions about her personal life. Then again, maybe all rich people were weird, nosy and thought themselves entitled to ask their junior staff members if they were single, if they smoked, and if they wanted children. She'd seemed pleased with Chloe's answers: Yes. No. And someday.

"I don't know why you're working here doing these windows, anyway," Jess continued. "You're almost finished school. You'll get a great job as a buyer or merchandiser as soon as you graduate."

"Unless I want my mother, sister and I to live on canned ravioli until that day, I have to keep some money coming in," Chloe retorted.

Jess suddenly bit her lip, looking sheepish. "Of course you do. Your mom still hasn't found a job?"

Chloe shook her head and turned away, not comfortable talking about her family's financial situation with anyone, not even a friend as loyal and supportive as Jess.

"Well, then," Jess said, "I'm glad you get to go on this 'business trip.' It'll be like a minivacation. After working so hard at night while going to school during the day, heaven knows you need it."

That was a nice thought, but Chloe didn't view this trip to the luxury resort as any kind of vacation. She intended to use the conference to soak up every bit of information she could about the retail industry in south Florida. She needed the exposure, experience and future career connections the conference offered, particularly since she was already four years behind her peers in getting her bachelor's degree.

It had taken several years of working in retail jobs full-time after high school to raise the money for college. Sure, she'd been offered scholarships—but scholarships wouldn't pay rent on her family's small house. Chloe's salary did.

Her mother's last job, in a legal office, had seemed like a dream come true a few years ago when Chloe had finally been able to start school full-time. Chloe knew her mother had tried to stick it out for her family's sake. She'd remained employed for three and a half years—the longest Jeanine Weston-Jackson-Smith had ever held a job in her life. During that time, she'd helped Chloe with her tuition. Plus, between the two of them, they'd managed to save a nice nest egg so her half sister, Morgan, wouldn't have to do as Chloe had done. Her little sister would start at a good private col-

lege when she graduated high school next year, no
matter what.

But for now, her mother was again happily unemployed, throwing herself into her latest artistic en-
deavor: ceramic lawn ornaments. And then again,
there was her most recent romantic relationship, with a
guy she'd met at a health food store.

Whenever the money got too tight, her mother
would wistfully bring up Morgan's college account,
but Chloe had made her promise they wouldn't touch
it. No way was she going to let her brilliant sister miss
out on any educational opportunity provided to her.
Jeanine had, despite the gleam in her eye when she
looked at the bank statement, agreed.

So for now it was again up to Chloe to support her
mother and younger sister as best she could. If she
could handle this night job until the end of the year,
she'd be able to graduate by Christmas and maybe
have a good-paying, full-time position by the New
Year—just in time to sock away the rest of the money
she'd need to send Morgan to school the following fall.

The connections she could make on this trip might
help that wish come true. But Jess was also right—she
could definitely use a couple of days lounging by a
pool at a pricey resort.

"Maybe you'll meet some fab man who'll make you
forget all your problems."

Chloe shrugged. "I'm beginning to think there's no
such thing as a fab man." She dropped her chin into
her palm. "The young, gorgeous, carefree ones only
seem to want *one* thing. The older, responsible, successful ones are either taken or impossibly arrogant. The
older carefree ones are usually gay."

"What about the young, responsible, successful ones," Jess said eagerly.

Chloe snorted. "Like Troy Langtree."

"I get your point." Jess sighed. "He gives new meaning to the word 'stiff.'" As if just hearing the sexy underlying meaning in her comment, her friend covered her lips with her fingers and began to giggle uncontrollably.

Chloe felt a flush rise in her cheeks. "He's not what I'm searching for. A guy who can hold down a job would be wonderful—but he has to at least be able to laugh at a good joke. I've never seen Troy Langtree crack a smile that wasn't prompted somehow by finances or sales figures."

"Well, you're right in terms of here at work," Jess said, thoughtfully tapping her finger on her cheek. "But I've been here a few months longer than you, and I have heard rumors about his after-hour activities. He might *not* actually be the conservative, respectable man he pretends to be here at work. Away from the store, he may not be exactly what he seems."

Chloe knew better than most that he wasn't what he seemed. Unfortunately, she hadn't seen him after hours in two weeks. "There are days when he's so stuffy, I can't picture him taking off his six-hundred-dollar suit even to barbecue in his backyard." *Unless, of course, he's changing a tire!*

"But I think I'd be able to overlook a lot of arrogance to come home to a man who looks like *that* every night."

Chloe didn't reply. Troy had been on her mind enough already; she didn't need to start talking about him to another man-hungry woman.

"Maybe you'll get lucky this weekend," Jess continued. "Maybe the rumor mill is right and he's a different man outside the store. He might just sweep you off your feet during the conference."

Chloe dropped a long, ivory-colored plastic leg onto her right foot, then hissed and hunched over in pain. "What are you talking about?" she finally managed to gasp. Wincing, she hobbled over to her desk and leaned against it to take her weight off her squashed toes.

"Well, you know, he's going to be there, too."

"No he's not. This meeting is more for marketers, buyers, and P.R. types. Not store owners."

Jess raised a perfectly plucked, heavily penciled eyebrow. "Yes, Chloe, of course he is. He goes every year. Besides, I heard him talking to his secretary about it this afternoon. I was trying to get him to sample some new Pico cologne, which, by the way, is so sweet and flowery, if I went out with a guy who was wearing it, I'd be checking for bra straps."

Chloe rolled her eyes. "Get back to Troy."

"He's going to the conference, too. You didn't know?"

She shook her head. "I had no idea. Is he going to be staying there? At the same hotel?"

"Well, sure." A smile crossed Jess's face as she obviously noticed Chloe's consternation. "Oh, so you *have* noticed him and you *are* interested, hmm?"

"Noticed, yeah. But I'm *not* interested. Like I said, he's not my type."

"Not your type for the long-term, maybe," Jess said, obviously warming up to her subject. She leaned closer, conspiratorially. "But why not have a sexy little fling while you're both out of town?"

"A sexy little fling? I don't do sexy little flings." *My*

mother is the sexy little fling person in my family. "And I seriously doubt Troy Langtree does, either."

"Just because you haven't doesn't mean you can't," Jess said. "Isn't it time to give yourself a break? Indulge in something delicious for a change? Okay, you know you and the stuffy one have nothing in common and couldn't possibly get seriously involved. So what? Nothing to stop you from getting mindless and fabulous in bed with him for a night or two."

Chloe tried to close her ears. What Jess suggested was simply impossible. Even if she was willing, Troy Langtree had never given her any indication he was attracted to her.

"Heck, I'd seduce him in a heartbeat if he appeared the least bit interested," Jess continued. "Unfortunately, judging by the women I've heard he's dated, I suspect he likes curvy, stacked bundles—like you—rather than stick-thin Amazons like me. Why don't you stop by the makeup counter on your way out and I'll get you some samples for this weekend?"

"Forget it," Chloe said with a snort. "This is about business, not pleasure. I'm not going to get personal with Troy Langtree, the managing director of this store."

Of course, if Troy Langtree the pagan tire changer shows up, I might just be persuaded.

"Okay, suit yourself," Jess said as she stood and prepared to leave the office. "But remember, if you keep putting off finding Mr. Right until after you finish school and get your mother and sister taken care of, you might find he's already married...or old and in need of Viagra!"

IN SPITE OF THE MERCILESS Friday afternoon sun sizzling against the bare skin on his back, Trent Langtree decided to go for one more walk of the resort grounds before calling it quits for the day. He'd been on-site since daybreak; it was now five. A long day, but a productive one. This job was definitely worth some long days—to Trent and to all his crew. Besides, long, hard days outside were still better than working in the family-owned department store like his twin brother Troy did.

The $200,000 job at the Dolphin Island Resort and Country Club was the biggest project his three-year-old landscaping company had ever landed and he was being damned ruthless in making sure it went off without a hitch. His workers weren't complaining too much about the long hours and demand for perfection. They knew as well as he how much was at stake with this job. And every one of them had a bonus riding on the outcome.

The stakes were even higher for Trent. The money would be nice, would keep the company in the black for a while. But even more important was the exposure and future clientele this work could bring in. The success of his company, The Great Outdoors, depended upon breaking into the upper-crust south Florida market.

"You could do that with a few phone calls," Jason, his most reliable crew foreman, liked to tell him. True. A few calls to his former friends and colleagues would probably bring in all the exclusive work The Great Outdoors could handle. But Trent didn't want it that way.

When he'd walked out of his grandmother's house, he'd told her he'd make it on his own—without the family name, or business, to prop him up. She hadn't been happy, but Trent had refused to back down. Her pleas and tears hadn't changed his mind; certainly her threats hadn't.

Trent loved the old woman, and the rest of the family, but he'd given them five years of his adult life trying to do things their way. Five years of wearing suits to work. Five years of going to meetings, trying to care about the buyers' predictions for the spring lines so the family-owned department store, Langtree's, would keep bringing in the almighty dollar.

Five years knowing he would never be happy doing what his family wanted him to do.

Trent had even gone by the store one rainy, miserable night a few weeks ago, just to remind himself of what was at stake. Like a bad omen, he'd ended up with a flat tire, which had amused his brother Troy to no end when he'd told him about it the next day at a family gathering. Troy had quipped that Grandmother probably set out the nails intentionally to trap Trent in the parking lot. When Trent had admitted he'd ended his tire changing with a refreshing bare-chested shower in the rain right outside the front windows of the store, his grandmother had not been amused. Then again, his grandmother was seldom amused by anything except sales and promotions.

Troy was cut out for that life. Troy liked the conservative, responsible atmosphere. He liked order and schedule and deadlines. Troy liked wearing ties to work, for God's sake! He definitely liked the money, which enabled him to keep up with the constant succession of women in his life.

Trent liked the heat of the sun on his back. Its blinding light in his eyes. The sound of the wind whipping palm trees during a storm. The lap of waves rolling onto a deserted beach and the smell of freshly cut grass on a summer afternoon. He liked his hands in the earth.

None of which made him the least bit qualified to take his place in the family business. All of which made his new venture—a landscaping company—his dream job.

No one had really understood. Not his grandmother, nor his retired parents. Not Troy. Certainly not Jennifer, the woman he'd thought loved him. His devoted fiancée. She'd worn his ring for less than twenty-four hours after he told her he was leaving the family business to "cut grass."

"Some things are better discovered early on," he muttered aloud. Like that your fiancée was a money-grubbing social climber who would go after your twin brother as soon as she realized you weren't going to be keeping her in Mercedes convertibles.

His broken engagement had been one of life's interesting lessons. He'd cared at first. Not anymore. He liked his life now, liked waking up in the morning and facing the day of honest work ahead. Trent planned to keep doing exactly that. But only if he could make it pay—and soon. His grandmother wasn't going to be put off forever.

"Until your thirtieth birthday," she'd said. "If you're not a complete financial success by then, promise me you'll come back to the store."

And, like an idiot, he had. He'd even signed a legally binding document to that effect. Three years ago, feeling like he'd explode from frustration if he had to sit through one more meeting with buyers and managers, he'd have agreed to just about anything. Now, with his thirtieth birthday—and his promised deadline—looming just weeks away, Trent was feeling the pressure.

This job could make him. It could also, however, break him. Considering the per-day penalty for late completion, and the narrow profit margin he'd budgeted in order to get the work, he knew there was no room for error.

As he walked over the newly sodded area his crew had installed earlier, Trent glanced up and saw heavy, late afternoon clouds rolling in. Typical. He inhaled, sniffing the electric scent of the stormy sky, liking it, knowing the newly planted grass would soak up the moisture and take root in the soil. He sucked in a deep breath of ocean air, cooled by the impending storm, and smiled, savoring the elements.

But standing outside near a Florida beach during a thunderstorm wasn't exactly wise. Waving goodbye to his crew, who'd loaded the last of the trucks and were preparing to depart for the day, Trent turned and dashed toward the main building of the hotel. Thankfully, he'd booked a room for himself for the weekend. He had important meetings scheduled with the contractor in charge of the new wing under construction, and he also wanted to personally supervise the critical work his crew had done on the side lawn. He planned to spend a few days here, on-site, for quality control. The resort had even picked up the tab for his room, a real surprise given the previously miserly attitude of the general manager.

Since he'd sunk every penny he had into his business for the past few years, Trent had no money for vacations or ritzy hotels. Not that this was a vacation—it was definitely going to be a work weekend. Still, there were worse places to work than a lush resort with golf courses, pools, spas, and hundreds of yards of pristine Florida beach.

As thick plops of rain fell from the sky, another flash of lightning cracked overhead. Trent reached the pool courtyard which overlooked the beach. The area was nearly deserted, most of the hotel guests probably having dashed inside as soon as the thick storm clouds had begun rolling in off the ocean.

One person remained.

"Crazy woman," Trent muttered as he watched a curly-haired brunette languorously rise from a lounge chair on the far side of the pool. Apparently oblivious to the metallic taste in the air, the drops of moisture beginning to reach the ground and the rumbling of thunder in the distance, the woman didn't even begin to fold her brightly colored beach towel. Instead, she turned toward the ocean, which roiled and churned a few dozen yards off the pool deck.

Trent watched her, noting the pronounced curviness of her body in the skimpy coal-black bikini she wore. "Nice," he murmured, liking the line of her hips flaring below a small waist, and the smooth, tanned legs and back. Her thick, curly mop of light-brown hair was clasped loosely at the nape of her neck and fell to just below her shoulders.

He suddenly wondered what color her eyes were. And whether, as she stared at the churning ocean and the heavy gray skies, she was smiling.

"You'd better come in before the storm gets worse," someone called. Trent glanced over to see a pool boy stacking chairs under a covered awning. He'd obviously been speaking to the woman, but she paid no attention. Instead, as Trent watched, she spread her arms out to her sides, dropped her head back, and lifted her face to the sky.

Trent watched, fascinated, wondering who she was, and, more important, why he found her so appealing when he had never even seen her face.

Then she turned, slowly, as if loathe to gather her things and go inside. From the other side of the pool, she noticed him. Her eyes met his. And she smiled the most gloriously joyful smile he'd ever seen in his life.

2

CHLOE DIDN'T KNOW HOW, didn't know why, but as she stared toward the other side of the pool, she knew she'd found her pagan again. Troy stood shirtless, wearing only tight, dusty jeans, watching her from a covered area near a closed outdoor bar. His stare was intensely curious, and she almost reached out a hand, crazily wanting to invite him to dance with her in the rain.

However, when another sharp bolt of lightning ripped the sky, followed almost immediately by a loud crack of thunder, she decided that wasn't such a great idea. As she bent to gather her things, she knew without looking that he'd come over to help. The storm wouldn't intimidate him at all.

Then he was there, retrieving her book, lotion and sunglasses, and shoving them into her beach bag. Chloe didn't even have time to yank on her beach cover-up before Troy grabbed her by the arm and tried to tug her toward the building.

"Next to a pool isn't the best place to be during a thunderstorm," he said, his voice raised over the wind that had whipped up into a frenzy in the past few moments.

Chloe nodded agreement, stopping only to grab her sandals before dashing with him toward the hotel entrance. She was not a bit surprised to see the laughter on his lips as they burst into the building just as the rain turned torrential.

"We made it in the nick of time." He shook his head hard, sending droplets of water from his hair against her already wet face, throat and chest. The contact was innocent, yet somehow intimate.

As he pushed back his thick, damp hair, Chloe caught a glimpse of something gold on his earlobe and realized for the first time that he wore a small pierced earring. She would never in a million years have guessed such a thing about Troy Langtree—she'd certainly never seen him wear it at work! Now, all she could think was how interesting it might be to nibble the bit of flesh beneath the gold stud. To tug on it with her teeth. To touch it with her tongue.

She shuddered.

"You okay?"

She nodded, still panting for breath. They both leaned against the papered wall of the hotel hallway inside the glass door. "I'm fine, thanks," Chloe finally managed to say. "I like storms. If it weren't for the lightning, I'd love to go down to the beach right now."

He nodded. "Feeling the strong, salty wind."

"Hearing the pounding surf."

"Getting the ocean taste in your mouth and feeling certain you've never breathed richer air."

"Sounds heavenly," she said with a sigh.

"Most people would think we're crazy." Then he laughed at himself. "But I have been called worse. How about a rain check? When there's no lightning."

"I'd like that."

As her ragged breathing returned to normal, Chloe paused to glance at him, and found herself face to collarbone with his amazing male chest. All bare. All flat and tanned and toned. He was broad in the shoulders, powerful across the chest, narrow and lean at the waist. Chloe caught her bottom lip between her teeth as she let her gaze travel lower, to the swirl of dark, curling hair on his muscled belly, until it disappeared into the waistband of his tight, wet jeans.

Exactly how long has it been since I've had sex?

She finally shook her head to clear her mind of all the erotic images invading it. Struggling for nonchalance, she risked one more glance at his bare chest. "Lose your shirt?"

He obviously noticed her staring. He smiled, a devastating, flirtatious smile she'd never once beheld on Troy Langtree's lips. Her heart skipped a few more beats, as much from his smile as from the intensity in those emerald-green eyes of his.

"Too hot outside. Of course, you're not exactly dressed either."

She followed his warm stare and glanced down at her body. Her bikini top, which had seemed almost modest in comparison to some she'd seen out by the pool earlier, now seemed too tight. The curves of her breasts pushed high above the fabric, rising and falling as she took deeper breaths. Her skin puckered with gooseflesh in the air-conditioned hallway. There was no mistaking the tightness of her nipples, right below the edge of her top.

Returning her attention to him, she saw Troy's much-too-kissable lips part and his eyes narrow as he continued to study her. Chloe nearly shuddered. "I didn't have a chance to put on my cover-up," she whispered.

He slowly shook his head. "Don't bother on my account."

She should. She knew she should. She was holding the darn thing in her fingertips; it would be easy enough to slip it on over her nearly naked, cold and damp body.

But Chloe couldn't move. Couldn't lift her hand. Couldn't keep a single coherent thought in her head. Troy's gaze moved higher, zeroing in on her face—her lips. *He's going to kiss me.*

"At the risk of sounding like a jerk with a pickup line, I have to tell you something. You have a *great* smile."

Smile? Yeah, like the moronic one she wore right now at the mental image of him dragging her into his arms and pressing that amazing mouth onto hers. Just the thought of feeling this man's arms around her, his hands on her waist, his tongue dancing with her own, and she went weak-legged and brainless.

"Thank you," she murmured. Then she tried to make a joke, tried to lighten the heavy atmosphere by referring to his normally reserved attitude. "So do you. Though, I certainly have never seen very much of it."

A hotel employee, the one who'd been stacking lounge chairs before the storm, walked toward them in the long, silent corridor. Chloe took a quick step back, trying to pull herself away mentally, as well as physically, from Troy's strong, sensual lure. She glanced around, but her eyes kept returning to him. His tanned, handsome face. The curve of his lips. The line of his jaw. The perfection of his bare torso. Even his hands. *His hands! Why have I never noticed the strength of his hands?*

"I guess I should go back to my room and change for the dinner banquet," Chloe finally managed to whisper as she noticed the amused, appraising glance they got from the passing pool boy.

"Meet me later. After your banquet."

She shouldn't. Something was happening here that had nothing to do with the store, or the retailers' conference. This was elemental, like the storm tossing the awning around outside. She should stop, back up, take a deep breath and remember what was important. School, job and family. Not a man. Not a gorgeous, to-die-for man who took her breath away.

She nodded. "Okay." Then she widened her eyes. *Who said that? Chloe, you idiot.*

"In the bar? At ten?"

Still having a mental argument over the stupidity of her actions, Chloe murmured, "I'll be there."

"Then it's a date."

A date? A date with the managing director? The guy who could toss you out on your rear at a moment's notice? Are you insane?

Maybe. But, damn, insanity had never felt so good.

Catching sight of the face of her waterproof watch, Chloe gasped at the time. "I have to go," she said. "Don't you, too?"

He raised a quizzical brow.

"I'll see you in a little while," she said, not waiting for his reply. Chloe clutched her bag close to her chest, turned and hurried away toward the elevator, fighting against her urge to look back at him one more time.

It didn't matter. Whether she looked back or not, she knew he watched her every step of the way. The excitement coursing through her body was all the proof she needed of that.

As she punched the button for the elevator, she

found herself softly repeating Jess's words. "Mindless and fabulous."

TRENT DIDN'T REALIZE until after the curvy brunette boarded the elevator that he hadn't learned her name. He chuckled, knowing he'd probably appeared as besotted as a teenager. But she'd agreed to meet him anyway. Later tonight he'd find out her name. Her name—not to mention everything else about her.

Though he'd been hit by a bolt of attraction watching her from behind as she stared at the stormy sky, Trent was even more interested now that he'd seen the rest of her. Her curly mane of light-brown hair surrounded a soft, heart-shaped face with blue eyes he thought he could get lost in. Her laughter, her obvious joy in the elements, her sense of humor—all intrigued him.

And the woman did some damn fine things to a black bikini.

Yes. This weekend of work was definitely looking up. After all, there wasn't much landscaping to be done after six o'clock at night. He had tonight and tomorrow night all to himself. To get to know her a *lot* better.

Trent couldn't remember the last time he'd felt as instantly attracted to a woman as he had today. It had been ages since he'd had the time to even date, much less get involved with someone. His business had been a twenty-four/seven commitment since the day he'd started it. Funny how having to pay rent for the first time in his life had made work more important than anything else.

He refused to think his broken engagement was the reason he hadn't allowed himself to get more than passingly interested in a woman in the past three years. Sex, yeah. That was easily available. But some-one he actually wanted to get to know? Well, that hadn't happened in a long time.

The mere idea that he was thinking along those lines startled him. No, the timing wasn't great—it sucked, in fact. The last thing he needed during these last critical weeks of this project was to get distracted by a curvy brunette with a heart-breaking smile. But Trent had never been one to let what he *needed* prevent him from going after what he *wanted*. Right now, he very much wanted *her*.

As he walked down the corridor, he suddenly wished he'd asked for her room number, in case she got cold feet and decided not to come tonight after all.

"She'll come," he told himself. Remembering the sight of her standing in the rain, he knew the woman was a risk-taker at heart. Much like himself. *She'll come.*

AT 10:05, CHLOE STOOD IN her hotel room, chewing a hole into her lip, staring at her own reflection above the bathroom sink. Troy hadn't shown up at the dinner banquet, so it had been several hours since she'd seen him. Yes, she'd had several hours in which to totally chicken out on their date in the bar.

"You can't do this. You know that, right?" she told the mirror.

It's just a drink.

"Baloney, it's not just a drink. You were there—you felt the heat, Chloe Weston. You meet him tonight and you might be with him until tomorrow morning."

Is that such a bad thing?

"Yes. It's a bad thing. You can't get involved with your boss. This job is too important. Losing it could very well mean dropping out of school and getting a day job to make rent money."

So when does living get to be as important as working?

That was the question of the hour. When did she get to live? Chloe had borne the emotional responsibility for her mother's and sister's well-being since she was twelve years old, right after her mother's second husband had walked out. That had been the worst year, when Chloe and Morgan had been separated from their mother for months. Once they got back together, Chloe had been determined they'd never be parted again.

So Chloe was the one who'd learned to fake a communicable disease when the landlord came to call. The one who'd bartered baby-sitting services with the owner of the kids' consignment store up the street to keep Morgan clothed. Through the other husbands, boyfriends, towns, people and jobs, Chloe had never let herself forget one thing: she was the one who had to keep it together. Morgan was too young and Jeanine too unpredictable.

Following her heart—or, in this case, her libido—was not something Chloe usually allowed herself to do. *So why not do it…just this once? You know you want to. Don't be a chicken.*

"Oh, shut up," she muttered aloud to the insidious voice. She sometimes pictured a little cartoon devil, complete with horns and a tail, sitting on her left shoulder whispering in her ear when she contemplated doing something really stupid. On her other shoulder, there perched not an angel, but a two-inch-tall version of Sister Mary Frances.

The sister had been her second-grade teacher during Chloe's single year at a parochial school—a year prompted by one of her flaky mother's religious experimentation periods. That was before her real father had split, when they'd had something of a normal life. Chloe had spent most of second grade sitting in a corner until she learned how to behave like a proper young lady. Instead of learning patience and obedience, she'd actually used the time-outs to imagine ways to get even with the Penguin, as the kids called her. So the Sister Mary Frances voice seldom won out.

Finally, sick of having a conversation with her own sun-pinkened face in the mirror, she grabbed her purse and slammed out of the room. The mental arguing continued, however. She talked to herself in the empty elevator all the way down to the first floor, then right up until she reached the bar entrance. The place was crowded, so she stopped mumbling and cast a quick glance around. She nearly convinced herself he wouldn't be here anyway, so it wasn't worth getting so hyped up about.

Then she spotted Troy waiting for her in a corner booth. Any thought of turning chicken, slipping out the door and running to her room like a scared little virgin evaporated. Not just because he'd seen her. No, it was because of that look in his eyes as he stood and walked toward her. Not a Troy look. Not a confident, I-never-doubted-for-a-minute-you'd-show-up look.

No, this look was relieved. Appreciative. Anticipatory. "I was afraid you were going to stand me up," he said, his voice husky and intense as he reached her side.

"I almost did." *Oh, gee, nothing like a little honesty to start an evening off right.*

"What changed your mind?"

Brushing a stray wisp of hair off her face, she struggled to seem nonchalant. "I was thirsty."

"I'm glad you were thirsty," he said with a teasing smile. "I was afraid you might have cold feet."

"My feet could sink the *Titanic*," she admitted ruefully.

He chuckled as he led her back to the intimate back-corner table, which was even more hidden by a few hanging plants and an indoor garden area, complete with softly gurgling fountain.

Candlelight. Flowery plants. Shadowy secluded corner. Chloe Weston, turn those wobbly three-inch heels of yours toward the door right now.

"Back off, Sister," she whispered under her breath.

He obviously noticed her sudden anxiety. "Is this all right? I asked for a quiet table so we could talk."

She gulped. "Uh, sure. Fine."

After pulling out her chair for her, he sat down opposite her. "Please, relax. I haven't got the wrong idea. I know you're here on business, you didn't come here for this. You never planned to meet with a man you don't really know in a hotel bar."

"A dark, candlelit hotel bar with low, sultry, danceable music," she muttered. His eyes widened and she shook her head. "No. This is *so* not me. I'm usually so boring. No adventures in hotel bars in my recent history. I'm an open book. A boring, what-you-see-is-what-you-get book."

Sitting across from her, he reached out and caught one of her hands, which she'd just lifted to again nervously brush back her hair. "I doubt that. I saw you by the pool, remember? I think there are some deeply hidden facets of you I'd very much like to explore," he said, his voice a seductive whisper.

Okay, that's it. You're in trouble now, missy.

As if he hadn't noticed her heart beating so wildly she thought the veins on her temples were about to explode, he continued. "Let's forget about who we 'usually' are for a while."

Chloe stared at him, trying to gauge his meaning. Obviously Troy knew something about hiding his real identity—he did such a good job of it even *she* hadn't caught a glimpse of the real tire-changing man beneath the business suits in the past few weeks. He'd obviously become adept at living a double life, slipping off his at-home persona as easily as he slipped off his sexy little gold stud earring.

Why shouldn't she give it a try?

He must have seen the indecision in her eyes. "Forget all the standard reasons we shouldn't be here together. You don't do this, I don't do this, we don't know each other. Just let it go. Tonight we're two people sharing an interesting evening together, getting to know each other. That's all."

"That's really all?"

"Yes." His voice lowered, his stare grew more intense. "Unless we both decide we want it to be more."

Heck, she wanted it to be more already. *Get out now, Chloe.*

He glanced toward the table, at her hand, which still held tightly to her purse. Chloe knew he realized she was poised to flee at a moment's notice. "So will you stay?"

Taking a deep breath, Chloe consigned the picture of Sister Mary Frances to the depths of her subconscious, briefly closed her eyes and nodded. "I'll stay."

"I'm glad." He reached over and gently tugged the purse free of her fingers, pushing it to the side of the table, still within reach, but not clutched like a lethal weapon.

He held a hand up, waving to a waitress. "How about a rum punch? It seems appropriately tropical. Okay?"

"Yes, but only one or I'll be dancing on the table."

"There's a sight I'd like to see," he said. "Particularly considering the length of your skirt." Chloe flushed as he laughed softly. "Don't worry. I didn't get the wrong impression. You look perfect. Sexy as hell—but still tasteful. Just right to show you're a desirable woman, without flaunting it."

"Well, I guess you know women's clothes," she murmured, feeling both embarrassed and at the same time very glad she'd worn the tight black miniskirt and sheer black hose.

"Now, should we introduce ourselves?"

"Excuse me?"

"We're strangers. Isn't it time for introductions?"

"Strangers in a bar?" she asked, catching on. This, obviously, was another way to separate themselves from reality—from the fact that they worked together in their everyday lives. That he was her boss, the managing director and part-owner of Langtree's Department Store, and she a window dresser. They would be strangers. No outside ties. No encumbrances. No expectations. Maybe even no repercussions. "I think I like this idea."

"My name's Trent," he said, as the waitress arrived with their oversize glasses. The woman leaned close to him as she placed their drinks on the table, her stare blatantly admiring. Chloe felt another shiver course through her. She was playing sexual games with this devastatingly attractive man—a man every other woman in the room had eyed at least once since Chloe had sat down with him. The anxiety Chloe had felt early in the evening began to slide away, replaced by something else. Excitement. Titillation. *Why the heck not?*

"*Trent*. How nice to meet you. My name's... Claudia."

He waited until the waitress walked away again before picking up his drink and raising it in a toast. Chloe lifted her glass as well and waited, expectantly.

"To stormy skies."

She nodded. "And strangers getting to know one another."

The first sip of rum punch was enough to convince Chloe she absolutely could not drink more than one. The thing tasted like straight rum, with a little cherry juice thrown in to give the alcohol a pink tinge. "Whew," she gasped once the burning sensation in her throat had stopped.

"Good?"

"Very. Just potent." She sipped again, noting the fiery sensation was no less strong the second time. But she was getting used to it. "So, uh, *Trent*, tell me about yourself."

He shrugged. "Not much to tell. I work too much. Eat all the wrong foods. Don't keep in touch with my family the way I should. I live in a beachfront apartment I really can't afford and have never seen such a wonderful blending of shades in a woman's hair before tonight." He reached over and brushed some curls back off her brow, stopping her heart. "Gold, brown, reddish highlights. It has to be natural."

Whoa...he's good. She picked up her drink and sipped

from it heartily, coughing and choking as the heat hit her belly again.

"You okay?"

"Fine," she choked out. "Now, uh, what do you do?"

He shrugged. "I own a landscaping business."

Well, that was stretching the fantasy a bit, in Chloe's opinion. Then again, it was his fantasy. And she'd already seen Troy Langtree's sensory attraction for the outdoors. So maybe it really was a deep-rooted wish, one he'd hidden from the world like he'd hidden his killer smile and the amazingly strong arms and chest. Not to mention the charming, flirtatious attitude.

"What about you, Claudia?"

"Hmm," she mused, playing along, trying to come up with her fantasy life, her deepest desire. What she'd do if she could be doing anything. "I'm a full-time grad student, and freelance graphic artist." She sighed with pleasure at the fantasy. Imagine, working for herself, only when she felt like being creative, and being able to afford to go to graduate school. Sounded heavenly.

"Any family?"

She contemplated continuing the fantasy, but in the end stuck with the truth, saying, "Yes. A beautiful, brilliant younger sister, Morgan, who's about to graduate high school. And a wonderfully creative—if a trifle irresponsible—mother who looks like she's my age. You?"

He nodded. "I have a few family members in this area. My parents retired and moved to Colorado a few years back."

Chloe sipped her drink, getting used to the strong brew and not choking this time. "No steady girlfriend?" she asked, not wanting to spoil the illusion, but needing to know just the same.

He seemed to sense that her nonchalance hid a keen interest. Reaching across the table, he took her hand. "I haven't been seriously involved with anyone for over three years. Too busy working. And I hadn't found the right woman yet."

"What would she be like?" Chloe asked before she thought better of it.

He didn't hesitate. "She'd have curly brown hair and amazing blue eyes. She'd love the beach, not be afraid of trying new things, like skydiving and windsurfing."

Chloe shuddered. "I don't do heights. High places make me nauseous. I'd feel sorry for whoever jumped out of the plane first and was below me on the way down."

He laughed softly. "I'll remember that."

"So you want an adventurous brunette?"

"Not entirely. Adventurous is nice. But she also has to have an amazing smile."

He was staring at her lips and she nervously licked them. She saw him pull in a deep breath, something hot and intimate flashing in his eyes. He finally looked away and picked up his drink.

"Anything else?" Chloe asked, feeling confused and yet completely fascinated by the intense heat she'd seen in his expression when he'd stared at her mouth.

He nodded. "Sense of humor is a *must*."

Okay, now he was getting someplace. Humor she could do. Chloe loved to laugh. Given the choice between a gushy, oozy chick flick and a bawdy comedy, she'd go for the grins any day. Her comedy movie collection filled several boxes in her closet.

Her mother called her ability to laugh at life, to find

joy in anything, her best feature. Chloe had once countered, "Thanks, Mom. Fabulous hair or a great figure would be nice. Heck, even brains! Sense of humor is almost as bad as telling the chubby kid she has 'such a pretty face.'"

Of course, Sister Mary Frances had called her sense of humor her ticket to a century in purgatory.

"Do you like old comedies? Laurel and Hardy?" Chloe asked.

He shook his head. "I'm more of an Abbott and Costello fan."

"Me, too. And Mel Brooks?"

"Oh, sure."

"So we share the same tastes in comedy," she said with a hopeful look. "Does that let me off the hook for skydiving?"

"Ever tried parasailing?"

"From what I hear," she replied dryly, "parasailing requires some elevation, too."

"Okay, I'll keep you on the ground."

You can keep me anywhere you want me...as long as you keep me. She took a sip of her drink and thrust the thought aside.

"This is good," she acknowledged as she sipped the last few mouthfuls of her punch. Funny how she'd begun to enjoy the rich, spicy flavors—probably because the alcohol had burned every taste bud right out of her mouth. But she wasn't complaining.

"I'm not opposed to seeing you dance on the table...or anywhere else. Would you like another drink?"

"Maybe I'd better have a glass of water," she said. *Okay, score one for Sister Mary Frances.*

"Let's make that two."

For the next hour, Chloe found herself thoroughly entranced by the man sitting across from her. Troy—er, Trent!—was funny and sexy, smart and irreverent. He laughed at her jokes and teased her about not being able to handle her punch. He seemed genuinely interested in hearing her brag about her brilliant little sister. He even got her to open up about her worries. Chloe found it easy to tell him about her desire for normalcy, and her concerns about her unconventional mother, whom she dearly loved, but who couldn't really be counted on for anything.

He once caressed a lock of her hair under the guise of pushing it off of her face, which had set her heart racing for several moments. He didn't talk much about himself, seeming to really want to focus on her, as if his own life was completely boring and she the most fascinating person on earth. That was an unusual feeling for Chloe, who was well used to sitting in the background while her flamboyant mother soaked up all attention like a paper towel soaked up spilled milk. She even finally decided she was ready to handle a second rum punch.

"You've got to be sick of hearing about my family, phobias, video collection, or the various lists of do's and don'ts by which I run my life," Chloe said.

He shook his head. "I don't think I could ever get tired of hearing anything you say."

This time Chloe was the one to break their stare first. Confusion washed over her. This wasn't quite the way she'd envisioned the evening. She'd been all set to be mysterious. To play along with his "strangers in a bar" suggestion.

But they'd gone well beyond playing sexy games.

Well beyond seductive flirtation. She'd known she was attracted to him. She'd never expected to like him.

"I want to know more about *you* now," she finally said. "Do you really like to do dangerous things like skydiving?"

He tilted his head to one side and lifted his hands up in helpless resignation. "Uh, yeah. I do."

"Yikes," she murmured, unable to picture the smooth, polished store businessman doing anything so impulsive. Trent, his alter ego, however? Well, yes, she could picture that.

"I don't really skydive very much anymore," he admitted. "No time, no money. I do still like to hang glide whenever I visit my folks out west. You really should try it, it could help you get over this problem you have with heights."

"If I'm more than ten feet off the ground, I'd better have a floor or a fully operational Boeing 747 underneath me," she countered. "Hang gliding, ha! It should be called strapping paper-framed wings on your back and pretending you're *not* attempting suicide."

He let out another laugh, and Chloe noticed, not for the first time, that every pair of female eyes in the place turned to look at him. Approvingly. Hungrily.

She reached across the table and touched his hand, sending a not-so-subtle message—*he's mine*—to the overhormonal bar bimbettes in the room.

He immediately responded by taking her fingers and entwining them with his own, sending shards of heat rushing up her arm. Chloe stared at their hands, marveling again at the darkness and strength of his against her own pale, soft skin. When she finally lifted her gaze to his face, she found him studying her, a half smile on his seductive lips.

"You ready to get out of here?" he asked softly, leaning close and lowering his voice to a more intimate level.

Chloe waited for the length of two heartbeats but felt like two hours for him to continue. *And go where?*

"The storm's over. We could go for a walk on the beach."

Chloe released the breath she'd been holding. "Sounds lovely." She meant it—a walk on the beach did sound perfect. But she still somehow felt a stab of disappointment. She told herself not to be an idiot. Even if he *had* issued a much more suggestive invitation, as she'd half feared—okay, half hoped—she wouldn't have taken him up on it. Absolutely not. Uh-uh, no way, never gonna happen.

Well, *probably* never gonna happen.

Remembering the quick stop she'd made in the hotel store before dinner, and thinking of the condom right now burning a hole in her small black purse, Chloe acknowledged the truth.

Okay. *Maybe* gonna happen.

3

TRENT HID A SMILE AS A variety of expressions crossed his lovely companion's face when he suggested a walk on the beach. He knew what she was thinking—exactly the same thing he was thinking. *We're strangers. This is too soon. What is happening here and why does it feel so right?*

Though he sensed he could stand up and lead her out of the crowded bar without another word, he didn't want to push her. "Your choice. We can stay here if you like."

"Hmm," she said, tapping the tip of her index finger on her cheek in obviously feigned indecision. "Stay here in a hot, loud, crowded bar with a bunch of other women who've been ogling you for an hour? Or go out onto a romantic, moonlit beach for a refreshing, private walk. Decisions, decisions. You don't make it easy on a girl."

He shrugged. "The story of my life. Making the tough choices." He leaned closer. "Besides, I haven't noticed any other women. I *have* noticed the three muscle-bound college boys at the bar who keep turning around to stare at your legs each time you shift in your seat."

Her eyes widened. She immediately turned to see. "You're sure they were looking at me? I mean, there are a lot of women in here who aren't sitting with other men."

"None of whom has legs like yours."

"Oh wait, I've got it," she said, ignoring his compliment. "You're the one they're interested in. They're gay. That'd explain why they haven't hooked up with one of these on-the-prowl females."

He chuckled. "Why is it so hard for you to believe you're on the mind of every single male in this room?"

An adorably disconcerted blush spread across her cheeks. She really didn't realize her own appeal. She had no idea how amazing she was. How her soft laughter could seduce a man. The way the brightness in her eyes brought energy to a lifeless room. The way every male with even a drop of testosterone in his blood saw those legs of hers and imagined them wrapped around him. Including him. Trent gulped down the last of his water.

She finally answered his question. "Maybe because I'm used to being the responsible, pretty-in-a-quiet-way, funny one who doesn't usually incite lustful males to riot in the streets—or in the bars." She smiled, glancing around. "You're sure it was me they were interested in?"

"Oh, I'm sure. Did you not notice the staring contest I got into with the one in the Florida Gators shirt a half hour ago?"

Deadpan, she asked, "Oh, you're an FSU Seminoles fan?"

He smiled. "No, NFL all the way—I'm not much into college sports. But I couldn't let that guy get away with drooling all over you like that. I guess I'm just one of those caveman guys who feels compelled to mark his territory."

She raised a brow. "Your territory?"

"I didn't mean that in the primal sense."

"Thank goodness. I think I've heard about how some male animals mark their territory in the jungle. We haven't even kissed yet, so I think it's a little early to start talking about that kinky stuff."

Instantly knowing what she meant, he threw back his head and laughed. The jocks at the bar turned to look. *She's gorgeous, she's bright, and she's funny as hell. Tough luck, boys.*

"So you ready to get out of here?"

She stood. "More than ready."

As he took her arm and led her out of the bar, Trent wondered what good deed he'd done recently to account for his incredible fortune. This woman, this stranger, was a dream come true. Not only funny, charming and self-deprecating, she was also beautiful and earthy. Honest and completely unpretentious. And sexy enough to make him shake in anticipation.

Claudia was his fantasy woman come to life.

"You okay?" he asked, noticing the slight wobble in her step. They'd just exited a back door of the resort, on the way to the pool and beach area.

"I don't do big girl shoes very well," she admitted. She sighed, giving her own feet a disgruntled stare. "High heels had to have been invented by a man. They're sheer torture."

Glancing down at the strappy, spiked-heel sandals beneath slim, black nylon-encased legs, Trent could only murmur, "Strap me to the rack."

Her giggle told him she'd heard.

"Yep. Definitely a male invention," she continued. "Like leg wax, chastity belts and brassieres."

"Seems like man was working against himself with those...except, of course, the leg wax."

"There are plenty of locations in the world where women don't feel the need to shave or wax their legs," she countered.

"Hopefully not at the Dolphin Island Resort and Country Club." Trent met her stare evenly, then let a teasing smile spread across his lips so she caught his meaning.

"Wouldn't you like to know," she retorted softly. Then, even softer, as if she was muttering to herself, he heard her say, "And wouldn't I just *love* to show you."

Knowing the alcohol might have gone a bit to her head, Trent doubted she even knew he'd heard. He grinned but turned away so she wouldn't see.

Well, yeah, he'd like to know. And he planned to find out. Particularly since the image of those long, tanned legs had been taunting him since the afternoon when he'd seen her in her bathing suit.

As they passed the pool and approached the wooden stairs leading down to the private, moonlit beach, Trent stopped. Since he was holding her by the arm, she halted, too. She stared at him curiously. Without explaining, Trent dropped to a crouch beside her. He reached for the straps of her shoes, unbuckling one, then the other. Taking one of her hands, he placed it on his own shoulder so she could balance herself. He noticed the way her fingers tightened, her skin burning through the thin material of his shirt. Feeling the touch throughout his entire body, Trent had to force himself to focus on the task at hand.

Impossible. He couldn't focus on anything but her.

Not only did her soft fingers brand his shoulder, but now his face was mere inches from her silky thighs.

His hands trembled as he tugged off each shoe. He was completely unable to resist gently stroking one ankle, stalling for time while he tried to control his body's response to her nearness. Her loveliness. And the sweet, elemental scent of her body.

Controlling the tides would likely have been easier.

"Better?" he asked as he finally rose to his feet.

She smiled and almost cooed her relief as she curled her toes on the cool surface of the pool deck. "Much."

"You wouldn't have been able to walk in the sand in these, anyway," he said, hearing the thickness of his voice. He struggled against the mental fantasy of sliding his hand up the sweet, vulnerable curve of her foot, curling around her calf, then moving higher. Over her knee. Between her thighs. Moving his mouth closer, to explore her softness and that intoxicating feminine scent filling his brain.

"You okay?" she asked when he fell silent.

He swallowed, hard, and nodded. "Fine. Just feeling stupid for not thinking beyond being alone with you on the beach. You're not exactly dressed for it. Your heels would have sunk three inches deep with every step."

Now, without the heels, he noticed how petite she was. The top of her head came to his shoulder, and she tilted her head back to meet his eyes with her amazingly blue ones.

"You'd have rescued me, wouldn't you?" she asked.

"Hmm?"

"I mean, you wouldn't have left me there, stranded, with my heels stuck tight in the sand all night, right? And me doing my impression of a beach umbrella?"

He grinned as a wicked thought crossed his mind.

Beach umbrella? I'd have no problem being underneath you on a beach.

She continued. "I don't suppose it's going to be too comfortable walking across sand in these."

Trent followed her glance down to her legs, still covered by a pair of silky-soft black hose. No way was he going to offer to help take *those* off. The next time he touched her legs, it would be to explore each inch of them with his hands, fingers and mouth. He hoped it would be in the not-too-distant future. But not here, a few feet away from a clear-glass hotel door, where anyone walking by could see them.

Before he could even offer to walk her back inside so she could change, he saw her reach under the bottom hem of her short skirt and start tugging.

"I was going to ask if you wanted to go back inside to change."

She paused.

"But this works too."

She went back to tugging.

Trent raised an eyebrow, watching with interest as the skirt rose higher and higher while she pulled. His anticipation rose right along with her hem. As did his heart rate. By the time she pulled the waistband free and was able to begin maneuvering the nylons down her legs, he caught a glimpse of something silky and red at the V of her thighs. *Lord have mercy* was the only thought he could manage in those infinitesimal seconds before she pushed the skirt back down, along with the nylons.

Then the silk, filmy things were off. She tucked them into her shoe. Giving him a cheerful smile as if she hadn't just sent every pint of blood in his body rushing to his groin, where it now pulsated and throbbed with urgent intensity, she said, "Shall we?"

He didn't reply. Instead, he took her by the shoulder and gently turned her until they faced one another. Staring down into her bright, amused eyes, he said, "Tell me one thing, angel."

"Sure."

"Are you really completely oblivious to what you're doing to me? Or are you just enjoying making me squirm?"

Her soft laughter was more seductive than the velvety night sky above them or the sound of the churning waves in the background.

"I think I have my answer."

"Let's say," she finally replied, her expression growing serious, "I am aware something's happening here. Frankly...*Trent*...when you were kneeling there, taking my shoes off, I was feeling a little more than simple appreciation. I had some pretty wicked thoughts going through my mind."

He groaned softly, imagining her thoughts, wondering if she'd wanted the same thing. Him touching her. Tasting her. Knowing her as intimately as it was possible for a man to know a woman. "So did I," he whispered. "If we hadn't been standing in plain view of the hotel, I might have helped you with the nylons." He leaned closer, until he felt her soft hair brushing against his lips. "And anything else you needed."

This time as she sucked in a deep breath, her lips parted. Trent zeroed in his gaze on them, anticipating the way they'd taste, the way she'd feel in his arms when they finally came together. Which they would. Without question.

She obviously saw him staring and her breaths grew

even more labored. The movement of her chest drew his attention lower, to the deep V-neck of her silk blouse—made deeper now because one tiny button had slipped free of its hole. He glimpsed the lacy edge of a red satin bra, one that matched the tempting bit of red caught between her thighs. His body reacted instinctively and he gritted his teeth in a vain effort for self-control.

"I probably would have let you," she finally admitted. "Help me, I mean." He searched for uncertainty in her expression or her voice, but noted none. "But I saw the glass door, too. We're not exactly in private."

"So...intentional torture." He gestured toward her bare legs. "Hence the nylon striptease?"

"I'm not an exhibitionist," she said with a tiny smile. "It's not like I pulled my skirt up over my waist or anything."

She obviously didn't know he'd seen more than she'd meant to reveal. He could be a gentleman and let her keep thinking that. Trent, however, had never really considered himself a gentleman.

"I really like red satin and lace."

She looked confused at first. After a few moments, her eyes widened in shock and her mouth dropped open. She immediately bent over to check her skirt, smoothing it to make sure she was completely in place. She also obviously noticed the loose button of her blouse and quickly fastened it. "I was *not* trying to flash you."

"And I was *not* trying to sneak peaks at your underwear." He paused. "Though I can't say I was trying real hard to look in another direction."

"Honesty. I like that in a man," she replied with a

good-natured nod. "I'm thankful I was *wearing* under-wear. Those panty hose can be worn without them."

She didn't wait for his response. Leaving him blinking and newly aroused at the thought of her completely bare under her short skirt, she dropped her shoes and hose at the top of the steps, then quickly skipped down them to the beach below. Trent followed, slowly, watching her run the several yards to the edge of the water and kick her feet in the lapping waves. He heard her laughter from the bottom step.

He walked closer, entranced by the shimmer of moonlight catching the gold highlights in her light-brown hair and by her smile. She was obviously savoring the strong ocean breeze blowing in off the ocean, which pushed the soft fabric of her clothes tightly against her body. As he reached her side, he could see the outline of her thighs beneath her short skirt, and the full curves of her breasts. Even the tightness of her nipples.

She turned and stretched her arms out wide, looking both languorous and excited. "This was a wonderful idea. I don't get to the beach much even during the day. You're lucky, living by the ocean."

"My one indulgence. Like I said, I can barely afford it, but it's worth waking up to those sunrises."

She stepped closer, grabbing his hand and tugging him toward the water. "Take off your shoes," she ordered. "Come on, get wet with me."

Now, there was a tempting thought. Getting wet with her. Not even thinking twice, Trent kicked off his shoes and socks, dropping them on the sand. He pulled up the bottom of his jeans, and together they stepped ankle-deep into the water. "Warm."

"Lovely," she agreed, kicking at the frothy water with her toes.

They walked down the beach, staying in the lapping surf, for several quiet minutes. Soon they found themselves in a deserted spot, with the lights of the hotel far behind them.

"I'd love to go swimming," she mused aloud.

"Feel free. I'll keep watch, if you want to skinny-dip."

"Keep *watching*, you mean," she countered. Her tone dared him to deny it.

"That, too," he admitted with an unrepentant shrug. "Seriously, if you want to get in, go ahead. No one's anywhere around, it's one in the morning, and your little red ensemble could be mistaken for a bikini anyway."

"Ensemble? Oh, so you saw the bra, too?"

He grinned wickedly.

"I have absolutely no secrets left," she said with a disgruntled sigh. She kicked water and sand at him, soaking the bottom part of his jeans.

Trent chuckled and splashed her back. Then, growing serious, he stepped closer until their bodies were separated by only an inch of moonlit night. "Honey, seeing what you're wearing beneath your clothes is only making me more interested in seeing what's underneath everything."

Her smile faded and something flashed in her eyes. Something excited and accepting. Ready. "You had me when you took off my shoes. You know that, don't you?"

Before Trent could reply, or even bend down to kiss her, she grabbed him by the hair and tugged his mouth toward hers. *Oh, yes, a woman who makes the first move* was his last coherent thought before his lips met hers. Then there was no thought. Only pleasure.

SISTER MARY FRANCES would probably be rolling over in her grave at Chloe's outrageous behavior. If, of course, she was in her grave, which was doubtful since she'd been a *youthful* mean-faced nun back when Chloe was a seven-year-old heathen. Somehow, though, Chloe didn't care in the least. She wanted to kiss this man. Now.

So she did. She didn't ask, she took, knowing he wanted to taste her as much as she did him. In an instant he was kissing her back. Oh, heavens, his perfect, smiling lips were touching hers, stroking hers, gently sucking and licking at hers. The mouth she'd fantasized about since the night she'd seen him smiling up into the rainy night sky was on her own. She'd never, *ever*, experienced anything more sensual.

Though she'd been bold and initiated the embrace, Chloe quickly gave up control. She felt herself grow weak in his arms as his tongue slipped between her lips to swirl against hers, tasting her, memorizing her, inhaling her. He tasted lovely—warm and intoxicating, like the rum punch. Fresh and clean and thoroughly male. Their breaths mingled as their initial frenzy slowed and they began to savor the kiss.

At first he'd tangled his hands in her hair, cupping her head, as she did his. Then, as they both began to move to the rhythm of the surf and the sounds of the night, their hands moved lower. Chloe's encircled his neck. His dropped to her hips. They swayed slightly, Chloe feeling almost mesmerized.

She gasped when he pulled her closer so she felt the

thick, rigid breadth of him pressing hard against his jeans. Hard against her body. "Oh that's... You're..."

"Yes," he growled against her mouth. "That's my..." Then he slid his lips to her cheek, pressing frenzied kisses there. "I asked you if you knew what you were doing to me."

She moaned low in her throat, completely unable to resist pressing against him, groaning at how good his powerful erection felt against her lower body. "I just didn't realize I was doing quite so *much* to you."

"I've been thinking about this since I saw you standing beside the pool this afternoon."

She didn't admit she'd been thinking about it since the night she saw him change his tire.

Chloe leaned into him, her body sparking with an intoxicating mixture of excitement and languorous need. Warm desire slid lazily through her veins, making her hot and cold all over. Making her arms feel almost too heavy to keep around his neck, and her legs too limp to hold her upright.

She felt literally weak with pleasure as she gave herself up to the sensation of lips and tongues meeting hungrily, of bodies pressed together from neck to knee. It suddenly seemed as if every word they'd exchanged before this moment had only been because there was *this* waiting for them at the end. This incredible delight.

"So, *Trent*, is this where playing strangers in a bar usually ends up?" Chloe asked when he moved his mouth from her lips down to her neck. She nearly sobbed when he pressed a hot, wet kiss in the hollow of her throat. And she finally got her wish and nibbled on the tiny gold earring, sucking his lobe into her mouth as she pressed closer.

"I'm not playing games," he said, lifting his head to

stare intently into her eyes. The heat she saw there melted every last bit of doubt she might have felt.

"I'm very serious," he continued, running his hands up her hips to encircle her waist. When he tugged her blouse free of the waistband of her skirt and slipped his fingers against her spine, she hissed.

"Check my bag and you'll see I'm serious, too," she finally managed to whisper. She wondered how she had the strength to talk when his fingers were doing such amazing things to the curve of her hips, and his mouth was busy pressing hot, needy kisses to her neck.

"Your bag?"

She nodded. "I stopped at the hotel store this evening. They carry lots of sundries."

"Sundries?" he laughed throatily and pulled away slightly, but Chloe followed his movement, not ready for him to stop nibbling one delicate spot below her right ear. "Any particular type of sundries?"

She should have felt embarrassed, but she didn't. "The rubber kind. I wasn't planning on this, but I believe in being prepared."

"I'm *very* glad," he whispered. "And, for the record, you're not the only one who believes in being prepared. The shop clerk must have been wondering why they were having a run on three-packs of condoms."

"Three?" She remained lethargic and dazed. "I bought a twelve-pack."

This time he threw his head back and laughed. "Thanks for the confidence in my abilities."

Chloe felt herself blush, knowing what she's just admitted, without really meaning to. "I mean, I was embarrassed and grabbed the first box I found. I didn't want to run into anyone from the conference and try to casually disguise a condom purchase," she explained with a laugh. "The box is in my room. But I did bring one in my purse." As soon as the words left her mouth she realized how that sounded. Like an invitation to take her right here and now.

Well, wasn't it?

She looked down, noticing the water lapping higher up her bare calves and his jeans. She had a sudden mental image of pulling him down on top of her, here in the rolling surf, making love while the waves washed over them in their never-ending rhythm. Seeing nothing but his face framed by the stars, his thick, dark hair softened in the moonlight. Feeling nothing but the weight of his body on hers, the warm water, the sharp sand. Tasting the salty air and the delicious flavors of his smooth, hot skin. Smelling the sea and the heady, musky fragrance of wild, frantic sex.

Happily fantasizing, Chloe leaned closer and began to tug his tight cotton T-shirt free of the waistband of his jeans, wanting his bare skin beneath the sensitized tips of her fingers.

He pulled away and Chloe nearly bit her lip in frustration. "Uh, honey, your purse..." he said. "It's not the one floating away right there, is it?"

Chloe followed his pointed stare toward the water. A black spot bobbed in the waves a few feet from shore. A few feet—and moving away fast. "Oh, no."

Before she could react, he dashed into the water, fully clothed, and dove beneath a breaking wave. Seeing him snatch her bag from the top of a wave just before it rode out of his reach, she laughed with delight.

"Oh, what the heck?" She ran after him, trying not to think about how much her red blouse had cost or that the black skirt was going to feel like shrink wrap when wet.

She didn't care, just dove under the warm saltwater. She rose with a smile on her face and saw him walking toward her in the knee-deep surf.

"You didn't have to come in. I got it," he told her as he reached her side, brandishing her soggy black bag.

"My hero."

Then, ignoring the purse, she slid her arms around his neck and pulled him close for another of those soul-surrendering kisses. Their smiles and laughter faded and Chloe once again lost herself in sensation.

When a wave washed over them, rising up to her thighs, he lifted her out of the water, pulling her legs around his hips and holding her there. He ran one flat hand in an open-palm caress along the length of her calf. "Silky smooth," he murmured. "Thank goodness."

"Razor. I'm too chicken to use wax."

"Feels perfect," he said, continuing to stroke her as if delighted by the textures of her skin.

She leaned back, knowing he'd hold her safe, trusting him to support her. His eyes glittered in the moonlight as he watched her reach up to unbutton her blouse.

"Red really is my favorite color," he said throatily as she let the blouse fall open. She reached for the front clasp of her bra, but before she could undo it, *he* did. With his mouth.

Chloe whimpered when he nuzzled the curves of her breasts and cried out when he finally took one hard, sensitized nipple between his lips. She jerked against him, grinding against his jean-covered erection. Only those jeans and her own thin, wet panties separated the neediest parts of them both. The friction felt so good she almost couldn't bear it.

"Here? Now?" he asked, his voice low and guttural with need.

"Yes, yes." She opened her eyes, staring up at the star-filled night sky, then down toward his thick dark hair, tangled around her fingers. His mouth still did crazy, wonderful things to her breasts and she thought if she moved against him one more time she was going to explode in orgasm.

She moved. And she exploded.

He heard her cries, moved his mouth up to hers, taking her sighs and catching them with his lips. "You're amazing," he whispered as he kissed her.

"I've never felt like this," she admitted, knowing she was probably admitting too much. "I want you so much I feel like I'm going to erupt."

"That makes two of us," he said, his voice loaded with suggestion and heat. "Can you get..."

She knew what he meant. Letting her shaky legs unwind from his hips, she lowered herself until she stood in front of him in the water. Her purse was looped over her wrist. She opened it to grab the condom, then bit her lip. "Think they're okay when wet?"

She realized how stupid her question was when he laughed with masculine confidence. He slipped his hand under her skirt, his fingers dipping beneath the edge of her panties into the core of her. With excruciatingly tender strokes, he showed them both just how wet she was. "I sure as hell hope so," he replied, his voice husky and full of need.

Drawing on every bit of experience she ever had at undressing male bodies—albeit plastic ones—Chloe deftly pulled his shirt off over his head and tossed it onto the beach, along with her purse. She then unfastened his jeans, biting her lip in anticipation as she brushed the back of her hand across the huge erection pressing against the heavy fabric.

He wore nothing underneath. When she felt his long, rigid warmth pulse against her hand, Chloe began to shake with anticipation and nearly fell. She completely forgot about the concept of needing to breathe to stay alive. Utterly breathless with desire, she knew he was going to fill her up so deep she'd remember the feel of him inside her as long as she lived. She could hardly wait.

When she squeezed his erection with her hand, he groaned. "I have to... Let me..." He pulled away, ripped the condom packet open with his teeth and tugged it on.

Pulling her blouse off her shoulders, and her bra along with it, he tossed them to the sand with the rest of their clothes. Then his lips were on her breast, sucking her achingly tender nipple, even as he picked her up again.

"Are you..."

"Yes," she demanded, pulling his lips to hers and tangling her hands in his hair. She pushed against him, taking him into her body with one fast, deep thrust.

Chloe could do nothing but throw back her head and howl at the moon.

4

THOUGH TRENT HADN'T planned it, he spent the night in her room. He certainly could have used a change of clothes after their wild encounter in the ocean, but when Claudia invited him to stay with her, he never even hesitated.

It was a good thing she'd bought the bigger box of condoms.

After they'd made love in the water, they'd haphazardly put most of their wet clothes into some semblance of order and made their way back to the hotel. Avoiding anyone in the lobby had been easy since they'd used a back, poolside door. The elevator was trickier—they'd gotten on with an elderly couple who looked at them like they were escapees from a mental ward. Luckily, the other people had gotten off the elevator on the second floor.

Trent was inside her again by the time they reached the fourth.

"Think they have cameras in these things?" she'd asked as she reached for the sandy, wet zipper of his jeans immediately after the door closed behind the elderly couple. "I might just need something to tide me over until we get to my room. A quick little sample of what's to come?"

At that moment, with her fingers brushing against his erection, he hadn't given a damn about cameras, witnesses, or anything else. He'd responded to her demand for a "sample" by pulling her skirt up, exposing her bare skin beneath, and plunging into her.

Hard to believe sixty seconds later, when they'd reached the seventeenth floor, they'd both been fully covered and feigning nonchalance. Just a sample...and he'd thought he'd go out of his mind if they didn't get to her room soon for the full treatment.

She'd consumed him. From the minute he saw her standing by the pool the previous afternoon, this laughing brunette with the blue-as-the-sky eyes had filled him with a stormy multitude of feelings he'd kept suppressed for three years—like excitement, lightning-strong attraction, enjoyment of someone else's company. He had no idea how long this crazy ride was going to last, but Trent was determined to stay on till the end. The timing was bad, the location worse. But he didn't care. He burned for her.

A night in her bed hadn't quenched the fire. It had fueled it. Because now, in the morning light, all he wanted to do was make love to her again. Watch her wake up. See the sun shining on the gold glints in her hair. Find out if he could make her come three times in a row again, the way he had a few hours before.

"I have to go," he whispered reluctantly when she curled against him in the bed.

"So early?" She nuzzled against his neck. "You're sure you don't want to stay for breakfast? Not even just a quick *sample?*"

"Stop tempting me," he ordered with a gruff chuckle. "I have a meeting in an hour. Besides, you don't want anyone to see me leaving your room, do you?"

He certainly didn't. The last thing he needed was for

Ripley, the tight-assed hotel manager, to hear he'd spent the night with a paying guest. Ripley viewed him as the hired help. Fraternizing was a strict no-no.

"I suppose not," she admitted, biting the corner of her lip. "So, what happens now?"

"I go to my meetings, you do what you have to do today. We meet back here or in my room tonight?"

She glanced away. "You want to see me tonight? Last night wasn't...all?"

Trent couldn't believe she'd even consider last night might have been all he wanted. What was happening between them was a hell of a way beyond a one-night stand. But it wasn't entirely his decision. As much as he hated to consider it, she might have been interested in no more than a brief fling during her weekend trip. "Not all. Not for me. What about for you?"

Rolling to his side, he propped his head up on his fist and stared down at her. When he saw a look of uncertainty cross her face, he steeled himself for the worst.

"I honestly don't know," she finally admitted. "There are such obstacles."

"What obstacles? No spouses. No commitments to the priesthood. No orders to run off and join the French Foreign Legion. We're adult, unattached and straight. I see no obstacles." He knew he sounded like a lawyer arguing a case, not that he cared. He wasn't about to let her get away. Not now that he'd found her. Not now that he'd *had* her.

"You make it sound easy." Indecision shone in her eyes.

"It is easy." Trent moved one hand to caress her hip, tracing its outline through the soft cotton sheet draping her naked body. "Listen, with everything we talked about last night, I think I understand what you're concerned about."

"I would imagine you'd have the same concerns," she said, her voice breathy as she shifted slightly under his hand.

"No, I don't. You're not your mother. I'm not one of your mother's boyfriends. I don't change my mind or lose interest at the drop of a hat." Trent continued to gently stroke her hip, moving his hand higher to curve over her waist. Warm color rose in her cheeks and her eyes closed as she instinctively stretched beneath his touch.

Watching her lips part and her breath deepen, Trent forced himself to stop. He was not above seducing her, but only as a last resort. Her eyes flew open when he pulled away and sat up in the bed, keeping the covers over his lap. "There was a lot more to last night than us ending up here," he finally said.

She rolled her eyes. "Yeah, there was us in the ocean. Us in the elevator. Us in the shower with those dual pulsing showerheads."

Trent smiled at the memory of their late-night encounter in the bathroom. She obviously noted his reminiscent expression. A sultry look crossed her face. Sliding up in the bed, she allowed the thin white sheet to fall from her shoulders and bare one perfect, tempting breast. She gestured toward the closed sliding glass door and said, "Us out on the balcony, hidden behind the towel draped over the rail."

She got the reaction she obviously wanted. Trent immediately hardened, reacting as predictably as one of Pavlov's dogs to the mental image her words evoked. "I don't recall us out on the balcony."

"Can you anticipate it?" she asked, her voice a purr

as she moved higher and allowed the sheet to fall completely away.

His heart rate kicked up a notch and he leaned closer, drawn magnetically to the allure of warm, naked woman. His hands nearly tingled just at the memory of cupping those beautiful, full breasts. And his mouth went dry as he recalled the way her dark, puckered nipples had tasted on his tongue. Sweet. Delicious.

Oh, yes. Oh, yes, indeedy, he had a feeling he'd be anticipating a lot more than one interlude on the balcony for the fourteen or so hours until he saw her again.

Which, he now assumed, was what she wanted. "Can I assume you don't want last night to be all?"

This time she only hesitated for a moment. Then she gave him one of those bright, sunny smiles. "Not on your life."

Laughing at her enthusiasm, Trent leaned forward to press a soft kiss to her lips. "Okay, then, I'll see you back here tonight. And in the meantime, if we bump into each other during the day..."

She rose to her knees, sliding her arms around his neck and pulling him close for another sweet kiss. "We smile," she whispered against his lips before moving lower to kiss his jaw. "We're polite." She moved her mouth to his earlobe and played with his earring—a souvenir from his outrageous, intoxicated twenty-first birthday party. That immediately got him even hotter. "Completely professional," she concluded, this time sliding her hands down his naked chest until they rested on his bare hips.

He gave her an evil grin, deciding to pay her back for deliberately torturing him when she knew he had to leave. "Right. And no one suspects that just a few hours ago I had my mouth on your..."

"Hey!" She pressed two fingers to his lips.

"You complaining?"

Her eyelids lowered. "Oh, no. No complaints." She stretched lethargically, silently inviting him to lie back down on the bed with her and adore even more of her body with his lips and tongue.

Trent forced his attention away from her. Oh, she was tempting and it took all of his self-control, but he did manage to get out of the bed. He walked toward the bathroom so he could pull on his still-damp jeans. As he reached the door and moved his hand to push it open, she cleared her throat behind him. Glancing at her, he noticed a wickedly retaliatory expression on her face.

"Today, when we're pretending you don't know how every inch of my body tastes," she said, her voice a sultry purr, "be thinking about the fact that by tomorrow morning, I'll be able to pretend the same thing about yours."

"I give up." Turning back around, he rejoined her on the bed.

TRENT'S MEETINGS Saturday morning with hotel management and the general contractor went well. They conducted a walk-through of the new lawn, discussing the irrigation system and the layout of some proposed landscaped areas. He thought he managed to do a good job hiding his distraction. Because as they toured through the planting beds, he kept thinking of the bed in which he'd spent the previous night.

After the walk-through, the contractor departed, leaving Trent alone with Ripley, the general manager of the hotel. "Did I see you with a blond-haired guest last night in the lobby?" Ripley asked as the two of them walked back toward the hotel offices on the first floor.

The man's question was intrusive, but not entirely unexpected. He answered truthfully. "A blonde? No. I definitely wasn't with a blonde last night."

"Coincidence, I suppose," the officious, suit-wearing little jackass replied. "Looked like you from a distance, though the clothes didn't seem right."

Ripley, who stood about five-foot-six and had more hair on the backs of his hands than he did on the top of his head, glanced at Trent's work boots, khaki pants and short-sleeve shirt with distaste. Trent hid a grin. Hell, this was what he considered dressing up for a meeting!

"You are prepared to discuss the progress of the project with the representative from the board?" Ripley asked.

"Fully prepared. I'll be there at two." Without another word, he walked away from the other man, deciding to go back to his room before lunch. His shower that morning had been rushed, to say the least. Not to mention cold. He'd needed to do *something* to cool his overactive hormones—his constant companion since meeting Claudia.

Resisting the urge to go up and see if she was in her room, Trent punched the button for his floor and leaned back in a corner of the spacious elevator. He couldn't stop a small sigh as he remembered being in just this spot about twelve hours before—with Claudia's leg wrapped around his jean-clad hips as he gave her a "sample."

"I'm ready for more," he mused aloud. Other people

had gotten onto the elevator with him, but he really didn't care what they probably thought of him talking to himself.

"I'll bet you are, handsome," a whispered voice replied. "So am I."

Glancing over, expecting to see the bright-eyed brunette with whom he'd spent the night, he instead found himself next to a blonde—a stacked blonde, whose curves spilled obscenely over the top of a two-sizes-too-small bikini top. When she met his gaze, she licked her plump lips.

Trent glanced around, wondering if she had indeed been talking to him. Among the other three people in the elevator, two were "suits" engaged in a deep conversation, and the third a woman who appeared to be about a hundred and two. So, yeah, the Pamela Anderson wanna-be had probably been talking to him. Twenty-four hours ago, he might have talked back. Not today. He leaned against the wall of the elevator and glanced away.

He didn't even pay attention as she moved closer. At least not until he felt her hand on his ass. "Hey!"

The old lady teetered and clutched her cane at his loud exclamation. The two men gave him oddly suspicious looks. And the blonde smiled like a cat that had swallowed a canary—wicked, predatory and self-satisfied.

Shocked that a strange woman had just goosed him in the public elevator of a ritzy hotel, Trent gave her a stern look, crossing his arms in front of his chest. She pouted, then pursed those obviously collagen-enhanced lips. When they reached the sixteenth floor and the doors opened, she sauntered out. Even the businessmen paused to watch her wiggle. Placing her hand against the door to prevent it from closing, she glanced over her shoulder at Trent and did a classic hair toss. "Sure you don't want to *get off* here?"

"Not on your life, lady," Trent muttered. He'd be willing to bet she'd gotten more men off on her floor than an old-time elevator operator.

The two businessmen stared at him like he was out of his mind. He thought he heard the old broad whisper, "Good boy."

The bimbo shot him a glare as the doors closed.

CHLOE FOUND IT DIFFICULT to maintain a calm, composed appearance when she left her room Saturday morning and went down to the conference facility. How could she appear normal? How could she walk among executives and buyers, merchandisers and managers, without the whole world seeing what she'd been doing for the past several hours?

Having a wild, passionate night with a man who was almost a stranger. Almost? Heck, the Troy she'd spent the night with was so different from the Troy she knew at work that he *was* a stranger. A delightful, charming, sexy, to-die-for stranger who'd given her more orgasms in a ten-hour period than she'd previously had in her entire life.

Is it possible to die of orgasm overdose? Well, heck, even if it is, what a way to go!

Somehow, she made it through the morning's workshops and breakouts without jumping up on top of a table and doing an impromptu tap dance to express her good mood. She sure felt like dancing though, especially when she thought of the night to come.

As seriously as she had considered ending things between them this morning—in an effort to protect not only her job, but now, she suspected, her heart—she was glad she'd changed her mind. Yes, she was vulnerable to him. Yes, she sensed the emotions building with the intensity of a tidal wave within her could overpower and eventually drown her. But she couldn't stop. Couldn't tell him not to come back. Couldn't imagine not spending just one more stolen night in his arms, exchanging kisses and whispers, love and laughter.

"One more night," she told herself. "Then back to life. Back to reality. Back to repressed store executive and harried window dresser."

The thought of tomorrow made her unutterably sad.

Chloe saw Troy a few times during the day, though they never actually came face-to-face. When they did see one another, he'd give her a nod, or a noncommittal smile from across the room. "He's good," she whispered under her breath when their stares met from several tables apart at the keynote luncheon. Just to shake him up a bit, Chloe glanced around to make sure no one else was watching, then gave him a quick wink.

He frowned, tilting his head to feign confusion. "*Really* good." She remained determined to get a rise out of him. This time she pursed her lips and blew him a kiss.

The surprise on his face made her grin. He had that prim and proper Troy persona going on. As his eyes widened and he glanced from side to side to see if anyone had seen, Chloe thought she detected a flush rising in his face. She cracked up. How could a man who, a few hours before, had introduced her to places on her body she didn't even know existed, get all stiff and indignant because she'd blown him a kiss?

He was one wonderful, sexy contradiction. Outrageous yet proper. Impetuous yet reserved. Introspective yet outspoken. Tender yet aloof. *You're a master at this double-life stuff!*

Not to mention a lot of other things.

With the rest of the afternoon filled with workshops, plus new displays in the exhibition hall adjacent to the conference center, Chloe tried, without much success, to put thoughts of her weekend lover completely out of her mind. She still had business to think about. And she wanted to be a complete sponge, soaking up everything she could about the industry.

She met some interesting people, buyers from the top department stores, promotional reps from national chains, and media people from the biggest newspapers in south Florida. When asked what she did, Chloe often found herself amused by people's reaction. Some were friendly. Some shrugged. One perfectly manicured and made-up woman, who said she was in management at a high end store, flared her nostrils as if she smelled something bad, then walked away without another word. The little devil Chloe half hoped the woman would trip in her *so* last-year lime-green pumps.

No, Chloe wasn't the only nonexecutive person at the conference. And she probably wasn't the only person involved in displays and exhibits in stores. Still, she would be willing to bet she was the only full-time college student and part-time window dresser in attendance. Another reason to thank Troy, who'd made this opportunity available to her.

A more suspicious person might have wondered about that, she realized. The insidious, doubtful voice of caution in her brain speculated about whether

Troy's decision to fund this trip for her had anything to do with the way things had turned out between them.

Absolutely not.

A slimier guy? Sure. But Troy Langtree? Mr. Picture of Propriety? No. And his alter ego, Trent, the charming, whimsical lover who held her hand, gently slipped her shoes off her feet and made her feel silly and wanton, sensual and energetic, all at the same time? *Impossible!*

What had happened between them the night before had been magical and perfect. Not calculated, not planned. Her mother would have said the planets were aligned and the moon was in somebody's Venus or something. Chloe didn't care about why, where or when it had happened.

All that mattered was the who—her rain-dancing charmer. And the how—how he'd made her smile, how he'd touched her hair, how he'd kissed her like he'd never tasted anything sweeter than her lips, how his eyes had glittered in the moonlight when they'd made love in the water. How he'd felt deep inside her body.

Chloe shivered. She had one more night. And while she somehow doubted she could continue fooling herself that what she had been feeling for Troy was mindless, there was no doubt the night ahead would be fabulous.

SATURDAY EVENING, when she didn't spot Troy outside the grand ballroom for the dinner banquet, Chloe took a chance and tried to call him. Using one of the courtesy phones on a lobby table, she asked to be connected to Troy's room. Unfortunately, she got his voice mail.

"Hi, it's me," she said. "I was wondering if you were

skipping the dinner because you wanted to rush right to the dessert?" Laughing softly, she continued, "Seriously, I am sorry if I embarrassed you earlier. You are so darn cute when you get all uptight and nervous. I can't wait until tonight. Still ten, right?"

Then she was cut off.

A few minutes later, while she tidied up in a ladies' room near the lobby, Chloe heard her cell phone ring in her purse. Worried something might have happened at home, she grabbed it. "Hello?"

"Hey, beautiful."

Troy. She instantly went warm and mushy. Cupping her hand around the mouthpiece to avoid being overheard, she said, "I've been wanting to hear your voice all day."

"Me, too. I hope you don't mind me calling. I saw the number written inside your phone case and jotted it down this morning before I left your room."

"I'm glad you did. I tried reaching you in your room a while ago. I left you a message."

"Really? I've been here for an hour. Maybe I was in the shower." He paused. "Nope, no light blinking. I hope you didn't leave some hot phone sex message for somebody else."

She laughed aloud, her voice echoing in the recesses of the large, empty, tile-floored bathroom. "No, no phone sex. But I guess I did leave it in the wrong room. Hope whoever gets it isn't rooming with a jealous wife or girlfriend!"

"Me, too. If we read something in the paper tomorrow about a man's clothes being tossed off a tenth-floor balcony, we might know why. Now, about that phone sex..."

She glanced up as another woman entered the

ladies' room. "Uh, now's probably not the best time or place. And, well, I'm not exactly experienced in that regard."

"There's a first time for everything," he cajoled. She could close her eyes and visualize his wicked smile.

"Let's talk about it tonight."

"I'll hold you to it."

As another group of women walked in, Chloe recognized one of the department managers from Langtree's. Though the woman couldn't possibly know who Chloe was talking to, she still felt nervous. "I'd better go. I'll see you later."

By nine-thirty, Chloe was back in her room, going through her suitcase for the tenth time. "Dress? Nightie? Shorts?" she said aloud as she wondered just how to greet him when he arrived.

"What does one wear to an affair?" she asked aloud.

Naked seemed appropriate. However, it wouldn't be an easy trick opening the door to him without giving quite a show to anyone else walking by in the hotel corridor.

I can't believe you're considering opening a hotel door in your birthday suit to greet a man you barely know!

"'Barely' being the operative word," Chloe whispered with a shrug as she stood next to the bed, glancing at the clock.

Finally, nervousness, propriety and the image of one of the buyers from Neiman Marcus walking by just as she opened the door persuaded her to wear clothes when she greeted her lover.

Lover. At least for one more night.

She couldn't think beyond tonight. Couldn't wonder what it would be like at work next week, walking past him in the shoe department, sitting across from him in his office, hearing him talked about over the water-cooler by the giggly single salesclerks.

"This is just a fling," she said aloud, remembering what her goal had been before this weekend. "A once-in-a-lifetime fling. We're not suited for the long-term." It was more difficult to believe that the better she got to know him, however. Because not only was the Troy Langtree she'd spent the weekend with a handsome, successful, stable, nice guy, he also definitely knew how to laugh. Possibly her ideal man.

Chloe didn't believe in love at first sight—not after seeing her mother, who believed in it totally, get burned time and again by a succession of "perfect" mates. Each time she believed he was the one. Each time she was left hurt, miserable and lonely in the end. No, Chloe didn't consider herself a romantic, or an idealist. She was content being a realist—though a happy one.

She hadn't fallen for Troy at first sight. She hadn't even *liked* him too much until the night she'd seen him in the rain. So no one could accuse her of doing what she'd sworn she'd never do—taking up with a complete stranger, like her mother had so many times before.

Funny how everything came back to that night in the rain. She'd gone from a faint dislike to a huge attraction in the time it took to voyeuristically watch him change a tire. If she hadn't been working that night, if she hadn't seen him and realized there was much more to Troy Langtree than the world realized, she would never have gotten involved with him this weekend.

It seemed almost impossible, but she now felt as if her entire world revolved around him. Like she had to grab this one additional night and wring from it every perfect moment she could because she was afraid she'd be left with nothing but the memory for the rest of her life.

It's the sex.

"No, it isn't the sex," she said aloud as she angrily swiped a brush through her hair.

Admit it. He rocked your world in bed.

Yes, he'd rocked her world in bed. And on the beach. And in the shower. "Okay," she muttered, "it's partly the sex."

She had to admit the truth, however—he also rocked her world whenever he flashed that amused grin. Whenever he gave a throaty laugh at one of her jokes. Whenever he clasped his fingers with hers as they walked together.

She could fall in love with him. She really could.

Could? Who do you think you're fooling? You're halfway there already!

Yes, she probably was. As impossible as it might have seemed just one day before, she might have found her one-and-only, once-in-a-lifetime Mr. Right. The question remained: was she ready to admit she really wanted more than this weekend?

And was he?

TRENT KNOCKED ON HER door at a few minutes before ten, gripping a fistful of flowers and a bottle of wine in one hand, and a pizza box in the other. He'd almost lost his grip on the flowers, more willing to drop them than the wine or, more important, the pizza. Then the door opened and she smiled that smile.

"I didn't imagine it," he found himself saying, forgetting the items in his hands.

"Didn't imagine what?" she asked as she immediately reached for the bouquet and the bottle, leaving him to save the pizza.

"The way your smile goes through me like a shot of whiskey," he admitted as he followed her into the room, kicking the door shut with his heel.

She raised an eyebrow. "I don't know about you, but on the few occasions I've done shots, I've always felt like I was going to lose my lunch."

Laughing softly, he put the pizza on a table in the corner, next to the wine and flowers she'd just deposited there. He took her by the shoulders and turned her around to face him. Shaking his head, he traced her lips with the tip of his index finger. "I start to feel all warm and electric. It's heady and intoxicating."

"The whiskey?"

"Your smile, angel," he whispered before bending lower to kiss her soft, parted lips. A tiny sigh escaped her mouth as they kissed—not a sigh of resignation, but one of completion. Satisfaction. Acceptance.

Her arms snaked around his neck as she tilted her head, silently inviting him to taste the deepest recesses of her mouth. Their tongues engaged in a lazy welcome-home dance. He felt her fingers slide through his hair, gently stroking his temples, then scraping along his jaw. He knew before she did it that she'd touch his earring—it had seemed to fascinate her the night before. And she did, taking the gold stud between her thumb and finger and twisting it, mimicking the movement with her tongue.

When the kiss finally ended, she stepped back. "Now I'm the one glad I didn't imagine it."

"What?"

"The way you kiss."

"Oh?"

"All men should be able to kiss like you."

He grinned. "I'm not offering lessons."

"I should hope not," she replied tartly. Perching on the end of the bed, she kicked off her sandals and tucked her legs up beneath her, allowing the fabric of her loose yellow sundress to fall over them. She glanced down, studying her hands, and casually said, "I suppose you would have to have a lot of experience to get so good at something."

She was so transparent. Sitting beside her on the bed, Trent took her hand in his. "I told you last night. I haven't been seriously involved with anyone for a long time."

She shot him a look out of the corner of her eye. He understood her unspoken question.

"Not casually involved, either," he admitted.

"I find that hard to believe." The look she cast at him—hot and admiring as she studied his face, then his body—told him she meant no offense.

"I've been driving myself pretty hard professionally, combined with having been burned personally. So maybe I don't trust people as much as I used to."

"But you're here with me," she pointed out.

Trent met her stare evenly for several long moments before admitting, to them both, "I trust you."

He did. He shouldn't, because he barely knew her. But for some inexplicable reason he felt sure of her character. It wasn't in her to be ruthless, mercenary or hurtful. No woman as physically giving and responsive could be an emotional recluse.

"I'm glad. I trust you, too," she finally replied.

"Trusting's not so easy for you, either, is it? With your family background?"

"Not really. Though, to be honest, my mother's

problems aren't always from getting involved with un-
trustworthy men. She just seems to fall in love at the
drop of a hat with commitment-phobic, irresponsible,
lazy, all-around jerks."

He chuckled as she shrugged in resignation.

"She's not really great on the whole responsibility
thing, either. My mother is trapped in the sixties. She's
very creative, but easily distracted. It's always been
simple for her to jump from one thing to the other, one
fabulous idea or overnight business sensation to the
next. When all I wanted was for her to find a nice safe
job as a secretary or something so Morgan and I could
go to the dentist once in a while."

Though he suspected she meant to sound as if she
was joking, Trent heard the hurt in her voice. "You
wanted stability."

"Absolutely. Stability and normalcy. I still do. I want
security, nine-to-five and no risk-taking."

That bothered him. Because nine-to-five he *wasn't*.
Nor did he ever want to be. And it sure didn't explain
why she was here with him now. "Aren't you taking
one major risk this weekend?"

She shrugged. "Maybe. Then again, maybe I'm just
recognizing a great guy when I've found him. Not
many men have shown up at my door bringing flowers
and food. Thank you for both. Now, are you hungry? I
didn't think I was, but the pizza smells yummy."

She stood, straightening her backless dress, giving
him a moment to appreciate the long, smooth line of
her tanned back. The bright yellow fabric rode low on
her waist, exposing the tender bones of her spine. Trent
slipped his hands on her hips, tugging her until she
stepped back between his parted knees at the end of
the bed. She still faced away from him.

"I'm famished," he said as he pressed one open-mouthed kiss to the soft, vulnerable spot right on the small of her back.

She jerked but didn't turn around. Finding a tiny zipper, Trent reached for it and slowly slid it down, careful not to catch the bare skin beneath. As the fabric parted, he followed the line of soft, exposed flesh with his tongue. He heard her moan, felt her shudder.

"You sure you're hungry for pizza?" he whispered as he finished unzipping her. Catching sight of the silky yellow thong she wore beneath the dress, he groaned and moved lower.

"Cold pizza's better any day," she mumbled as she shivered beneath his hands. Trent watched as goose bumps formed where his breath touched her body. When he caught the elastic loop of her panties with his teeth, she swayed as if she'd fall. His hands at her waist helped her regain her balance.

"Keep trusting me," he whispered.

Not stopping the tiny love bites to the backs of her hips, he reached down and slipped his hands beneath the bottom hem of her dress. The muscles of her slim legs went taut in anticipation as he brushed his fingers against her calves. Gently nudging her with his own knees, he watched with satisfaction as she immediately slid her feet apart, opening her legs for him.

He caressed his way up her thighs, drawing closer and closer to their apex, hearing her breath grow choppier with every inch his fingers traveled. She swayed, almost imperceptibly. Forward, toward his hands, which came ever closer to where she wanted them. Then back, toward his mouth, which still teased the elastic of her thong and the curvy hips and backside beneath.

When he finally reached that damp triangle of silk covering her mound, she moaned, low and deep. Her moan turned to a gasp when he bunched the silk fabric into a thin strip and tugged it tighter against her.

"What are you...oh," she sighed, obviously noticing how nice the friction felt as the silk slid across her most sensitive spot. Pulled forward by his fingers, then back by his teeth.

"Please..."

He knew what she was asking for. What she was nearly begging for. It was as much his pleasure as hers to give it to her. Slipping his fingers beneath the silk, he brushed them through her curls, finding her throbbing center. She moaned again, louder than before. Remembering the way she'd played with his earring earlier, he caught the tiny bud of flesh between his thumb and index finger, gently—ever so gently—teasing it until she started to shake.

"Turn around," he ordered against her back, knowing she was close. He wanted to see her when she climaxed, wanted to taste her ultimate pleasure on his tongue.

She began to turn, lethargically reaching to unfasten the dress at her neck. It fell to the floor, puddling around her feet as she finally faced him. Her eyes remained closed, her body pliant and ready. Reaching for the twisted elastic of her thong panties, he pulled them down, letting them fall to her feet. Then he drew her closer, knowing the feel of his warm breath on her thighs, her curls, was making her crazy.

"Grab my shoulders and hold on tight if you feel like you're going to fall. Because I'm so hungry it's gonna take a long time for me to get my fill."

A smile of wicked anticipation crossed her lips. He

moved closer, so close her scent filled his head like an intoxicating incense. Her thigh muscles quivered as he came close. So close.

Just a millisecond before he could reach out and indulge in her sweetness, he heard a loud, jarring nose.

His cell phone.

5

"ANSWER THAT AND YOU'RE a dead man."

He might have laughed at her vehemence if he hadn't wanted to punch himself for forgetting the phone. Reaching toward his belt, where it was clipped, he fumbled to find the power switch so he could turn the damn thing off. Before he could do so, however, a buzzing sound emerged from his pocket. "My pager."

She groaned. "Somebody just shoot me."

"Not many people have these numbers." Not wanting to, he cast a quick look at the screen of his pager and recognized the number. "My grandmother's house, with a 911 after it."

"That could be her calling on the cellular, too."

They both cast horrified glances toward the phone, as the mental image of his stern-faced grandmother intruded.

"You'd better answer." She grabbed her dress, dressing quickly, like a teenager caught making out in her parents' car.

"Yeah, you're right," Trent muttered. "Shit." Punching the answer button on his phone, he said, "If this isn't an emergency, then this is a recording and this telephone is not in service."

Unfortunately, it was an emergency.

After a three-minute conversation with his grandmother, Trent disconnected and turned toward the woman to whom he had been about to make love. She sat on the other side of the bed, fully dressed. She appeared concerned, and a little disappointed.

"Is everything okay?"

"My dad's in the hospital up in South Carolina. He and my mom are on a golfing trip and he collapsed on the course earlier this evening. They think it was a heart attack. Not major—he's conscious and talking—but my mother's pretty upset."

"Of course she is! Are you going?"

He nodded. "Yeah. My grandmother has booked a flight for all of us. I'd better grab my stuff and go straight to the airport."

"Is there anything I can do? Do you need me to call anyone?"

He shook his head. "No, but thanks for asking."

They both stood. Her makeup was smeared and her lips still swollen from his kisses. She was disheveled and beautiful.

Noticing one strap of her dress was twisted over her shoulder, he reached out to straighten it. "I'm sorry as hell about this. I definitely had other plans for tonight."

"It's okay, really. I just hope your dad's all right."

"I'm sure he will be. Grandmother said he's complaining about missing his tee time tomorrow." He still touched her shoulder, taking his time to fix her dress. "Talk about bad timing."

She rolled her eyes. "Tell me about it. I think I'll go take a shower after you leave. A cold one."

He brushed his fingers against her cheek. "Why not a nice warm bubble bath? You can soak and relax, then think of me as you wash yourself—very thoroughly."

A flush of color rose in her cheeks and she blinked her eyes rapidly. "I, uh, don't... That is..."

He laughed softly, liking her confusion, her innocent embarrassment. ''Tell me you will. Promise me you'll lie there in the tub and touch the places I want to be touching. Give yourself pleasure the way I wanted to tonight. It'll give me something intriguing to think about on the plane.'' He remembered their earlier conversation. The idea of erotic telephone talk seemed even more enticing now that he knew he was going to have to leave her much too soon. ''It would also give us something interesting to talk about the next time I call.''

Her face was flushed, her breaths coming in shallow gasps. Before he could apologize for putting her right back on a cliff of sexual need, she reached up, slid her fingers into his hair and tugged him close for a long, slow kiss which both offered comfort and sought it. Her tenderness overwhelmed him. Her sweetness enthralled him. And when she pulled away, letting him see the suspicious damp sheen in her eyes, her tears moved him.

''Now you have something *else* to think about.''

''I'll miss you. You're staying here until tomorrow?''

''Yes. Will you call and let me know how your dad is?''

He nodded as he went to the door. When he reached for the handle, he turned around for one more kiss. This time there was no way she could hide the tears. He knew what was wrong.

''This is not goodbye. We never got to finish our conversation this morning about what we both want. But there is no question this isn't over. I'll see you soon.''

She looked skeptical. Trent wanted to reassure her, but there was no time. He couldn't tell her everything he was feeling, how much he liked her, how much he wanted her, how sure he felt that something unique and amazing was happening between them. There wasn't time for all the words.

Instead, he reached for his earlobe and removed his gold stud earring. She watched questioningly, but didn't say a word. Palming the jewelry, he reached toward her own ear and gently unfastened the small gold hoop she wore there. A smile of understanding crossed her lips as he replaced her hoop with his stud. She touched it with the tips of her fingers, twisting the metal the way she had when he'd been the one wearing it.

"Let me," she said, reaching for her own thin, gold hoop, which still rested in the palm of his hand. Taking it from him, she stood up on tiptoes and slid it into his ear, carefully fastening it, then caressing his lobe.

"A constant reminder," he said softly, glad her tears were gone. "We'll trade back soon."

"I'll count on it."

Pressing one more light kiss on the tip of her nose, Trent turned and left the room. She stood in the doorway watching as he walked down the quiet, carpeted hall, blowing him one last kiss as he turned a corner and lost sight of her. "Very soon," he repeated as he pushed the call button for the elevator.

When the doors opened, he stepped into the elevator and saw a person already inside. Jerking his head, he did a double take and broke into a rueful grin. "I don't think this elevator's mirrored. And if it were, I sure as hell know I wouldn't be wearing a monkey suit. So you're not my reflection."

The other man raised a condescending brow. "Nor would I be caught dead in those faded jeans."

Trent could only shake his head and stare at his twin brother, Troy. His mirror image. His closest friend.

"Well," Troy said, crossing his arms over his chest as he leaned against the elevator wall. He appeared completely unfazed by the coincidence of them coming face to face in an elevator miles from home. "I'd say small world, but it's awfully cliché."

"More like welcome to the *Twilight Zone.* What are you doing here? Have you heard about Dad?"

Troy's smile faded. "Yes, I got a call from Grandmother. I immediately contacted the hospital and they told me he's doing well. They're doubtful it even was a heart attack, but they're running tests. Of course, I want to go anyway."

Trent sighed with relief, glad his brother had thought to call the hospital directly. His own first instinct had been to go. Troy's had been to research. Typical.

"So you're heading to the airport now?" Troy asked.

"Yeah. I'm gonna run to my room for my stuff. Need a ride?"

Troy shook his head. "I've got my car. Not that I'd even consider riding in that monster truck rally heap of yours, anyway. I'm on my way back to my room to pack my things as well."

Trent ignored the jab about his truck—normally he would have commented on Troy's pansy Jaguar. "You were somewhere other than in your room when you got the call?" Trent asked instead, wondering if Troy had been as pleasantly occupied as he'd been when their grandmother had called.

A reminiscent sigh was his brother's only response. Trent chuckled, used to Troy's revolving-door romantic life. They'd each had their own means of escaping the confines of the Langtree legacy. Trent through his business; Troy through his women.

Troy finally said, "So what are you doing here? I assume you're not attending the retailers' conference."

"You know my company's doing the landscaping job here."

"Oh, right. How's it going, Trent? Are you doing all right? I know this is a big job for you."

Trent nodded, seeing the genuine concern his brother seldom revealed unless they were alone. "It's fine. It'll be a raging success, just in time for our thirtieth birthday."

Troy grinned. "Grandmother's going to have to cancel your birthday, slash, welcome-back-to-the-store party."

The elevator stopped again, though not on either of the floor numbers lit up on the panel. As the doors slid open, they glanced out. Trent saw the back of a platinum-blond head and a voluptuous body poured into a tiger-stripe minidress. The woman was turned away, talking to someone who was down the hall.

"Shut the door, quick." Troy sounded almost panicked—an emotion not often seen in Trent's always-in-control twin brother.

Trent didn't have time to react before Troy reached around him, punching the "door close" button. His brother backed into the front corner of the elevator, hidden from the open doorway. He raised a finger to his lips, telling Trent to stay quiet.

"Why do I feel like we're twelve and playing secret agent?"

"Would you shut up!?" his brother snarled, his voice low.

"We don't have to wrestle to see who gets to be Mac-

gyver, do we?" Trent asked, getting a real kick out of
seeing his ten-minutes younger brother squirm.

Troy glared, then jabbed the button on the control
panel harder. Trent watched as the blonde began to
disappear behind the slowly closing doors. Finally
seeming to notice the elevator, she turned, looking
startled as she caught sight of Trent inside.

He waved.

Somehow, it came as no surprise that she was the
blonde with the grabby hands from his elevator ride
this morning. Her eyes narrowed and he heard her
snarl something. It sounded suspiciously like, "You
think you can blow me off," before the doors slid completely closed and the elevator moved again.

He heard his brother's sigh of relief. "Wanna explain
that?" Trent asked.

"Stalker," Troy replied, slowly shaking his head.
"Or all-out *Fatal Attraction* psychopath."

Trent almost laughed at his brother's relief at having
eluded the woman. "You know her?"

"Well, know's not quite the word I'd use."

"Oh, so you *did* her. And she didn't take the 'last
night was fun, baby, here's a gift certificate to the store,
go buy yourself something nice' bit too well?"

"You're so very amusing, do you know that?" Troy
said with a smirk. "You should really be going to
clown college instead of digging up bushes."

Trent shrugged, crossing his arms in front of his
chest and smiling innocently. "Seems to me you're the
one who should stop planting in so many gardens, little brother."

Troy sighed. "She seemed normal when we met."

"And when was that?"

"Last night. Then today she starts calling my room accusing me of blowing her off—which I hadn't!"

"Yet."

"Yet," his brother conceded. "Then I get a message from her this evening acting apologetic, saying we're supposed to meet at ten—which we weren't."

"Because…"

Troy shrugged. "Because I was meeting someone else."

Trent just rolled his eyes. Then he thought back to his encounter with the woman earlier. "Uh, sorry to tell you this, but I think I might have done it."

"Might have done what?"

"Blown off the bimbo." Trent held his hands up, palms out, as Troy frowned. "Sorry, man, I had no idea you were here. And when she copped a feel earlier, I basically told her to get lost."

"She thought you were me."

Trent nodded. "Most likely."

Troy finally seemed to realize what Trent was admitting. He raised an incredulous brow. "And you seriously weren't interested? You didn't take her up on it?"

Trent shook his head at the near miss. "No, thank God. Twin brothers within twelve hours? That woulda been just plain skanky."

"Are you really my brother? Really the man who gave my number to all the girls whose hearts he'd broken in college?"

"College was a long time ago, bro. Gotta grow up sometime."

"If growing up means turning celibate, I think I'll stay young."

"Nobody said anything about celibate," Trent said,

knowing his own secretive smile was going to drive his brother crazy.

Not that he'd tell him a damn thing. No way. What had happened to him this weekend at the resort was private and personal. Too new to share. Certainly too rare to degrade by exchanging locker-room talk with his perpetually horny brother.

He reached up and touched the small gold hoop in his ear, smiling.

"SO, TELL ME ABOUT THE conference. Did you meet any interesting people? Do anything fun?"

Chloe recognized Jess's voice behind her as she worked in her workroom Monday evening. It was her first night back after her long weekend. She'd dreaded coming in, both because she knew Jess would be full of questions and because she hated walking around the store knowing she wouldn't see Troy there. He'd left a message on her voice mail earlier, while she was in class, saying his father was doing fine but he'd be spending a couple of days in Myrtle Beach to help his mother out.

She hadn't been in the store ten minutes before her friend had come knocking. She wasn't the least bit surprised.

You can do this, Chloe. You can be discreet and mysterious. She doesn't have to know a thing!

Well, that was debatable. Even her teenage sister, Morgan, had taken one look at her face the previous afternoon and instantly known Chloe was hiding something. She didn't know how long she could put Jess the bloodhound off.

Gulping, she took a deep breath before turning around to face her sharp-eyed friend. Luckily, the lighting wasn't so great in the room. So maybe, just maybe, Jess wouldn't be able to read the sultry happiness Chloe wore on her face like rouge.

"It was fine," Chloe said, proud of herself for the calm, cool tone of her voice. She turned to face her friend, fighting to keep a self-satisfied grin off her lips.

Jess took a step closer, crossing her arms in front of her chest. "What aren't you telling me?"

"Nothing. Nothing at all. I met some great people. Attended some great workshops." *Had some great sex!* "I was really impressed by what the marketing rep from Macy's had to say about how their store is refocusing their Christmas promotion."

"Macy's."

"Yes. And the hotel was lovely. Nicest place I've ever seen. Right down to mints on the pillow."

"Both pillows?"

Chloe raised a brow.

"Yours and his? You know, you and whatever guy you shacked up with?" Jess obviously saw Chloe's wide-eyed shock. She snorted a laugh. "Remind me never to tell you when I'm planning a surprise party. You absolutely cannot keep a secret."

"I didn't say a thing!"

"You don't have to, honey. It's written all over you. You've got that 'I am woman, hear me purr' look on your face."

"You're imagining things."

Jess kept laughing. "You'll tell me sooner or later. At least gimme a hint—anyone I know?"

Chloe wasn't about to answer.

"Hmm, who from the store was going? I can't see you doing the mattress mambo with a complete stranger. It can't be Troy because I heard he was *busy* himself. Then he got called away."

Shooting for casual interest, Chloe asked, "Oh, really?"

"Some big, major family emergency or something. He's out of town. I hear he won't be back for quite a while," Jess replied, forgetting her inquisition for the moment to focus on the gossip about Troy.

Chloe could have told her Troy would be back by the end of the week. At least, so he'd said in his phone message earlier. But she played dumb. "What a shame."

"Yeah. Apparently a really big shame for Leila. She was fit to be tied. I hear she was so mad she left the conference early."

"Leila from advertising? What's she got to do with it?"

Jess glanced toward the open door of the storeroom, then leaned closer. She paused to build the tension of the forthcoming dish. "Well, I hate to gossip..."

Chloe snorted. "And the Pope hates to pray. Just tell me."

"Well, apparently she and Troy got pretty *close* this weekend, if you know what I mean."

Close? Close? How close?

"I'm not following," Chloe mumbled as a tinge of concern crawled up her spine.

"You know. *She* wasn't afraid to go after something a little mindless and fabulous," Jess explained with an impatient sigh.

Chloe's jaw dropped. "No way."

"Way," Jess replied with a nod. "One of the girls from accounting told me she'd heard Leila telling someone else that the two of them hooked up Saturday night."

"Hooked up?" she repeated dumbly. "What do you mean?"

Jess blew an impatient breath. "Get with it, Chloe. I'm telling you the two of them did the wild thing."

The wild thing? How the heck much of a sexual appetite could one man have? "You're wrong."

Jess stiffened, obviously offended. "It was a reliable source. She says Leila was right there in bed with him, doing the deed, when he got the call about his family emergency." As if noting Chloe's continued reluctance to believe the story, she threw her arms apart. "For heaven's sake, she said she wished she'd hidden his phone until after the grand finale!"

The haze of red which had descended somewhere behind Chloe's eyes during their conversation receded. "Right there, in the act, when he took the call, huh?"

Jess snickered. "Talk about your major coitus interruptus."

"Isn't Leila the one who claims Brad Pitt asked her out when he was in town for a celebrity fund-raiser last year?"

"You think Leila's bullshitting?" Jess sounded disappointed.

"I definitely think Leila's bullshitting."

Correction. I know she is.

BY ELEVEN, CHLOE HAD finished changing the floor displays in the children's department and was preparing to leave the store for the night. Alone in her workroom, she grabbed her purse and swung the strap over her shoulder just as her cell phone began to ring. Answering it, she held her breath, hoping it was him.

It was.

"Hi there. I hope it's not too late to call."

"No problem," she replied, dropping her purse to the floor. She sat on an old sofa in a corner of the room, shoving some miscellaneous mannequin arms and legs out of the way. They landed on the floor with a thud.

"What was that? Are you okay?"

"I'm fine. How about you? How's your dad?"

"Leaving the hospital in a couple of days. They've decided it wasn't a heart attack, it was a heart *episode.* A warning. Now he's pitching a fit because the doctor told my mother not to let him have red meat. The man's a steak fanatic."

She laughed softly. "I'm glad everything's all right."

They both paused, the silence not uncomfortable, yet loaded with expectation.

"Did you..." he began.

"Are you..."

He chuckled. "You first."

"I wondered if you know when you're coming home."

"Need your earring back?"

"Something like that." Her fingers rose to touch his gold stud. She'd touched it many times in the past few days, liking the connection, liking feeling almost branded by something of his. "You're still wearing it?"

"I promised. It's not coming off until you take it off me."

The certainty in his voice warmed her. She curled up on the lumpy old sofa. "Now, what were you going to ask?"

"Want the truth?"

Her heart beat faster as she sat up. "I think so."

"I was going to ask if you took a bath Saturday night."

She curled again, feeling suddenly warm. "Yes."

"And?"

"And what?"

"Tell me about it."

She cleared her throat.

"You're blushing. I can tell."

"You can't hear a blush."

"You're not blushing, not feeling all warm and liquid?"

"Well, maybe you're right," she admitted.

He paused. "Tell me about your bath."

Chloe bit the corner of her lip for a second, not sure if she could do it. Chloe Weston engaging in phone sex? What if she sounded stupid? What if she did it all wrong?

Don't you do this...only bad girls do things like this. Don't you even think about it!

Well, that cinched it. "I used lots of bubbles. I lit some candles I'd picked up earlier in the evening, hoping you and I could use them. And I soaked for more than an hour."

In his hotel room in Myrtle Beach, Trent smiled and lay back in the unfamiliar bed. "Tell me more."

"The bath oil the hotel left smelled like lilacs," she offered. "It made my skin feel so soft after I dried off."

He didn't want to think about her drying off. Not yet. First he wanted to think about her wet...glistening. "How did it feel before you dried off? Slick? Smooth?"

He almost heard the purr in her voice. "Very slick. I could slide the palm of my hand over my body so easily."

"Your stomach? Your thighs?"

"Yes."

"Your breasts?"

"Uh-huh. The tub wasn't quite deep enough, though, so when I lay back, the water didn't cover my breasts completely. And the air in the bathroom was cool. My nipples stayed so hard."

Trent bit back a groan, knowing by the dreamy tone in her voice that she'd forgotten her shyness. She was lost in fantasy.

"Did you touch them with your slick fingers? Warm them with the oil?"

"Yes."

Trent closed his eyes, picturing her. Getting hard for her though she was hundreds of miles away. "And what were you thinking when you touched them?"

"I was thinking of how much better your fingers feel than mine. How much I like it when you touch me. How it feels when you put your mouth on me and suck deeply, swirling your tongue over my nipple. It's like there's an electric cord that goes from the tip of my breasts right down my body, ending between my thighs. And the current shoots straight through me."

"You're killing me."

She gave a throaty laugh. "You started this."

"I wish I was there to finish it. Where else did you touch?"

"A few other places." She sounded coy.

"Did you wash the spot on the back of your knee that's so sensitive you howl when I lick it?"

"I don't howl." She sounded indignant.

"You definitely howl, angel. Did you use a wash-cloth? Or your hands?"

"Both. And a loofa sponge."

"One of those rough, seaweed-looking things?"

"Sometimes rough can feel good."

He shifted, swallowing hard. "Oh?"

She nearly purred. "Like the roughness of the calluses on your fingers, compared to the tenderness of your touch."

Trent unbuttoned his jeans. "Go on."

"Some places are too delicate to wash with the sponge."

"You used your hands?"

"Uh-huh."

Trent couldn't speak for a long moment. He lay in his shadowy hotel room, picturing her, remembering the curve of her face and the softness of her shoulders. The way her skin felt beneath his hands. And always that smile.

"I have a feeling I'm going to have some pretty wild dreams tonight," he finally managed to say, hearing the hoarseness in his own voice. "*If* I ever get to sleep after the long cold shower I'm gonna have to take as soon as we hang up."

"Why a cold shower? Why not a hot bath?"

"I don't need anything to heat me up. I need to cool down."

"A warm shower would be nice. Cool down gradually. And be sure you wash as thoroughly as I did the other night."

He had a feeling he was going to have to do exactly that.

THOUGH HE'D TOLD Claudia he would be home Thursday evening, Trent actually came home Wednesday afternoon. His father was doing fine and had ordered both his sons to get back to Florida where they belonged. Trent and Troy had flown home together, landing in Miami at around three.

Claudia's number was the first he dialed as he drove away from the airport. He thought fleetingly of calling his office or his foreman, but somehow felt they could wait. She could not.

When a female voice answered, Trent said, "I'm back and I'm dying to see you. Tell me where we can meet so I can rip your clothes off."

"Uh, sorry, pal," the voice replied. "If you're looking for my sister, the owner of this cell phone, you missed her. If you're a sick, whacko prank caller, do not pass Go, just go straight to hell."

The sister. The teenage sister. Perfect. "You must be Morgan. Listen, I'm really sorry..."

"Forget it," the girl replied with a laugh. "I have a feeling I know who this is. You guys met at that conference she went to last weekend, right?"

Hoping she wasn't merely fishing, Trent admitted, "Yeah. Can you tell me where she is?"

"She came home after school then went to work at the store for the evening. I noticed her phone sitting here on the kitchen table. Guess she forgot it."

"The store?" Trent remembered her mentioning doing some design work, but she'd never said where. "Which store, exactly?"

"Langtree's."

Trent jerked so hard, he nearly drove his truck onto the shoulder of the highway. "Langtree's? In Boca?"

"Yep. Do you know how to get there?"

Feeling dazed at the incredible coincidence, Trent mumbled, "Yeah, I do. And, Morgan, if you hear from your sister, don't tell her I called, okay? I'll go by the store and surprise her."

CHLOE SPOTTED TROY standing in the doorway to his office, talking to his secretary as she went to clock in Wednesday afternoon. He was distracted, looking the other way, and didn't notice her. Good thing. She didn't know if she would have done a decent job pretending she wasn't eating him up with her eyes. Nor did she want to see him before she had a chance to pull her hair out of its ponytail and run a brush through it.

She hadn't even known he was coming back today. He couldn't have been here long, otherwise Jess would have said something the minute Chloe arrived. He'd probably beaten her to the store by no more than a few minutes.

He'd be coming to see her soon. She knew it.

The low heels of her sandals clicked on the tiles of the floor as she quickly made her way through the housewares and clothing departments. Her anticipation grew with every step—as did her trepidation. Because now, for the first time since their magical weekend, they would be together in the real world.

By the time she reached her little private corner of the store, she'd tugged her hair free and fluffed it, dug a tube of lipstick out of her purse and touched up her lips, and spritzed some perfume on her wrists and throat.

Finally alone in her shadowy workroom, she paused to wonder which Troy was going to come walking through her door. She sent up a silent prayer that he would be her weekend lover—that being here, in this closed-in, stuffy environment hadn't forced him to slip back into his staid, conservative persona. She didn't think she could bear that. She wanted to see his wicked grin, to watch his eyes darken with appreciation when he saw her. She mostly wanted him to kiss her like he couldn't get enough of her.

Sitting down on a sofa facing the doorway, she carefully arranged her short skirt showing just enough leg. Then she waited for him. She waited. And waited.

He's not coming. "Yes, he is. He sounded ready to explode last night." Their late phone call the night before had been even steamier than their first one. She smiled at the memory, whispering, "This whole phone sex thing is actually pretty fun."

Nope. You blew it. He's avoiding you the way a woman who cheated on her diet on the weekend avoids the bathroom scale Monday morning. It's over.

When she glanced at her watch and realized it had been more than an hour since she'd spotted Troy in his office, she took a deep breath and picked up the phone on her desk.

"This is Chloe Weston. May I speak to Mr. Langtree please?"

"He's terribly busy right now," Troy's pit bull—er secretary—replied. The older woman guarded her golden boy from the evil minions working the floors of the store like a kindergartener guarded his cookies.

"It's important."

The woman harrumphed. Chloe had never really heard a harrumph before, but there was no question that's the sound the old bat made into the phone. Finally she said, "All right, I'll tell him you want to talk to him and see what he says."

The next voice she heard was Troy's. When he answered with a distracted, "Hello," Chloe was so glad to hear his voice, she didn't hesitate. "I'm waiting for you. And my panties are coming off right now. So get back here and greet me properly."

Silence.

"Troy? Are you there?"

He cleared his throat. "Uh, Chloe? You've, uh... caught me by surprise. I have someone in my office right now."

She grimaced. She should have known better than to engage in sexy, playful talk here at work. "Whoops. I'm sorry. Forget I called. Come by when you're free, okay?"

She hung up, feeling like an idiot. Poor Troy. She could just imagine how red in the face he must be and hoped he wasn't in a meeting with a room full of executives or something. The thought brought an irrepressible giggle to her lips.

The next thirty minutes crawled by at a snail's pace. Chloe tried sketching, but couldn't focus and dropped her sketchpad to the floor. Curling up on the sofa, she kicked off her shoes and tucked her legs beneath her, feeling almost as if she could take a nap. That wouldn't be too surprising, considering the lateness of the previous few nights. Plus her classes at school were brutal right now with impending final exams.

It wasn't until she heard the clearing of a male throat that she realized she actually *had* dozed off. Disoriented, she opened her eyes, gazing around the shadowed room, and saw him. Troy.

He stood a few feet away, watching her, absently brushing the fingers of one hand against his jaw. He looked contemplative, speculative and definitely interested.

She followed his stare. While she'd relaxed on the couch, her skirt had risen well above its normal knee-length, revealing her thighs all the way to the hem of her panties. Her cotton top had come untucked, and had twisted around so one shoulder was nearly bared and the curve of her right breast was exposed.

"You're back," she said softly, feeling somehow unsure in spite of how glad she was to see him. She sat up straighter, fixing her top and smoothing her skirt.

If he'd smiled, if he'd winked, if he'd crossed the room and held out his arms, she would have been in them in a flash, all her worries gone. But he didn't. He still stood there, conservative and professional in his perfectly fitted suit, staring. Okay, it was definitely an *interested* stare. But not an I-missed-you-like-crazy, you're-the-woman-for-me stare. "Troy? Is everything okay? You seem...different."

He cleared his throat, his gaze still moving over her legs, down to her bare feet and ankles, a small knowing smile finally appearing on his beautifully curved lips.

Suddenly self-conscious, she slipped her shoes on. "Sorry, I was waiting and I guess I drifted off."

"Don't apologize," he finally said. "I'm glad I was held up," he said, his voice silky and seductive.

"Oh? Why's that?"

He stepped closer, not answering. His eyelids lowered as he studied her rumpled clothes, her mussed hair. She probably looked like she'd just gotten out of bed. And he looked like that's exactly where he wanted her to be. "If I'd come any earlier, look what I'd have missed out on. Though, I suppose I should scold you. You obviously told a fib."

She raised a questioning brow.

"As far as I could see, you're definitely still wearing your underwear." He crossed his arms and tilted his head, giving her an arrogant, challenging stare.

Feeling more confident, Chloe stood and took one step until their bodies were inches apart. "Maybe not

for long. Now are you going to kiss me or keep on looking?"

In the split second before she grabbed him by the
hair and tugged his lips down to meet hers, Chloe saw
his jaw drop open. She might have giggled if her
mouth weren't so busy kissing him. Then he began
kissing her back, drawing her tightly against him and
boldly cupping her backside in his hands.

She waited for the fireworks. Waited for her legs to
lose their strength and her breasts to get all tingly and
heavy. Waited for the explosion of desire.

Nothing. Nada. Zero explosions. Zilch on the
fireworks.

Oh, it was nice, kissing Troy couldn't help being
nice—the man was a great kisser. But it wasn't body-
rocking like it'd been the weekend before. *It's this place.
He's back to Stuffy Store Manager. Might as well kiss those
multiple orgasms goodbye right now!*

She almost burst into tears at the disappointment of
not rediscovering those amazing feelings she'd had
with him just days before. She wanted her rain-
dancing pagan. But she had the Southern Retail Executive of the Year.

Chloe instinctively reached up to his earlobe, seek-
ing her own tiny gold hoop. Though she half expected
it, she couldn't help a sharp stab of disappointment
when she realized it wasn't there. Despite his promise,
Troy had taken it off.

Tilting her head as he moved to press hot, somewhat
overly enthusiastic kisses on her neck and throat, she
opened her eyes. Had he replaced the hoop with something smaller and more unobtrusive? Or had he chickened out altogether and not worn anything since he
was coming back to work?

She blinked and did a double take. *That's funny.* He wasn't wearing an earring. But what was really bizarre he had no earring hole, either! Chloe felt pretty sure she would have remembered if the man's ear had been pierced on the gay side, but she jerked her head around to be sure.

Still no hole.

Troy finally seemed to notice her distraction. Not removing his hands, he lifted his head and stared at her. "Chloe?"

Squeezing her eyes shut tight, she gave a firm shake to her head just in case she was still asleep over on the couch and this was some weird surrealistic dream. Maybe she'd dozed off on top of one of the mannequins, and a pair of plastic hands were the ones latched onto her butt.

She reopened her eyes. No dream. Still no earring hole.

"What the hell is going on here?" she asked aloud.

"That's exactly what I'd like to know."

Troy hadn't answered. Well, actually Troy *had* answered—but he hadn't done it from three inches in front of her. Rather he'd spoken from the doorway, several feet away.

Still wondering if she was dreaming, Chloe slowly turned and looked toward the door and saw...

Another Troy.

6

TRENT FELT SUCKER PUNCHED. As he watched his brother and Claudia spring apart, he blinked twice and tried to make sense of the situation. Of all the things Trent had imagined happening when he reunited with Claudia, finding her in his brother's arms—with his hands on her ass—definitely wasn't high on the list. Actually, that wasn't on the list at all, unless he decided to list his worst nightmares.

To give her credit, she looked like he suddenly felt—sick to her stomach, as if she'd swallowed a glass of rancid milk. Her mouth hung open, her eyes widened into saucers. Confusion warred with dismay in her expression.

"Troy?" she asked, staring right at him.

"Yes?" his brother answered. Troy shifted his gaze back and forth between the two of them. Trent noted the annoyance on his twin's face at his interruption. It was about to be replaced by shock because in about twenty seconds flat, Trent's fist was going to be greeting his brother's jaw.

"Troy?" she repeated, this time her stare focused squarely on Trent's twin.

"Yes," Trent answered. He stepped into the room, where Claudia and Troy still stood too close together. Then again, the same state was too damn close as far as

Trent was concerned. He pointed to his brother. "He's Troy."

"He's Troy?"

"Is there an echo in here?" Troy asked.

She ignored him and turned toward Trent. "So you're..."

"Trent."

"There's really a Trent?" She looked stunned.

"Yeah. That'd be me. Trent Langtree."

The obscenity she muttered made Troy's eyes widen. But since Trent couldn't think of another way to sum up this unexpected turn of events, he figured the four-letter expletive worked as well as anything else.

The words she'd uttered just as he'd walked in made it clear she knew something was wrong with his brother's kiss. She'd sounded thoroughly confused. Her shock at seeing him in the doorway cemented it. So he had to discount his first nasty, niggling little suspicion that for some reason she'd wanted *both* brothers.

She wouldn't have been the first. Hell, one old college girlfriend had wanted them both at the *same time*, which had given Trent a serious case of gross-out. Even Try-Them-All Troy had drawn the line at that one.

"Does someone want to explain what's going on here?" Troy asked, still sounding highly annoyed at the interruption of his storeroom tryst. The thought made Trent's fingers clench into fists again.

"I was about to ask you the same thing," Trent replied. "Any particular reason you're trying to stick your tongue down Claudia's throat when she's *mine*?"

"Yours?" Claudia said, her voice carrying an edge.

He knew his announcement probably made him sound like the worst kind of caveman. *Tough.* "Mine."

"Who's Claudia?" Troy asked.

Her eyes grew wider. "You thought I was really Claudia?"

"Just who else would I think you were?"

"Anyone going to tell me who Claudia is?" Troy asked again, looking completely confused.

"I'm Claudia," she mumbled. "At least he thinks I am." She raised a hand to cover her eyes, then almost stumbled over to the lumpy old sofa in a corner of the room. "Of course, I thought he knew I really wasn't."

"How could I know that when you said your name was Claudia?"

"Chloe, why did you tell him your name is Claudia?"

"So it's Chloe?" Trent thought the cute name suited her.

"Yeah, *Trent*, my name's Chloe!"

"I don't understand what's happening here." Troy shook his appearing bemused. "I feel like somebody's going to ask 'Who's on First?' at any moment. Can someone explain what's going on?"

"I don't know…" Trent began.

"Third base," Chloe mumbled.

Trent thought he heard a snorty, somewhat hysterical chuckle from her as she quoted from the famous comedy routine. "You really are an Abbott and Costello fan. Not many people know the actual lines." More evidence that she was the girl for him, in Trent's opinion.

In spite of her laughter, she still appeared stunned. Dazed.

Trent looked at his twin and tried to explain. "I'm beginning to think Claudia here—or, Chloe—is a little mixed-up about our identities. Sort of like our ninth-grade teachers were."

Troy thought about it, then nodded. "You mean the year we switched places so I could haul your sorry butt through Algebra?"

"Yeah, and so I could make sure you didn't flunk out of World Cultures."

"Maybe if you'd learned math you'd want a real job making real money and wouldn't be spreading fertilizer around all day," Troy said with a condescending smirk.

Trent offered his brother an obnoxious smile. "And maybe if you'd learned something about geography you'd resent being stuck in this mausoleum Grandmother built for us and go out and experience the rest of the world."

"Would you two please shut up?" the woman on the couch said. "I'm having a bit of a *moment* here."

Trent and Troy both stared at her. Feeling quite sure his brother hadn't been told to shut up by anyone in quite a long time, Trent waited for his reaction.

"There's no reason to get hysterical." Troy crossed his arms in front of his chest and tilted his head back in his most patronizing look. The pose usually managed to either entirely piss off or merely silence anybody who didn't know Troy well enough to tell him to get over himself.

Chloe might not recognize his intentionally intimidating stance—but Trent had no doubt she had the guts to stand up to his sometimes pretentious brother. Heck, her openness and courage were some of the things he'd liked best about her from the moment they met. Plus her smile. Which, he noticed, was conspicuously absent at the moment.

"Hysterical?" Chloe said as she leapt to her feet. "Who's hysterical? Hysterical would be breaking something." She punctuated her remark by kicking one foot in frustration, accidentally making contact with the ankle of a naked mannequin leg. It slid under the sofa until only the toes and heel were visible. She glared at it, then at them. "Hysterical would be running out into the shoe department asking if anyone had a nice combat boot they could kick me with for being such a blind idiot."

Troy looked at Trent. "She's hysterical."

"She's gonna hit you if you call her that again."

Chloe's eyes narrowed. "Am I the only person in the world who didn't know there are two of you?"

"You must be," Troy replied. "But don't feel bad. Other people have been confused by how alike we are."

Trent shook his head and shrugged. "We're nothing alike."

"Of course you're not, other than physically," she retorted, as if the idea was ridiculous. "I can't believe I didn't figure it out sooner. You're complete opposites."

Her understanding about how very different he was from his twin—when even some of his own family members hadn't caught on yet—warmed Trent. It didn't change her expression, though. She still looked like she wanted to murder him.

She continued. "How is it possible I didn't hear about the two of you? I had no idea Troy had a twin brother."

"Yeah, I've figured that out," Trent said. As he voiced the words, Trent realized his anger had nearly evaporated. Yes, it still rankled having seen his brother's hands on a woman Trent had already decided was his. A woman he truly felt could be the one he'd been waiting for all his life.

Once he could forgive, given the situation. But if Troy ever touched her again...

"So what now?" Troy asked.

"You get out," Trent replied. "Beat it. Right now."

His brother's eyes narrowed, a competitive light shining in them. "Seems to me I was the one she was kissing just now. So why should I be the one to leave?"

Trent didn't even flinch. "Maybe because *I* was the one in her bed last weekend?"

Out of the corner of his eye, he watched Chloe throw herself on the couch and cover her face with her hands. *Not very tactful.* He'd apologize later, during the long conversation they'd have to have as soon as he got his brother to leave.

"Last weekend? At the conference?"

"Yeah," Trent admitted. "Now, will you get out? Go harass some salesclerk for smacking her bubble gum, or chew out a buyer for ordering too many size fives."

Troy ignored him, casting an interested look toward Chloe. She remained as motionless as a sack of flour. Trent wondered if she'd fainted but knew she hadn't when he saw her fingers begin rubbing at the corners of her eyes.

"And yet she kissed me...thinking I was you...who she thought was me," Troy said thoughtfully.

"You're giving me a headache," Chloe mumbled from the sofa, still not uncovering her face.

"Right. She just kissed the wrong brother."

"Or she *slept* with the wrong brother," Troy countered with a suggestive raising of the eyebrow.

"Give it up, Troy. Find some other poor woman whose heart you can break. Chloe's off-limits to you."

"Poor woman?" Chloe sat up and stared at him. "Off-limits? I'm sitting right here, you know. You two sound like a couple of third graders arguing over a Pokémon card."

"Well, you can clear this whole thing up easily, can't you?" Troy asked. "Choose."

Trent really hated the confident smirk on his brother's face. It was going to be a real pleasure to see him deflated in the next few seconds when Claudia...er, Chloe...shot him down.

"Choose? Good grief, should I pretend you're a couple of rump roasts in the grocery store meat section?" she said. "Are you two always like this?"

"It's not a big deal, angel," Trent said with a comforting smile. "He's not bad. He's just got a big head. Tell him to get lost and we can straighten this out. The two of us have set ground rules for this type of situation. We have ever since we both decided we wanted to marry Melanie Jones in the first grade. Once the choice is made, the other has to back off."

"Poor Melanie probably had a nervous breakdown and ended up being the only six-year-old making pot holders in the nuthouse," Chloe muttered, sounding extremely disgruntled.

"Come on, *Chloe*, tell him to get out of here so we can talk," Trent said, even as he shook his head in amusement.

She paused, staring back and forth between the two of them. As the silence dragged on, Trent began to frown. *This is taking too long.* He took a deep breath, knowing he couldn't have been mistaken about what had happened between them last weekend. Mixed-up identities or not, she could never have faked those responses to their lovemaking. She wanted *him*. No question about it. *So what's the holdup?*

"Well?" Troy prodded. "You got my twin brother when you thought you were getting me. The question is, which one of us did you really *want?*"

She crossed her arms, closing her eyes. "I can't believe this is happening."

"She wanted me," Trent finally snapped. "Not an anal retentive suit-and-tie-wearing manager who only removes his fingers from his calculator keys long enough to unzip his fly!"

Troy remained unfazed. "Oh, so you're saying she wanted the irresponsible grass cutter who chucked his family business in favor of shoveling cow manure?"

Well used to the verbal insults from a lifetime of lobbing them back and forth, Trent didn't take offense. He and Troy might get some serious enjoyment out of belittling one another, but he knew damn well there was no one else in the world as loyal to him as his twin. And the feeling was completely mutual.

The two of them broke into rueful grins. "Just because you're my brother doesn't mean you're not an asshole," Trent said with a reluctant chuckle.

"And just because you're mine doesn't mean I'm going to back off and let you win," Troy retorted every bit as pleasantly.

Trent supposed that to someone else it might appear they detested one another, so it wasn't a total surprise when Chloe said, "You two are unbelievable." She sounded disgusted with them both. "I've decided who needs to leave," she continued as she bent to slip her shoes back on her feet. "Me."

Trent still stood in the doorway. He debated preventing her from going, or insisting on accompanying her. One thing stopped him. A lone, forlorn tear slid out of the corner of one of her beautiful eyes, making a moist path down the silky smooth cheek. The tear was accompanied by a single whispered word. "Please..."

He knew what she asked. *Please give me room. Please let me escape without screaming or bursting into tears. Please don't make me have this conversation right now when I'm feeling so humiliated. Please give me time.*

He stepped aside. Reaching toward her cheek, he gently brushed the tear away. "I'll call you later."

She touched her own face, following the path his fingertips had traced, and gave him a watery smile. Then she nodded and hurried out, leaving Trent and Troy alone in the storeroom.

"Interesting. I never noticed how attractive the little window dresser is," Troy said. "She always seemed so sedate, quiet and...bookish."

"As opposed to your normal preference for platinum blond, easy and stupid?"

Troy shrugged. "Who would ever have imagined sweet-faced Chloe would be so enticing. The blinders are off now, though."

Trent took a few quick steps across the room until he was nose-to-nose with his twin. It was like glaring at his own reflection. Only the slightly shorter hair, the absence of a bit of gold on his brother's earlobe, and the speculative curl of Troy's lips, proved they were two different men.

Well, that and their completely different personalities.

"Troy, I'm telling you now, forget it. She's mine. You don't have a chance."

Troy rubbed a hand against his jaw. "Hmm, you're sounding awfully territorial. You can't have known her very long, or she'd at least have figured out your real name."

Trent narrowed his eyes. "You're on thin ice."

"Oh, come on, you barely know the girl. Are you telling me you won't step aside gracefully if she decides I'm the one she's really interested in?"

"You're not." His tone revealed Trent's certainty. "She was confused. She'll straighten this whole thing out once she's not feeling quite so embarrassed."

Troy shrugged and touched an index finger to his lips. "Perhaps. But can you be sure?" Troy stopped smiling, staring at him intently. "Trent, all kidding aside...have you given any thought to the possibility that what happened last weekend was not quite a mistake. Maybe it was intentional?"

Trent didn't follow.

"I mean," Troy continued, "maybe she set out to get my attention during this conference, long before the two of you ever met. Not for emotional reasons, but for financial ones. And then she ended up with you by accident?"

Trent's teeth clenched in his jaw. "You're way off-base."

His brother persisted. "Look, I'm not trying to score any points off you here. Maybe you're right, and it was all some bizarre misunderstanding. Maybe it will lead to true love, the three-bedroom house and the SUV—that nauseating utopia so sought after by the middle class."

Trent had to laugh at Troy's disdain of marriage and commitment. It'd be interesting to watch his brother cut down to size by some woman someday.

Apparently not noticing Trent's distraction, Troy continued. "Trent, she wouldn't be the first woman to judge the differences between us solely by the size of our bank accounts."

"Huh. You *hope* that's the only size comparison women are making," Trent tossed off, still thinking of Troy's accusations.

Troy caught the insult and smirked. "We're twins, remember?"

Trent hid a grin. "Maybe. But I think I definitely got the lion's share of the *southern* genes, little brother."

"Seems like I'm the one who never lacks for female companionship."

"I wouldn't be bragging about that. One of these days, you're going to get blindsided by some woman. I just hope I'm around to see it."

Troy looked skeptical. "I seriously doubt that day will ever come, but if it does, I hope you enjoy it every bit as much as I'm enjoying today." He then lowered his voice, sounding more sincere. "And I hope I'm wrong about Chloe."

Trent shrugged, remembering what his brother had implied. He didn't like it, but the niggling seed of suspicion did plant itself somewhere deep in his brain. He knew it was going to be there for quite a while, or at least until he got to talk to Chloe alone. "I should go find her."

"I don't think she wants to be found. Besides, it's your first day back. Have you even gone to the resort to check on your crews? Or to the storage unit you call an office?"

"Not your company, not your concern," Trent replied.

"I'm worried about you. Is that allowed?" Troy asked.

"Thanks, Troy," Trent said his voice softening. "I'm

doing okay. You don't need to worry—although I can see why you wouldn't want me to fail and come back here. Then you'd be out of a job, little brother."

Troy barked a laugh. "Some days that doesn't seem like such a bad thing. Maybe it would make my life easier if The Great Outdoors sank back into the compost pile from which it arose. Then Grandmother could turn her corporate—not to mention matchmaking—eye on her other grandson for a while. The woman really seems determined to get some great-grandchildren."

Despite his comments, Trent knew full well his brother didn't want him to fail. Not out of any great liking for Trent's fledgling company, but out of respect for Trent's courage in striking out and making it happen. Trent knew his brother didn't envy him—but he did respect him.

The feeling was mutual. The two of them had often talked about the stifling lack of freedom in their family. It was no secret Troy was not always happy in his role as heir apparent. But if not happy, at least he was content. Not to mention dedicated. Trent had to admire his brother for that. He didn't think he could have been as gracious were their roles reversed.

"So Grandmother's not going to get her wish. The grass-cutting guru is not about to come crawling back to the fold?"

"Nope. You get to be the king of this retail castle for the rest of your life. I'll remain the minor stockholding prince."

"I think you mean jester." Troy turned toward the door.

Trent rolled his eyes. Before they left the room, Trent

said, "By the way, stay away from Chloe. You kiss her again and you're dead meat."

Troy's evil chuckle said his brotherly niceness quotient was fully used up. "Seems to me she hasn't officially made her choice yet. Until then, the field's wide-open."

Knowing his brother was just trying to get on his nerves, Trent ignored him and left the room.

Though he'd fully expected Chloe to be long gone, Trent cast a quick look around outside as he left the store anyway. He saw her right away. She stood beside his truck, her arms wrapped tightly around her body, one hand wearily rubbing her brow.

"Claudia," he shouted as he strode across the parking lot toward her. He offered her a sheepish smile when he reached her side. "Sorry. I mean Chloe. It's going to take me a while to get used to your real name." He tilted his head, looking at her. "But it suits you."

She bit her lip.

"I'm glad you waited," he continued, not wanting her to run off again. She looked as though she wanted to do exactly that, as if with one misspoken word, she'd dart off and never trust him enough to even speak to him again. More proof, as far as he was concerned, that she was nothing more than the open, genuinely trusting, honest person he'd perceived her to be from the moment they'd met. "Let's go someplace and talk. Away from here. Away from Troy and the store and everything else."

She twisted her hands together and looked at the ground, scuffing the pavement with the toe of her sandal. Then she finally met his eye. Her stare asked for nothing but the truth. "Tell me one thing, okay? One thing before I go someplace by myself to think over this whole *awful* thing—which is exactly what I'm going to do in about two minutes."

"It wasn't all awful," he said softly, trying to comfort her. "I remember one or two very nice things that have happened since we met Friday night."

She frowned, creating an adorable, unfamiliar line above her brow. He wanted to kiss it away. Wanted to kiss her lips until they spread into a beautiful smile. Since he'd left her so abruptly Saturday, he'd been thinking of nothing else but getting right back to where they'd been when his cell phone had interrupted them. Their late-night phone calls had done nothing but fuel the fire of his desire for her.

Right at this particular moment, however, she looked fully prepared to punch him if he so much as touched her arm.

"That's the problem," she finally whispered. "You believed we *met* Friday night."

"We did meet Friday night."

"According to you. Not to me."

He nodded, seeing her logic. "Okay, you obviously didn't realize Friday was our first meeting."

She looked exasperated. "Well, that's the point."

He shook his head. "I'm not following."

"You had just met me, yet you...we...."

He suddenly understood. "Well, you had just met me, too."

"But it's not the same thing." Her words ended in a near wail. She immediately lowered her voice as someone pulled up in a parking space nearby. "I thought I knew you. I did not realize I was with a complete stranger."

Trent recognized her anxiety. "And I did."

"Exactly!"

"So now you want to know if I make a habit of this, if I go around picking up beautiful brunettes in hotel bars and having wild sex with them on the beach?"

She sucked her bottom lip into her mouth, looking almost ashamed, then defiantly nodded. "Yes."

"Nope. Never have before. Never will again. You were my one and only bar pickup."

"Oh, thanks," she muttered. "Should I feel complimented that I transformed you into a lounge lizard?"

He grinned at her obvious disgust. "Look, Chloe, I'm being completely honest with you here. No games. No pretense."

"There's a first in our relationship."

He ignored her pessimism. "I'm not a saint. I'm not exactly proud of some of the things I did in my younger years. But I can tell you one thing for sure— what happened between us Friday night happened because we instantly clicked. I knew right away we were perfect together." He crossed his arms. "You know, if I were a less confident guy, I might take offense at being thought of as cheap and easy."

She gulped. "So you didn't think...that is, you didn't assume I was some tramp on the prowl?"

Her words brought Troy's allegations to mind. He thrust them away. "No. I was too busy being glad I met you to question why we ended up together." He lowered his voice, leaning closer until he saw her hair move under his breath. "I'm still glad, Chloe. Nothing has changed for me. Nothing."

She froze for a long, heavy moment, her body swaying unconsciously toward his. Then she took a quick step back, again wrapping her arms around herself. Finally she nodded. "Thank you for clearing things up, but I still have some thinking to do. I need to figure out how I am going to deal with what happened. Taking up with a complete stranger isn't something I've ever considered doing, Trent. This is *not* me!"

He touched her cheek with the back of his fingers, noting the pale translucence of her skin. "You can be whoever you want to be, Chloe, and it isn't going to change the way we reacted to one another. It can never erase what happened between us last weekend. And what *else* is going to happen between us."

Her breathing deepened as he leaned closer to brush a kiss on her temple. "There's an else?"

"Uh-huh," he whispered against her jaw. "Definitely an else. But I think you need to come to that conclusion yourself."

She stepped back. "I'll call you." Then she hopped into a small car parked in the next spot and sped away.

It wasn't until after she left that he spotted her purse on the ground beside his truck.

AFTER LEAVING TRENT, Chloe debated where to go. Home was out. Her mother and sister would take one look at her and know something was wrong. Her mother would then try to help by chanting or filling her with herbal tea. Meanwhile, Morgan would listen and tuck all that adult information into her young, impressionable, teenage brain. She'd see yet another example of how pathetic the love lives of the women in their family were.

Chloe instead drove the few blocks to the beach. Ignoring the dire threats of towing and prosecution, she parked illegally near one of the highbrow hotels and walked to the nearest access ramp. The last time she'd stood on a beach had been just a few nights before. With Troy. "No, Chloe, with *Trent.*"

Staring at the churning surf, she felt tears flow from her eyes in earnest. "You're an idiot, Chloe Weston, and you should have listened to Sister Mary Frances." She waited for the little voice of dissent that would let her off. It didn't come. "See, even your subconscious can't defend you, because you're a major screwup."

A young couple walking on the beach glanced at her. *Don't mind me, I'm just a good girl gone very bad. Someone call Jenny Jones. I see a big story: women who sleep with a complete stranger while thinking they're sleeping with their boss.*

"Trent was really Trent," Chloe mused. He really was the guy who liked to strip off his shirt and dance in the rain. The skydiver. The risk-taker. The one with the killer smile and the gold stud earring. The one who could bring her from blasé to fully aroused in two-point-nine seconds.

And Troy was really Troy. The store owner. The businessman. The nine-to-five, open-mouth-insert-silver-spoon millionaire. Although, from some of the insults the brothers had tossed around, she had to wonder if there was more to Troy than she'd ever suspected. Heck, she didn't really know *either* brother.

Chloe pulled her sandals off and walked down the wooden crossover to the nearly deserted beach. The vacationers were likely back in their rooms, slathering on the Solarcaine. Soon they'd head out in their limos for an expensive dinner. They'd never spare a moment to worry about mundane things like rent, health insurance, or clothing their young children.

They were the rich people. The spoiled people. People like Troy Langtree. But *not* like his twin.

Having spent a good portion of her childhood wondering whether her mom was going to be able to pay the phone bill before the service got cut off, Chloe couldn't understand someone simply walking away from financial security. Saying thanks but no thanks to a great job. Yet that's what Trent had done. He'd walked away. And not merely from security—he'd walked away from wealth!

Wealth doesn't matter. True. Chloe didn't pine for yachts, or want to eat caviar. But she'd like to think she'd soon see the end of boxed macaroni and cheese and hot dogs for dinner.

Now, especially, with her mother unemployed and their savings running out, Chloe felt particularly confused by anyone who'd toss away success. She sighed, staring at the ocean.

If her mother would just get a job to help cover the rent, things could improve greatly. But Jeanine was so wrapped up in her latest business venture—and her latest romance—that Chloe had stopped asking if she'd gone through the help wanted ads. Chloe had also taken the precaution of hiding the passbook for Morgan's college account. Heaven knew she loved her mother, and generally trusted her, but Jeanine sometimes acted before thinking. Jeanine had been hinting quite a lot about how much easier things would be if they tapped into that fund, saying they could replace it with the fortune she'd make on the shop she wanted to open.

Chloe was not about to risk Morgan's future on another one of their mother's pipe dreams.

So is it the money? Is that why you were so shocked that Trent and Troy are two different people—and Trent's not the rich, successful guy you thought he was?

"No. It isn't." She didn't believe herself a shallow person. And she knew, deep in her heart, that she hadn't been interested in Troy when he was only a rich, stuffy department-store owner. No question, the desire had been all for Trent. Wonderful, dazzling, seductive Trent spinning shirtless in the rain.

Her heart beat faster just thinking of him. She remembered in the store when he'd brushed away her tear, looking at her with the tenderness of a man who truly cared about her. And, of course, she'd noticed the earring. He still wore it, as he'd promised.

"Knock it off, Chloe, this isn't some sappy Fred and Ginger story." More like a twisted Tennessee Williams's play. *Girl sees boy. Girl wants boy. Girl gives herself to boy. Girl learns boy is a stranger who could very well have a pair of wives somewhere.*

"Okay, now you're just being morose," Chloe said aloud.

Her instincts about Trent couldn't have been so completely off-base. Still, getting involved with him was exactly what she'd sworn she'd never do: taking up with a complete stranger. After her mom had taken up with Tanner the trucker, then found out he liked to wear women's underwear, Chloe had decided she'd never so much as kiss a guy unless she knew his address and date of birth. Troy had seemed safe, since she'd thought she knew a lot about him—and look how wrong she'd been about him!

As for Trent, she'd slept with him and didn't even know his middle name, phone number or age. Plus, the more she learned about him, the more Chloe feared he was exactly the opposite of the type of man she always thought she wanted. He liked risks, he was impulsive, he saw something he wanted and went after it. The kind of person who didn't mind uncertainty, who wouldn't worry about what happened tomorrow when today could be so glorious. Just like her mother.

Three words described getting involved with Trent Langtree: wrong, wrong, wrong.

Funny though...the only way she could remember him making her feel was completely and totally right.

7

TRENT HATED TO INVADE Chloe's privacy by going through her purse. But it was either find her address that way or try to get Troy to give it to him out of her personnel file. Snatching her black leather wallet out of the mysterious depths of her female armament bag seemed the lesser of two evils. He even managed to avoid plucking out any scary-looking feminine products.

When he pulled up outside her house in Coral Springs, he made a few assumptions. First, Chloe hadn't exaggerated the modest circumstances from which she came. The house appeared neat, but had seen better days. An old Florida bungalow, its faded lime-green stucco exterior cried out for fresh paint, and its old-fashioned casement windows needed replacing.

Also, someone in the house had one bizarre liking for ceramic animals. The landscaping bed next to the front door was overrun with frolicking squirrels, chipmunks, alligators and hedgehogs. He expected Snow White to come skipping out of the house at any moment. Eyeing one cumbersome rabbit crushing the fronds of a really nice-looking sago palm, he stepped closer, but the door opened before he could save the poor plant.

"You're not the pizza guy." A teenage girl wearing

thick glasses and a frown spoke to him from the front step.

"No, I don't come bearing pepperoni and mushrooms."

"Meat. Ugh," she said with a shudder. "Spinach, onions, and double garlic. Not that it's any of your business."

"Nope, not my business. Though I have to ask...you don't have a date tonight, do you? I mean, double garlic and onions? Or do you plan to scare off some vampires?"

"Just 'cause you're cute doesn't mean you can comment on my choice of pizza. Now who are you and what are you selling?"

He ignored the "cute" remark. He sensed it wasn't a compliment. "I'm not going to try to sell you something."

She smirked. "Sure you're not. Look, buddy, the blue-haired set in this neighborhood gets a little antsy about hunks in tight jeans going door to door peddling stuff."

"I'm really *not* a salesman," Trent began to explain.

"Well, you're not in a suit, so I guess you aren't here to try to save my soul from the fiery pit, either." She peered owlishly at him through the glasses. "Oh, wait a second, are you the guy who called a while ago looking for Chloe?" The girl broke into a smile. The sharp angles of her face softened, revealing a sparkle in blue eyes that he now realized looked like her sister's.

"Yeah. I'm Trent. I brought her purse." He held up Chloe's small bag.

"I'm Morgan, her sister. She's not here." She snickered. "I thought you were going to rip off her clothes, not her purse."

Remembering what he'd said when Morgan had answered Chloe's phone, Trent felt his face go red. Morgan saw. "You're even cuter when you blush. Come on in and wait for her."

As soon as they stepped in the door, a pizza delivery truck pulled up outside. Trent paid for the pizza. He then proceeded to devour a third of it while he and Morgan got to know one another in the kitchen of the small but neat house.

"You know, you probably shouldn't have eaten this pizza if you and Chloe have a date tonight."

"Chloe has a date tonight?"

Trent started as another woman entered the kitchen from a side door. He instantly recognized where Chloe and her sister got their blue eyes. "You must be Chloe's mother."

The woman nodded, smiling as she looked him over head to foot. "Yes, I'm Jeanine. You're really here for Chloe? Well, isn't that the grooviest thing to happen all week."

Groovy? Given the loose, flowing dress, the long purple scarf and the dangly crystal earrings, Trent figured the woman was stuck a few decades in the past. If he hadn't known she had a daughter in her mid-twenties, Trent wouldn't have imagined Jeanine could be old enough to be a sixties flower child. Her youthful, unlined face didn't hint at her real age. The dreamy look in her eyes said she was also more than a little spacey.

"Mom, did you eat anything today?" Morgan asked as she set another plate. "You've been in your studio for hours."

Janine absently waved a hand in the air, as if the issue of food was a mere trifle. Trent watched with interest as Morgan gently sat her mother in a chair and put food and a drink in front of her. He had the feeling this wasn't an infrequent occurrence.

"Studio? Are you an artist?" Trent asked.

"Ceramics. My latest passion. My studio is the garage."

"Ah, the menagerie in the front yard."

"Better than the naked dancing school," Morgan muttered, shoving her glasses higher on her nose with the tip of a finger.

"It was artistic dancing, Morgan. Performance art."

Morgan snorted. "It was naked fat guys trying to look like the elements while gyrating to Earth, Wind and Fire."

Trent bit another piece of pizza to hide his laughter.

"I enjoyed helping people discover their inner talents and beauty," Jeanine said, her expression gentle and introspective.

"They mighta had inner beauty, but there was some serious outer ugly among your dance students, Mom."

Trent chuckled again, liking Chloe's sister more and more.

So, Jeanine was the irresponsible dreamer who, he remembered Chloe saying, hadn't had the best of luck in the romance arena. Morgan was the tough teen who'd obviously had to grow up a lot sooner than most kids her age. Where did that leave Chloe? His delightful, smiling, laughing Chloe? He had a sinking feeling he knew exactly where it left her—right in the middle. Being the adult in her relationship with her mother while trying to help her sister continue to be a child.

He now wanted to be with her more than ever. To get to know her, all about her. Her secrets, her true wishes, dreams and desires. To tell her he understood her need to be wildly free and uninhibited if only for the space of one all-too-short weekend. She'd wanted to lose herself with him for a few days at a distant, romantic resort. He didn't imagine she'd had much opportunity in her life to truly indulge her own fantasies. He hoped he'd have the chance to help her indulge in a few more.

"So, Trent, what do you do?"

Before he could reply, the phone rang. Morgan answered and waved to let him know it was Chloe. She didn't tell Chloe he was here, seemingly too busy listening. The girl winced, then rolled her eyes. After a minute or two, she hung up and looked toward Trent. "Feel like going back up to Boca? Chloe's in trouble."

Trent was on his feet, walking toward the door before Morgan could utter another word.

"Oh, he's a gentleman," Jeanine said approvingly.

"You wanna know where she is?"

He paused only long enough to hear Chloe's location. Then he turned to leave again.

"Hold up." Morgan scooped Chloe's purse up off the kitchen table and tossed it to him. "She'll probably need this. She's going to have to pay the towing company."

If she lived to be a hundred, Chloe would never ignore a No Parking sign again. That no-no now had a spot high on her life's list of stupid things to avoid at all costs. It was positioned at number three, below ever getting another spiral perm, and two down from going looney-as-a-bedbug over a complete stranger.

"Thanks for lending me the money to make the phone call," she said to the man who was about to leave her stranded. She knew the tow-truck driver must have heard her grudging tone, but didn't care. It was like thanking the toll booth attendant for allowing you to pay to drive on a public road. Like thanking the cop who just wrote your speeding ticket. Some things shouldn't get gratitude.

"No problem," the guy said with a smirk. "The lot address is on the card. You can leave the phone call money with the office when you come to get your car tomorrow."

So much for the kindness of strangers. He drove away, towing her dull but reliable hatchback along behind him.

When she'd returned from the beach to find him hooking up her car to his truck, she'd immediately begged him not to. Desperate, she'd offered him a promise to be gone in twenty seconds, leaving him with fifty bucks, to forget all about her.

Chloe had opened her door to get her purse for the promised fifty. She'd kept that much out when she deposited her paycheck earlier, planning a grocery run. Remembering she'd stopped for a burger and fries at lunchtime, she hoped the guy wouldn't mind forty-seven in bills and three in coins she'd have to dig out from under the seats of her car or the bottom of her purse.

No purse. No fifty dollars. No nice wave from a paid-off driver. To top it all off, Chloe couldn't even dig up the coins to make one lousy phone call and had to bum it from the man.

After he'd gone, Chloe sat dejectedly on the wooden steps of the beach crossover, her head lowered, forehead cupped in her hands. This ranked up pretty high on her list of bad days. Certainly not as high as the day her father had walked out. Or the day Morgan's had. But it was definitely a bad one.

When she heard a rumbling engine, she didn't look up. It couldn't be her mother. Jeanine's ancient Volkswagen Beetle made a distinctive putt-putt-sputter sound. She shuddered at having to ride in the thing, which her mother called the Love Bug.

At age nineteen, Chloe had finally gotten Jeanine to explain the name. Learning that Morgan had been conceived in it, Chloe had refused to ride in the Beetle from then on, unless it was unavoidable. Precocious, ten-year-old Morgan had looked up the word conceived in the dictionary, asked her mother if she was a contortionist, then boycotted the car as well.

Her mother had called them her Prudey Pollies. Chloe preferred to think of them as normal girls who were grossed out by the thought of their mother having sex, much less having sex in a vehicle in which they'd ridden hundreds of times.

"A purse for your thoughts?"

She knew that voice. Jerking her head back so hard she heard her neck crack, Chloe looked up in shock to see Trent—yes, definitely Trent, not his twin—standing above her. Before she could reply, he plopped down next to her on the step.

"How...what..."

"You dropped your purse at the store. I took it to your house and was there when you called for help."

"Thank you. I can't imagine how I dropped it without realizing." *Probably because he's fried your brain cells!*

Here they were, alone again at a romantic beach. A dangerous situation all the way around. But she had to be genuinely grateful. He'd gone to a lot of trouble—

first driving to her house, then all the way up here to return her bag.

"You even saved me from the Love Bug," she mumbled. He gave her a curious look, probably thinking she was referring to the pesky insects that descended upon Florida twice a year. The creatures went flying around in swarms, thousands of pairs of them conjoined in connubial bliss until they splatted en masse onto every car windshield in the state. For the first time ever, Chloe began to sympathize with them. *At least they go out happy and don't have to deal with the morning after.*

"Let's take a walk," Trent said as he grabbed her hand and pulled her to her feet.

"I don't know if that's such a good idea. You and me alone on a beach again?"

He gave her a wolfish smile. "Yeah."

"Wouldn't we be asking for trouble?"

"Just to talk, Chloe, okay? I promise."

She thought it over, then frowned. "Sure, we'll go down and walk on the beach, only to come back in time to find your truck being towed away. Then we can both try to figure out how to get home tonight."

"There's a hotel right over there where we could stay if we get stranded." He tilted his head toward the building behind them, looking so boyishly hopeful she had to grin.

"I somehow got the impression five-star hotels are out of the price range of Trent the landscaping guy."

"And Chloe the window dresser."

"Touché. So we were both fish out of water at the Dolphin Island Resort."

"Maybe that's why we connected," he said, leaning closer until she could feel his warmth. "Weren't we both looking to be a little crazy for one outrageously wicked weekend?"

One outrageously wicked weekend. One outrageously wicked *interrupted* weekend. Chloe swallowed hard, very much aware of his long, lean body nearly touching hers from shoulder to hip. She searched for some inner willpower that would allow her to remain impervious to the sensual lure this man had held for her since the first moment she'd seen him. There was none. As she'd discovered last weekend, when it came to Trent Langtree, she had the strength of will of a three-day-old kitten.

She still gave it her best shot, trying hard to sound like a cool, collected, put-together grown-up. "The weekend's over, Trent—over and best forgotten."

"Yet here we are, still together." He leaned closer, his intimate smile flashing white in the near darkness of the late Florida sunset.

"By accident," she managed to whisper.

"Don't the best things always seem to happen by accident?" He raised his hand and cupped her arm, his thumb stroking the cool skin at the hollow of her elbow.

She gulped, then jerked back. "Hands off, mister." *So much for cool and collected!* "I mean, please, we need to talk. Not..." *Walk down to the beach and go for another salty, sweaty, sexy swim?* "Not touch."

He held up his hands, palms out. "Okay. No touching. Talking only."

A car pulled into the lot, its headlights nearly blinding them as it drove toward the last row of parking spaces near where they stood. Chloe raised a hand to her eyes, turning her face. Trent had just done the same thing, so the two of them ended up staring into each other's eyes.

"We'd better get out of here before the greedy tow-truck guy comes back," she finally said, forcing herself to look away.

"We'll go somewhere else to talk. Are you hungry?"

Her growling stomach answered his question. Her fast-food lunch had worn off hours ago. "I guess."

"Well, let's go get you some dinner," Trent said as he took her hand and turned toward his truck.

"I don't think so. But I would appreciate a ride home."

Trent grimaced, looking sheepish. "You can't eat at home because the pizza's all gone."

Chloe frowned. "Pizza? You've been sitting down at my house eating pizza with my family?" Not waiting for him to answer, she rose up on her tiptoes and sniffed, searching for evidence that he really had stolen her dinner. Before she knew what he was doing, he'd swooped down and pressed a kiss on her mouth, licking lightly at her lips.

The contact was electric, not to mention spicy. She pulled away and shook an index finger at his face. "You rat! Spinach, garlic and onions. You did eat all my pizza."

"Guilty," he said with a teasing laugh. "Tastes a lot better than it sounds. And since it got me a kiss, I can't truthfully say I'm sorry for eating all your pizza, Chloe."

Well, in the interest of being completely honest, neither could she. There'd been zing, pow, explosions galore just from the briefest brush of her lips against his. No question, Trent called to some deep, inner part of her which his brother Troy had left completely unaffected.

That didn't mean she was even *thinking* about kissing him again. Uh-uh. No way. Not until she'd gotten her head together and set some ground rules—first of which was actually getting to know the man. Until she at least knew his middle name, shoe size and date of birth, his way-too-kissable mouth wasn't coming anywhere near hers again.

"Okay, well, since you ate my pizza, and I never got to the grocery store today, you *can* get me something to eat then." She dug into her purse and pulled out a piece of minty gum. "And here!"

He laughed as he opened it. "Thanks." Then he put it in his mouth and chewed, still grinning. Heck, even the rhythmic motion of his jaw as he chewed gum was too sexy for her peace of mind.

Together they walked to his truck, which was so high he had to help her up into the passenger seat. She'd bet her last dime his little push to her fanny with the palm of his hand hadn't been entirely necessary. Entirely enjoyable, yes, but not necessary.

Alone in the dark, cozy cab, she sidled close to the door and clung to it as if stuck there with Velcro. She heard his low chuckle in the darkness. He'd obviously noticed the invisible wall she was trying to erect between them. They drove in silence for a few minutes, Chloe not quite sure what to say to this man, with whom she'd been so intimate a few days before.

"You okay?"

"Yeah," she whispered, wondering how he'd known she was upset. She really *shouldn't* be feeling upset. Embarrassed, yes. A little stupid and blind, yes. But upset to find out Trent was not Troy? The fact that he wasn't the straitlaced store manager should have made things better, not worse.

Trent was the same sexy, amazing lover who'd brought her to such astounding heights last weekend. He certainly already knew her better than any man had ever known her. They'd gone well beyond shyness, beyond any possibility of playing coy. They'd intimately gotten to know one another's likes and dislikes. Where to caress. When to speed up or slow down. What spot on his body could elicit a groan when touched with her lips. Where he could touch her in return that changed her moans into screams of pleasure.

No. He hadn't changed. He was the same man. The same man...but a complete stranger. A stranger who, as it turned out, was exactly the type of man she'd sworn to never become involved with. A risk-taker. A daredevil. A man who walked away from security and stability and embraced uncertainty. The kind of guy who could never be happy with the steady, conservative, steady life Chloe had longed for since childhood.

"What are you thinking?" he asked.

"I'm still wondering if this whole thing was a nightmare and I'm going to wake up," she admitted.

"Now you've gone and hurt my feelings."

Instantly contrite, she turned toward him. "I'm sorry, I didn't mean it was *all* awful."

His gentle smile told her he'd been teasing. "Gee, that's comforting. So, what part wasn't so awful? Friday night on the beach? Saturday night in your room?" He paused, lowering his voice. "The phone calls?"

Though the air conditioner was on, blowing a steady stream of cool air into the darkened cab of the truck, Chloe felt sweat bead on her upper lip. She shifted, the loose, filmy fabric of her skirt suddenly feeling too confining, the slick leather seats almost uncomfortably firm beneath her overly sensitive body.

The phone calls. Only one night ago they'd been exchanging erotic whispers on the phone, fantasizing together in a long, sultry call that had lasted nearly two hours. When she remembered telling him how she sometimes wondered what it would be like to be made love to while gently restrained with soft, silky scarves, she felt her face grow hotter.

Then she recalled the raw need in his voice as he'd told her how much he thought about Saturday night. How he fantasized about finishing what they'd started. The way he'd stand her in front of him and slowly strip off her thong. Taste her until she exploded, then, while she still shook, stand up and enter her from behind, holding her around the waist, cupping her breast with his hand, driving into her until they both fell to the bed in completion.

She shuddered.

In the darkness he took her hand. She clutched it, saying nothing. Chloe needed the tenderness he silently offered and took the reassurance his gentle touch provided.

"I'm sorry. I shouldn't have mentioned that," he finally said, his voice low and gravelly, as if he, too, had allowed himself to get lost in sensual memory. "I didn't track you down to seduce you, or to ignore what you're going through."

Seduce her? Heck, if he kept rubbing the tip of his index finger on the fleshy skin of her palm, she was going to be ripping her own clothes off before they got to I-95. And she'd feel a whole heck of a lot better if he'd roll down the window and spit out the piece of gum, which still made his jaw roll in a sexy, lazy rhythm that had her shifting in her dampening panties.

"Thank you. Look, I think it's best if you just take me home. I can have something to eat there. I'd really like to be alone for a while."

Get me home. Get me out of this truck with my underwear still on and my libido in check!

He appeared about to argue, but didn't. They drove in silence for several minutes, his hand still lightly resting on hers. She used the cover of darkness to study the strength of his profile, his sculpted jaw, his strong chin. His mouth.

She forced herself to look away, staring at the black pavement passing beneath the tires. But her gaze kept returning to him. How could she ever have confused him with his brother? They were identical yet so completely different in every way that mattered.

When they'd nearly reached her neighborhood, Trent broke the silence. "How long are you going to need to come to grips with this? Can we get together tomorrow?"

"I don't know."

He sighed in frustration. "So tell me, talk to me. What's bugging you the most? Are you embarrassed? Worried Troy is going to say something? Because he won't, I can guarantee that. I've got way too much on him for him to shoot off his mouth."

Two lotharios. "How reassuring." She thought about his question, what was most bothering her about the situation. "I don't like feeling I'm not in control."

"Are you always in control, Chloe?"

She laughed softly. "No, not usually. But I like to pretend I am. And I like to let other people around me think I know exactly what I'm doing at all times."

"So getting caught in a little case of mistaken identity…"

"A *little* case of mistaken identity? That's like saying Mount Everest is a little hill."

"Chloe, you aren't the first person to get me and Troy confused. Even though I'm much better looking and a hell of a lot more pleasant."

She managed a grin. "Yes, you are. And ever so modest."

His fingers tightened around hers. "So this issue of being confused isn't really an issue, because I'm the Langtree you want to be with."

When she hesitated, his hand started to loosen.

Yes, *yes*, she wanted to be with him in terms of being naked and hot and sweaty. But be with him forever? Let herself love him the way she'd believed she could last weekend, when she thought he was the stick-around type, the nine-to-five businessman who might want the wife and the kids and the house in the burbs? She simply couldn't say.

"Chloe?"

"I don't know what I want right now," she admitted softly.

"You think you might be able to explain this to me?" His voice carried an edge.

She wasn't sure she could, but had to try. "Trent, there's no question my body wants you, and has since the beginning."

He hesitated, then said, "But your brain doesn't?" She hesitated, and he continued. "Or is it that your brain is interested in one brother and your body in another?"

This time there was no mistaking the anger in his voice or the stiffness of his shoulders in his tight shirt.

His muscles bunched under his sleeve, reminding her of his coiled strength.

She immediately wanted to deny his accusation. She hated the way his words had sounded, hated angering or, worse, hurting him. But his words weren't *entirely* inaccurate.

Physically, there was no doubt which man she wanted. Trent. And mentally, well, she knew full well she didn't want Troy in any way, shape or form. But she couldn't deny she'd wanted what she thought Troy represented—stability, security, safety.

They pulled into her driveway before she could respond to his accusation. She saw by the tenseness of his jaw and the flash in his green eyes that he'd read into her silence and found an answer not to his liking.

Chloe started to speak, but he'd already opened his door and hopped out of the truck, coming around to help her down as well. As always so thoughtful, even when he was obviously bloody furious with her.

Her body slid against his as he helped her down, creating delightful friction and instant heat. Her breasts brushed his chest, her thighs his legs. Showing no reaction to the moment, he stepped back and took her arm, walking her to the door.

"Trent..." she began to say, knowing she couldn't leave things like this. She had to explain, had to make him understand. She didn't want him getting back in his truck tonight thinking she really had any interest in his brother.

Before she could say another word, however, the front door opened. "You're back," her mother said with a wide smile. "And just in time." Jeanine stepped inside, holding the door wide to usher them both in. Trent remained on the porch.

"Good night, Chloe."

"You're not coming in?" Jeanine playfully wagged her index finger at him. "You big romantic, don't you even want to see how lovely the flowers you sent look?"

"Flowers?" Chloe asked.

Trent just stared.

"Uh, Mom, maybe you should let Chloe come in and read the card," Morgan said. Bless her perceptive little sister's heart, she'd obviously taken one look at Chloe and Trent and read the tension between them.

"Don't be silly," Jeanine said with a wave of her hand, oblivious to anything except the whiff of romance in the air.

Jeanine grabbed Trent's hand and tugged him inside. Chloe followed, watching as her mother waved her arm toward a huge bouquet of long-stemmed red roses standing on a coffee table in their small living room.

She knew they weren't from Trent. She'd seen that instantly by the controlled yet almost amused look on his face. Feigned amusement, most likely. The tightness of his smile told her he was still angry about her thoughtless silence in the truck. The flowers weren't helping one bit.

"How wonderfully extravagant of you, Trent," Jeanine continued, nearly gushing.

Mother, shut up!

"They're not from me."

Jeanine had the grace to flush. Trent chuckled wickedly as he walked over to the vase, plucked the card out of the flowers and tossed it over his shoulder to Chloe. She caught it in midair but didn't have to read it to know it was from Troy.

Trent plucked a single rose out of the bouquet. "My brother was always such a show-off. He's never learned the value of simplicity." He turned to Jeanine, handing her the rose and giving her an intimate look. "A single bud placed into a woman's hand is much more personal."

Her mother visibly melted. Chloe eyed him warily.

Removing a spray of baby's breath from the bouquet, he walked across the room to stand in front of Morgan. Tucking it into her hair with a gentle smile, he whispered, "Understated appreciation is always more genuine than blatant flattery."

Unflappable Morgan actually blushed.

Chloe waited, her heart stuck in her throat, as Trent went back to the table and pulled the remaining flowers out of the vase. Unsure what he'd do next, she froze as he moved toward her. Her breath caught. Her pulse sped up. Her eyes widened as she watched him walk around her to open the door.

Then he pitched the entire bouquet out onto the darkened front lawn.

Behind her, Jeanine gasped as Morgan snorted with laughter.

Trent turned to Chloe, taking her by the shoulders. "Flowers can never say something as powerfully as this."

Completely ignoring the presence of her mother and sister, he hauled her up onto her tiptoes, catching her mouth in a kiss that turned her into a big pile of quivering jelly. Boneless. Liquid. Completely saturated with desire as he plumbed the recesses of her mouth with his tongue. He tasted her secrets, sipped, then drank deeply of her, using his expert mouth to bring her to one large, living, breathing, raging hormone. He kissed her like she'd *never* been kissed in her life.

Then he simply let her go and walked out of the house.

The moment the door slammed shut behind him, her wobbly legs gave out. Chloe slid down the wall to land on her butt on the foyer floor.

"I'd rather have gotten what you got," Jeanine mused with a little shrug and a wink. Sniffing her flower, she breezed out of the room.

Morgan cleared her throat and gave her head a hard shake, as if to wake up from a dream. Finally she turned to follow their mother. Giving a shaky sigh, she said, "Me, too."

Chloe couldn't say a word.

8

AFTER HE DROVE AWAY from Chloe's house, Trent spotted a convenience store nearby and pulled into the parking lot. He needed a cold drink, not only because he was overheated, but also to wash down the wad of chewing gum he'd quickly swallowed just before kissing Chloe in her living room. Remembering his mother's dire warnings during his childhood, he wondered if kissing Chloe would be worth seven years of gummed-up kidneys.

"Yep. That kiss was definitely worth it." A reluctant grin curled across his lips at the memory as he hopped out of the truck and went into the brightly lit store.

Trent couldn't ever remember being so emotionally wrung out. First off, he'd been craving her for days. Then, tonight, he'd been mad as hell at her for what she *hadn't* said on the ride home. Add his annoyance with his brother, the tension in the room, the stressful week...and his restraints had simply snapped. He'd acted on instinct, anger and need, and found himself turning into some kind of possessive neanderthal.

Five minutes later, back in his truck with a can of soda in his hand, he headed toward the interstate for the drive home.

"Getting all worked up in front of a woman's mother is seriously uncool," he muttered, his thoughts returning to what had happened at Chloe's.

He couldn't believe he'd become so instantly aroused. He'd been lost to everything else, ready to pick her up and carry her to the nearest flat surface— preferably a bed, though the kitchen table would have sufficed. He'd barely even remembered they stood right in front of her mother and sister.

"Moron." As if the woman hadn't been embarrassed enough already today. What had happened at Langtree's that afternoon would have to go onto one of Chloe's lists, the ones she'd talked about during their long, playful conversation in the bar last Friday night. He wondered if he should start a list of most humiliating moments. Just today he would chalk up a few good entries.

He really hadn't set out to embarrass her. Then, remembering her silence in his truck during their ride back to his house, he shrugged off his guilt. "Something needed to wake the woman up. She's obviously not thinking straight."

Either that, or she was one hell of an actress who'd really managed to snow him about her true feelings and desires.

He should wash his hands of the whole situation. Walk away, tuck the memory of last weekend away for his old age when he could be a dirty old man and cackle about his wilder younger days. Remember one hot, wicked weekend with a beautiful stranger who had a captivating smile.

He shook his head. "Screw that." No way was he letting her go. She might not have been jumping up and down to assure him she had no interest in his brother, but Trent knew she really didn't. She certainly hadn't been melting into Troy's arms earlier at the store. And

Chloe was much too bright and down-to-earth a woman to want a smooth operator like Troy.

No, there had to be something else holding her back. One way or another, he was determined to find out what.

TRENT COULDN'T BEGIN his plan of figuring out just what was going on in Chloe Weston's mind on Thursday because he worked a thirteen-hour day. He spent the morning driving all over north Broward County to check on his regular crews. The grass-cutting contracts at a number of the pricier homes in the area, plus maintenance commitments with a number of small businesses, were the bread and butter of The Great Outdoors. They wouldn't make him rich, but they did allow him to cover the weekly payroll.

The Dolphin Island Resort and Country Club job was a different story. That was his E-ticket ride out of the ranks of struggling landscaping guy and into the realm of successful business owner. So he spent the bulk of the day there. It was a good thing, too. In the few days he'd been gone, one of his crews had accidentally struck a water line with a posthole digger. Another had planted some pricey magnolia trees so close to the beach they'd be dead from the salt spray in two months. And a supplier had delivered three-hundred Andorra junipers when he'd ordered blue rug.

"How could things go straight to hell in five days?" he asked Jason Richter, his chief foreman on the Dolphin Island job. The two of them stood in the construction trailer on the north edge of the resort grounds.

"I'm sorry, boss. I can't be in ten places at once."

Trent shook his head. "I know. It's not your fault—

it's mine. I should have been here. Has Ripley been all over you?"

Jason laughed in spite of his obvious weariness. "Uh, did you know Ripley has some serious allergies? He came strutting out to the west lawn one afternoon when we were planting some flowering trees and turned a very interesting shade of blotchy red. Haven't seen him since."

Trent chuckled. "I'll have to remember that."

The two of them spent another thirty minutes scheduling these last few critical weeks of the project. He couldn't afford any more mix-ups, delays or human errors. The targeted completion date was fast approaching, with either its huge bonus, or the start of its hefty late fines.

Finally seeing Jason smother yet another yawn, Trent glanced at his watch. It was nearly eight in the evening. "Come on, let's get outta here."

Jason didn't have to be asked twice. Trent watched him get in his car and leave. Alone again, he went for one more walk-through of today's work area, relieved to have had something else to think about besides Chloe for a few hours. Not an easy thing to do lately, particularly since he was back at the spot where they'd met.

Finally calling it a day, Trent wanted nothing more than to go straight home to take a forty-five minute shower. But he had one more stop to make. His grandmother had arrived back from South Carolina today. Her estate was on the way, so he decided to go by for a quick visit.

Though a feisty woman who'd been called a five-foot-tall lump of silk-encased iron, his grandmother Sophie had been genuinely distraught over her son's health scare. Trent believed his father would be all right—like the doctors said, he'd had a wake-up call. Trent was also, however, certain his grandmother was sitting at home fretting. Nothing upset her more than not being in complete control of the lives of everyone around her. And not even Sophie Langtree, south Florida's own Queen Mother, could control another person's heart.

When he arrived, he found his grandmother in her study, helping herself to a generous portion of brandy. "You made it home in one piece, I see?" he said as he walked around the desk to kiss her cheek.

A flash of pleasure brightened her eyes, then she narrowed them. "You couldn't even stop to clean up before visiting your grandmother?"

"You want me to leave?"

"Don't you dare. Sit down, young man, and tell me something. How is your father going to manage all the way on the other side of the country, far from all of us who love him? We have to find a way to get them to move back here."

Same old song and dance. Trent knew his mother would sooner give up an arm than move back to Florida to live under her mother-in-law's rigid thumb. His mother was the first one who'd even come close to supporting Trent's need to leave the store, and the estate, and strike out on his own. She hadn't been pleased about him taking such a big risk, but she'd at least tried to help his father and brother understand, since she'd needed to escape, too.

"He's going to be all right, Grandmother. You heard the doctors. It was a warning to eat right and take better care of himself." He took her arm to walk her across the room. "Which is exactly what Mom's been telling him to do for ten years."

"That western air," she muttered with dour, knowing certainty. "It thickened his blood."

Trent didn't try to argue against the implacable old-lady logic. It simply wasn't worth it. "I just wanted to make sure you arrived home safely. Are you feeling all right? Is there anything you need?"

"Yes, I need someone to fly to New York to meet with a new designer about a private label for the store," the woman said, slipping in the request as easily as she'd have asked her housekeeper for a cup of tea.

"I'm sure Troy can handle it," Trent replied smoothly. "And, by the way, I'm doing very well, thanks so much for asking."

Sophie shrugged delicately, then sat on a leather sofa, patting the seat next to her. Trent sat down, hiding a smile as his grandmother took his hand and squeezed it. "I know you are, silly boy. Do you think I don't keep tabs on you?"

"I'd be surprised if you didn't."

His grandmother sipped her brandy, casting him a quick, nonchalant look out of the corner of her eye. "So, is there anything else happening in your life? Meet anyone new?"

If only she knew. Chloe had consumed him for days. But he wasn't about to give his grandmother any more ammunition in her campaign to get her grandsons married and procreating.

"Quit being nosy," he said as he put an arm around her thin shoulders and gave her a quick hug. "Though, we all know butting in is your favorite pastime. Second only to checking your bank statement."

She gave him a look of hurt innocence so overly sincere he almost laughed. He'd seen that look before many times.

"Why, Trent, I can't imagine what you're talking about. When have I ever interfered in your life?"

AT 1:00 A.M. SATURDAY morning, Chloe sat in the darkened recessed front window of Langtree's Department Store, looking over her latest creation. "This one's going to raise some eyebrows," she said with a satisfied nod.

She'd fully intended to try something different this week. She'd planned to focus on the new high-end kidswear line the store was starting to carry. Getting people to spend fifty bucks for a pair of size 2T jeans would definitely require some creative marketing and she felt fully up to the challenge.

When she got to work Friday night, however, she found yet another message from Troy, along with a box of pricey chocolates. He probably hadn't paid for them, since the store sold them. Still, she supposed the sentiment was nice.

Today's offering, along with the flowers and lovely gold bracelet he'd left for her yesterday, should have made her feel at least somewhat flattered. Instead, they bothered her immensely. The mangled flowers had gone in the trash. The bracelet had ended up back on Troy's desk, along with a note telling him politely but firmly to please leave her the heck alone.

Troy didn't appear to be living up to his own code of behavior. She'd told him—once in writing, and once in person when he'd come by her workroom last night for a visit—that she was simply not interested. Seeing him had been embarrassing, to say the least. The man had, after all, had his hands on her fanny and his tongue in her mouth.

He'd laughed at her blush, then listened to her rejection. But he hadn't backed off.

Funny, the Langtree twin she didn't want seemed determined to get her. And the one she did want hadn't bothered to do more than make one unsuccessful attempt to reach her on her cell phone in the past two days.

Of course, his brief message had stopped her heart when she'd listened to it. "How much longer are you going to make us both suffer?" he'd said in a husky whisper. "Chloe, I want you so bad I can't sleep at night."

His simple words had done a lot more to send Chloe's pulse racing than his brother's attempt to buy her interest. Still, remembering the way they'd seemed almost amused by the idea of fighting over her, she didn't enjoy the competition. Chloe couldn't help feeling like a piece of meat caught between two hungry dogs, or a toy between two stubborn toddlers.

Hence the window display.

"Troy's gonna have a cow," she said aloud as she ran one last quick test of the new lighting configuration. Unlike the soft, dreamy, ivory-colored lights from the past few weeks, this one required something a bit more obvious. Red. Bright red lights to illuminate the woman mannequin, who was being tugged in different directions by two identical males.

The poor, wide-eyed female looked like she was going to be split right in half, with her arms completely extended to her sides, and her toes barely touching the floor. She was dressed in a stylish, adorable Liz Claiborne dress that had caught Chloe's eye. Her suitors were fully decked, too. One in a suit that cost more than Chloe made in a month. The other in jeans and a sexy, sleeveless muscle shirt.

Chloe's one concession to where her true feelings lay was in ensuring that the female looked longingly at the hunk in the jeans, not the overbearing suit-clad one.

The result was striking. Hip and simplistic. Certainly not subtle, but definitely satisfying.

As she packed up her things and prepared to leave, Chloe found herself hoping her mother would be asleep when she got home. Jeanine had been weepy and emotional this morning, and Chloe figured she and her latest boyfriend had broken up. She wasn't up to nursing her mother through another shattered relationship. Not tonight. Not while she was so torn over her own convoluted love life.

Chloe heard an engine rumbling outside. A strong sense of déjà vu washed over her. She pushed the drapes apart in time to see Trent's black pickup truck pull up outside. Biting her lip, Chloe was mentally jolted back in time to a few weeks ago when she'd first seen him. First watched him. First wanted him.

Double-parking at the curb, right where he'd been that night he'd had the flat, he killed the engine and got out of the truck. Chloe remained still, peering through a slit in the drapes, just wanting to watch, to see if history could repeat itself. Could he possibly make her feel as restless and aroused as he had the last time?

Unfortunately, it wasn't raining so his shirt didn't start sticking to all the lovely contours of his chest and washboard stomach. Plus he obviously suspected she was there. He must have spotted the muted lighting in the box window, because he came close and tried to peer in, cupping his hands around his face as he tried to see through the dark glass and darker curtains.

He couldn't possibly see her. But the slow smile spreading across his sultry lips told her he knew she was there. Somehow, he knew. He knocked on the glass, then tapped on his watch with his index finger, as if to tell her it was quitting time. Turning, he hopped up into the back of his truck. Wondering what he was doing, she saw him unfold an outdoor lounge chair and set it up. He lay down on it, crossed his hands over his chest, and prepared to wait.

"You're crazy," she said with a helpless laugh, certain he'd sit there all night if he had to. Her heart began to race and she hurried to go out to him. "Crazy and wonderful," she mumbled as she prepared to shut off the spotlights.

Then she hesitated. Knowing he'd see or hear about what she'd done in the window sooner or later, she decided to go for broke. Keeping the display fully illuminated, she tossed her purse out onto the floor of the store, stepped down, then slowly pulled the cord of the drapes to part them.

Chloe bit her lip as she watched Trent sit up in the chair. With the streetlamp illuminating his face, she had a good view of his expression. She saw him shake his head, then break into an amused grin. Though she couldn't hear a thing, she knew he was chuckling.

Then Trent rose from his seat, obviously catching sight of her inside the store. Giving her an intimate look, he bowed his head politely, as if acknowledging his part in inspiring her creation. Finally, he brought his hands up and began to clap, applauding her ingenuity.

"I knew you'd understand," she whispered, smiling

so broadly her cheeks hurt. She hurried to find the night watchman so she could get outside.

Exiting through the rear of the store, she hopped into her car, which was parked nearby, and drove around to the front entrance parking lot. Trent had returned to his seat in the battered lawn chair, probably realizing when she'd switched off the display lights that she was coming out.

"I'll bet no one has ever accused you of hiding your feelings," he said with a laugh after she'd parked beside him and gotten out of her car.

"You're not exactly Mr. Subtle yourself," she countered as she walked up to the truck and stuck her hand up for his help. He obliged, not just helping her but lifting her up into the metal bed of the truck.

The streetlight reflected a definite twinkle in his eye. "Hi, Chloe Weston. It's nice to meet you."

Chloe's heart skipped a beat as she recognized what he was doing. Taking them back. Starting things over. Offering them a clean slate. Who could ask for more? "Hi, Trent Langtree." Chloe smiled. "I guess this means we're not strangers anymore."

"And no more games," he added.

"We still don't know each other very well," she pointed out.

"Which is why I'm here. No time like the present to get acquainted. It's not too late, is it?" He sounded so reasonable, standing in the back of a truck in the middle of the night.

"Absolutely not. This job has made me a night owl." Since she didn't have school the next morning, Chloe didn't really care if he kept her out until dawn. As long as he kept her.

Chloe knew she might live to regret getting further

involved with him. But she also knew she'd regret it even more if she didn't take this amazing, passionate opportunity now, while she had the chance. *Deal with the future when it gets here for once.*

"Do you have to get home right away?" He hadn't stepped back, remaining so close she could almost feel his body touching hers, though a full inch of hot Florida night air separated them.

"No. Why? You have something in mind?"

"I wondered if you like to dance."

She hadn't expected that. She'd anticipated a sexy proposition, maybe—well, *hopefully*—but not an invitation to go dancing. "You want to take me dancing? Now? Isn't it a little late?"

Instead of answering, he walked toward the front of the truck and reached through the open rear window into the cab. Then he stepped back. Hearing the languorous music come from the inside speakers, she laughed softly.

"Dance with me?" he asked, holding his hands out in invitation. She stepped into his arms as smoothly and instinctively as the night embraced the stars.

And they danced. To the slow, bluesy instrumental notes coming from the car radio. To the sounds of the night. To the rhythm of Chloe's own steadily beating heart.

"You're a wonderful dancer," she said, not lifting her cheek from his shoulder as they swayed.

"My mother made Troy and me take lessons when we were six."

"I have a tough time picturing Troy in tap shoes."

They fell silent again, still moving as one soft ballad gave way to another. The wind picked up, blowing a strong breeze across their bodies. Chloe felt the loose cotton fabric of her summery dress mold against her, cupping her thighs and her hips. She shivered a bit, but he tugged her closer so she felt nothing but his solid warmth.

"Do you think the security guard can see us from inside the store?" Chloe asked.

"Is Charlie still the night guard?"

She nodded.

"Then no. Not a chance. I'm quite sure he went right back to his nap as soon as he let you out."

"So management does have an idea what goes on down on the sales floor?" she asked.

"I'm not management anymore."

"Definitely not. I can't imagine that, you know. Simply cannot visualize you being like Troy. Walking around scolding salesgirls whose earrings are too long or who wear too much makeup."

"He's gotten better," Trent said with a deep chuckle. "He campaigned for uniforms for a while. We butted heads for months on that issue."

She paused, then asked, "You don't miss it, do you?"

Wondering if he remembered all she'd said the weekend before about wanting stability and a reliable, successful, steady nine-to-five type of man, she held her breath for his answer.

"No. I don't."

His honesty didn't surprise her. She'd expected nothing less.

"I hate being cooped up inside all day," he continued. "Something about recycled air stifles me. Plus I like building something of my own, being challenged and excited."

He sounded like her mother. *Is he just as easily bored, as readily distracted?* She shoved the thought aside.

"I'd say our relationship has been challenging and exciting, so far," she offered with a forced smile.

"Absolutely." He pulled her even closer "I suspect that's why Troy is the way he is. I get what I need out of flying without a net in my business and financial life. He gets it out of his sex life."

Made sense. Didn't make her happy, but it made sense. And heaven knew she wouldn't want to change the man, because she'd fallen crazy in love with him just the way he was.

In love? Since when? Chloe, are you insane?

Probably. But she wouldn't trade what she was feeling right now for the entire world.

They continued to dance, cocooned by the store on one side, and, on the other, a long row of pine trees separating the parking lot from the nearby highway.

"So we're completely alone and we can't be seen."

He raised a brow. "Uh-huh."

"Think you could maybe kiss me, then?"

She didn't have to ask him twice. Still dancing in that expert three step sway, he lowered his head and brushed her mouth with his.

She sighed, deep in her throat, and brought her hands up to tangle in his hair. He didn't immediately deepen the kiss, seeming content to gently taste only her lips. She closed her eyes, tilted her head and let herself feel nothing but him. His arms around her. His body pressing against her. His lips sipping hers like she was a fine wine.

When he finally ended the kiss, she slowly opened her eyes to find him staring down at her tenderly. Then he brushed his lips against hers once more. Lightly. He was teasing her, she knew, making her wait for more. She shivered in anticipation.

"Cold?"

She shook her head. "I've never felt warmer."

After a few more moments, when one song had ended and another begun, Chloe softly spoke. "I saw you that night. Do you know that?"

He gave her a questioning look.

"The night you had the flat tire. I saw you out here. I watched you from the window."

"You did?" Sudden understanding lit his eyes. "The window...the mannequins. I heard about the picture in the paper, but I never made the connection."

She nodded with a sheepish grin. "I was the voyeur who took your private moment and put it on display for the whole world to see."

He frowned and scolded, "You couldn't even come out and hold up an umbrella for me while I changed the flat?"

"Sorry. Not enough time to wipe the drool off my chin. I was quite busy ogling you, I'm afraid."

He laughed softly, still holding her. Still dancing. Still embracing. Still so tender and intimate she wanted to cry from the pleasure of being back in his arms.

"You must have thought I was Troy," he finally murmured. "You didn't know there were two of us then."

His quick understanding of the situation made it easier to explain. "You're exactly right. Before then I'd never given your brother a second thought. But that night...well, that's what made me want you."

He remained silent for a moment, obviously interpreting her meaning. Then he said, "So there was never any question about who you were interested in."

She stopped moving, tilting her head to stare up at him, wanting to make sure there was no more confusion, no more doubt about her motives. "None, Trent. It was *you* before we ever met. What happened at the resort would not have happened if I hadn't seen you standing across the pool during the storm and recognized the passionate, amazing man I saw the night you had the flat."

"What about Troy?"

"Absolutely *nothing* would have happened between your brother and me at the conference. It was always you." She stepped close again and they resumed their slow, sensual dance.

He pulled one of her hands up to his lips and pressed a soft kiss on the back of her fingers. His other hand rested on the small of her back, stroking, lightly caressing her, building her intense longing for him to an even higher pitch.

Casting aside her doubts, her worries and her fears, Chloe admitted the truth. "It's *still* you I want, Trent."

"I think you'd better tell my brother that," he said with a lazy laugh.

She sighed in annoyance. "I've been trying to."

"Have you come right out and told him you've chosen me?"

"Well, no, I guess not in those words. I figured telling him I wasn't interested in him should be enough."

He shook his head. "Nope. Sorry. Troy isn't used to being told no. Plus he's having a lot of fun trying to make me squirm. He's going to follow our rule to the letter."

"You two are twisted."

"Nah. Just guys."

"I'm glad I had a sister."

"Your sister's adorable, by the way. I liked your mom, too."

"Thanks. They're unique," she admitted with a shrug. "I wouldn't trade them for the world."

"I'm sure they say the same about you."

"What about your family?"

"Pretty much like yours," he admitted. "Eccentric. All very different. My grandmother's probably the most like Troy. Very strong willed and likes to get her own way."

"I don't imagine she was happy when you quit your job."

He barked a laugh. "Unhappy doesn't begin to describe it. But it worked out all right. Troy has done a good job."

"Speaking of Troy...I'll tell him tomorrow."

"Tell him what?"

She paused. "That I'm all yours."

"Are you?"

"I think so."

"Let's keep dancing and work on figuring it out."

Though no thunder rumbled and no lightning flashed across the sky, a soft summer night's rain began to fall. Chloe felt a drop hit her forehead and slide down her face, then felt still more droplets gently strike her hair.

Trent leaned closer, kissing the moisture from her temple. He continued to hold her tight as they swayed to the song on the radio and the new music created by the falling rain.

"You're getting wet," he murmured.

"So are you."

They continued to sway.

"Do you care?" he asked.

"Not a bit." Shaking her head, Chloe curled her fingers around his neck, reaching up to play with her gold hoop earring, which he still wore.

"Me neither."

9

THOUGH CHLOE DESPERATELY wanted him to, Trent did not make love to her Friday night. They spent hours dancing in the rain and beneath the gradually returning stars. After those intimate moments in his arms, exchanging long, slow, wet kisses that never seemed to end, she would have been quite willing to risk arrest for public indecency by getting naked with him in the back of his truck. All he had to do was ask.

He didn't ask.

Nor did he ask the next afternoon when she met him at his apartment and they sat out on the beach. His hands rubbing slick oil into the skin of her back made her shake. Watching him stand beneath an outdoor public shower to rinse the sand off his long, lean body, savoring the cool relief against his hot skin, made her drool. Going into his small but beautiful apartment and seeing his huge bed made her tremble.

But still no sex. Not Saturday. Not Sunday, either, when they drove down to Fort Lauderdale and he somehow managed to convince her to try parasailing. After that horrible experience, Chloe doubted he'd ever want her again. *Not many guys are really turned on by a woman almost throwing up from ninety feet in the air.* To her complete mortification, she'd had a couple of close calls, actually gagging into the hand she'd pressed against her mouth.

Trent was tender and sweet when taking care of her afterward as they sat on a bench near the beach. "I'm sorry," he whispered as he poured more cold bottled water onto a paper towel to replace the one on her forehead. "You warned me about your problem with heights."

"I'm not feeling sick anymore, you know," she replied from under the paper towel. "I'm just never taking this off my face because I'm so embarrassed."

"Lots of people have a problem with heights."

"Do lots of people punch the guy driving the boat after they land?"

Trent shrugged. "He deserved it. You screamed for ten minutes for him to bring us back down and he just sat on deck laughing as you turned green."

"He's gonna sue me."

"I have a good lawyer. Besides, he's not going to sue you because he'd have to haul himself into court and admit that you, who are no taller than his collarbone, gave him a black eye."

Monday's trip to an aquarium was fun and platonic. Tuesday's dinner and a movie were sweetly romantic but just as platonic. Finally, Wednesday, when they met for lunch between her classes, Chloe had reached her breaking point for maximum lust buildup. One more romantic, nonsexual encounter and she'd explode.

"Trent, what is going on here?"

He chewed and swallowed the fry he'd just popped into his mouth. "I'm eating your fries. Sorry, I thought you were done."

"I'm not talking about the French fries."

"Was your burger okay? Overcooked?"

"Forget the fries and the burger," she bit out. "I'm

talking about this. Us. You and me. What are we do-ing?"

"I believe we're having lunch." When she groaned, he added, "Sorry. I couldn't resist."

"So are you going to answer me?"

"What was the question again?" He held his hands out defensively as she glared. "Just kidding."

She crossed her arms, waiting.

He shrugged. "Chloe, I was under the impression that you absolutely refused to get involved with some-one without getting to know him first. Wasn't that the issue? That we didn't know each other? That you weren't sure who I was?"

Her mouth fell open. These past few days, when she'd wondered if he'd just stopped wanting her, if he was no longer attracted to her, he'd been trying to let her get to know him? She didn't know whether to thank him or smack him.

"So that's what we've been doing?"

"Yes." He grinned. "I think it's called dating."

"I think we have moved a little bit beyond dating."

"Who says you can't start dating after you have sex?"

Chloe leaned back in her chair. She wanted to ask him just when their dating was going to progress back to at least some seriously heavy petting. It didn't, how-ever, seem very ladylike.

Across from her, Trent continued to pick at the rest of their lunches, looking completely relaxed. She saw a twinkle in his eyes and knew he was fully aware of the struggle going on inside her. *He's expecting you to throw yourself at him.*

Too much longer, and that's exactly what she would do. But she was woman. She could hold out. After all, weren't females the strong ones in this particular battlefield? Women didn't need sex the way men did, right?

"Baloney," she muttered as she reached for her glass and downed the last of her iced tea. Lowering her glass, she slipped her tongue out to lick the corner of her lips, catching a drop of moisture there. Trent watched her every move. His eyes narrowed. His lips parted. Beneath his shirt, she saw his shoulders tense. She realized he was hanging on by as thin a thread as she.

Gotcha, sweetheart.

"Okay. Dating it is," she said with an exaggerated sigh.

Meeting his stare, she let him see the heat in her expression. She silently let him know that nothing had changed. Chloe wanted him. Badly. But the next move was his.

"So what's next on the dating checklist? Miniature golf?" she asked, knowing he probably heard the sour tone in her voice.

He laughed softly. "I think I'll surprise you."

TRENT WORKED OUT THE details for Friday night the way a general might plan a battle. He was supposed to see her Thursday, but had canceled. No way could he spend more time with Chloe without giving in to that liquid, limpid *take me now* look she got whenever they kissed. Heck, whenever they looked at each other!

He didn't want to weaken, didn't want to make love to her again until it was the right time and the right place. That meant staying away from her until Friday night.

Not making love to her had been pure hell. But if it

gave Chloe the confidence to know she could trust him, and trust the feelings between them, it was worth it. *She* was worth it.

He thought about her constantly. When he should have been sleeping, when he should have been working. During meetings and walk-throughs. Jason had had to repeat a question three times during a phone conversation Thursday afternoon. Trent had even forgotten about plans he'd made to meet his brother for drinks. Troy had understood. More than likely Troy had gotten distracted by a tight skirt and hadn't shown up, either!

There was no disguising the truth—he'd fallen hard for the woman. After his broken engagement, Trent had wondered if he'd ever understand the meaning of real love. During the past two weeks, since he'd met Chloe, he figured he'd come damn close.

By Friday night at eleven, Trent was ready. Chloe didn't expect to see him until the following afternoon, so he pulled his truck around to the back entrance of the store when he arrived. Charlie, the night watchman, greeted him at the employee entrance. "Come on in, Mr. Langtree. Thanks for the night off."

Trent handed the man a hundred bucks and the tickets he'd gotten through a connection at the stadium. "Here you go."

"Me and my buddies have been wanting to get to one of these games all season. Monday's home game will be great."

"I hope you enjoy them. Remember, just between us, right?" Trent held the door open so Charlie could exit.

"By the way," Charlie said before walking away, "she's in the storeroom. She hasn't gotten to the front display yet."

After the other man got into his car and drove away, Trent locked up and reset the door alarm. Then he got to work.

The floor plan of Langtree's hadn't changed in the past few years so he had no trouble making his way through the darkened store. He made some side trips on the way. Having stopped in yesterday to scope things out, he knew which racks to visit in certain departments. He made quick visits to the electronics, sporting goods, and gourmet foods areas of the store, as well as a few more. And lastly—most importantly—bridal.

When he was finished, he moved toward the employees-only corridor that led to the storage rooms and loading dock. He paused at a lighting control panel to turn the entire first floor lights on, but on the lowest possible setting.

Following the sound of some loud music playing on a staticky radio, he reached Chloe's workroom. The door stood partly open, revealing a sliver of light from within. As he pushed the door in and entered the room, Trent spotted her immediately.

Ricky Martin was singing, and Chloe Weston was dancing. Holding the torso of a headless female mannequin—whose head and limbs lay on the lumpy sofa—she bopped around the room, gyrating and doing a provocative bump and grind, all the while holding a running conversation with the dummy.

He laughed. She didn't hear over the blaring music.

It appeared Chloe liked to live "La Vida Loca" in the late-night hours in the closed department store. Thank goodness. Tonight they were definitely going to have to go a little crazy.

"Am I interrupting?"

She dropped the mannequin. "Trent, you scared me half to death! Didn't anyone ever tell you not to sneak up on a person in a dark place in the middle of the night?"

"Someone must have overlooked that life's lesson. Maybe it was the same week you were supposed to learn not to peek at people from darkened windows?"

"Shut up and kiss me hello," she said with a cheeky grin.

He quite happily obliged, drawing her into his arms to give her a deep, languorous kiss that left them both breathless. When their mouths finally broke apart, she wobbled and leaned closer. There came the look again. *Take me now.* He took a step back.

"Ready for our next date?"

"Now? I'm sorry, I can't leave. I haven't even started the front window."

"Who said anything about leaving?" Grabbing her hand, Trent pulled her with him out into the hallway. "Come on."

"Where are we going?"

"We're going lots of places tonight, Chloe." He led her through the softly lit store, keeping his fingers entwined with hers, enjoying her confusion. "I think we'll start with what you suggested the other day."

She didn't appear to remember. So when they arrived at the sporting goods area, and she saw the golf clubs, balls and putting matt, she burst into laughter. "Miniature golf?"

"Sorry, no fountains, elephants or Sphinxes to make it challenging. But it should do for tonight."

"You're out of your mind."

"No. I just like to play." He lowered his voice, cajoling her. "Don't you? Say you'll play with me, Chloe. All night long."

She raised a brow. "All night?" Then she glanced from side to side. "The guard's around here somewhere, you know. And there are security cameras."

He shook his head. "Charlie's gone. We're locked in here alone. The cameras and motion alarms are all off until seven o'clock tomorrow morning. I took care of it myself as soon as I got here."

He watched her bite her lip, obviously tempted, but unsure. "What if someone finds out? What if someone walks in on us?"

"Impossible." He leaned closer, close enough to breathe in the flowery scent of her cologne. "Besides, doesn't the slim possibility of getting caught make it all the more exciting?"

Her pulse beat faster in her throat and her lips parted as she drew deeper breaths. Temptation and excitement brought a sparkle to her eyes and a flush to her cheeks. She nodded. "All right. I have thought about it before, you know—how interesting this place could be after-hours."

"That's the spirit." He bent over to pick up a club, placing it in her hands. "Come on. You can go first."

"Okay, but I'm not the world's best golfer."

"I can tell," he said, glancing down at the club in her hands. "You're holding that putter all wrong. Loosen up."

She raised a brow and gave him a pouty look. "You're complaining about how I hold your putter? Funny, Trent, I thought you liked it nice and tight."

"Knock off the sex jokes. This is strictly first-date stuff," Trent scolded, trying to look stern, knowing he failed.

Frowning, she neatly tapped the ball, sinking it on the first try. She grinned. "I lied. I'm the Putt Putt Queen of Deerfield Beach. I was just following the cardinal first-date rule for girls—let the guy win because men don't like to lose."

"You didn't let me win."

"Sorry. It's not in my nature to pretend I'm hopeless."

"Too bad. I'd kinda looked forward to showing you how to play." He stepped behind her, turning her so her back was pressed against his chest, and her curvy rear end nestled against his groin. "You sure you don't want me to help you with your stroke?"

She gasped. "I think I could definitely use some tips on keeping it smooth and making those long, deep drives."

No way could she not feel his hard-on. And no way could he not know she intentionally bumped against him, tempting him mercilessly in a fully clothed game of up-the-sexual-ante.

Their miniature golf game lasted only a few minutes. Unable to continue watching her curling her hands around the shaft of the club, Trent pointed to a nearby bench. "Wanna skate?"

She looked, her eyes widening as she saw the in-line skates he'd placed there. Matching his and hers sets in the appropriate sizes. Then she shook her head. "I can't skate."

"I'm not falling for that again."

"I'm serious. You won't be the one falling, I will."

She proved to be right. Chloe definitely could not skate. She was barely able to stand up, much less move. They'd gone about six inches from the edge of the seat when her arms windmilled and she nearly crashed to the floor. Trent grabbed her by the waist, their weight sending them back to the surface of the bench where she landed in his lap.

Their laughter faded as they faced each other, nose to nose, each fully aware of every inch of touching bodies. "I think we'd better try something else," she whispered.

Nodding, Trent eased her off his lap into her own seat, and began unlacing the skates. When they were both finished, he pulled her to her feet. "Ready?"

"Where are we going now?"

"It's a surprise."

She gave him an arch look out of the corner of her eye. "How about up to the third floor?"

"What's on the third floor?"

Chloe gave him another one of those heavy-lidded stares that made his blood rush through his veins and his resistance skid away in chunk, then said, "The bedding department."

Swallowing hard, Trent forced a look of disinterest on his face. "No. I have lots of other plans tonight. I should tell you right now, Chloe, *none* of them include a bed."

Her eyes widened and she quickly turned her face, a blush rising in her cheeks. Trent saw her sigh and bite her lip. It took every bit of self-control he had not to laugh or just kiss her senseless when he heard her mutter a frustrated curse.

The night was just beginning. And she had no idea what else he had in store. He could hardly wait.

VIDEO GAMES ON SOME BIG screen color TVs were next. Chloe, whose childhood arcade experiences had involved simple stuff like Ms. Pac Man and Donkey

Kong, got thoroughly trounced in a martial arts night-mare that left her feeling queasy. "These things have gotten pretty realistic, huh?"

"You didn't like Ninja Warrior Hacksaw Killers?"

She shook her head and gulped. "One too many flying intestines for my taste."

Trent just laughed as he took her arm. "You hungry?"

"Splattering blood and gray brain matter on a fifty-six-inch screen. Who wouldn't be hungry after that?"

"Maybe we'll eat later." He started to walk right past the gourmet food department when she spotted a large white sheet spread on the floor, complete with picnic basket and cooler.

She paused. "A picnic?"

"Thought you weren't hungry."

"What did you bring?"

"Only the best chocolate the store sells," he said with a noncommittal shrug. "Plus raspberries and champagne."

Chloe sat down. "Maybe just a tad." Spotting a long, crystal flute glass, she held it out while Trent popped the cork of a pricey bottle of champagne he'd removed from the cooler.

As they shared the champagne and chocolate, Chloe began to feel more relaxed, more lethargic. The golf, skating and games had been fun, but she somehow sensed the mood was changing, shifting into a different phase. They'd progressed beyond the playful first dates, which, she imagined, was exactly what he planned. She admired his ingenuity. And she knew quite well what he was doing. Trent was giving her what she thought she always wanted. Time. A slow buildup. A chance for her to feel she really knew him before they got more seriously involved.

All of that might have been just fine if they hadn't *already* been seriously involved. It was hard to pretend holding his hand while skating was enough when she really wanted him naked and thrusting into her, completely out of control and frenzied.

The night is young. She turned her face to hide her smile. Yes, the night was definitely still young. They had hours and hours alone in this wonderful, silent playground.

"I never imagined how romantic this place could be after hours," she said. Chloe sipped her champagne, letting the moisture coat her lips, knowing he watched her every move.

He slowly leaned closer until they were sharing the same breath. When she could barely stand the tension, he finally kissed her, licking the champagne away.

"Good?" she asked in a husky whisper.

He nodded. "Try a raspberry."

She needed no second invitation. Chloe plucked one plump, juicy-looking berry from the cooler and brought it to her mouth. Trent made no effort to disguise his interest as she opened her lips and slipped the fruit between them. Biting into the fruit, she moaned at the sweet, tart juices spurting against her tongue. "Delicious. Want some?" she murmured as she slipped the rest of the fruit into her mouth.

He answered by leaning forward to kiss her again, tasting the berry with her, their tongues sharing the succulent treat.

Though she was more than ready to lie back on the floor with him and finish their picnic the way all romantic picnics should be finished, Trent pulled away and rose to his feet.

"We're leaving?" She wanted to cry.

"Yeah. Let's go." His voice was husky, telling her he hadn't found it easy to end their kiss and stand up.

"Where now?" she asked as he took her hand to help her up.

He kept their fingers entwined as they walked farther into the store. "Would you mind being a private model for me tonight?"

Model? The idea tempted her. Chloe had often thought about trying on some of the exquisite clothes the store carried. Since most were out of her window-dresser price range—and anyone who worked in the store knew it—she'd never felt comfortable doing it during the day. Now might just be perfect.

For some reason, though, as they neared the ladies' clothing departments, Trent didn't slow his pace. He kept right on walking. She hurried to keep up. "Uh, where are we going?"

"You'll see." He passed juniors, sportswear, and business attire and ignored racks of swimsuits. Then he finally paused when they reached the last of the women's departments.

She stopped and stared, raising a skeptical brow. "Bridal?"

"Go to the first dressing room. I left something for you."

She bit her lip. "I don't know that I really feel like trying on wedding gowns."

"I promise you. It's not a wedding gown. I'll be waiting for you in the alterations area." Before he walked away, he said. "By the way, consider it a gift. I bought it for you yesterday."

A number of possibilities flitted through Chloe's mind as she walked toward the dressing rooms. The bridal area also included the store's entire selection of ball gowns and formals. She wondered if he was going to outfit her in an extravagant dress and take her dancing again.

Dancing would be nice. But remembering how aching with need she'd felt after last weekend's dance session in his truck, she didn't know if she could go through it once more. Right now the only dance she wanted to do was a horizontal one.

You're the one who wanted a nice guy!

"There's such a thing as too nice," Chloe muttered as she pushed open the swinging doors.

The low lighting did not permeate into the dressing rooms, so it took a moment for her eyes to adjust. Blinking a few times, she finally saw what was hanging on a hook. What he'd left for her. What he wanted her to model for him. *Oh, my.* There was one more thing the store offered for sale in the bridal selection. Luscious, seductive lingerie fit for any bridal trousseau.

Clenching her fists and raising them over her head in an expression of pure triumph, Chloe shouted, "Yes!"

Trent had obviously finished playing the look-but-don't-touch game. Because there was no way he was going to be able to look at her in this and *not* touch.

She quickly undressed, dropping her clothes into a heap on the floor. Then she reached for the padded hanger, almost afraid to handle the delicate silk and lace. When she did, she nearly cooed at the sensation of liquid fabric caressing her skin. "You wicked man," she murmured as she changed.

Since Trent hadn't turned the lights on in the dress-

ing room area, she could barely even make out the
dark color—black? Burgundy? She didn't know.

The push-up bra fit her snugly, barely covering the
top curves of her breasts, the lace scraping against her
sensitized nipples. She donned a matching pair of
high-cut lacy panties. Only after she had them pulled
snugly against her body did she feel a suspiciously stiff
seam and realize the panties were zippered right down
the middle. *Outrageous!* "Oh, yeah."

A garter belt and the silkiest stockings she'd ever felt
came next. Then she slid on the short matching robe
and belted it at her waist, noting the plunging neckline
that gapped to well beneath the bottom of the bra. Finally, she slipped her feet into a pair of obscenely high-
heeled pumps that completed the seductive ensemble.

When she was finished, Chloe tried to glimpse her
reflection in the mirror, but was unable to see much in
the darkness of the tiny cubicle. Running her fingers
through her hair to loosen it around her shoulders,
Chloe bit her lip and took a deep breath. This sensual
game was exciting, but also a little frightening. Unable
to see herself clearly, she couldn't stop to build her confidence, couldn't tell her reflection that she was worthy
of the effort he'd undergone for her tonight.

You are, Chloe. Just as Trent was worth any anxiety or
insecurities she was battling now.

Exiting the dressing room, Chloe followed a carpeted aisle around a corner to the alterations area. She
didn't see Trent waiting for her. But she definitely saw
what he'd prepared.

As in every bridal department there was an alcove
with a raised dais, surrounded on three sides by tall
mirrors. Brides usually stood here, trying on gowns,

getting a good view from every angle, then waiting patiently to be measured and fitted.

Trent obviously had something else in mind. He'd covered the broad step with an ivory satin sheet. And white tapered candles were lit in front of each mirror, providing soft illumination. A single overhead spotlight shone down on the center of the platform.

"Are you here?" she asked, remaining near the corner, not stepping fully into the light.

"Go stand on the platform."

His voice came from near the counter, but she still didn't see him. She bit her lip. "Where are you?"

"I'm here. Please, Chloe, go to the step. Let me see you."

Taking a deep breath, she walked to the dais and gracefully stepped up on it. She looked over her shoulder for him.

"No. Don't look for me." His whisper was huskier than it had been a moment before. Chloe looked down to see her body brightly lit by the tiny, overhead spotlight and knew he was studying her from head to toe. She shivered.

"Look in the mirrors," he continued.

She looked. Then she looked again. Chloe's lips parted as she struggled to breathe in spite of the shock of the mirrored images surrounding her. Silk-clad Chloes were reflected on all sides, within the depths of every mirror. Her reflection repeated itself over and over. The effect was amazing. The jewel tone of the glittering sapphire-blue lingerie against the softness of her skin was both striking and sensual. Incredibly dramatic. Seeing the pronounced curves of her body beneath the silk, she pictured him somewhere out there, watching her from the darkness. Her heart rate kicked up, blood surging through her veins until she could almost hear it. "Is this what you want?"

"Oh, yes."

Though she sensed his voice was closer, Chloe didn't turn around. She kept her gaze on the mirror directly in front of her, almost not recognizing the woman there. A confident smile crossed her lips as she reached for the loose sash of the robe.

She heard his sharply in-drawn breath. He was even closer now.

"Shall I stop?"

"If you want me to kill myself."

She laughed softly, then untied the sash, letting the robe slip open. A soft groan just behind her said he'd stepped to within a few feet. She didn't turn around, nor search for his reflected form in the mirror. Chloe had never even considered how addictive the erotic power of making someone desire her could be. She felt it now, though, and liked the feeling. It was intoxicating. Heady. Overwhelming. Matched only by her own body's elemental response.

She wanted him so much she ached.

"More?" Not waiting for his response, she allowed the robe to slide to the edge of her shoulders. It hung there, covering none of the front of her body, which was now fully reflected.

"You're amazing. Do you see yourself the way I see you now?"

Chloe shrugged her shoulders, allowing the robe to fall off.

Then she looked forward, studying her mirror image. She'd never considered herself a truly beautiful woman. Certainly she'd never thought herself an exotic, sensual one. Now, standing before the mirrors, wide eyed, pink lipped, barely clothed, she *was* exotic, beautiful, sensual. And she knew it. He'd made her see it.

Almost in awe at the reaction he'd inspired in her with nothing but a darkened room, some clothing and whispered words, Chloe moved her hand to her neck. She touched the skin there, watching all the while. Next, she traced the flat of her palm across her shoulder and arm.

"You're thinking of me touching you."

She nodded, moving her hand again, skimming slowly over her breast. Lower. Then stroking the smooth skin of her belly until her pinky finger dipped into the top elastic hem of her panties.

"More," he demanded when she paused.

She shook her head, dropping her hand to her side. "It's not my hands I want on me."

Chloe waited for a moment that could be counted in mere seconds, but which felt like hours. Then in the blink of an eye, she looked at her reflection and saw his dark, masculine hand slip over the curve of her hip to her stomach. As she savored the warmth of his flattened palm against her skin, she never stopped watching. His tanned fingers contrasted sharply against her white flesh as he stroked her.

He remained behind her, out of the circle of the spotlight, blocked from her view in the mirror by the darkness and by her own body. But she made no effort to turn around, enthralled by the sight of him touching her. She held her breath as his fingers came tantalizingly near her breasts. When they slid past without making contact, she whimpered. Then he moved lower, across the panties, to trace a light path on the front of one thigh.

"Please." He didn't reply. Did he want her to beg? She would. The pleasure was so intense it nearly pained her and she melted when she finally felt his breath on her body. His warm lips touched the tender bit of flesh where her neck met her shoulder. Chloe closed her eyes and tilted her head to the side to give him access. She was rewarded by the feel of his warm, wet mouth pressing a hot kiss to that vulnerable hollow.

He moved behind her, stepping up onto the platform. She felt his clothes against her naked skin and knew he hadn't removed his jeans or T-shirt. He remained fully dressed while she trembled, vulnerable, nearly naked before him. She didn't give a damn. "Stop touching me and I might just lose my mind."

"I've barely begun," he whispered. Stepping closer until his body met hers from top to bottom, he brought his left hand up to cup her other hip. His slow, steady caresses made her close her eyes and moan, and that pressure, that hot, solid feel of him pressing against her from behind, made her utter a helpless cry.

"Open your eyes, Chloe."

She obeyed, her desire increasing even more. He watched her from over her shoulder, his eyes glittering in the shadows, his face a mask of pure need. She tilted her head back, resting it on his shoulder, thrusting her breasts higher in invitation. Trent moved his hands up to catch them, undoing the front clasp of the bra with one flick of his fingers. When the silky blue fabric fell to the floor, he caught her breasts in both hands.

"Oh, yes." She writhed as he touched her, drawing near the sensitive tips, but not touching them as she wanted. "Please," she whimpered, needing more. He immediately complied, taking both taut nipples between his fingers and enticing them to even tighter peaks. Her lips parted. "Yes. Like that."

Pressing more kisses on her neck, he continued a delicious survey of one breast with his hand, while moving the other down her body toward her panties. Her hips jerked forward, inviting him on. He unerringly found the tiny tab of the zipper at the very top of the elastic and began easing it down. Carefully, so cautiously, obviously not wanting to hurt her. But also drawing out the tension until she felt sure she'd go out of her mind if she didn't have him soon. Raising one arm, she draped it back across his shoulder as she tilted her head to kiss him. Their mouths met, open, wet and ravenous.

Hearing the slight hiss as the zipper parted, she whimpered when he bent lower, sliding his hand between her legs to completely open the slit in the garment. The coolness of the air touched her wet flesh. Then she felt the warmth of his fingers.

"Watch, Chloe. Look at us."

She did, staring again at the mirror, watching his fingers slide through her curls into the slippery folds of her body. He found her clitoris, stroked it, teased it until she shook, then moved his fingers deeper, sliding them into her. She didn't know which was more erotic—feeling his fingers inside her, or watching them disappear. Her legs started to give out.

"I've got you." He steadied her, holding her at the waist.

With expert touches, Trent brought her to a shocking climax within just a few moments and Chloe could only throw back her head and cry out at the pleasure of it. Before she came back to earth, she demanded, "I want you now, just like this."

He didn't hesitate, stepping back only to remove his clothes. When she heard the tear of foil, she shivered, knowing her wait was almost over.

"Like this? You're sure?"

She nodded, meeting his stare in the mirror as he moved close behind her and again began kissing her neck and shoulders. Chloe pressed back against him, inviting him, hissing as she felt his thick, hot erection against her bottom. "Very sure."

Wearing the stockings, shoes, garter belt and panties, she knew she must look utterly wanton. She loved that he made her feel that way. Wanton felt right, at least for now.

Standing naked behind her, he again reached around to cup her breasts, then lower, to spread her thighs. She welcomed him, letting him lift her up onto her toes while he bent at the knees and slowly eased into her from below. Helpless little cries emerged with her every breath as he filled her up. Slowly. With agonizing restraint. Until he thrust home and she howled.

Trent groaned as Chloe arched further, leaning to press hot kisses against his neck. He felt her teeth tasting his skin as she pushed against him, tempting him with the sweet curve of her backside, while taking him deeper inside her.

He'd never seen a more breathtaking sight than watching her tonight. Never conceived of a more erotic encounter than this one. "I've been thinking about making love to you for days."

"I thought I'd dreamed it. I thought it couldn't possibly have been as good as I remembered," she whispered.

"It was." Then there was no talking, only smooth strokes, wet, open-mouth kisses and gasps. Wrapping his arm around her waist, cupping her breasts, he drove until they both were weak. Trent knew he could lose control much too easily like this. He didn't want it to end too soon, even though he planned to make love to her many times, in many places, before the night ended.

She whimpered. "I want to see you. Really see you."

He pulled back, almost groaning at leaving her warmth. She turned in his arms to face him, slipped her hands behind his neck, then drew him closer to kiss him deeply. Then she pulled him down with her onto the satin-covered step, lying on her back and parting her legs invitingly.

Glad the brief interruption had slowed the frenzy somewhat, Trent held her hips and paused at the hot entrance of her body.

She gazed up at him, wonder and longing in her eyes.

"Chloe, do you remember the second night we talked on the phone? When I told you my fantasy?"

She paused, then nodded, a sultry smile curving on her lips.

"Thank you for fulfilling it," he said.

"The pleasure was all mine." She wrapped her stocking-clad legs around his, thrusting up to take what he wasn't giving her.

He plunged to the hilt, catching her cry with another soul-sharing kiss. "By the way, angel, I didn't forget your fantasy," he murmured against her lips.

His body began to take over, instinct replacing thought. He drove into her, hard, then harder. The hot, pounding strokes made her writhe, but he saw her brow tighten as she tried to remember what he was talking about. She'd obviously forgotten just how provocative she'd been, whispering about being gently restrained.

"I don't remember...I can't think..."

"I do. I can. And I definitely will."

Then passion took over and they both hurtled wildly out of control toward their climaxes. Right before they reached them, her eyes flew open. She obviously remembered. "You mean..."

"Yes, Chloe. I have the silk scarves all ready," he said.

Judging by her rapturous cries and twisting body, his words pushed her over the edge one moment before he exploded, too.

10

SINCE CHLOE HAD BEEN TOO distracted to finish all her displays the night before, she came into the store Saturday afternoon. Trent had to work, though he said he'd try to get out early and meet up with her this evening. She could hardly wait.

Every department reminded her of where she'd been the night before with him. Though they'd cleaned up and hidden the evidence of their long, sensual tryst, she couldn't help wondering if someone knew. Did every person who nodded and smiled somehow suspect she'd been here, spending hour after hour in sensual euphoria, just one night before? A grin lurked behind her lips with every step she took.

"Hi there," Jess said as Chloe passed the perfume counter. "The window's amazing today. That's definitely going to raise some eyebrows. Girl, you've got guts."

"Thanks. Maybe I was feeling a little...wild last night."

Jess probably heard the secretive tone in Chloe's voice. "What are you up to? That window wasn't, uh, *reality*, was it?"

Chloe merely shrugged before walking away.

The only real work Chloe had accomplished the night before had been the front window. Trent had helped her, the two of them laughing as they completed the romantic story Chloe had begun in the display box just a few weeks before. The public deserved to know the female mannequin had made her choice. She was dressed in wicked, sapphire-blue lingerie with her jean-clad lover standing directly behind her. Shrouded in darkness. Only his hand was visible on her bare stomach. Well, yeah, Jess was right. Some eyebrows were definitely going to shoot up with this one.

A few hours later, after she'd finished changing some back-window displays, Chloe returned to her workroom to gather her things. She hadn't heard from Trent yet, though she fully expected to. Whistling as she entered the room, she froze when she saw someone else already there.

"Mrs. Langtree?"

The elderly woman, who'd been glancing curiously at some promotional plans Chloe had been working on at the desk, greeted her with a patrician smile. "I hope you don't mind me waiting for you in here. And you may call me Sophie, if you like."

Feeling like the Queen of England had just invited her to address her as Lizzie, Chloe eased into the room. "You were waiting to see me?"

"Yes, I was. May we sit down and speak for a few moments?"

The elderly woman glanced around, obviously trying to find somewhere else to sit other than the ratty tweed sofa. Chloe walked over to her desk and pulled out her chair, offering it to the woman. Chloe took a seat on the couch, wondering why Sophie Langtree wanted to see her. "Is there something I can do for you?" Then a thought struck her. "Is this about the window?"

"Not really," the old woman replied. "Though I

must say, that was very nicely done. Provocative. It should bring people into the store. Is Troy paying you well?"

Chloe straightened. "Well enough."

"Well enough? Spoken like a woman who has bills to pay and an inadequate salary with which to pay them."

"I'm fine, and thankful for this job. It allows me to work at night and not interfere with my class schedule at school."

"Yes, you're nearly finished at the university."

Chloe frowned. "How did you know that?"

"I know quite a lot about you, Chloe. I make it my business to know about anyone closely *involved* with my family."

As heat flooded her face, Chloe tightened her fingers in her lap and took a deep breath. "Involved?"

The woman waved a hand in the air. "I know all about you and Trent. Heavens, Chloe, the entire world should know about you and Trent considering you've had your romance on display in the front window for the past month. I assume, from this morning's effort, that the two of you have, uh, progressed in your relationship?"

Chloe coughed into her fist. *This is his grandmother!*

"Don't worry. I do approve. Your family background might leave something to be desired, but you appear to have talent and ambition. And there's a kindness about you that would be a nice complement to Trent's own generosity of spirit."

She didn't care about the praise. "My family background?"

The old woman stared piercingly at her. "Your mother is a little...unusual, is she not?"

Chloe straightened in her seat, meeting the older woman's stare. "What is it you want, Mrs. Langtree?"

"Why, nothing, dear. Just to get to know you, and let you know I'm glad things have worked out between you and my grandson. You'll be a good influence on him. You might even help him correct some of the mistakes he's made in his life."

"Mistakes?" Chloe asked, still confused by just what this woman could possibly want from her.

"Trent is much too impulsive," Sophie said with a frown. "He leads with his heart, not his head. He takes risks, lives dangerously. He needs someone stable, like you, to keep him grounded. To keep him from going off and wasting his talents on foolish ventures...."

Chloe couldn't help but notice the parallels between the Trent the older woman described and her own mother. The comparison didn't help matters. "Foolish ventures like his business?"

The woman's eyes narrowed. "What an outrageous waste of time. He could be hurt, or ruined. He needs to come back here where he belongs."

"Trent is very happy with his work, Mrs. Langtree."

The woman glanced at her hands. "And you, Chloe? Are you satisfied with Trent's...profession?"

Chloe didn't hesitate. "I just want him to be happy."

"How loyal of you. I wonder, does that loyalty ever waiver? When you're bone tired after eight hours of school and five hours at work? When you sit down to pay the bills and wonder how you'll manage? Do you ever wonder what it would be like to be with a man who could take all those troubles away from you?"

"I don't need a man to take care of me," Chloe replied, hearing anger in her voice. "I can take care of myself."

"And what about Morgan and your mother? How long can you keep taking care of them?"

Standing up, Chloe paced across the workroom to her desk. "I don't think that's any of your business. And I have to go."

"I only wondered, of course, because of what's going to happen now. With your mother's problems."

Chloe froze, looking at the woman who stared all too innocently at her own handbag. "What are you talking about?"

"Oh, she hasn't told you?" Sophie tsked. "Too ashamed, I suppose. I wasn't trying to pry, Chloe, honestly. I just asked my lawyer to have someone make a few inquiries into your background. One can't be too careful, you know." Frowning, she mumbled, "Particularly with some of the women Troy has brought around."

"Get back to my mother."

"Well, it appears she's gotten herself in a bit of a fix. A man she was seeing recently, a Mr. Howard, apparently talked many people into investing in a new venture—a shopping center filled with arts and crafts stores?" She paused, looking at Chloe for confirmation, but Chloe didn't respond. "Your mother helped him, encouraging others to invest. And now he has disappeared, taking all their money with him."

Chloe sighed, leaning against her desk as she shook her head in dismay. She'd known something was wrong with Jeanine. She just wished she'd bothered to try to find out what it was. "My mother is guilty only of being a very openhearted, trusting person."

"Yes, I'm sure she is. And hopefully the police won't be too hard on her, though of course she is being investigated as an accomplice. But since she lost so much money as well, perhaps they'll be more understanding about her involvement.''

Chloe's legs weakened. She slowly lowered herself to the surface of the desk, sitting there in shock. Sophie watched her every move, looking both forthright and a little sympathetic.

''What money did she lose?'' Chloe managed to ask, hearing the shakiness in her voice.

''My sources say she withdrew a rather large sum from a college trust the two of you had set up a few years ago.'' As tears came to Chloe's eyes, Sophie rose from her chair and walked over to pat her on the shoulder. ''I'm sorry, Chloe, but she emptied the account.''

She didn't want to believe it. ''How could she? She promised...''

''I know,'' the woman continued. Obviously not used to comforting anyone, Sophie stopped patting and returned to her chair. ''I'd like to be able to help you, Chloe. All of you—your mother and Morgan as well. That sister of yours sounds remarkable, brilliant. She deserves much more than years of working while she goes part-time to the community college.''

Now she gets to the point. ''Why don't you just say what it is you came here to say?'' Chloe asked as she rose from the desk. She kept her arms clutched tightly around her waist. ''Are you trying to bribe me? I convince Trent to give up his dream and you pay my sister's tuition and get my mother out of legal trouble?''

The woman shook her head. ''Bribery? No, of course not. But think how much easier it would be to help your sister if you're married to the top executive of Langtree's. And how the Langtree connections could obtain the best lawyers for your mother.''

''Do you always try to control the members of your

family like this? My God, no wonder Trent had to get out."

"I'd do anything for any member of my family."

Chloe just shook her head, barely listening as she still reeled over her mother's recklessness. *I'll do double shifts. If I drop out of school, go back later, after Morgan's taken care of...*

Trent's grandmother continued. "Including giving them little pushes in the right direction on occasion. Like, for instance, when the perfect girl is right under their nose, but they just can't see her."

That got her attention. "What are you talking about?"

A smile appeared on Sophie's face. She looked like a child who'd gotten just what she wanted for Christmas. "Did you never wonder why Troy sent you to the retailers' conference?"

"Of course I did. Did you have something to do with it?"

The woman nodded. "I asked him to. And I made sure the management of the resort offered Trent a room for the weekend."

Chloe still didn't completely understand. "But why?"

"Because of the window, of course. The same day the window appeared, Trent told me he'd broken down in the rain right in front of the store the night before. The window proved you saw him and were attracted to him. Once I met you, I realized he'd be mad for you. It just took a little pushing to get the two of you in the right place at the right time."

Chloe couldn't even speak.

"It worked, didn't it? Everything is coming along exactly the way it's supposed to. Now you just need to finish the job."

TRENT ARRIVED AT THE store at around four o'clock Saturday, deciding to surprise Chloe at work. It had been a long, grueling day on-site. His crews were weary and clumsy after several sixty-hour work weeks in a row. They were primed to foul up, so he sent them all home after lunch—shortly after he'd arrived, due to his late night with Chloe. He'd spent the rest of the afternoon catching up on backlogged paperwork. It amazed him how quickly things could get out of hand. Not for the first time, he wondered if he was going to be able to pull it off.

Even that seemed less important than the one other thing on his mind—his relationship with Chloe.

Trent could have called her, or met up with Chloe at his apartment later, as they'd planned, but he didn't want to wait. Last night had cemented what he'd suspected for weeks. He loved her. And he was ready to tell her so. Besides, he wanted to make sure Troy had seen the display window and gotten the message.

When he arrived, he ran into his brother on the sales floor. "You lucky bastard," Troy said with a grin before Trent could utter a word.

"You saw?"

"I saw," Troy admitted. His brother lowered his voice. "Tell me, was it really the blue outfit...the one with the zipper?"

"I'm not telling you a damn thing."

Troy sighed. "Ahh, it's the real deal, as they say?"

"Definitely. So stay away from her."

"Done," Troy replied as he walked toward the office area. Seeing Troy stop to eye a stunning redhead shopping in the jewelry department, Trent laughed as he walked away.

When he reached Chloe's workroom, he heard voices from the partially open doorway. At first he figured she was listening to the radio again. But when he heard a familiar voice, he froze with his hand on the knob, wondering just what job his grandmother wanted Chloe to finish.

"What is it I'm supposed to do?" Chloe asked.

"Well, there are several ways to accomplish this little task. It could be as simple as you just asking him nicely. Let him know that if he really cares about you, he'll do it."

"Forget it," Chloe replied. "I can't convince Trent to give up his business."

A twitch started beating in Trent's temple.

"It might not even come to that, Chloe. Trent is already so distracted by you that his company is probably going to fail anyway. He's down to the wire on this resort project, and if he can't complete it on time, he will go under. If you keep him busy, this can all come about quite naturally—just in time for his thirtieth birthday, our agreed-upon deadline."

Though it was difficult, Trent forced himself to remain silent, needing to hear Chloe's response. He didn't want to believe it was true. Didn't want to imagine her ever agreeing to do such a thing.

"How do you know the project's not going well?" Chloe asked.

"I have my sources," Sophie replied. "Do you really doubt I can find out this type of information?"

"No, I don't question the lengths to which you'll go. You're very thorough, aren't you? You've been so careful, setting this whole situation up, sending me down to that resort so the two of us would meet and get involved.''

Now the twitch turned into a full-blown throbbing. He'd been set up? His grandmother had conspired with Chloe to distract him from the most important job of his life?

Worse, he'd let them do it.

"I didn't force Trent to do a thing," his grandmother replied. "You're both adults. If he allowed his relationship with you to prevent him from focusing on his work, doesn't that prove what I've been saying? He's not as dedicated to his little lawn service business as he protests. He's ready to come back, Chloe. You just need to help him figure that out."

Trent walked away, not able to stand and listen to any more. That his grandmother would do this came as no real surprise. He'd grown up in her house—he knew she fought dirty, always in the name of love and family loyalty.

But Chloe? He didn't want to believe it. Had she been in on it from the beginning? Obviously she must have been, if his grandmother had intentionally sent her down to the conference.

Sophie had been right in one respect—she might have been able to put them in the same proximity, but what happened afterward had been entirely due to him and Chloe.

One thing didn't make sense. There was no way Chloe could have faked her shock when seeing he and Troy together for the first time. So it seemed impossible that she could have been *hired* by his grandmother to hook up with him at the conference—she didn't even know he existed!

Knowing he was going to drive himself crazy until

he just confronted the woman he loved, he stopped right in the middle of the shoe area and turned back toward her workroom. One way or another, he would find out the truth.

By the time he got there, Chloe was alone, sitting on the sofa with her face in her hands. Hardening himself against her tears, he entered the room.

She immediately looked up. Her face was not tear-stained, but her eyes glittered with moisture. "Trent." Though she stood, she didn't immediately step into his arms. "Have you been here long?"

He nodded. "Long enough. Did you have an interesting visit with my grandmother?"

"You...you heard our conversation?"

He nodded again, remaining silent.

"Aren't we a pair?" She laughed bitterly. "My, what a couple of family trees we fell out of."

Trent crossed the room to her desk, glancing at the paperwork there. Then, no longer able to control his anger, he swiped his hand across her desk, sending the papers flying. "How could you do it? How could you scheme with my grandmother to ruin me? I thought what we had was real."

She froze. "It is! I didn't... Trent, how much of our conversation did you actually hear?"

"Enough to know you're supposed to keep distracting me so I lose my shirt and have to come crawling back to this crypt." The hurt look on her face gave him pause, but he couldn't suppress the harsh tone in his voice. "Did I misunderstand? Isn't that what you and my grandmother were discussing? Ways to ensure I crash and burn?"

She shook her head, tears falling from her eyes in earnest now. "That might be what she wants, Trent, but I wasn't agreeing to do it. I had absolutely no idea she planned for us to meet, that she got Troy to send me down to the conference."

"Yeah, I figured out that much," he admitted bitterly. "So, did she come to you later, when she saw how nuts I was over you, asking you to keep me busy while my company fell apart around me?"

She shook her head, crossing her arms as if hugging herself, keeping a tight grip on her shoulders. "No, Trent, I promise you, this is the first time she approached me."

"You've never spoken to her?"

"Well, once," she admitted, "but it was before I met you. She asked me a bunch of questions, complimented me on my work and that was all." She took a step closer, reaching out one hand, but not touching him. "Please, Trent, you have to believe I would not have deceived you. I had no idea your project at the resort isn't going well. Is that true?"

He ignored the question. "She didn't ever ask you before today to keep me from focusing on the job?"

She shook her head, giving him a simple, honest answer. "No."

He believed her. She hadn't agreed to sabotage him before today. That didn't completely resolve things, though. "So," he asked, crossing his arms in front of his chest, "are you going to go ahead with Plan A? You blow my mind in bed, make me fall crazy in love with you, then ask me very sweetly to support you in the style to which you'd like to become accustomed?"

This time she flinched. "I don't deserve that."

No. She didn't. He'd regretted the words as soon as he said them. "I'm sorry, Chloe. I shouldn't have said that."

"I never wanted to be rich, Trent. I never thought less of you for not being as wealthy as your brother."

He shook his head. "I know. It was never about being rich, was it? It was about security, stability, being the nine-to-five, boring guy in a minivan you've been wanting since you were a little kid."

She straightened, tears now running down her face. "Don't make it sound so ridiculous. Right now, a nine-to-five guy seems a hell of a lot more appealing than someone who might one day decide to empty our kids' college account and open up a parasailing school."

Is that what you think of me? Chloe, how did we ever get here? When did things get so out of control?

"So, be honest now. You can do that much. Do you want what my grandmother wants?" He stepped closer, lowering his voice, needing the truth. "Do you really want me to come back here, to be like Troy? Would that solve your problems, fulfill those dreams of yours?"

Her face grew more pale and an anguished look appeared in her eyes one moment before she looked away. "Have I ever asked you to do that, or made you think it's what I wanted you to do?" she said softly, rubbing a weary hand across her brow.

"No. You haven't," he admitted. "But you've never tried real hard to convince me you don't care that I'm not the successful, wealthy, stable man my brother is."

The ball was back in her court. All she had to say were two little words. *I don't.* As her tears continued to fall, she remained ominously silent.

"I guess that says it all."

Trent turned and walked out the door.

As soon as he'd gone, leaving her wide-eyed with shock and dismay, Chloe realized what Trent had been asking for. He'd wanted a denial, wanted her to tell him he was wrong. He'd been looking for confirmation that she didn't want him to change, didn't want him to be like anyone other than his wonderful, outrageously sexy self.

He'd asked for her faith. And she hadn't even understood the damn question. Chloe had been so torn up and intent on her family situation that she'd been inattentive during what was possibly the most important conversation of her adult life.

Go after him.

She should. Follow him, assure him that she loved him—truly loved him—just the way he was. After all, she did. She'd loved Trent Langtree since before she even knew who he really was.

He thrilled her, amazed her, made her feel beautiful and adored. She loved being with him, looking at him, even just sitting in silence. She was, quite simply, crazy about the man.

But he also scares you to death.

"You got that right," she whispered.

Today, finding out what her mother had done, what her family now faced, Chloe's emotions about Trent were even more confused than before. Yes, she loved him. She just didn't know if she wanted to live like this forever.

Did she want to wake up one day twenty years from now, hearing the same kind of news about her husband that she'd heard today about her mother? True, Trent wasn't as irresponsible as Jeanine, but he was passionate. A dreamer. A daring risk-taker. Trent would always go with his gut, not his brain, and make lots of mistakes along the way.

He'd excite her. Oh yes, living with him would always be a thrill. But Chloe had been telling herself for years that she didn't want thrilling, she wanted safe. Being with Trent would definitely be a roller-coaster ride of a life.

"So, now's the time to put up or shut up," she muttered. "Do you want to be the kind who rides the fastest roller coaster, or the kind who stays at home and never even goes to the park?"

Did she have enough strength for the ride? Enough courage? Enough love?

Yes.

"Now you're on my side, Sister?" Chloe knew it was the honest, levelheaded part of herself whispering in her subconscious. The wild, unpredictable side was telling her to run like hell.

A slight pounding in her head, which had begun when Trent left, became as intense as a jackhammer. "I can't do this now."

Not yet. Her mind still full of her mother's problems, she knew she had to sort out that mess first. And maybe, somewhere along the way, as she dealt with the latest debacle, she'd decide just what it was she really wanted from her future.

Taking a deep breath, Chloe grabbed her purse and

left the store, heading home. Her mother might already have been arrested. It wouldn't be the first time Chloe had to make bail for her outrageous parent. Jeanine's previous offenses had usually only involved minor things like breaking antinudity ordinances, or refusing to leave a peace rally.

This time, however, she might be in real trouble.

TRENT HADN'T INTENDED TO confront his grandmother about her interference in his life. When he saw her emerging from his brother Troy's office, however, he just couldn't leave the store.

Her eyes widened in surprise when he approached. "Trent, I had no idea you were here."

His twin, apparently as in tune to Trent's emotions as ever, looked at his face and said, "Let's go back into my office."

"Why don't we go to dinner?" Sophie smiled innocently.

"I'm not hungry," Trent bit out. "Unless you want some dirty laundry shaken out right here, I suggest we go into the office."

She obviously got the point. Without another word, she turned on her heel and preceded him into the room. Troy entered last, shutting the door firmly behind him. "What's wrong?"

Trent didn't even glance at his brother, instead focusing on their grandmother. "Our agreement's off."

She raised a brow. "Whatever are you talking about?"

"Don't play coy. You broke the rules. No more deal."

Troy walked around his desk to sit down. "What happened?"

"Our arrangement said no interference, Grandmother. And you definitely interfered." Trent paused for a moment, crossing his arms. "I heard your conversation with Chloe. You've lost."

His grandmother widened her eyes. "I didn't interfere in your business, Trent. I promised you I wouldn't blackball you, wouldn't ask business associates not to hire your firm."

"You interfered by having the hotel put me up for the weekend to ensure I'd meet Chloe."

Troy leaned back in his chair, putting his feet up on his desk. "Now, this is getting interesting."

Trent rolled his eyes. "Don't you have a store to run?"

"Practically runs itself."

"I mean it, Grandmother," Trent said. "I was so furious with you at first that I almost missed the significance. You interfered. That makes our agreement null and void. No matter what happens by my thirtieth birthday, I'm not coming back here."

His grandmother frowned. "I didn't interfere with your business. So I tried to do a little matchmaking..."

"And then you tried to bribe Chloe into either asking me to quit, or to keep me so busy that this resort job would fail."

When Troy whistled in disbelief, their grandmother shot him a glare. "Trent," she said, "I've only ever wanted what's best for you. You tried this lawn service, and obviously it hasn't worked out. You're going to lose every penny on this project, anyway."

Troy removed his feet from his desk and sat up. "You're not going to make it on the Dolphin Island job?"

"The job will be fine." If he had to work eighteen

hours a day, seven days a week, he'd make damn sure of that! "And actually, Grandmother, I should thank you. You've done me a favor. You handed me a way out with your scheming. According to our legally binding agreement, I'm off the hook."

Sophie gave it one last shot. "Chloe didn't accept the offer. She wouldn't do anything to hurt you. I haven't affected your business at all."

A sense of relief darted through him, though he'd already surmised as much. "Doesn't matter, Grandmother. The wording in our contract was very specific. It didn't say your sabotage had to be successful, just that you had to try it. And attempted bribery qualifies. So I'm outta here for the last time."

"Until your next date," Troy muttered under his breath.

Trent was too busy enjoying his grandmother's shocked silence to tell his brother to shut up.

For once, the woman was silenced. Her lips moved, but no sound came out. Finally, she resorted to tears. She dabbed at her eyes with a tissue. "I only ever wanted what was best for you."

Trent didn't fall for it. "What's best for me is the woman you might have just helped me lose."

"Impossible. She's insanely in love with you. Believe me, I knew it the minute I saw her first display in the front windows." Sophie bit her lip. "I'll talk to her."

"Just butt out, would you? Chloe's got to be the one to decide what she wants. Something's obviously bothering her."

He noticed his grandmother grab her purse and clutch it on her lap. "Uh, Trent, did she tell you what was wrong?"

"No. But I am sure it has to do with her background.

The things she's always thought she wanted. She hasn't had the most normal family life."

His grandmother lifted a brow. "I wonder if you're fully aware of how unusual her childhood really was. It amazed me, you know, that she wouldn't leap at the chance to bring you back to the family, to try to get herself a wealthy husband."

"Chloe knows money doesn't matter." He turned to leave.

"Spoken like someone who's never truly done without it," his grandmother retorted tartly. "Your Chloe has, though. Did you know she and her sister spent time in foster care? That they were taken by the state because they and their mother were living in a beach shack with a bunch of hippies? That was right after her stepfather abandoned them and their house was foreclosed."

Trent stopped and studied his grandmother, seeing no deceit in those bright, knowing eyes. "You had her investigated."

She shrugged. "Of course. After your brother brought that stripper to our Christmas party and she tried to walk out with one of my Fabergé eggs in her purse, I investigate anyone who comes in contact with you two."

"She said she was a Rockette," Troy mumbled.

"She was a thief," Sophie snapped.

Trent ignored their sniping. "She never told me that."

"I imagine it's not something she likes to talk about. It certainly does make you think, doesn't it? How nice it would be for her to never have to worry again. To feel safe and secure, never wondering if she and her family are going to be homeless, or if her children are going to be hungry." She hesitated for a moment, then drove the point home. "Like she was."

Trent listened for slyness in his grandmother's voice, but there was none. She wasn't trying to trick or cajole. She didn't need to. The truth was quite enough.

CHLOE HAD JUST PULLED into her neighborhood when her cell phone rang. Praying it wasn't her mother making her single phone call, she yanked it to her ear. "Yes?"

"Chloe, it's Trent."

She bit her lip, wanting so much to talk to him. The timing was pretty bad, however. "Hi."

"Can we talk?"

Reaching an intersection, she stopped and didn't proceed through. "I'm almost home, Trent. Uh, listen, there's a lot going on. Can we meet later?" She lowered her voice. "I do want to talk to you. I don't want you to think...I want you to know..." *Dammit, how to do this on the phone?*

A car horn sounded. "Yeah, yeah, I'm going," she muttered.

"What?"

"I'm sorry. Traffic. Look, you're right, we need to have a long, serious discussion. But I can't right now. I have to...." *Save my mother yet again?* "I have to think."

"Okay, I know. I just wanted to give you one more thing to think about, Chloe."

"Yes?"

"I just told my brother I want my job back."

He cut the connection before she could say a word.

The guy behind her laid on the horn, long and loud, because Chloe couldn't move. She sat with her car half-blocking the intersection and absorbed what he'd said.

He'd given up? For her? Tears rose in her eyes.

"No, Trent. No." That he thought her worth such a sacrifice awed her. But she couldn't let him do it.

Finally, when another driver joined in the chorus of honks, Chloe hit the gas and drove home. She would have continued reeling over Trent's revelation if she hadn't seen the car parked in front of the house. "Crap. Can things get any worse?"

A blue and white police cruiser took up most of the entrance to their tiny driveway, so Chloe parked in the street. Jumping out of the car, she ran into the house. "Mom, don't say anything without a lawyer," she yelled as she burst into the front door.

Jeanine and the man sitting beside her on the sofa looked up from their steaming cups of tea. "Hi, Chloe."

Not trusting herself to speak to her mother yet, Chloe stared at the officer. "Did you read her her rights?"

The officer, a rather attractive older gentleman with a thick shock of salt-and-pepper hair, stood and extended his hand. "You must be Jeanine's other daughter. And no, your mother didn't need to hear her rights. She's not in any trouble."

Maybe not with you!

"Chloe, maybe you'd better let me explain," Jeanine said.

"I know, Mom. I know what you did and why. We can talk about that later." She looked at the cop. "So, you're not here to charge my mother with any type of crime?"

He shook his head. "Oh, no. Your mother was the first one to come to us with her suspicions about Mr. Howard. Alias Mr. Hilton, and Mr. Howell. He's wanted in several states. She helped us contact the other victims, and then gave us enough information to track the suspect to his sister's house in Orlando. He was arrested this afternoon."

Chloe dropped to an overstuffed chair by the door, so relieved she couldn't even remain standing. She forced herself to take a few calming breaths, then looked up again. Her mom and the cop were exchanging warm smiles. *Oh, great.* "So you caught him. Did you get the money back?"

Morgan walked in and heard the question. "Nope. Apparently, he was a gamblin' man. It's all shot, including ours."

Morgan didn't seem overly distraught, but Chloe jumped up and hugged her sister. "We'll figure a way out of this, honey."

Her little sister allowed the embrace, then pulled away. Morgan wasn't the demonstrative type. "It's covered. Mom's got a new job, I can work all summer, plus there's the reward."

"Reward?"

Jeanine, who hadn't said much since Chloe arrived, explained, "It's not as much as we've lost, Chloe, but it'll replace most of Morgan's college fund."

The officer picked his cap up off the coffee table and said, "I think I'd better let you all talk things out. Jeanine, thank you so much for the tea. I'll see you at work on Monday."

Chloe raised a brow.

"I got a job at the police station," Jeanine explained. "With my experience at the law office, they hired me on as a receptionist." Jeanine exchanged a warm look with the cop before he left. Chloe exchanged a weary one with her sister.

Once they were alone again, Chloe turned to her mother. "Morgan and the police might be dealing with this okay, but that doesn't mean I am."

Jeanine took her hand, pulling her over to the sofa. "Chloe, this isn't your worry. For once, I recognized what was happening myself. I started realizing something was wonky with Ted a few days ago. I didn't wait for someone to bail me out this time. I did something about it."

Though she'd been prepared to have a major blowup with her mother, Chloe stopped. "Yes. You did, didn't you?"

Jeanine nodded happily. "I knew how you'd feel. I knew you'd want to fix this mess. But I am capable of learning from my own mistakes, Chloe. I am capable of changing. I want to do that. For you." She turned and looked at Morgan. "For both of you."

"Changing?"

Jeanine looked down at her hands, which were clenched in her lap. "I already packed away my ceramics equipment. I had my suits cleaned. I can be who you need me to be again."

As she listened to the sincere tone in her mother's voice, Chloe was shocked at her sudden sense of loss. Her mom in suits. No longer floating around making her happy little animals in the garage with a smile in her face and a kind word on her lips. Going back to the lifeless, bored woman she'd been until she quit her job a few months before.

"I don't want you to change, Mom," she whispered.

Chloe couldn't believe she'd spoken those words aloud, but she knew it was true. For the first time in her life, she allowed herself to admit it. In spite of her occasional frustration, anger and worry, she blessed every minute she'd had with her irrepressible mother.

"I love you for who you are, not who I want you to be." Certainty and relief washed over her as she continued. "I care enough about you to want you to be truly happy. Isn't that the way it's supposed to be?"

Morgan nodded approvingly. "Finally, someone other than me makes some sense in this house."

As easily as that, the answer to Chloe's dilemma was perfectly clear. She had no dilemma at all. She loved Trent for who he was.

And she wouldn't change him for the world.

THOUGH IT WAS ALMOST SIX, Trent didn't go home after his brief phone call to Chloe. In spite of being bone tired, he drove back down to the Dolphin Island Resort. He might be quitting, but he was going to finish this job—and finish it *well*—before he went. Even if he had to plant single-handedly all three hundred of the blue rug junipers his supplier had finally delivered yesterday.

He needed to work, needed to dig and pound and hammer. Keeping his body busy would ensure that his mind couldn't spend every moment wondering where Chloe was and if she was all right, what she was thinking and what she'd decide.

Once at the resort, Trent went into the on-site trailer and wrote a few notes for Jason for Monday morning. Digging out his keys to the fenced storage lot where the nursery materials were kept, he stripped off his shirt and prepared to go do some planting. He wanted to sweat, wanted his muscles to ache, so maybe tonight he'd be tired enough to actually sleep.

"Doubt it," he mused as he walked out.

He had just reached the gate to the lot when he saw a car pull into the construction entrance. "Chloe."

He froze, watching her park, then emerge from the car. Her somber expression gave no indication of her mood. He didn't really know what to expect. Jubilation? Disappointment? Understanding? A little of everything?

"Hi," she said softly as she finally reached his side. "I kinda figured you'd be here. I couldn't reach you any place else."

He shrugged. "Still plenty of sunlight."

She crossed her arms in front of her chest. "Did you mean what you said on the phone? About wanting your job back?"

He gave a curt nod. "Yes. I told Troy I'm coming back."

Her eyes narrowed. "You didn't answer my question. Do you *want* your job back?"

"I want *you*," he said, after a moment's hesitation.

He watched her lips soften into a smile. "You have me, Trent. You've had me since the first time I saw you out a rain-streaked window on a stormy summer night." She stepped closer, reaching up to caress his face with her fingertips. Then she moved her hand to his ear, touching the small gold hoop he still wore. "I love you."

He turned his head to kiss her palm. "I love you, too, Chloe. And I want to make your dreams come true."

She smiled. "You've given me a whole new set of

dreams, Trent. A whole new understanding of love and loyalty." She slipped her arms around his neck, stepping even closer. "But there's something you should know. I have no intention of being the wife of a boring, suit-wearing, retail kingpin."

He froze. "What are you saying?"

"I'm saying," she explained, "that I want to be with a man who can stop traffic on the highway just by standing on a construction site with his shirt off." She lowered her gaze to his chest and licked her lips. "Yum."

"Be serious."

"I'm being completely serious. Trent, I fell in love with you for who you are, every glorious bit of you. I don't want you to give up your dream because you think you have to for me to have mine. I want us to be together...to build new ones." She grinned. "Just promise that if you get too reckless, I do have permission to be the voice of reason."

"This from the woman who punched the guy driving the boat."

He kissed the laughter right off her lips, telling her without saying a word how much he adored her.

"Now," Trent said when they finally broke apart, "did I hear you say the word wife?"

She raised a brow. "You might have."

"Can we get married on the beach?"

"Are you proposing?"

"I thought you did."

She fisted her hands and put them on her hips. "Well, ya know, it's a little more natural for the guy to ask!"

Trent pulled her into his arms again. "I'm not good at asking for what I want, Chloe," he whispered as he lowered his lips to hers. Right before they met, he said, "Sometimes, I just take." Then he kissed her again. Deeply. Tasting her, inhaling her, getting to know her all over again—now not just as a lover, but as his life mate.

"And yes, we should definitely get married on the beach," she whispered when he moved to kiss her neck and earlobe.

Before he could reply, they both heard more cars pulling into the parking lot beside the trailer. Dropping an arm across her shoulders, Trent watched as a small VW Beetle parked next to Chloe's car. Behind that came his brother's jade-green Jaguar. "Somebody forget to invite me to the reunion?"

Jeanine and Morgan waved as they climbed out of the Beetle. Glancing toward Chloe, he saw her laugh and shake her head. "Want to explain this?"

"Well, uh, when I was trying to track you down a little while ago, I called the store and spoke with Troy. I told him to keep his lousy job because you were much too busy being an entrepreneur to go back to stuffy old Langtree's."

"I'm sure he loved that."

"I think he was amused, at least until I told him I couldn't wait to see some woman have him running around in circles."

"I told him the same thing."

She chuckled. "He also confirmed what your grandmother told me about this job, Trent. I'm sorry it's not going well. And if your grandmother was right, and

I've been the cause of that, I'm even more sorry. I want to try to help. So I didn't just come here to propose to you, I came to work."

For the first time, Trent noticed what she was wearing: khaki shorts, a tight T-shirt and work boots. Not Chloe's usual style. "Work?"

"We're ready. Where should we put the herbal tea and rice cakes for our break time?" Jeanine asked as she and Morgan strolled up. By their attire, they also appeared ready to do some physical labor.

Morgan rolled her eyes. "She insisted on packing us a cooler, tons of water, and those little fans you can wear on your hat. Like it's noon instead of dinner-time."

Before Trent could reply, he saw Chloe's jaw drop open. Following her stare, he watched as Troy approached. His own eyes widened when he saw what Troy was wearing. "My brother in jean shorts and sneakers?"

"He's got the legs for it," Jeanine commented with an appreciative sigh.

"The shorts definitely work for me," Morgan added.

Jeanine and Morgan continued staring back and forth between Trent and his twin. Trent chuckled when he saw Chloe roll her eyes.

Troy glanced at them both. "Thank you, ladies. We sell this line at Langtree's." Then he glanced at Trent. "Which is a good thing, since I certainly wasn't going to ruin a suit out here helping you plant a few hundred bushes in the ground."

Trent met his brother's eye, ignoring Troy's sarcasm. He sent him a silent message of thanks, knowing his twin understood what was in his heart. For once, Troy didn't smirk, didn't toss off a condescending remark. He simply said, "You're welcome." Then Troy looked at the others. "Let's get to work."

"Okay, *brother*," Chloe said.

Troy raised a brow. When Trent nodded, confirming their engagement, Troy grinned. "At last. Grandmother can now turn her eye on you two. I'm sure she'll place an order for great-grandchildren as soon as she hears. And maybe she'll leave me and my sex life alone."

Chloe's mother didn't appear to catch on to the news—possibly because she was still busy ogling Troy. But Morgan's fine blue eyes brightened with pleasure behind her thick glasses. She leaned over and gave Chloe a kiss on the cheek. Seeing the surprise on his fiancée's face, Trent assumed that wasn't a frequent occurrence.

"Okay, crew, let's get busy," Chloe said, looking happier than he'd ever seen her. Bending, she picked up a shovel, which was lying beside the gate. She tossed it toward Troy. "You're going to need this."

Troy caught it easily. "I do know what a shovel is."

"Good. Now Troy, remember, when you're planting, the brown part goes in first. The green part stays up." She grinned wickedly. "And don't forget—these kinds of beds are for planting in, not playing in."

He hadn't seen his brother at such a loss for words for a very long time. Chloe was definitely just what the Langtree family needed. Thanksgiving dinners might never be the same.

Looking to the clear blue sky above, Trent smiled and shouted, "I love this woman."

Chloe leaned up on tiptoe, cupped his cheek, and tilted his face toward hers. Gazing tenderly into his eyes, she pressed a sweet kiss on his lips. "This woman loves you, too."

*   *   *   *   *

Who better to bring down wicked
Troy than outrageous bad girl
Venus Longotti, from Leslie Kelly's
March 2002 release

INTO THE FIRE.

Don't miss their story, launching the

BAD GIRLS

miniseries with
Harlequin Temptation, early 2003.

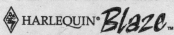
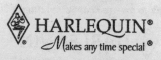

TRUEBLOOD, TEXAS

Coming in July 2002...

DYLAN'S DESTINY
by
Kimberly Raye

Lost:

One locket. A locket that certain people want badly enough to kill for, and Julie Cooper is the only one who can lead them to it. She's been running for months with her baby. But now she's tired.

Found:

Freedom. Dylan Garrett has loved Julie from afar for years and there's no way he's going to lose her again. He'll do anything to protect his love and her precious son.

It is up to Dylan to crack the case, so that he and Julie can finally find their destiny...together!

Finders Keepers: bringing families together

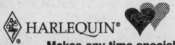

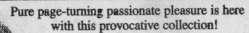

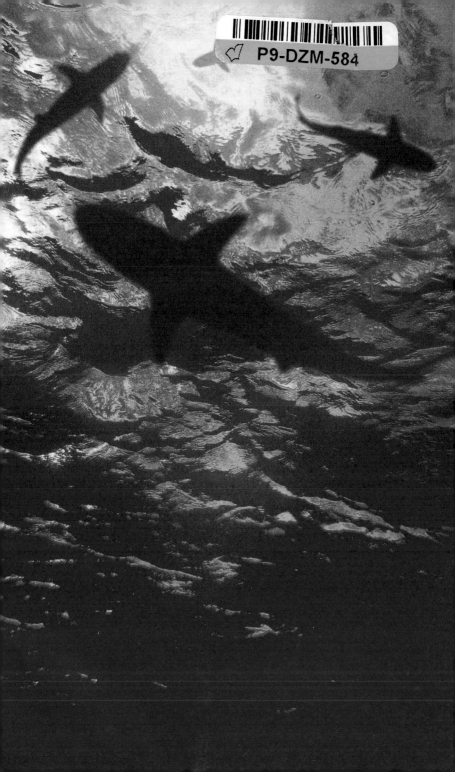
P9-DZM-584

Also by Michael Northrop

Gentlemen

Trapped

Plunked

Rotten

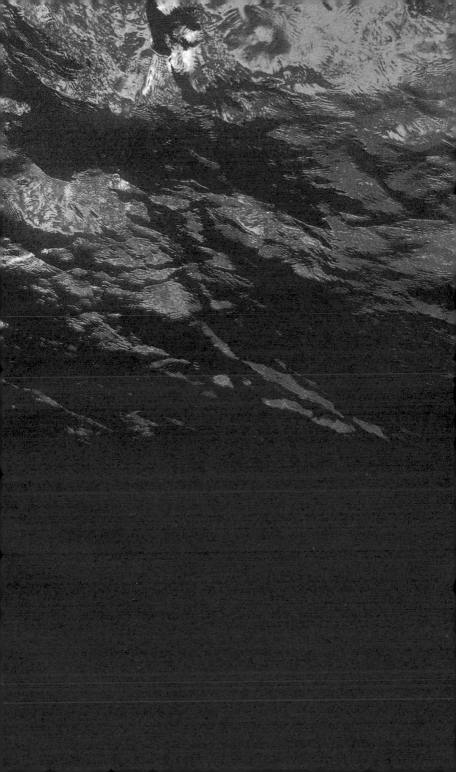

SURROUNDED BY

SHARKS

MICHAEL NORTHROP

SCHOLASTIC INC.

ISBN 978-0-545-78054-4

Copyright © 2014 by Michael Northrop.

All rights reserved. Published by Scholastic Inc. SCHOLASTIC and associated logos are trademarks and/or registered trademarks of Scholastic Inc.

12 11 10 9 8 7 6 5 4 3 2 1   14 15 16 17 18 19/0

Printed in the U.S.A.   40

First Scholastic paperback printing, September 2014

Book design by Phil Falco

For my agent, Sara Crowe,
and my editor, Anamika Bhatnagar,
who have kept me afloat in some very perilous seas

PART ONE

CARRIED AWAY

1

Davey Tsering opened his eyes and looked up at an unfamiliar, cream-colored ceiling. He'd slept fitfully on a steel-framed canvas cot, and his body felt a little like he'd just fallen down a mountain. He heard his family before he saw them. His dad was snoring loudly and his younger brother was echoing him like a smaller version of the same revving engine. Davey groaned softly and turned to look around the overcrowded hotel room.

He saw his mom and dad, Pamela and Tam, lying next to each other on one of the room's two double beds. His mom's face was turned down in a grim frown as she slept. Davey peered at the alarm clock on the night table between the two beds. He squinted, but it was too far away for him to read the little glowing numbers. He carefully reached down to the floor for his glasses. The little cot was noisy, and the last thing he wanted was to wake someone up and have company.

He put his glasses on and everything in the room became a little clearer. It wasn't an improvement. There was drool at the corner of

1

his dad's mouth, and his mom was balanced precariously on the edge of the bed.

Davey's younger brother was splayed out in the next bed, the one that was supposed to be Davey's tomorrow night. Davey looked at him for a few moments. He was surprised by how young he looked lying there, and how peaceful. He still looked like the little kid who used to follow Davey around everywhere. But Davey wasn't fooled. He knew that as soon as Brandon woke up, he'd become "Brando." That's what he liked to be called now. Now that he'd turned into a Class-A pain in the neck, now that he'd started arguing with their parents. Like those two didn't argue enough already.

Davey couldn't imagine what that would sound like in this little room. And who needed imagination? He was sure he'd find out before the week was over. He took a deep breath and regretted it immediately. The room was slightly but unmistakably funky. Four people had been in here all night, sleeping, snoring, drooling, and . . . *Oh no,* thought Davey. *Oh Dear Lord . . . Had someone been farting?*

Another breath, this one quick and cautious, confirmed his fear. He assumed it was Brando, but there was no way to be sure. Was it his dad? His *mom*? It was too horrible to think about.

Finally, he remembered why he'd put his glasses on. He looked at the clock: 6:47. *That's it?* he thought. *That's it?* It would be hours until everyone was awake and ready to get moving. He knew what they'd say: "We're on vacation. Let us sleep."

He had to get out. Thirteen and a half was too old to be stuffed into a room with his entire family. One day in, and he already needed a vacation from this vacation.

Slowly, very slowly, he reached down and pulled the thin hotel blanket off his body. His heart started beating faster. If either of his parents woke up, they'd stop him. If his brother woke up, he'd want to come, too. He had to be quiet. Spy quiet, ninja quiet. Ninja-spy quiet.

He pushed his feet slowly over the side and cringed as the cot creaked under his shifting weight. He glanced over at the beds: no movement. He reached out and put his left hand on the windowsill, taking some of the weight off the cot. In one quick, smooth — well, kind of smooth — movement, he stood up.

Davey had slept in a T-shirt and his swim trunks because . . . well, basically because his brother had. If pajamas are too babyish for your younger brother, they are, by extension, too babyish for you. And he had to admit it was a pretty solid plan. His swim trunks were the one thing he could wash himself as the week went on, just by going in the water. They were in the Florida Keys, after all. The Internet described this place as "a sunny tropical paradise with white sand beaches and crystal-blue water." It didn't seem like paradise so far — and it definitely didn't smell like it — but Davey was 100 percent sure the March weather here was going to be better than it had been in Ohio.

Still, he wasn't really a beach person. He was skinny, and he wouldn't call himself nerdy, exactly, but he did like his fantasy books. He leaned down and silently pawed through the little pile of paperbacks he'd set up next to the cot. All the books except one were by J. R. R. Tolkien. Davey was such a big fan that he knew what all the initials stood for. And the one book that wasn't by John Ronald Reuel Tolkien was by his son.

Davey made his selection: *The Silmarillion.* The bookstore lady had told him it was "for serious Tolkien fans only," and so it was his new favorite. He stuffed a few other essentials in the white-mesh pocket of his swim trunks and surveyed the path ahead. He had to walk right by the beds — why on earth had he set up the cot by the window instead of the door?

He walked carefully, minefield-style. The carpet was thick and easily absorbed his weight. Halfway across the room, he heard someone turn over. He knew it was his brother before he even looked — his parents had no room for such large maneuvers. He looked back slowly and was relieved to see Brando in a slightly different position but still just as asleep. The shifting of his blankets had revealed something else, though. Brando was definitely the one polluting the atmosphere. In a way it was a relief.

Davey saw a sliver of morning sunlight through a gap in the curtains. That was his goal. He needed to reach it. He needed to get to a sunny, warm place that didn't sound like dueling chain saws and wasn't contaminated by the burrito grande his brother had eaten at the airport. He turned back toward the door and kept going. He was past the beds now. A few more tense steps and he was at the door.

He pressed down on the handle with slow, even pressure. He knew there would be a click. The question was how loud.

Click.

Not too loud. He didn't hear anything behind him and didn't turn to look. He was too close to his goal. He pushed the door open and quickly stepped through.

2

In open ocean approximately four miles to the southwest, a very different individual was also up early. Although "up early" wasn't exactly accurate in this case. It had been up all night. It had been up all of its life. But now, in the fresh light of morning, it was on the hunt.

Galeocerdo cuvier. The tiger shark. The distinctive stripes that earned the species its name had faded as this one reached adulthood, but there was a second reason for the name. The sea tiger was at least as fearsome a predator as a tiger on land. It was a massive, muscular brute of a fish. It was sometimes called the man-eater shark, but that wasn't entirely accurate, either. It would eat anything, from sea snakes to sick whales to discarded lunch boxes.

As the sun speared through the warm top layer of the ocean, all of the shark's senses were alive. Its eyes scanned the water as its ears listened for rhythms. It smelled the water constantly with powerful nostrils that had nothing to do with breathing, had no other job. If you were in the water a thousand yards away, it could taste you already. It could tell if you had a sunburn. But it was doing something else, as well.

Small jelly-filled pores along the shark's head were alive to any electrical charges in the water. With them, the shark could sense the tiny charge given off by the muscles of a fish as it flicked its tail. It could sense the vast humming of an ocean current. With a threshold of around five one-billionths of a volt, it could sense nearly anything that moved down here. And that's how it knew it was close.

It had been on the trail all night, gliding patiently through the water. It wasn't sure at first: a faint smell, and far off. And even when it knew — *blood* — it still wasn't willing to expend much energy. The sea was vast and hungry. Food was often gone by the time the shark arrived. The body would be gone, even the scraps, leaving it with nothing but the smell and the knowledge that it was once again too late.

But not today. Its prey was just up ahead. The broken rhythm of an injured animal swimming rang through its senses like a church bell:

Whump-whump-wahamp-*whump* . . .

Whump-whump-wahamp-*whump* . . .

Whump-whump-wahamp-*whump* . . .

The shark could see it up ahead now. It was a loggerhead sea turtle, a rich feast of fat and muscle if the shark could catch it. And there was something wrong with it. One of its flippers was injured. Yes, the shark could see that now. It could see it and smell it and feel it and sense it and taste it.

It could've been hurt by a fishing net or another shark. It could've been anything out here, but it didn't matter now. After all those miles of slow, patient swimming, the shark had closed to within a few dozen yards. The turtle knew it was there now and swam harder.

Whump-whump-wahamp-*whump-whump-whump*-wahamp-*whump*

The effort came to nothing. The tiger shark exploded through the water, closing the distance almost instantly with an impressive burst of speed. And then it was on the turtle and feeding. Its powerful jaws clamped down on the injured flipper. Dozens of broad, backward-curved teeth, serrated like kitchen knives, found their marks. And again. And again.

The turtle weighed close to 250 pounds. The shark was five times that, but the turtle would still have been enough to fill its stomach — if it weren't for the others. The tiger shark swam by itself for hundreds of miles, but when there was food, it was never alone.

As it circled around for another bite, a second shark flashed up from below. It was smaller and faster and just as hungry. It tore chunks of its own. And then another one appeared. With it came a cloud of the little scavenger fish that frustrated the big shark. They were too small and quick to catch, but big enough to snap up some of its kill.

The turtle was torn to pieces and devoured in a storm of blood.

3

Davey made it past the hotel's front desk — really a chest-high counter — without any trouble. Admittedly, there was no one there, so the only trouble would've been if he'd run into it. He didn't. He read the small RING FOR SERVICE! sign and he didn't do that, either. Then he pushed through the front door and stepped out into a truly gorgeous morning.

He could hardly believe it. In front of him, just past the hotel grounds, was a beach and then the ocean. The blue of the sky and the blue of the water met at the horizon. It was like another world, a fantasy realm.

He hadn't really seen the beach the day before. The coolest thing he'd seen then was the Cincinnati airport, where he'd been able to watch a few jets take off. It was too late to see much by the time they'd gotten to Florida. The taxi driver in Key West told them the sunset had been really great — and that they'd just missed it. The guy who piloted the little boat over to this island said the same thing. The boat ride was kind of cool, but there

9

wasn't much to see in the dark. Davey's main impression of Florida so far had been of a nice thing he'd just missed.

He saw it all now, though. First up, a palm tree. Until that moment, palm trees had been one of those famous things he'd seen on TV but not in person. Palm trees, polar bears, riots . . . He stood there looking at it for a few seconds. It was just like on *Hawaii Five-0*. So far, he'd made it exactly four feet from the hotel.

He looked to the sides: more palms trees and a sandy walking path in both directions. He listened closely and could just hear the little waves curling and falling and retreating at the ocean's edge. He turned around and saw the sign on the front of the hotel. Swooping blue letters on a white background spelled out ASZURE ISLAND INN. *Two points off for spelling*, he thought, though he knew it was the same way on the map.

He picked a direction — left, just to be different — and started walking. It took him a few steps to register the temperature. Normally, he'd step out a door and right away his body would tell him that it was too hot or too cold. It was a lot of both back in Ohio. But this time, his body had no complaints. It was warm but not too hot. The light breeze was refreshing but not too cool. Davey knew it would probably heat up as the day went on, but he figured that would just make the breeze feel nicer.

So, yes, he was impressed. But then he spotted the flaw in the plan after a few more steps: There was nothing to do on this island.

Still in front of the hotel, he could already see the end of it. Not the end of the hotel; the end of the island. It was that small. He looked at the hotel again, just now realizing that it was the only one on the island. This was a one-horse town, and the hotel was that horse.

Wow, he thought, *Mom wasn't kidding.* The first time she'd told them about this trip, she'd described it as a "remote island retreat." Brando had groaned. Two of those words basically mean the same thing as *boring.* After that, she'd started calling it a "family retreat" to "recharge." You weren't allowed to groan at a "family" anything, and who didn't like to get charged? Anyway, it hadn't been up for a vote. They'd already purchased the tickets — some great deal online.

Davey kept walking, and then he saw something. It was some kind of stand, just off the path. *Hey now,* he thought. It was closed, but then it wasn't even seven in the morning. With the wooden shutters locked, it was impossible to tell what it sold, but it had to sell something. He squinted into the distance and saw another one. *Maybe there are some the other way, too,* he thought.

Davey didn't need much. At home, he spent most of his time in his room, and a lot of that reading. And he had his favorite books with him. His parents could recharge, and he could reread. A few weeks earlier he'd overheard his mom calling him "kind of monk-ish," but he didn't think she meant it entirely in a bad way. They had monks in their family, actual Tibetan monks. His parents' business sold arts and crafts from Tibet. Though if you wanted to know what most of the arguments were about, they didn't sell nearly as many as they used to.

It didn't take Davey long to reach the second stand. This one had metal shutters that were closed tight with big padlocks. There was a sign on top: ASZURE ISLAND BAR. Davey considered it. He'd been hoping for a place that sold comic books, or even regular ones. He knew that Ernest Hemingway used to live on Key West. He could see Key West from here, a fuzzy lump on the water. Davey hadn't read any of Hemingway's books yet, but he knew he wrote about bullfights and wars and other potentially interesting things. He flexed his left hand and felt the familiar weight of *The Silmarillion*.

A bar was okay, he decided. They'd have pretzels and potato chips and probably a few different kinds of soda. Plus, it would be fun to tell his parents, "Back in a minute, just going to the bar!"

Davey smiled for the first time in days. And then he heard something: voices, headed his way. He was at the far end of the island, where it came to a tip before bending back toward the other side of the hotel. That's where the voices were coming from. He'd had the whole island to himself until now, but not anymore. The voices were getting louder. Not wanting to go toward them, he looked around for an alternative.

4

Drew Dobkin wanted the world to know that she was being held here against her will. She'd wanted to go to Madrid or Miami or Mykonos. It didn't have to begin with an *M*; those were just examples. But it should have been somewhere with excitement and music and boys with tans to look at. She was fourteen now and needed to go on holiday somewhere appropriate. Well, she'd be fourteen in two months, but she was always one to round up.

But had she been asked? She had not! Her parents had simply found some great deal online and packed her up like so much luggage and shipped her here straight from England. Now they were stumbling around some little walking path with only a vague idea of what time it was. She checked her phone. No service, of course, but it worked as a watch. It was 12:28 in the afternoon back in Knutsford, and apparently 7:28 in the morning here. And what was this, anyway, a deserted island? Like the ones in the cartoons? They hadn't seen a single person since they'd left the hotel. And come to think of it, they hadn't seen anyone there, either.

"Lovely, though, isn't it?" said her mom, Kate.

Her dad, a man universally known as Big Tony, grunted in agreement. And then she got the distinct, annoying impression that they were waiting for her opinion on the matter. She flicked her eyes around a bit. She supposed it was quite pretty, in a boring sort of way. Instead of admitting it, she asked, "Can we go to Key West today?"

Her best friend, Becca, had told her that Key West was where the party was at. Her exact words: "Key West, that's where the party's at." Drew didn't need a full-on party, just some excitement and a bit of fun. Wasn't that what holidays were for? It made no sense to her to leave England to rest — England was already the sleepiest place on earth!

"Now hold on, then," said Big Tony, his first words of the day. "We just got here last night!"

"It speaks!" said her mom, acting astonished.

And then there they went, joking around and talking about anything other than Key West. Drew let them have their fun. She'd spotted something interesting up ahead. It was a little . . . what did you call it? A pier, or was it too small for that? A dock, maybe?

"Here's the boat place," she said. She pointed out over the water, a little farther up the path. There was a single boat tied up alongside.

"That the one we took last night?" said her mom. They headed off the path and toward the worn wooden dock. The boat was painted white and had the hotel's name on the back in blue, just above the blocky outboard motor.

"Don't think so," said her dad.

They crossed a little sliver of sand and stepped carefully onto the end of the dock. Drew expected it to shift and possibly sink, but it was sturdy enough. She looked down as she walked and could see the ocean sloshing underneath through the planks. She gave the weathered wood a closer look. "Pretty worn down, isn't it?" she said.

"Adds to the charm of the place, I'd imagine," said her mom.

"And the cost!" joked Big Tony.

"This must be where they bring the people over," said Kate, pointing to the side opposite the hotel launch. The wood seemed even more scratched up and worn out there, and there was a thick rope tied to the far post. It was just like the one securing the hotel boat, but this one was coiled up, waiting for the next arrival.

"Nice work, detective," said Big Tony.

Kate smiled. Drew flicked her eyes to the side and saw Key West, hazy in the distance. Then she smiled, too.

The family turned and headed back toward shore, with Drew last in line. At the end of the dock, they met someone. "Hello there, luv," said Kate to the little boy. "Where are you off to?"

The boy looked to be ten or eleven. He pointed out to sea, back toward Key West. Drew glanced at him. Technically, this was a boy with a tan, but definitely not what she'd meant.

15

"Well, that will be quite an adventure for you!" continued her mom.

The boy just nodded and took a seat on the edge of the dock.

"Little pirate, that one," said Big Tony as they resumed their trip along the walking path.

Drew took one last look over her shoulder and saw the boy's parents appear from the hotel grounds with their luggage. *They must be waiting for the first boat to show,* she thought. *There must be a schedule somewhere.*

"Dad?" she said.

"Yeah, luv?"

"How much was the boat last night?"

"One million pounds!" he said.

Her mom gave him a swat.

Her parents held hands and looked out at the water. Drew clasped her own hands together as a joke, but there was no one to appreciate her humor. She kicked at a seashell with her flip-flop. She was wearing a parentally approved combo of shorts and a light T-shirt. ("You can't just go walking around in your bathing suit all day," her mom had said. "You're English!") Even as early as it was here, she already felt the sun on her arms and legs. At least she'd get a tan. Those were hard to come by in Knutsford.

She looked out to sea, too, but it all sort of seemed the same to her. She tried the island side, and there, sitting up against the trunk of a palm tree, was another boy. This one looked older, almost her age. He was somewhat tan, too, but she thought it might be the natural kind with him. He was in the shade and reading a book, after all.

He raised his head as she passed, but looked down quickly when he saw her.

Quiet as a church mouse, that one, she thought. *He'll be no fun at all.*

Her parents didn't even notice him. They'd just spotted the bar.

5

Davey stood up and brushed the sand from his butt. He was just going to have to move if there were going to be English people running all over the place. It was distracting. He'd heard enough to identify their accents and not much more. He had a pretty solid grasp of English accents from PBS.

This family didn't have the posh accents from *Downton Abbey* (his mom's favorite show). They sounded more like some of the characters on *Mystery!* (his dad's). And by some of the characters, he meant the criminals. And the guy who played Gimli the Dwarf in the Lord of the Rings movies. He didn't think they were really criminals, the way the parents held hands and joked around. And they definitely weren't dwarves.

The problem — the distraction — was their daughter. At least he assumed it was their daughter. Whatever branch of the family tree she fell off of, her T-shirt was so light that he could see her bathing suit right through it. Or, wait . . . was that *her bra*?

Yep, waaaaay too distracting. Their voices had faded away at this point, but he figured they'd be back. Or someone else would, probably wearing a tiny bikini or something else that would make it impossible for him to concentrate on reading his book. Plus, he was sitting, like, twenty yards from the bar stand. What if it opened up and he got drunk on the fumes? It seemed possible. He knew from science class that alcoholic solutions were prone to evaporation. He took a deep breath as he started walking back toward the pathway. The air did smell a little different. Was that the ocean or just a whole mess of rum? Man, he'd be in trouble then. Stumbling back into the hotel room completely blitzed on alcohol vapors.

He'd be in trouble anyway. He'd realized that right around the time he'd fully woken up, just outside the hotel door. One of his parents was going to wake up and see that he wasn't there. Then that one would wake up the other one so they could both have a mutual parental freak-out about it. He rehearsed possible excuses in his head:

"I was just sooo excited to get started on our awesome vacation!"

"I saw a beached whale from the window and went out to help."

"Brando was farting."

He didn't think any of those would cut it, so to speak. He tried to think of others, but the best he could come up with was: "Where was I going to go? It's a frickin' island!"

It was hopeless. He was thinking about that girl again. He wondered what her name was. Had they said it, in their criminal dwarfen accents? The only thing he remembered them calling her was "luv." And if he called her that, he'd straight up get smacked.

Luv . . . Now there's something he didn't hear in his family, not anymore. He picked at that thought for a bit until he saw the next family. They were sitting quietly on their luggage at the edge of a little dock, just off the walking path.

"Out for a walk?" called a very tall man.

Davey looked at him. The only thing louder than the man's voice was his shirt. A Hawaiian shirt in Florida . . . Those were some weak geographical skills right there.

"Yeah," Davey called back. He tried to think of something else to say so he could walk away from them without seeming rude. "Waiting for a boat?"

"Yeah," called the man. "First one of the day. We're not exactly sure when it's supposed to get here, but we've got an early flight."

That hadn't worked. Now he had to respond to that, too. He took another look at the little group. The lady was glancing over her shoulder and out to sea, as if mentioning the boat might've made it appear. There was a boy there, too, younger than Brando. The boy nodded at him, and Davey nodded back. He realized he still hadn't responded.

"Well, good luck with that!" he called. He gave a quick wave and started walking again before they could say anything else.

Once he was a safe distance away, he looked back. There was a white boat tied to the end of the dock. He sort of wanted to check it out. He also wanted to walk to the end of the dock and look into the deeper water. He bet there'd be fish and stuff. But he couldn't with all those people camped out at this end of it. What was it, rush hour all of a sudden? He kept walking, looking for a quiet spot to read his book.

The pathway connected to another one leading to the back of the hotel. There was a pool, which made no sense to him. The whole place was surrounded by ocean. He kept going and was all the way at the other end of the little island when he found it. A little path split off from the main one. He followed it through a thick stand of scrubby bushes and salt-stunted trees and emerged onto the most beautiful little beach he'd ever seen. The most beautiful, and the most private. There was absolutely no one there, and looking back, he could no longer see the walkway or the hotel or really much of anything.

In fact, the only evidence that anyone had *ever* been there before was a large sign, nearly falling over in the sand. The paint was sun-blasted and peeling, but he could still make out most of the letters: NO SW MM NG.

He played a quick game of *Wheel of Fortune* in his head, bought a vowel: *No Swimming*.

6

Brando got up to go to the bathroom. He was so sleepy that he didn't notice his brother was gone until he got back. For a few moments he just stood at the end of his bed looking at the empty cot. At first he thought that something exciting might've happened. Maybe his brother had been carried off by a gator or captured by drug smugglers. He'd watched enough TV to know that Florida had both.

He walked over to the cot, knelt down, and looked underneath. Davey wasn't camped out under there. He looked over at his own bed: comfortable and warm. He could just go back to sleep and forget about it, but now he was curious. He knew his older brother well — he'd lived with him his entire life — so he knew what to look for.

He checked the floor on both sides of the cot, everywhere within an arm's length or so. Sure enough, Davey's glasses were gone. And where was that book he'd been carrying around all week, *The Silma-something-or-other*? He found Davey's little stack of books and checked each one. It was gone, too.

So he took his glasses and his book, thought Brando. *Probably his key card for the room, too.* That pretty much ruled out gator attack or kidnapping. Brando shrugged it off. That had been a long shot, anyway. So that meant . . .

Davey had snuck out of the room. It didn't surprise Brando that much. His brother was always wandering off to hang out by himself these days. He'd become so boring. But this was different. This wasn't heading straight up to his room after dinner. He could get in major trouble for this.

Brando reached down and felt the cot. The plan was for them to alternate nights on it. Their dad had called it an "army cot," trying to spin it into something cool. Brando wasn't fooled. He touched the metal frame and coarse canvas and could tell it would be seriously uncomfortable.

A plan took shape. If Davey got in trouble, he should have to sleep on the cot all week. That was only fair, right? Brando could just quietly suggest it at some point. He liked the plan, but now he was all kinds of conflicted. He was many things, most of which he'd admit with pride: loud, moody, maybe a little devious around the edges. But he was not a rat. And he had a lot of opinions about his older brother, who never wanted to hang out with him anymore. But he didn't hate him.

He looked back at his parents. He knew his dad was still asleep because he could hear him snoring, so he only really had to check on his mom. She was motionless, balanced on the very edge of the bed. How did she sleep through that noise at point-blank range? For a second Brando wondered if he snored, too. *Nah,* he thought. *Not me.*

He looked directly at them and thought, as hard as he could:

WAKE UP.

WAKE UP.

YOUR SON HAS FLOWN THE COOP — WAKE UP!

Nothing.

Brando made a deal with himself: He wouldn't intentionally wake them up. That would be the same as ratting on his brother. He'd just behave totally normally. If they happened to hear him and wake up before Davey got back, well, Davey had made his cot, and now he had to lie in it. All week.

Brando went over to the little desk, pulled out the chair, and sat down. He spent some time reading the room service menu. He considered his breakfast options. Then he got up and walked over to the mini fridge on the other side of the room. It was fairly close to his dad's head, but he wasn't especially careful opening it.

His dad didn't seem to notice. Brando pushed through all of the expensive stuff the hotel was trying to sell: the five-dollar pack of M&M's, the mixed nuts for seven fifty. He took out the half-full bottle of Coke he'd picked up in Key West and put in there last night. He undid the cap, but it was too flat to hiss or fizz or anything.

He wasn't supposed to have soda in the morning, but this was a no-lose situation for him. If his parents woke up right now, he wouldn't be the one in trouble. He stood right next to their bed and took a long drink. Still nothing. He put the cap back on and put it back in the mini fridge. He closed the door kind of hard. Wouldn't want to waste electricity.

His dad shifted in the bed. He started to roll over, but his body seemed to remember that it had nowhere to go and stopped. It amounted to a shoulder fake, one way and then the other. He even stopped snoring for a moment. Brando held his breath, but his dad went right back to snoring. His mom hadn't moved an inch.

Brando walked back across the room. He sat on the edge of his bed. It really was comfortable. He lay back to consider his next move. A minute later, he was snoring, too.

7

Davey was surprised how warm the water was. He was standing at the very edge of the breaking waves, up to his ankles. He'd kicked off his sneakers and walked right past the NO SW MM NG sign, which was fine because he wasn't sw mm ng. He still had his glasses on, still had the book in his hand. He was just testing out the water for later.

He figured he'd go in that afternoon — if he wasn't hotel-grounded, anyway. That would be fine with him, too. That was Davey's secret weapon. Most of the things his parents could do to punish him — send him to his room, revoke TV privileges — he did to himself anyway. If they really wanted to get to him, they could take his books away. That might work, but no parent ever did that. In parent logic, that would be like forbidding him from doing his homework.

The little waves curled around his ankles, clean and clear and warm. They seemed almost friendly. It was like being licked by a giant kitten, he thought — except not as weird or creepy as that. He looked out over the water and could see all the way to the horizon. He felt like an explorer. There was nothing in between him and the edge of the world. He remembered the sight of Key West off in the distance from the other side of the island. He pictured the image of Aszure Island he'd seen on Google Maps. If Key West was east of here, then he was looking at the open ocean to the west now. Next stop: Mexico, a thousand miles away.

A larger wave broke in front of him, sending water halfway up his shin. He reached down and ran his right hand through it as it rushed past, clutching his book to his chest with his left. It was like a bath, like stepping into a vast, gently rolling bath. The water tugged at his calves as it rushed back out to sea, and he stood up to steady himself.

Maybe this week won't be so bad, after all, he thought as he walked out of the water and back up the beach. If he stood right in the breakers the whole time, he'd hardly be able to hear his family. Or maybe if he just didn't tell them about this little spot . . . He looked around the little beach. He had it to himself and could sit anywhere. He chose a spot at the edge of the trees, where he could be half in and half out of the sun.

He sat down, opened his book to the page he'd dog-eared, and got started. He read for a while, but he wasn't quite as lost in it as he had been the first two times he'd read it. He kept looking up at the sea. He watched the little waves build themselves up and fall over. He watched the foamy white breakers that had pushed and pulled playfully at his ankles.

He decided to go in again, maybe just a little farther this time.

He hadn't put his sneakers back on, so he didn't have to worry about them. Sand clung unevenly to his feet like threadbare socks. He took the key card and the eight dollars — a five and three ones, folded neatly — out of the pocket of his swim trunks. He looked around to make sure there were no witnesses and took his T-shirt off. He figured he'd go in up to his waist.

He looked down at his little pile of stuff and then looked over at the mouth of the path. No one else had come through it so far, but it was just a couple dozen yards from the main walkway. Better safe than sorry. He bundled up all his stuff, sneakers included, and walked back to the line of trees. He found a bush that was a little greener and less patchy than the others and stashed his stuff underneath the far side. He got a nasty scratch on his arm from one of the sharp little branches. It turned red with tiny pinpricks of blood as he walked across the sand. It didn't bother him. He used to get a lot of cuts and scratches back when he and his brother used to roam around the neighborhood, climbing trees and crashing through bushes. When he turned around, he couldn't see his stuff at all. He was satisfied, except . . .

He reached up and took off his glasses. Just in case. He'd only had them for a year. He'd gotten them when he'd started having trouble seeing what his teachers were writing on the board. He jogged over and put them under the bush as well, careful not to scratch himself this time. He kicked the sand around as he walked back so there wouldn't be an obvious line of footprints heading right toward his eight bucks. He stopped after a while. The sand was too fine to hold a shape for long.

He passed that sign again. *Relax, little sign,* he thought. *Don't lose any more letters worrying about me. I'm just going to wade around for a few minutes.* The sign was probably just there because there was no lifeguard on duty or something dumb like that anyway.

He marched right into the water this time. He didn't even pause at the line of breakers. It was so great because he didn't have to hold his breath for that first shock of cold, the way he did at the lake back home. He didn't have to go slowly, waiting for his body to adjust. He just strode forward like a hero heading into battle.

He braced himself for the force of the first wave. It hit him at the knees and splashed up the front of his trunks. The waves were bigger now. The tide was coming in.

8

Drew was on the roof of the hotel. She'd found the sun deck. It was still too early for proper sunbathing, she supposed, but it was a nice opportunity to give her parents the slip. They were in the lobby waiting — dead serious — for the gift shop to open. As if they didn't have all week. Plus, she could give her bikini a test run before they all headed to the beach later.

She was standing at the railing and looking out over the little island. She could see nearly all of it from up here. "I am the master of all I survey," she told herself, "the queen of my castle." But then she gazed out over the water and saw the hazy lump of Key West, and she knew the truth. A queen, maybe, but in exile.

She lowered her gaze and saw the dock again. She tried to find the little boy from earlier, but it was impossible. He was just one small figure among many now. There were other kids, and other parents, too. A small crowd had gathered, still waiting for the first boat of the day.

A pile of luggage was growing at the edge of the dock. Drew looked at the pile, looked at the people, looked back at the pile, added it up. It wasn't enough luggage for the number of people. That meant some of them were just going into Key West for the day. She heard her friend's voice: "where the party's at." She needed to figure out how to get on that boat.

Her parents would never let her go alone. She had to give up on that dream right now. They simply wouldn't. And if she snuck off and hopped on the boat right before it left, they'd hop right on the next one. They'd comb every square centimeter of the place until they found her, shouting "Drew-Bear! Drew-Bear!" the whole time and embarrassing her to high heaven.

No, she'd have to bring them, and even that wouldn't be easy. She'd have to work on them, convince them. She made up her mind to start later that day. A few casual comments here and there, just to plant the seed.

She wandered over to the railing and looked out into the distance. It was open ocean as far as the eye could see: clear blue tropical water, shadow and light and wind playing over its surface. Her mom was right; it was quite pretty.

She took one last look over toward Key West as she tugged her shorts up her legs, and there it was, a fat boat making slow progress across the water. The little crowd was more animated now, as if someone had stepped on their anthill. She pulled her shirt over her head, found her second flip-flop, and headed down to find her parents. The restaurant would be open now, and she was hungry.

*　　　*　　　*

Down at the dock, the fat-bottomed boat bumped to a stop against the rubber tires strung along the side of the pilings. The day manager of the hotel was there to meet it and throw the rope.

"Hey, Zeke," he said to the boat's captain.

"Hey, Marco," said the captain.

Zeke's real name was Jonathan Palpen, but he'd learned long ago that the tourists preferred something a little more down-home. He'd picked Zeke off a show about gator wrestlers.

"Hold on now, folks," Zeke called. The tourists on board were already standing up and trying to get off the boat. The ones onshore were already rumbling down the dock, jockeying for position. Sundays were always the worst. "Let me tie up first!"

There was a little edge in his voice that made them listen. Zeke had been out at the local bars the night before. It was what they called "a late night" in most places, but in Key West they just called it Saturday. He tied up, fore and aft, and then squinted up into the sunlight. He eyeballed the count: maybe a dozen, most with luggage. It would be close to capacity.

"Let 'em off first," he called, as the inbound passengers began to file off the boat. He didn't bother to soften his voice. The tourists liked that, too. Captain Zeke, with his tattered white captain's hat, short temper, and faint smell of booze — so authentic!

"Marco, my man, can you help me collect the money?" he called, even louder. "Five bucks a head, no exceptions!"

"Sure thing, Zeke!" called Marco.

They always did it this way because some of the outgoing guests would give Marco one last tip, a few dollar bills to go along with the fiver for the boat. Marco would then quietly slip some of the haul over to Zeke, along with the outgoing mail and any FedEx packages that needed to be dropped in the box at the marina.

The tourists bumped and jostled their way along the dock, out of and into the boat. Luggage was dropped from the boat onto the dock and vice versa. And all that sound was conducted into the water, through the wood of the dock or the bottom of the boat. It was a thick bass beat, an irregular, spastic drumming, an entire rhythm section of commerce.

It carried through the water, and it didn't go unnoticed. Some days, Zeke would see a small shark come right alongside the boat to investigate, maybe a spinner or even a blue. Some days he saw something larger. Today, he mostly just saw luggage. He eyed the tags as he stowed the cases: *EYW* for the little airport on Key West, *FLL* or *MIA* for the larger ones in Fort Lauderdale or Miami. That last one always seemed unlucky to him: *MIA* . . . missing in action. Maybe that's why he never made it up that far.

Some of the passengers greeted him. They remembered him from the trip out or the year before, or even the day before for the day-trippers. He grunted a response. The truth was they all sort of blended together after a while, different faces every day of every week of every year.

Soon the money had been collected and the luggage stowed. The ropes that had just been thrown on were thrown off. Marco gave them a theatrical wave. "Thanks again for choosing the Aszure Island Inn!" he called as the old boat began to putter away. "Tell your friends!"

The passengers waved back at him and then turned around to face forward. Most of them had long trips ahead, long trips to cold places. Zeke kept his eyes on the water ahead. A long, dark shadow crossed paths with the boat sixty yards out and slipped silently underneath. A part of the creature's primitive brain told it to follow this noisy thing. It knew what it was now. But it was too small. It was the big ones that sometimes left food in their wakes. It was the ones as big as a dozen whales that were worth following. Not this one.

The shark glided silently on.

9

Davey was in up to his waist. That's as far as he'd planned to go, but the breakers were coming in right at stomach height and really letting him have it. He decided to wade out a little farther, just past them. It's not like he would get any wetter. The waves had already declared a splash fight and won handily. When Davey pushed his hand back through his hair, he was surprised to find it slick as an otter's. He didn't care; he was having fun. He waded out a little farther.

He'd just been through an entire Ohio winter: bleak and gray and cold. He'd spent almost all of it inside, and most of that in his room. This felt good. Splashing around in the sun. The water gave him a little tug under the surface, and he let out a little bark of laughter as he regained his balance. The splash fight was over, and the sea had just challenged him to a game of tug-of-war.

He wasn't even sure which sea. His best guess was the Gulf of Mexico, but there was a chance it was the Caribbean. He made a mental note to check when he got back to the hotel room. As soon as he thought about that dark, crowded, smelly little room, he knew he'd made the right decision. Whichever sea it was, even if it was still just the Plain-Jane Atlantic, everyone back at school would be impressed.

He walked parallel to shore for a while. He looked back at the beach. It looked smaller than he remembered, and he had no trouble taking it all in. He was still alone. He saw the sign leaning over in the sand. He couldn't read it from here without his glasses, but he knew what it said. He thought about swimming a little anyway. Just a few strokes to say he did it. He was a pretty good swimmer. He and Brando used to go down to the lake every day, back when he did things like that.

The ocean had gone quiet around him. He was so lost in thought that it took him a while to notice. When he did, he looked out to sea. The surface was flat in front of him. He assumed it was because he was out past the surf line. But when he looked in toward shore, the surface was flat there, too.

It was the strangest thing. There were breakers on both sides of it, and then this band of flat water in between. It was as if something was knocking the waves down here. And something else seemed weird. It was the breakers; they'd moved so far in toward shore.

He got a sick feeling in his gut.

He took a breath and told himself not to panic.

The breakers hadn't moved farther in. He'd gone farther out. Much farther than he'd intended. Much, much farther. The water was up to the middle of his chest, and suddenly that seemed way too deep.

He stopped walking and felt the same tug under the surface that he'd felt before. And now the panic flooded through him: It had never stopped. He'd been walking against it this whole time. It had pulled him a little farther out with each step, leading him along like a bad friend. He looked down. The water was so clear that he could see his feet. He could practically count his toes. But he was so far from shore. The slope had been gentle up to this point, but it could drop off five, ten, twenty feet at any moment. He'd be in over his head — over his head in some sea he couldn't even name.

He started in toward shore. At least he tried to. He took a big step, and then another. He pushed his legs through the water as hard as he could. But the water pulled back just as hard. Every time his feet left the bottom, the sea tugged him backward. After half a dozen steps, he was sure he was no closer to shore.

His forehead was still slick with water, but he felt the sweat break out along it in little pinpricks. He decided to swim for it. He lunged forward and began kicking before his face even hit the water. Once it did, he began throwing his arms forward.

His fear wanted him to flail away, to scratch and claw at the surface. He didn't let himself. He needed to do this right. He remembered his lessons, maintained proper form. He kicked with his legs and pulled his outstretched hands through the water in full, even strokes. He looked to the side to get his air.

And he needed that air. His lungs began to burn almost immediately. It had been a long time since he'd swum to anything farther out than the raft at the lake. And even that was a while ago. He'd barely gone to the lake at all the summer before. He remembered the swim in from the year before that. How he would run the length of the raft and dive headfirst. He'd glide and kick to see how far he could go underwater. By the time he'd come up, he'd be halfway to shore.

The memory was so strong that Davey expected to be halfway to the beach by now. He was tired and needed a break anyway, so he broke his rhythm and took a quick look forward. If he'd had enough air in his lungs, he would've screamed. The beach was farther away now. It looked so small, like he could hold it in his hand. So small, and so empty. He wanted to call for help, but there was no one there.

It had been a mistake to swim. He knew that now. He stopped kicking and let his feet fall back underneath him. He pushed his arms sideways through the water to keep his head and shoulders steady. In a few moments, he was straight up and down in the water. But he wasn't standing. His feet could no longer reach the bottom.

He kicked a few times, just to stay afloat. He took a few quick gulps of air. And then he began kicking and throwing his arms forward. He scratched at the surface of the water. He clawed.

10

Panic turned to desperation and Davey turned that into effort. He was cranking out more effort than he ever had. Swimming had been a mistake — this whole thing had been a mistake! But here he was, and swimming was all he had now. He just needed to try harder, to get back to where his feet could touch.

But desperation is a fast-burning fuel. His muscles ached as he threw them forward. His lungs screamed for more oxygen. His rhythm fell apart. He turned his head to the side to breathe, but he got greedy. He was still sucking in air as his head turned back down. He inhaled bitter salt water and coughed facedown in the sea. More water slipped in. He spit out as much as he could and kept going.

He was no quitter. He never had been. He could read an entire book in one sitting. A lot of people have probably done that, but for Davey, the book might be four hundred pages and the sitting six hours. He'd won races in gym by being kind of fast for longer than his classmates could be really fast. And Davey was pretty sure that if he stopped trying now, he would die. Keep trying or die. It wasn't even a question.

As he got farther from shore, he approached a sandbar lurking under the surface. That's what had caused this. As the ocean had pushed forward and the waves had piled onto shore, tremendous pressure had built up for all that water to get back out to sea. The sandbar had shifted, as it did sometimes, and a gap had opened up. The water had found the gap and rushed back through it. People called them riptides, but they weren't really tides at all. Rip current was more accurate. That's what they were: currents, shifting and dangerous.

Davey had started counting his strokes in sets of four. It helped calm his raging mind and gave him something to focus on. He couldn't keep swimming forever, but he could do another four. On the fourth stroke of his next set, he forced himself a little farther up out of the water. He sucked in a lungful of much-needed oxygen and risked a quick look forward. With water in his eyes and without his glasses, the beach was a blur of color far away. Still so far away. He fell back into the water. Higher up meant deeper down, and now he was under the surface.

It was quiet under here. Even his aching muscles eased a bit in the warm churn. It was almost peaceful. *This is how I'll die,* he thought. *Under the warm, clear water.* They say that, right before death, your whole life flashes in front of you in seconds. And if a whole life takes seconds for an adult, how long does it take for a thirteen-year-old? And how long does just one memory take? It flashed into Davey's mind fully formed, like a fish pulled from the water.

It was his family's last vacation, two years ago. They'd skipped last year. They were staying with relatives in Colorado and had spent a day riding down a fast-moving river on inner tubes. They were all bundled in fancy, neon-yellow life jackets. Fallen tree branches had snagged on the river bottom and collected into big bird-nest-looking tangles in some places.

The family had sailed past the first few with their dad calling out orders: "Watch out!" and "Left, left, left!" or "Right, right, right!" But Brando had managed to bull's-eye the third one. He rode the fast-moving current right into the center of it, and his tube stuck fast. Brando popped right out of it and into the water. His life jacket had been way too big for him, and he'd bobbed down the river like a yellow rubber ducky. Their mom angled over and scooped him up. No harm, no foul, except that now his tube was hung up on branches back upstream.

They'd left a security deposit, and their dad was determined to get the tube back. The rest of them angled their tubes over into the shallow water along the bank and watched. He took off his life jacket, dove into the water, and swam for it.

Tam was a good swimmer. At first, he made some progress. It was two steps forward with every powerful stoke. But the current would push him one step back on every little pause in between. He made it maybe ten feet back upriver before the ratio started to reverse. One step forward with every stroke, two steps back with every pause. Pretty soon he was right back where he started. He'd looked at his family, surprised to see them right there. Davey remembered his father's face, exhausted and embarrassed.

Tam had dived back in. Tried again. But this time he hadn't even made it five feet, not even the length of his body. In the end, he had to walk through the bushes and prickers along the bank, wearing just his shorts and life jacket. He got scratched and cut and stung by a bee. He got upstream of the tube, dove back in, and got a hold of it, but he never said another thing about it.

Davey pushed back to the surface. His muscles roared with outrage. They thought they were done with effort, done with everything. But he battled on. He breathed in quick gulps, but water still slipped in, this time through his nose. He cleared it as best he could, but he could feel himself beginning to hyperventilate. He pushed his muscles to the point of exhaustion and then past that.

All that effort, and this time he was the one who couldn't make it five feet. A river in the sea. That was the only way he could understand it: He was in a river in the sea. How could he fight a thing like that? How could he win when even his dad had given up?

He gave up and the current took him. The sun pushed light through his closed eyelids. He was barely conscious, floating backward. Some primitive part of his brain — not even human, really — kept his systems going. The rest of his brain — all the higher functions, the brain that had been able to read a fat book in one sitting — could hold only one simple thought now: *Stay afloat.* His legs twitched when they could into something like a kick. *If you can, stay afloat.*

And he was carried out to sea.

PART TWO

BOY AND SEA

11

Brando fell off the bed. It was bound to happen. He'd fallen asleep on the very edge of the thing. He rolled one way to get more comfortable. Then he rolled back and onto the floor. His head pumpkin-thunked on the soft carpet.

"Corn dog!" he blurted. It's what he said when his Spider-Sense told him his parents were around.

They'd been close to waking anyway. Now, as if they were garage doors activated by the words *corn dog*, they rose. His mom sat straight up in bed like a zombie rising from an autopsy table. His dad finally stopped snoring. In the sudden quiet, Brando could hear him throw off the covers on the far side of the bed.

Pamela was the first to speak. "Brando?" she said. "Davey? Was that you?"

From her perch on the bed, she could see neither of her sons.

Brando rubbed his head and heard himself say, "Davey's not here."

And, oh boy, that did it. Pamela followed his voice down. She wasn't especially surprised to find her youngest on the floor in between the beds. Then she looked over at the cot and her mouth dropped open.

"What do you mean, 'not here'?" she said at the exact same moment that Tam said, "Well, where is he?"

Brando got to his feet. His mom's face was puffy from sleep. The side of his dad's face was a web of red lines from where it had been pressing against the pillow. Brando almost felt bad for them. They'd been awake for seconds on the first day of their first vacation in two years and they already had something to be mad about. He was just glad it wasn't him. "How should I know?" he said.

Three minutes later, they were at the front desk. Marco, long back from the dock, was on the other side.

"Has our son been past here?" said Tam.

Uh-oh, thought Marco, but what he said was: "What does your son look like?"

Tam waved his hand toward Brando. "Like this one, but a little bigger," he said. "Has glasses."

Marco looked at Brando and tried to picture him older and with glasses. "Sorry," he said. "Not this morning."

"How long have you been back there?" said Pamela, still tugging at the sundress she'd thrown on.

"Do you mean behind the desk?" said Marco. For some reason, he didn't like the phrase *back there.*

"Yes," she said. "Obviously."

Marco didn't like that *obviously*, either, but he took a deep breath and told her, "About half an hour."

"That's not very long," said Pamela.

Marco did not like this lady.

"Who was here before you?" said Tam, trying to edge back into the conversation.

Marco knew this would set the lady off, but he said it anyway. "No one. It's ring for service during overnight hours."

"What? That's . . . I've never even . . ." sputtered Pamela before collecting herself. "I've never been to a hotel that didn't have *someone* on duty!"

Marco wanted to say, *Well, you've probably never been to a hotel on a tiny island before. We don't get a lot of walk-in business from frickin' dolphins!* Instead, another deep breath. "Well," he said, "I can tell you that he didn't ring the bell."

Pamela glared at him, but Tam pulled her away. "Thank you very much," he said. "I'm sure he's just checking things out."

Marco nodded and gave them a halfhearted smile.

Brando followed his parents toward the front door. He was close enough to hear his dad whisper to his mom, "Don't make him mad. We might need his help this week."

"I hope not," she whispered.

They pushed through the glass double doors and began calling out Davey's name. Brando trailed after them, mortified.

"Davey!" shouted Tam. His voice was blunt and loud.

"Davey!" called Pamela, her voice sharper and still a little raspy.

Brando kept his mouth shut. An older couple out for a walk turned and stared at them, and Brando burned with embarrassment. *Yep,* he thought, *the Tserings have arrived.*

His parents looked around and stopped shouting. They could see the whole front of the hotel and most of the main beach from here, and the old couple were the only people in sight.

"Least he won't get lost in the crowd," said Tam.

"We should've gotten coffee first," said Pamela, batting his arm.

That's when Brando realized that they weren't all that concerned. And why should they be? It was an island. How far could Davey go? They weren't even especially mad. Brando exhaled. *Good,* he thought. *Maybe they won't kill him when they find him.*

"Maybe there's somewhere out here that sells it," said Tam. "I think I see some kind of stand up the path."

He pointed to the left. Pamela leaned over to look around him. Two sharp thumps carried through the air as the stall's storm shutters were thrown open. "Looks like they're opening up."

Without another word, they began walking in that direction. Adults and their coffee. Brando didn't understand it: The stuff tasted like motor oil. But he knew that they were now looking for two things: one was served in a cup, the other wore glasses.

He looked around as they walked. It was seriously nice out here, and it felt good to be outside without a jacket. He looked up at his parents. They were looking around, too. He followed his mom's eyes out to sea and saw that she had the beginnings of a smile on her face. That was good for her, especially these days. He was now ready to contribute to the search.

"He took his book," he said.

"What's that?" said Tam.

"He took that book. It wasn't with the others."

His parents were quiet for a few moments, and then Tam broke the silence. "Ha!" he barked.

Pamela smiled, a real smile this time. "Our outlaw son," she said. "Sneaking off to read."

They both laughed. They didn't look at each other when they did, but they still kind of shared a laugh. Brando hadn't seen them do that in a long time, and it made him feel good.

"Keep an eye out for the reflection off his glasses!" he said, and got a few more little laughs out of them. They were making the most of it, but the mood started to change after that. The farther they went with no sign of Davey, the tenser they got.

"I was sure he'd be right outside," said Tam.

"On one of those chairs out front or maybe that little patio," said Pamela, picking up the thought.

Their heads were on a swivel now. Their lazy looks to the side had become sharp turns toward the slightest sound. They began stepping off the walkway to look behind trees or down side paths.

And then they began calling out again. His mom stuck with his name, just "Davey! Davey!" over and over. His dad mixed it up sometimes with a "Where are you, champ?"

It didn't bother Brando as much anymore. He wasn't too worried. Davey had been going places without his parents — the lake, the store, the library — since he was nine or ten. And not just going to those places, but taking Brando there, too. So he wasn't exactly worried. Not exactly. But he wasn't embarrassed by the calls anymore, either.

He saw a woman walking along the edge of the beach with a baby slung to her front in a harness. He pointed her out, and his mom walked over and did the talking. "Have you seen a young boy? About this tall? With glasses?"

Even from back on the walkway, Brando could see that she was embarrassed. She'd lost her boy, and here this woman was holding her child closer than her purse. His mom didn't like being embarrassed at all. She wouldn't do it if she wasn't at least a little worried.

The stand they'd seen opening up did sell coffee, but the first batch wasn't quite ready when they got there.

"Five minutes," said the man, who hadn't seen Davey, either.

They could already smell it beginning to brew, but they didn't wait.

12

Davey opened his eyes to a nightmare. Ocean. Ocean forever. He tried to figure out how long he'd drifted and how far he might have gone. But his memories were vague and dreamlike. He remembered floating on his back when he could and treading water when he had to. He remembered flickering on the edge of consciousness, slipping under the surface, pushing his way back.

He didn't know how far he'd gone or even in which direction. All he knew for sure was that the current had finally let go of him, and he was very far from land. He straightened himself up in the water. His legs felt rubbery and numb as they churned slowly underneath him. They moved just enough to keep his mouth above the water. When he needed to, he flapped his arms to help. They hurt more, weren't as numb. He wasn't sure if that was good or bad.

Little waves pushed him around, and fear punched him in the gut. He was out here alone, in deep water. Anything could be in here with him. It could be just below him, or just behind. *Sharks.* The word popped into his head. He looked down into the clear blue depths. Under the surface, his legs somehow looked both short and far away. At the end of them, he saw his feet, moving slowly back and forth. He saw no other shapes. But there was another fear lurking inside him, this one as big as the entire ocean. He tried not to give it a name, but it already had one. *Drowning.*

He squinted into the distance. He looked at the horizon the way he used to look at the board before he got his glasses. *His glasses.* The thought gutted him. How was he supposed to see land when he couldn't tell the difference between an *E* and a *Z* from twenty feet away? Still, he had to try. His arms, his legs — they wouldn't last much longer out here. The small swells were making him work harder, sapping what was left of his energy.

He pushed his arms clockwise through the water and kicked a little harder with his right leg. Slowly, he began to turn. He squinted into the distance as he went. *Please, please, please,* he thought.

Nothing this way.

Nothing that way.

Nothing that way, either.

And then, when he was sure he must have gone all the way around already, he saw it. Had it been there before? Had he missed it? It wasn't much, just a hazy blue-gray lump off in the distance. *Thank God,* he thought. *Thank God.* He didn't know if it was the island he'd come from or a different island. And he didn't care. It could have been the Island of Boy-Eating Monsters and he would've been thrilled.

He stopped squinting. It got a little fuzzier. But now that he knew where to look, he could still see it. The next question, the big one: Could he reach it? The thought of swimming filled him with a profound and heavy tiredness. He felt like he'd already swum enough for a lifetime today.

He couldn't let himself think about it. If he didn't swim now, he wouldn't get another chance. It really *would* be enough for a lifetime. He lowered his head. He told his legs to kick, told his arm to rise up and fall forward. He didn't know if any of that would happen until it did.

Slowly, and just barely, he began to swim. It seemed so crazy to him because he was pretty sure he was heading right back in the direction he'd just come from. Why did he expect this time to be any different?

He pushed the thought out of his mind. He tried to replace it with something better. He thought about what he'd do when he got back to land. First, he'd just lie on whatever beach he washed up on for a very long time. Maybe a day. Then he'd get up and walk or crawl or roll or whatever he could manage until he found his parents. He pictured his mom and dad, and the first thing he thought was, *I'm in trouble. They're going to be so mad.* A second later, that seemed funny to him. *In trouble? Ya think?* Facedown in the water, just for a second, he smiled.

And then he thought, *I'm definitely getting that bed tonight. Brando can have the cot, and he'd better not say anything about it, either. I'm a year and a half older, and that's that.*

He looked up to make sure he was still headed in the right direction, and he was surprised to see how much bigger the island looked already. It seemed like a weird shape for an island, but then he'd never seen one from out on the water before. He dropped his head down and kept going.

The burning ache was returning to his muscles now. It wasn't as bad as before yet, but it wasn't good, either. How many strokes did he have left in his arms? he wondered. How many kicks did he have left in his legs? Would it be enough?

He stopped thinking about it, and for a while he just swam. He made slow, uneven progress. He wouldn't have been surprised if jellyfish were passing him. But at least he was headed in the right direction. At least he was making progress. He might even make it.

He made himself wait before he looked up at the island again. It was a waste of energy, and it threw his rhythm off. But it was the only thing that kept him going. He made another deal with himself: Four more good strokes and he could take a quick look. He wanted to see how big it looked now. He wanted to know that he was getting closer to his destination.

And he was. He was getting so much closer, in fact, that on the third stroke, he hit the island with his head. It made a hollow plastic *BONK* that he could hear right through the water.

13

The second stand was a lot like the first. It was about the size of a toolshed back in Ohio, but made of weathered wood with no-nonsense metal storm shutters on the front. The big difference was that the shutters were still closed on this one.

"No coffee here, either," said Tam. He looked back down the walkway. The coffee would be ready back at that first stand by now.

Pamela pointed to the sign on top: ASZURE ISLAND BAR. "Might have Irish coffee," she said.

"*Mom,*" said Brando. He was twelve, and he already knew you weren't supposed to make jokes about the Irish drinking.

"That's what it's called," she said.

"Really?" He filed the information away. Irish coffee: a joke you were allowed to make because it was true.

The stand faced out onto a beach, which more or less faced a bigger island off in the distance. "What's that?" asked Brando, pointing to it.

"Key West," said Tam.

"Bet this beach is popular," said his mom, nodding in front of them.

Brando looked around. "There's no one on it now," he said.

She smiled. It was a small, not particularly happy smile. "The bar's not open yet," she said.

They were moving on when they heard something from inside the stand. It was a loud thump followed by a sharp voice. That meant the same thing in Florida as it did in Ohio: Someone had just dropped something.

Tam ducked his head around the far side of the stand. Sure enough, there was a door there, and it was slightly open. He looked over at Pamela, and she nodded. He walked toward the door, and Brando followed a few steps behind. He'd never seen the inside of a bar before.

Brando could hear more sounds inside as they approached: footsteps, shuffling. Someone was moving stuff around in there. He watched his dad knock. The sounds stopped. Whoever was inside was playing dead. Brando had done the same thing himself when people came to the door, muting the TV, lying low. Davey basically did it all the time now, up in his room. He nodded toward his dad: *Don't be fooled.*

Tam knocked again, and the guy gave up. More shuffling, and then the door swung outward. Tam stepped back quickly, narrowly avoiding getting door-punched. A man ducked his head out and said, "Come back at eleven. Mimosas and Bloody Marys. Full bar at noon."

He began to close the door. Brando couldn't help but stare at his head. He had silver-gray hair, which Brando had seen plenty of times before. But his skin was something else entirely. It was tanned now and had probably been tanned steadily for the last five or six decades. Which is to say, it was something like leather. Brando smiled. *Davey would love this old dude. He's just like the characters in his books.*

"Wait," said Tam, and he grabbed the door.

Already staring at the man's face, Brando could see he wasn't happy about it. The man looked at Tam's hand. Then he ducked his head out a little farther and looked at Tam's face. "Like I said," he snapped. "Can't serve you till eleven!"

"We're not looking for drinks," said Tam. His voice wasn't hard or angry, but it wasn't soft, either. "We're looking for a boy."

The man seemed confused for a second. He had the look of someone who hadn't gotten much sleep. To Brando, he looked kind of like a tired wallet. "We don't sell those, either," said the man. "Maybe in Miami."

He looked over and caught Brando staring.

"You already got one, anyhow," he added. He still didn't look happy, but he'd stopped trying to pull the door closed.

"No, another one, our other son," said Tam.

"It's just that he's . . . Well, he's wandered off," said Pamela.

Brando and the man were equally surprised. Neither one had seen her walk over from the path.

The man's grim expression softened some. Maybe it was because he'd figured out what was going on or maybe it was because the mother of the boy was present. "Well, I'm sorry, ma'am," he said, "but I ain't seen no boy around this morning. 'Cept this one here." He nodded toward Brando. Brando nodded back.

Tam's hand fell from the door. The man searched his morning-clouded mind for something encouraging to end on.

"Small island; you'll find 'im," he said. Then he tugged the door shut behind him.

Tam immediately knocked again.

"I'll keep an eye out!" the man called from inside, and that was the end of that.

They continued down the walkway, turned the corner, and headed down the other side of the island. *So far, it's shaped like an eye,* thought Brando.

Very quickly, they came across the dock. There were already a few people gathering for the next boat. They headed off the path to go ask them the same question they'd asked everyone else.

"We should print out a picture," said Pamela. "We could just show it to them."

The thought really bothered Brando, but he couldn't say exactly why.

"Let's at least go all the way around the island first," said Tam. Brando could tell from his voice that the idea bothered him, too. "We're not even halfway."

"I think we are," said Pamela under her breath.

Brando looked over just in time to see their flat expressions blossom into big fake smiles for the people at the start of the dock. And that really bothered him.

"Hello there!" called Tam. Pamela chipped in with a friendly wave.

Brando watched as a man stepped forward to greet his dad. They were about the same age and height. For some reason, they shook hands.

"What's all the excitement here?" said his dad.

"Waiting for the boat back, unfortunately," said the other man, as if he was trying to sell them a car. "Our time is up. Great week!"

"There's a boat this early?" said Tam.

"Oh, sure," said the other man. "Think this is the second one. Should be here any minute. Busy day at the checkout desk."

A family of four joined the group as he was talking, proving his point nicely.

"Well, I won't keep you," said Tam. "The thing is — craziest thing — our oldest son seems to have . . ."

Brando didn't listen to the rest. Behind him, his mom was already asking the new family the same thing. Instead, he walked out onto the dock.

"Don't fall in, sport!" called his dad.

"Be careful!" called his mom.

Their voices were a little too eager, their calls directed more toward the small crowd than their son. The message: *We are not bad parents!*

63

Yeah, yeah, thought Brando, holding up his hand. He was looking at the boats. There was the white hotel launch, which looked new and sleek and cool. And there was another boat tied up next to it now.

It was an old motorboat. Everything about it was battered. The paint was largely gone and the engine looked primitive, like the first one ever invented. Looking at it, Brando thought there was a small chance it was powered by steam. Even empty and tied to the dock, the boat listed alarmingly to one side. All of which made this boat, of course, much, much cooler.

Brando knew immediately that it belonged to the weather-beaten old man at the bar stand. It was like the boat version of that guy. He looked back over his shoulder. His mom and dad were done working the crowd. They waved at him to come back. From the looks on their faces, he knew that they hadn't gotten any information.

He had a new idea. He'd ditch them, too. He'd ditch them and spend the whole week hanging out with the old guy. He'd ride in the dangerous boat at top speed and listen to stories. Not the kind of stories that Davey liked, but real ones. Stories about people who drank Irish coffees, people who weren't even necessarily Irish.

He thought about it some more as he rejoined his parents on the shore. When they left all the people behind and continued down the walkway, he wondered where they were all going. For a few moments, he thought about both things at once. He thought about anything, in short, other than the fact that his brother was still missing. He thought about anything other than the fact that he had known before anyone and had done nothing about it. He already knew that.

14

Davey recoiled the way you do when something hits you in the head. Think dodgeball. The difference being that he was in deep water, in every sense. He stopped his legs midkick. He flapped his arms under the water — once, twice, three times. His head moved backward above the water as his feet continued to drift slowly forward underneath it.

The thing floated in the water in front of him. It was still bobbing lazily from the impact. Davey just stared at it. It's not that he didn't know what it was. He knew exactly. It was a water cooler bottle. Replacing the empty ones in his parents' home office with full ones was one of his standard chores. Brando still wasn't quite big enough — or careful enough — to do it without spilling half a gallon on the floor.

But he didn't expect to head-butt one in the Gulf of freaking Mexico. It took him a few moments to figure out what it was doing there. Then he realized that it was trash, washed out to sea just like he had been. It was partly submerged and tilted on its side, maybe a third full of water. It rose up and over each little swell that washed past them. It was the same cheap kind of bottle that his parents had downgraded to recently. It was made of thin, transparent, blue-gray plastic instead of the thicker, bluer, more opaque plastic of the name-brand bottles.

Davey looked at its humpbacked profile, its neck pointing up just enough to keeps its open mouth above water. *Yep,* he thought. *That's the shape I thought was an island.* He felt like he'd just failed a test. He wasn't getting closer to an island. He was getting closer to a water cooler bottle. He was treading water again, his legs rubbery and spent. He made his right hand into a fist. Then he reached out and smashed down on the top of the bottle. Stupid bottle!

The force of the blow pushed the mouth of the bottle underwater. Ocean water poured in. The neck tipped back up a moment later, and the bottle found its balance. It continued bobbing along on the water.

Davey did the same, but with more effort and a worse attitude. As his surprise faded, he made the obvious connection. He coughed up a single sharp laugh at himself for thinking a disposable plastic jug was an island. He was happy all of a sudden, almost overjoyed. *This thing floated!*

He leaned forward, kicked his legs, and grabbed the bottle. He hugged it with both arms. Love would not have been too strong a word. Now, the big test: He stopped kicking his legs. He began to sink, taking the bottle with him. He angled the opening of the bottle up into the air. They kept sinking. He held his breath as his mouth neared the water. The bottle stabilized. Most of it was underwater, but the neck stuck up alongside Davey's head. He glanced over. It looked like the periscope of a little plastic submarine. More important, it was keeping them both afloat.

He let go with one arm and smashed the water three times. The first two were just sheer happiness and relief. The third was more like, *In your face, ocean!*

And now that he was thinking a little more clearly, he realized that he could make this even better. He gathered the little strength he had left. As tired as he was, it felt great. Because he knew he'd be able to rest after this, at least for a little while.

He waited for a little swell to pass. The bottle carried him up and over. Then he reached down and grabbed the bottom of the bottle. His mouth and nose dipped under the surface, so he moved fast. He lifted the bottle up and out of the water, kicking fiercely. His whole head was underwater now. Everything was under the water except his arms and the bottle. Above the little waves, he tipped the bottle down.

He tipped it down the same way he did when he replaced one in the office: just enough. It began to empty but stayed above the surface. He heard the splash of water on water. He wished that it really was full of bottled water, instead of salty brine. He would've drunk it all. As the bottle emptied, it became lighter. Even as his kicks grew weaker, they lifted him farther out of the water. Soon, his head was above the surface again. Then his shoulders were.

Then he was holding a big empty bottle, way up in the air. The sun was shining through it, making crazy patterns.

He flipped it back around, top up, and dropped it back in the water. It floated higher now. Even when he grabbed hold again, it floated higher. Even when he allowed his tired legs to stop kicking, it floated higher. The top third of the thing was above the surface. He leaned down and rested his head along the top and his cheek along the neck. This didn't solve anything. He knew that. He flicked his eyes forward and still saw nothing but a hazy blur of horizon.

But right at that moment, he didn't care. Right at that moment, and for quite a few after it, he rested. He hugged the big plastic bottle tight — his own little island — and rested.

15

The Tserings were nearing the far tip of the island when they realized someone was chasing them. He wasn't exactly running after them; it was more of an urgent walk that occasionally broke into an awkward jog. Brando was the first to notice.

"I think that guy from the hotel is after us," he said.

His parents turned and looked. Once they recognized him, they stopped and waited for him to catch up. There was nothing around. Just the ocean on one side of the walkway and the far corner of the hotel grounds on the other. There were no other people, and the only sounds came from the small waves and gentle breeze.

Once he'd been spotted, Marco slowed down. He tried to act casual as he walked toward them, but the sweat on his forehead gave him away. He gave them a small wave. Then he reached up to wipe his forehead in an exaggerated way, trying to make a joke out of it.

Word had gotten back to him at the main desk that there was a family out beating the bushes for a lost boy. That was not, in any way, good for business. He was in charge of things today. The owners of the hotel would have his hide if this blew up. Every advertisement they ran, from the brochures at the airports to the header on the website, used the phrase *family friendly*. He didn't want to spend the next year answering the phone and saying, "Oh, no, we hardly ever lose children. A very small percentage, really." And he didn't want all of the families checking out today going back home saying, "The craziest thing happened at the Aszure Island Inn. A boy just disappeared!" He didn't want the families checking in to worry about it the whole time, either. He needed to help this family find their kid — and hopefully get them to shut up about it until they did.

Pamela was looking at him like he was a stray dog. He wished he hadn't gotten off to such a bad start with her. It was hard to undo a bad first impression. He plastered on a big, toothy smile and gave them another wave. Only Brando waved back.

"Did you find him?" asked Tam hopefully.

Pamela perked up a bit. The possibility hadn't occurred to her.

Marco just shook his head. Tam and Pamela turned away from him to hide their disappointment, but Brando watched him closely.

"I should've gone the other way around," said Marco. "Just walked three-quarters of the island trying to catch up."

"Well, if you don't have any news, why did you bother?" asked Pamela.

Marco looked at her. *Big smile,* he told himself. "Wanted to help you look!"

"Wanted to shut us up, probably," said Pamela.

A bad attitude and smart, too, thought Marco. *How am I going to handle this one?* His smile flickered and then fell from his face.

"We both want the same thing," he said. "Any idea where he might've gone?"

Brando looked from his mom to Marco and back again. She seemed satisfied with his answer.

"No," said Pamela.

"And you've checked . . ." Marco made a little circle with his left hand.

"Yes," said Tam, "we've checked everything up to here."

"Everything?" said Marco.

"Every last grain of sand," said Tam.

Marco was sure that included asking every last person they came across. He cringed at the thought.

"Well, might as well keep going," he said, pointing down the walkway with his chin.

They continued on in the direction they'd been heading. They had an extra person now, but not much use for him. Brando looked around. This part of the island was even quieter — and that was saying something. There were no bar stands or docks, no little clusters of people. In their place was an extra helping of trees and scrubby little bushes. He watched as Marco made a show of helping. He leaned over to look behind a tree and then leaned back to look up into it.

"My brother isn't a monkey," said Brando.

Marco looked down and flashed his big smile at him, but Brando wasn't buying it.

"Where does this little path go?" said Pamela. She was a few steps ahead of the rest of them and pointing down at a little gap in the undergrowth.

"Goes to a little beach," said Marco.

"We should check it out," said Tam, but Marco had already caught up with them and started down the path.

Without another word, they turned and followed him. It was a narrow path, and they had to walk single file to avoid the saw grass. Marco moved quickly, barely looking down. He knew the path well. Hotel employees sometimes hid out back here, extending their breaks as long as they thought they could get away with. *It is definitely a place a kid could go and not be noticed,* he thought.

But when they reached the mouth of the path, there was no one there. No employees, and no missing boy. Brando pushed past him on the left as Tam and Pamela pushed past him on the right. He followed a few steps behind, and they all fanned out across the little beach.

"Davey!" called Pamela.

"You here, champ?" called Tam. "Where are you? We're not mad!"

Brando let out a little burst of air. *Yeah, right,* he thought. But his eyes scanned every inch of the beach.

They all noticed the same things in a different order. Brando saw the No Swimming sign and then scanned the line of surf. Pamela scanned the surf first and then saw the sign. Tam was still staring into the deep shadows along the trees at the beach's edge and nearly tripped over the thing. He read it.

"He's not, uh . . ." Marco began, nodding toward the sign. He didn't even want to think it, much less say it. But he had to. "Your son, he's not much of a swimmer, is he?"

Pamela looked at him, horrified.

"No!" she said. She disliked him more now, just for saying that.

"No, he used to, but he doesn't even . . ." said Tam. He was distracted, just now scanning the surf. He snapped out of it when he finished. "No, he used to go to the lake, but I don't think he went at all last year." He turned to look at Brando. "You guys go to the lake last summer?"

"Not much. Maybe twice," said Brando. "He never wanted to."

What he didn't say was that he still wasn't allowed to go alone. His parents already knew that, and Marco figured it out from his tone of voice.

"Yeah, Davey's in more of an indoor phase right now," said Tam. "And he definitely wouldn't ignore a sign like this, either."

"That's true," said Brando. In the last year or two, his brother had become the sort of freak kid who walked around fences instead of climbing over them.

"You should get a new sign," said Pamela, frowning at the faded letters. "Or at least stand it up straight."

"Not hotel property," said Marco.

"I don't care whose property it is," she said, looking directly at him. Marco looked down and saw an old cigarette butt in the sand. He had an eagle eye for them at this point. He looked around, wondering if there was anything else he was missing.

Brando saw his eyes searching the ground and did the same. It occurred to him to look for footprints, but the beach was full of them now. Four fresh sets. He looked up and tried to see the beach the way Davey would. It was quiet, and there was shade over by the trees. It would be a good place to sit and read.

"He'd like it here," he said. But the adults were still squabbling about who did or did not own the beach and didn't hear him. He went up to where the first trees met the sand. He stood under one. Then he sat down. He positioned himself so that his legs were in the sun and the rest of him was in the shade. He pretended he had a book in his lap.

"Come on, Brando," called Tam. "You can rest at the hotel later."

Brando looked over. They were back at the mouth of the little path. He took a quick look at the bushes and trees behind him.

Even with the sun burning bright overhead, they were stuffed with shadows. He looked closer. "Davey?" he said.

There was no response. He stood up and brushed the sand off his shorts. Twenty yards away, the grown-ups started back down the path. Brando hurried to catch up.

16

Drew was waiting in line at the breakfast buffet. She was going to get one of those big meaty American meals she'd heard about. The smell of bacon wafted her way, and her stomach rumbled for it. She'd barely eaten anything since she'd arrived on the island. She was beginning to wonder if she ever would. So far all she had on her plate was silverware and a stiff cloth napkin. Her dad was talking to the guy in front of them and holding up the works.

"You can't have just one slice of bacon!" said the man. He had some sort of accent. Drew ran through the different sorts of American accents she knew, all from movies or TV. She pegged this guy as either a cowboy or a redneck, possibly both.

"Now hold on a minute!" said her dad. "I'm watching my boyish figure!"

She could hear him making his own accent bigger, playing to his audience. She rolled her eyes. *Come on,* she thought.

"Well I'm sorry to say that horse has left the barn," said the man. Now Drew was thinking cowboy, just because of the horse thing. Her father laughed. The "horse" was his boyish figure. It had gotten away. Boy, had it. Everything about Big Tony was big these days, and that included his stomach.

"That a Texas accent?" asked Big Tony.

"Louisiana," said the man.

Drew wasn't exactly sure where that was, but she knew it wouldn't matter. Her dad would just pretend the guy was from Texas, anyway. She looked at the man. All he had on his head was a bald spot, but it would be a giant cowboy hat when her dad told the story. *This big bloke from Texas told me to have more bacon. Had to oblige before he drew his pistols!*

She could reach the scrambled eggs from where she was, but she held off. If she put them on her plate now, they'd just get cold. She could already tell the other man was just like her father: a big talker. There was no telling how long this would go on. She let out a long sigh. It contained as much annoyance as air, but no one heard it. The man was talking again.

"How about you? That's not a Liverpool accent you're slinging around, is it?"

Oh no, now he's done it, thought Drew.

"I'm no bleeding Liverpudlian!" bellowed her father. She could practically hear heads all over the dining room turning to look. So embarrassing. "I'm a Mancunian to the core!"

"You live in . . . Manchester?" said the man.

Her father raised his eyebrows. He was impressed. "Just outside," he said. "Manchester's not a place you live. It's a place you come from and go back to for football."

Drew watched as the man nodded. She could tell he was still picking the words out of her dad's thick accent.

"That's soccer to you," he added, but it wasn't necessary.

"United or City?" said the man.

Here we go, thought Drew.

"United!" thundered her dad. She risked a look over her shoulder. There weren't that many people in the dining room yet, but they were all either looking over or, worse, making an effort not to. "When I die, my face'll turn red, not blue!" her dad was saying, referring to the colors of the two teams.

Drew picked her plastic tray up off the metal railings. This had gone on long enough.

"Seen a few games myself," said the man. "They show them here on —"

Drew dropped her tray down onto the railings. *BANG!*

The man looked over. "Looks like the natives are getting restless," he said.

Drew had no idea what that meant.

"This one's always restless," said her father. He reached over to ruffle her hair, but she ducked him. She wasn't ten anymore! "This is my daughter, Drew."

"David," said the man. "I was just telling your old man here to have more than one slice of bacon."

"You can bet I'm going to," she said. Then she bumped her dad's tray with hers.

The men laughed. Her dad took two more strips of bacon.

"There you go," said David. And amazingly, there they went, filling up their trays with bacon and eggs, some sort of potato thing, and the odd piece of fruit.

"Come on over and sit with us," said David, as they neared the end of the buffet. "My wife and I have that big table all to ourselves."

"Right," said her dad. "Go get your mum, will you, luv?"

Drew looked over at her mom, sitting alone at another table. She'd had the good sense to beat her husband to the buffet line and was already halfway done with her food. Drew headed over.

"Dad's made a friend," she said. "From Louisiana."

Kate chuckled. "I heard."

"Whole room did," said Drew. But now that she had her food, she really didn't mind. She waited as her mom gathered up her things. Then they went over and sat at the new table. Introductions were made all around.

Drew began eating immediately. The bacon was wonderful. She didn't worry about talking. She knew it would be taken care of. There were two men at the table who very much enjoyed the sound of their own voices. She wondered who would go first. Maybe her dad would want to keep talking about Manchester United. It was by far his favorite topic.

But no, it was David who began. He wanted to talk about a missing boy.

"Just up and vanished from the room this morning, apparently," said David. "Just gone. Poof! And now his parents are out circling the island, calling his name."

"His name is David, too," added the wife, Julia.

"Yes, that's right," said David. "Just a little guy. Very sad. His parents, even his little brother, they're out there asking if anyone's seen him."

Drew put down her fork. More dropped than put down, actually. It clattered against the plate.

"Yes, luv?" said Kate.

Drew looked around the table and realized everyone was looking at her.

"Think I saw 'im," she said.

Big Tony looked at the empty air ahead of him, as if he kept all his memories floating there. "Yeah, that's right," he said. He nudged Kate. "Remember?"

She nodded slowly and looked over at her daughter. "You're right, luv," she said.

But they were talking about two different boys.

17

Davey clung tightly to the water cooler bottle. It wasn't that he thought it would go anywhere; it didn't look like either of them would. It just felt reassuring to have something else that was solid in all this endless water. A little swell came and he let the bottle carry him up and down again. His legs hung down, pointing straight into the deep. The sun was hitting him square. It was hitting everything out here.

Now that he didn't have to work constantly just to stay afloat, he could think more clearly. Mostly, he was thinking about rescue. He was sure his family had noticed he was gone by now. He was wondering if they would find his things on the beach, or if someone else would.

He ran over other ways that people might figure out what had happened to him. Someone else could get caught in the same rip current. It would have to be someone who knew what to do and could make it back to shore. Then they might report it. Then people might search the beach more closely, might find his things. Might, might, might.

The odds were bad. He knew that. He wasn't stupid. But he floated there stringing together events that could lead to his rescue. He did it for the same reason he hugged the bottle. It was comforting. And if he thought about it hard enough, he could almost believe it.

He scanned the skies for rescue planes. He listened closely for a helicopter. For one amazing moment, he thought he heard one. But it was only the gentle churn and chop of the ocean.

He scanned the horizon. His eyes were too weak to see land in the distance. But now that he had something solid to hold on to, he thought he could feel himself drifting. Maybe he'd drift into range. Or maybe he'd see a boat. A big tanker, a fishing boat, a Navy ship . . . He wasn't picky. But he saw nothing.

Davey was nearsighted, which meant he could see things close to him. He looked down and was surprised to see a little fish. It was the size of a goldfish, but a plain gray color. It was hanging in the water just in front of him, a foot or two below the surface. As he looked, he saw another. As he watched that one, he saw a third, partly hidden by his shadow.

"Little guppy guys," said Davey. He was speaking mostly to himself, but to tell the absolute truth, partly to the fish. It came out as a raspy croak. He knew his mouth was dry, but he had no idea his voice was so bad. He gathered up some spit. It tasted like salt. Somehow, he'd even gotten some sand in his mouth.

He spat into the ocean. One of the fish came up to investigate.

"Gross," said Davey, and he sounded better this time. He made a mental note to use his voice every now and then. He needed to keep it in working order in case that Navy ship arrived.

The fish dipped its head and flapped its tail, powering back down to its friends. Davey watched them for a while. He'd spotted a fourth now. They were hanging out under the water cooler bottle. *For the shade,* he thought, *or maybe the shelter.*

The truth is, small fish follow floating objects in the open ocean for both reasons. These ones had probably been following the bottle long before Davey showed up. But it was even better now. Much of the sunlight shined through the bottle, but Davey cast solid shade. And there were other advantages.

Davey felt a little tickle on one of his toes. He didn't think much of it. He'd been in the water for a long time now, and his whole body felt a little weird. His fingers were beyond pruned. But then he felt another little tickle. He looked down through the crystal clear water and saw one of the little fish in front of his foot.

Davey pulled his foot away. The little fish advanced slowly, maintaining about an inch of distance. It looked like it was locked in a staring contest with his big toe. And then it swam up and took a quick nibble. Davey felt the familiar tickle.

"Dude!" he said.

He kicked his foot hard. The fish retreated, its tiny mouth still working on the flake of dead skin it had scavenged. The fish stayed under the bottle for a while, but a few minutes later he felt another tiny mouth at work. It was on his other foot this time. He couldn't tell if it was the same fish or if that one had somehow told the others about the new restaurant in town.

He shooed them away, pumping the water cooler bottle up and down over their heads like a piston and unleashing a few quick, choppy kicks. The fish swam off in a little diamond formation.

They stopped a few feet away. They just hung there in the water. Fish are not the smartest creatures, and it was quite possible that they'd already forgotten the whole thing. Then one of them saw the bottle again. The bottle and the boy and the little floating island they formed.

They all swam back to it. This time they approached in an uneven line, two slightly ahead, two slightly behind, like pawns advancing up a chessboard. Davey pumped the bottle again — down, up, down.

The little fish retreated and returned.

Davey gave up. He went back to thinking about rescue. But beneath him and all around, the percussive plastic thumps he'd made with the bottle were still carrying through the water. It was an odd sound out here, the sort that would attract attention.

18

David and Julia had quickly worn out their welcome, but Drew's family still hadn't been able to shake them. Now they were all leaving the restaurant together. Drew gave her mom a quick, worried glance: *Are they just going to follow us around all day?* It seemed possible.

Finally, her dad executed a daring escape move. He walked several steps past the elevator bank. David didn't so much as look over at it. He didn't break stride, and he certainly didn't stop talking. He'd barely stopped once he'd gotten going. It was a mystery how he'd been able to clean his plate without spraying the table with egg bits.

"Oops, just got to pop back up to the room," said Big Tony.

Drew smiled. *Well done,* she thought, and it was. David and his better half had already walked past the elevators. They couldn't claim they needed to use them now, too. It was a clean break. Almost.

"All righty," said David. His tone was breezy but forced. He was struggling to come to terms with the loss of his audience.

"We'll just be at the concierge desk. We've got some questions for that lady."

Good, go talk her ear off, thought Drew. *At least she gets paid for it.*

Julia flashed them a quick, slightly desperate smile. It was like she was secretly being held hostage and trying to communicate the fact with her teeth and eyes. She'd barely said a word during the meal. But now she surprised them all with some actual information.

"Oooh," she whispered. "That's them!"

She pointed over toward a group standing near the computer and printer set up along the wall for guests to use. She and her husband both made exaggerated bug-eyed expressions at exactly the same moment. *How about that?*

She's no hostage, thought Drew. And then, mercifully, they walked away. Drew and her parents stayed put, pretending to wait for the elevator.

"Gah, I thought he'd never leave," said Big Tony.

"Thought he'd never shut up," said Drew.

"Still hasn't," said her mom. She nodded over toward the concierge desk, where David was already peppering a stylishly dressed young woman with questions. In sharp contrast to the scene a few hours earlier, the lobby was fully staffed now, bustling with activity.

Their eyes landed back on the family of the missing boy, still waiting for the computer to free up. A quick look at their body language made it clear how impatient they were. A man with headphones on was seated at the lone computer, completely unaware. He was video chatting with what looked to Drew like a ball of frizzy hair in a dark room.

Drew was the first to figure out what they were doing. "They're waiting to print out a picture," she said. "Like a missing person advert."

Kate gasped.

"Shame, isn't it?" said Big Tony.

"We should say something," said Kate.

"Right thing to do and all that," said Big Tony. "Should we, uh, should we all go, then?"

"You go," said Kate, waving him on. It had always been understood that he was the most social, the one to talk to strangers. He was the one who'd gotten them trapped at a table with David, after all. Now he had to make good.

The elevator dinged and opened up. No one got out, and they let it close again.

"Go on, then," said Kate.

He walked slowly over.

Drew turned to her mom. "Bit awkward, isn't it?"

*　　*　　*

Brando stared at the back of the man's head. *How clueless can this guy be?* he thought. It was bad enough he was chatting away with this frizzy-headed, Muppet-looking woman. It was much worse that they had to hear him do it. Brando fantasized about walking over and plucking the man's earphones right off. He couldn't decide what he'd do after that. Strangle him with the cord, maybe.

Brando looked around the lobby for what felt like the eighty-fourth time. This time, he saw a man heading straight for them. He was a big guy, and kind of tough-looking. He had a head that was either shaved or bald, maybe some of each, and a gut just shy of sumo-level.

Good, thought Brando. *If he wants to use the computer, too, maybe he'll body-slam lover boy here.*

"Pardon," he said.

Tam and Pamela turned around. Brando gave him a closer look. The man raised a big meaty hand and gave them a surprisingly dainty wave.

"Yeah, sorry to bother you," said Big Tony. His accent was so thick that all of the vowels seemed to be off by one. "My family and I . . ." He motioned over to two people standing by the elevator. Brando looked and saw a lady about his mom's age and a girl who looked like she might be in high school. He thought he could just see her bathing suit top through her shirt. He missed the next several sentences.

". . . so when we heard that, we thought we should let you know," Big Tony was saying when Brando tuned back in.

"Let us know what?" said Pamela.

"We saw the boy. Well, we saw *a* boy, anyway."

"When? Where?" said Tam.

"He was by himself," said Big Tony. Brando was paying close attention now. They all were. "He was down by the dock. Where the boat comes in, know what I mean? Just waiting there."

"Waiting for the boat?" Pamela said, a hint of panic rising in her voice.

Big Tony looked at her. "Couldn't say. Could be. He was just sitting there. We didn't think much of it, know what I mean? Called him a little pirate."

He had no idea why he'd added that part, but he couldn't unsay it now. Tam and Pamela looked at each other.

"Well, anyhow, thought you should know," he said, wrapping up.

"Yes, thank you!" said Tam. "Thank you so much."

Big Tony gave another little wave and started to retreat. At the last second, he changed his mind. He took a few quick steps forward. He reached down toward the man sitting at the computer and pulled the headphone away from the man's right ear.

"Hey! Chatty!" said Big Tony, louder now. "Time's up."

He let the headphone snap back. The man looked up, his expression shifting quickly from surprise to fear.

"Cool," said Brando, as Big Tony walked back toward the elevator.

"Did you tell 'em where he was?" asked Drew when her dad returned. In her mind, that was sitting under a tree by the bar stand, reading.

"Course," said Big Tony. In his mind, that was by the dock.

"Well done," said Kate. She meant ousting the man from the computer.

They were all on their own page, really. They didn't stick around as the missing boy's family printed out pictures from the newly available computer. They'd done their part. When the next elevator came, they took it.

On the short trip up to the fourth floor — the top floor of the hotel — Drew saw her opening. "We should take that boat into Key West today." She said it casually, as if the thought had just popped into her mind. "You know, just for a few hours. Then we'll know if we like it or not."

She thought they'd shoot her down immediately, but they didn't say anything at first. She held her breath as her parents looked at each other. As the elevator door dinged open, her dad shrugged. "Guess we might," he said. "Kind of depressing around here, kids disappearing and all that."

"I don't know," said her mom. "I was hoping for some quiet today."

Drew had an answer for that. "Good way to get rid of that David, isn't it?"

Check and mate. Kate conceded with a nod.

"Just don't you go vanishing on us!" said Big Tony, and then they all disappeared into their suite.

19

Now that he'd had some time to watch the little fish, Davey decided that they were more silver than gray. Every now and then, one of them would turn and catch the sunlight streaming down through the water just right. It would flash a brilliant silver, then turn and flash again. Sometimes he didn't even see the fish, just the flash. As clear as the water was, the surface got in the way. It bent the light and obscured everything below it, especially when there were ripples or swells.

Then he made a discovery. He was resting his head against the water cooler bottle, as he had been for a while. He usually looked around it, scanning for the boats that refused to show, for the land that refused to appear. But this time he looked through it. He thought maybe it would act like the lens of his glasses. Instead, it worked like the glass sides of a fish tank. Looking below the waterline, everything was much clearer.

Davey used it as a funky sort of swim mask. He tilted it forward and looked down. One of the little fish swam by. It grew slightly as it passed the middle of the bottle and then slipped by. Davey tilted the bottle more and found it again, swimming down to join its friends.

He spent some time watching them. They looked a little blurry, because the bottle wasn't perfectly clear. But apart from that, he had a good view. They made small moves in unison. They'd all turn to the right and then back to the left, or vice versa. Or they'd swim up a few inches and then back down. There didn't seem to be any reason for the moves, but they did them together, like a tiny boy band.

He shifted his body down a little lower in the water. It improved his view, but soon he felt a shiver go through him. As warm as the water was — close to eighty degrees — it was still twenty degrees below normal body temperature. The more time he spent in it, the more obvious that became. He scooted himself back up the bottle. He grabbed it near the top and pushed it farther down into the water.

The sun hit his back again. It took just a few minutes to burn the water off and start warming him up. He felt the skin there getting tight and knew he was already beginning to burn. But what choice did he have? He needed the heat.

He looked up at the sun. Was it directly overhead? Not quite, he decided. He realized he could tell the time with it. He was pretty sure that straight overhead meant noon. He decided it was around eleven o'clock. *That's it?* he thought. It felt like he'd been out here for twice that long. He wondered how long it would've felt like if he hadn't found the bottle. He wondered if he'd still be feeling anything at all.

He looked up at the sun again. It flashed like the biggest silver fish there ever was. Could he use it to figure out directions, too? A phrase flashed through his head: *rises in the east, sets in the west.* But he couldn't make it work because he couldn't figure out which way he was facing. Or if he was facing a different direction now than he had been five minutes ago. There were no fixed points to go by. There were a few clouds, way up, but they were moving, too. And he was being carried. He was sure of it now. He was drifting along in some larger current.

Is this the Gulf Stream? he wondered. He didn't think so; not yet.

He was sure about one thing, though: It didn't matter which direction was which when it was the sea deciding where he went.

As the sun continued to crawl across the sky, Davey went back to looking for boats or land. He went back to listening for helicopters or planes. The report came back the same each time: none, none, none, and none.

20

The only subject that was even half as interesting to Davey as rescue was this: What had he done wrong? He kept picking at the question like a scab. And it was a big scab, because he'd made a lot of mistakes.

Should he have stayed in bed? Yes. Could he have read his book there, even with the snoring and toxic gas? Yes. Did those things seem like dumb reasons to sneak away now? Of course.

But he had.

So should he have left a note in the room? No, he decided. He'd meant to be back before anyone woke up. And he wouldn't have known about the beach then anyway, so what good would a note have done?

Should he have stayed out of the water? One thousand percent yes. Had the sign told him to? Yes! Duh! *Oh my God, I'm an idiot!* For a while, that seemed like his biggest mistake. He beat himself up about it pretty badly. And then, just floating there and feeling like an idiot, he thought of a bigger mistake.

He was remembering the moment he gave up, how he'd been thinking about his dad giving up in that river. It reminded him of something, and then it was all so obvious.

A few months after the family had gotten home from the tubing trip, his dad tried to buy something called a never-ending pool. His mom had said it was because he was embarrassed that he "couldn't swim to that stupid tube." His dad would only admit that he "needed more regular exercise."

He still remembered the exact words because it had been one of his parents' first big fights. It had still been a new thing. Davey and his brother — still Brandon then — could hear it all, even though they were upstairs and their parents were downstairs.

The business had just started to go bad then, to "slow down." That was another thing he knew from those first arguments — and from a lot of the ones since then. In any case, things weren't going well, and they'd just gone on a vacation. His mom wouldn't let his dad buy the little pool.

Tam had gone to the showroom anyway, one day when Pamela was out. He'd taken Davey and Brandon. Even at the time, Davey knew his dad was trying to get them on his side. They brought their swimsuits and tried it out. Except for Brandon. The salesman said he was still too young. Anyway, it was kind of cool.

It was like a little tiny pool, not much bigger than a person. It had a motor at the front that created this powerful current, like one continuous wave. And you just swam against it and swam against it and swam against it for exercise. You could swim for an hour and not get anywhere but healthy. Well, if you could swim for an hour you were probably already super healthy, but that was the point of it. Davey had only lasted a few minutes, and that was after the salesman had turned the motor down for him.

He hadn't thought about it much after that day. He was pretty sure they'd never get one. His mom had only said they'd talk about it "once the business came back." They'd never talked about it again.

But now he wished they'd gotten the stupid thing. He wished they'd sold the minivan to pay for it. Because if he'd done it more than once, he would've remembered. You could swim forever and never reach the end of that thing. That's why they called it a never-ending pool. But all you had to do was take a few quick strokes to the side to reach the edge. That's how you got out.

He felt so stupid.

He'd swum against the rip current, trying to reach the end. He should've swum sideways. That's how you got out. He felt like someone had just kicked him in the stomach. And worse, he felt like he deserved it.

He tilted the bottle down. He watched the fish for a while, trying to distract himself from himself. He found three of them quickly and was looking for the fourth. That's when he saw it. It was farther down. It was hard to say how far. Maybe twenty feet, he thought. It was the quick flick of a tail, the black flash of an eye.

This was no little fish.

21

Holy cow, they're calling the cops, thought Brando.

A wave of hot panic nearly knocked him down. *They're going to question me. They're going to find out that I knew he was gone and went back to sleep. Should I just tell them now? Should I just tell Mom and Dad before the police arrive, before it's . . .* He searched his head for the phrase, the one they used on TV. *Before it's a* criminal matter?

He looked up at his parents. If either one of them had looked down at that moment, he would've told them. But they didn't. They were both busy. His dad was taping another picture of Davey to the wall. It was a digital picture Pamela had emailed to one of her friends. It was the first and best one they could find, and they'd cut it in half to crop out Brando. Now the oddly shaped photo — a tall rectangle with one sloping side — was centered on plain white paper. Underneath it read:

MISSSING BOY

DAVEY TSERING

PLEASE CALL!

The hotel's main number was under that, followed by their room number, since there was no cell phone service out here. No one had noticed the extra *S* in *misssing* before they hit print. Fifty pages later, no one cared that much.

Brando looked over at his mom. She was talking to the hotel manager, Marco. He'd resurfaced as soon as they'd started taping up the flyers. Brando could tell he didn't like it. Every time they put one up, Marco gave them a look like they were spray-painting swear words onto the wall. For a while, Brando kept a close eye on him to make sure he didn't take the flyers right back down.

"The island doesn't have any police," Marco was saying.

"You have to have police," said Pamela.

"The island doesn't have its *own* police," Marco clarified. "We call Key West if there are any . . ." He let his voice trail off, not sure how to finish the sentence.

"Well, that's good!" said Pamela.

Why is that good? thought Brando. *In what possible way could that be good?* Then he remembered: Key West. That's where they thought he'd gone. That was their new "theory," because of what the big English dude had told them. That he'd seen a boy waiting by the boat dock early this morning.

That didn't sound right to Brando. It didn't seem like something Davey would do. He looked around. He could see close to a dozen of their flyers from where he stood. There were four on the front doors alone: two facing out, two facing in. *If he's still on the island, that oughta do it,* he thought.

"Do I just dial 9-1-1?" asked Pamela, holding up her phone.

"That won't work here," said Marco. He let out a long breath. "You can use the phone at the desk. I'll get the number."

"I could just dial 9-1-1," said Pamela as they headed toward the desk.

"Please don't," said Marco.

They kept talking after that, but Brando couldn't hear them. Everyone in the lobby was talking. Every time Brando looked around, he caught people staring. He knew what they were talking about.

His dad finished putting up a flyer. He'd used long strips of Scotch tape on all four edges, with extra strips in the corners. If a hurricane came through, the roof would blow off, but these flyers would still be up.

"Where'd everyone go?" said Tam.

"To call the cops," said Brando.

His dad nodded his head. "Good."

If Brando was going to tell him anything, this would've been the time. But he didn't, and the time passed. Ten minutes later, they were heading back to the little dock. Tam and Pamela looked at the ground carefully as they approached, as if they were tracking a wild animal, as if they knew how. Finding no Davey tracks, they stepped onto the dock.

Tam tried to put up a flyer on one of the thick wooden pilings, but it was too breezy and the wrong kind of tape. They headed for the far end of the dock. There were no other people waiting because another boatful had just left.

Marco stayed behind on the sand, talking quietly into a little walkie-talkie. Brando was sure he was telling someone to take down all the flyers. He stared hard at the little yellow walkie-talkie. He wished he had Magneto's powers, or Jedi powers maybe. He'd crush the thing with his mind. He tried anyway. Nothing. Marco kept whispering, and the thing kept delivering little bursts of static in response.

Brando headed down the dock to join his parents. He looked over at the bar guy's battered, lopsided boat as he passed it. He wished he could just take it and go searching for his brother, but he knew that wouldn't end well. Instead, he waited with his parents. They didn't have to wait long.

Brando sat down on the end of the dock. He let his legs hang over the end and wasn't even all that curious why he felt his butt getting wet. It was a dock, after all. As soon as he looked up, he saw the little powerboat heading their way.

It knifed through the water in a straight line at first. Then it began arcing toward the dock, like an arrow on the way down. The boat bounced crisply over the little six-inch swells and left a long white wake behind it. Despite everything that was going on, despite all the bad things, Brando couldn't help but think: *That's frickin' awesome.*

As the police launch got closer, Brando could make out more details. It looked like an inflatable orange boat made permanent, with a metal frame reflecting the sun and a little cockpit in the center that looked just big enough for a person to stand up in. Soon, he saw the outline of the man's head and shoulders through the little window.

The man cut the motor and the boat drifted the last fifty yards to the dock. The launch bounced lightly against one of the tires hanging down along the pilings. The man stepped out from the little cockpit, picked up a line, and secured the boat. He pulled himself up onto the dock.

"Morning," he said.

Tam and Pamela said hello, but Brando didn't respond. He'd never seen a police officer in shorts before. He looked back down at the boat, just to make sure it was an official police boat. The words stenciled on the side in white spray paint seemed to leave no doubt about that, and there was a flasher and siren on top of the cockpit.

He looked back up at the guy. He looked young. Not like a kid, but not 100 percent like an adult, either. His shorts were hitched up too high, and he had a sunburn. It wasn't a tan, like Marco and most of the other people who worked on the island. It was a burn, like he was a tourist himself. A spray of messy blond hair stuck out from under his police cap. *This is the guy they sent?* thought Brando. *He looks like a Cub Scout troop leader.*

Marco thumped loudly down the dock, his dress shoes pounding the wood. He was still stuffing the walkie-talkie into his pocket with his left hand as he reached over with his right to shake the young cop's hand. "Hey, Jeff," he said. "Sorry to drag you out here on a Sunday."

Oh, great, thought Brando, *they know each other.*

He tried to use his mind powers again, even though he was pretty sure he didn't really have them. This time he was going for less Magneto, more Professor X. Jedi would still work, too. He thought as loud as he could: *Come on, Davey. Where are you? This isn't funny anymore. It was never funny. You need to get back here.*

The adults began to talk all at once. Brando stood alone on the edge of the dock. All he could see was clear blue water.

Where are you?

22

Davey was two and a half miles offshore, drifting to the southwest in a countercurrent. It was a bad situation, and it had just gotten worse.

That was a shark. He was sure of it now.

He replayed the images in his head. There was the first quick one, just a blur as it turned quickly and vanished. If that had been it, he could've told himself it was something else. It could've been some other big fish, a tuna maybe. But then he'd seen it again. It was moving slower this time. It was in no hurry at all, and why should it be? This was its home, not Davey's.

It glided slowly by, ten feet down. He saw its pointed head and its knifelike body. The water and plastic between them warped its shape slightly as it slid by, but he followed it and got a good look. He could see its fins, as clear as any nightmare he'd ever had. The dorsal fin angled straight up like a sail; the pectoral fins projected out like wings. Its mouth hung just slightly open, a line of black in all that blue.

He lost sight of it. He turned the bottle, tugged it through the water, tilted it farther down. Nothing, it was gone again. He began to see stars and realized he'd been holding his breath the whole time. He gulped in air and tried again. This time he dunked his head under the water and tried it without the bottle. He opened his eyes, but all he saw was water.

The little fish had scattered, not because of the shark but because Davey was moving the bottle all over the place. He saw them now, just off to his left. They were four little gray blurs, moving in unison. They skittered a few feet farther away as he watched them. *It's behind me!* he thought.

He jerked his body around, kicking his legs and pushing through the water with his right arm. His left arm was draped over the top of the water cooler bottle, and it was slowing him down. *By the time I see it, it will have its teeth in me.*

But when he completed his turn, there was nothing there. The endless ocean faded to a featureless blur in front of him. The ocean pressed in. He let out a few bubbles to keep the salt water out of his nose. He looked to his left, to his right, and then down past his feet. He surfaced, blowing out air as he went.

He checked to make sure no water had gotten into the bottle during the commotion. He wanted to climb up on top of the thing. He wanted to stand on it, like a lumberjack rolling a log. But he couldn't. It would sink, and then where would he be?

He told himself to calm down, not to panic. Yes, it was a shark, but it was small. It didn't look much more than three feet long. There was no way to be sure at that distance, but that's what he decided: three feet. Four feet, tops. He was taller than it was. *I'll punch it in the face if it tries anything!* That made him feel better.

For a while, he alternated between scanning under the water for the shark, scanning the horizon for boats, and scanning the sky for a plane or helicopter. He made them Official Survival Tasks and kept himself busy with them. He thought about how he'd signal if he saw a boat: He'd wave the bottle, splash around, shout as loud as he could. Same for a plane, he decided, except there wouldn't be any point in shouting.

The worst of his panic subsided, but his nerves were still stretched as tight as guitar strings. He heard a splash off in the distance, and it was like someone had strummed those strings with a hammer. He whipped his head around but saw nothing.

He wanted to scream, more out of frustration than fear. He had no idea what had caused the splash. Had something jumped out of the water? Why? He forced himself to go back to his Official Survival Tasks. Task 1: Look for shark. Task 2: Look for boats and/or land. Task 3: Look for planes and/or helicopters. Task 1: Look for shark. . . . Half an hour later, he had one other task to take care of.

Davey was the kind of kid who got out of the water to go to the bathroom under normal circumstances. These were not normal circumstances. The little fish had returned, and he apologized to them as the water got ever so slightly warmer.

It's hard to say he'd just made an enormous mistake. What choice did he have, really? Still, sharks are legendary for their sense of smell. Less well known: the fact that urine in the water is nearly as intriguing to them as blood.

Eventually, there would be that, too.

23

"You'd be the family of the boy, then," the officer was saying.

Brando noticed that he didn't say *missing* boy. Everybody noticed that.

"Yes, I'm Tam Tsering, his father."

"I'm Pamela Marcum Tsering, his mother."

The officer pulled a notebook out of his pocket. Brando had seen a hundred cops do that on TV. They'd pull a little notebook out of the back pocket of their pants or, if they were detectives, the inside pocket of their sports coat. This guy pulled it out of the side pocket of his cargo shorts.

"Well, I'm Jeff Fulgham. Deputy Jeff Fulgham — always forget that part. You can call me Jeff, Deputy, whatever you're comfortable with."

He was fishing around in his pocket again. This time he came up with a pen, but he didn't write anything. He turned toward Marco and asked, "What time's the next boat?"

Marco looked down at his watch. "Twenty minutes," he said. "Or whenever Zeke gets here."

"Yeah," said Deputy Fulgham. "This isn't the best place. People are going to start lining up, anyway. Let's go somewhere to talk."

"We can go out back by the pool," said Marco. "Nice place to sit. Should be quiet."

Who cares if it's a nice place to sit? thought Brando, but no one was asking him. The deputy hadn't even asked him his name.

They were all rumbling back down the dock now. Marco and the deputy were in the lead, talking low. Brando picked up his pace a little. He wanted to get close enough that he could hear what they were saying, but not close enough that they'd notice him. He watched the handle of the deputy's gun move back and forth as he walked. The gun was black, and so was the holster. When Brando looked closely, he could see the long rectangular edge of the magazine.

But he couldn't hear what they were saying. The footsteps, the breeze, the distance . . . They all conspired to keep things secret.

It took them just a few minutes to arrive at the pool. Deputy Fulgham looked around and pointed at a table. It had a glass top, a beach umbrella built right in, and five seats: just the right number. Tam and Pamela filed past and took seats next to each other. Brando took a few steps and then knelt down next to Marco and the deputy and pretended to tie his sneaker. He listened closely and heard the last words Marco said: ". . . no divers. Please. Not yet."

No divers? What does he mean by that? But Brando barely had time to think about it, because Marco nearly tripped over him on

111

his way to the little table. Deputy Fulgham headed over, too. Brando had untied his lace for his act and now he really did have to tie it. When he finished, he pulled out the last chair and sat down. The interview was already in progress.

"Can I keep this?" said the deputy. He was holding one of the flyers.

"Sure," said Tam. "Course."

"And how old is he?" said the deputy, folding the flyer.

"Thirteen," said Tam.

"And a half," said Pamela.

"So almost fourteen?" said the deputy.

Pamela just looked at him, like, *Obviously*. The deputy didn't notice. He was jotting something down in his little notebook. Brando looked over. He squinted. He thought he could just make out the first —

"What's your name, little dude?" said the deputy.

Brando looked up; the deputy was looking right at him. He was so startled that he nearly tipped his chair over backward. "Brando," he said.

"It's Brandon," said his dad.

Oh my God, thought Brando. *Did I just lie to the police?*

"He prefers Brando these days," said Pamela.

They were talking about him like he wasn't there. He hated that. *Also,* he thought, *did he just call me "little dude"?* He didn't feel guilty anymore. He felt mad.

"And how old are you?" said the deputy. Now he was talking too loud. Brando hated that, too. He hated when adults spoke LOUDLY and CLEARLY to him. How was that supposed to help? He wasn't seven — or deaf. His grandmother shouted at him, too, but he didn't mind that so much. She actually was deaf.

"I'M TWELVE!" he said.

"All right, little dude," said the deputy, jotting it down. "No need to shout." He turned back to Tam and Pamela, so he missed the look Brando gave him. The deputy had a talent for ducking looks.

"And when was the last time you saw" — Deputy Fulgham looked down at his notes — "Davey?"

"Last night," said Tam.

"When we went to bed," said Pamela.

"What time was that?"

"Around ten," said Tam. "Maybe ten thirty. It was a long day."

"You got in yesterday? From?"

"Yes," said Pamela. "From Cincinnati. We live right outside."

"And you were all in the one room?"

"Yes," said Tam.

"And you didn't notice he was missing until this morning?"

"No," said Tam.

"No," said Pamela.

And then everyone was looking at Brando. He felt his face getting hot. His stomach tightened up. Panic grabbed at him with a thousand sharp little fingers. But then he thought about the question, the actual words of it. The little fingers let go.

"No," he said. And that was true. He hadn't noticed Davey was missing until this morning. The deputy hadn't asked him *when* this morning.

"And what time was that?"

D'oh!

"About eight thirty," said Pamela.

Brando was stewing in his chair again. The umbrella built into the table was keeping the sun off them, but he still felt like he was in a microwave. The deputy didn't even look over at him, though. The microwave clicked off.

"So he could've left anytime after ten thirty last night?" said Deputy Fulgham. He looked over at Marco, who shook his head.

"There's someone at the desk until at least midnight."

"That when the bar closes?" asked the deputy.

"Yes," said Marco. "Kitchen closes at ten, but the bar stays open at least that late."

It was quiet for a few minutes as the deputy scribbled furiously in his notebook. Finally, he looked up. "Who was at the desk last night?"

"Debbie," said Marco. "Debbie Reyes. You know her."

"Oh yeah . . . And?"

"Nothing," said Marco. "Already called her. She remembers

checking them in, that's it." Brando remembered the lady who had checked them in: She was tall, and her hair was taller. "And she definitely would've noticed a boy wandering around by himself at that hour."

"Okay, so . . ." said the deputy. More scribbling.

"Listen, Deputy," said Tam.

The scribbling stopped. He looked up.

"Our son wouldn't . . . I mean, he wouldn't leave the room in the middle of the night. Where would he even go?"

"Right, right, of course," said the deputy. "Just trying to establish a time line here."

More scribbling.

"So you think it was this morning?"

"Yes," said Tam.

"Of course," said Pamela.

"Yes," said Brando. "He took his book."

"He took his what?"

But before Brando could repeat it, the loudest family on the face of the earth arrived. At least that's what they seemed like to Brando. It was two enormous adults and a little girl in water wings.

"Don't go in the pool yet!" called the man.

"Not yet, baby!" called the woman.

"I wanna go in the water!" shrieked the child.

"Now, you wait for Mommy!"

The whole table watched them. There was a brief cease-fire in all the yelling as the family began to unload their stuff next to the lounge chairs on the other side of the pool.

"Yes, this morning," said Pamela, tired of beating around the bush. "Someone saw him by the boat thing. . . . By the . . . the dock."

"What was that?" said the deputy, suddenly all ears. "Come again?"

"Yes," said Pamela, taking a deep breath before proceeding. "It was an English family. They told us in the lobby."

Behind them, there was a splash, a scream. "Don't go in the deep end!" called the little girl's mother.

No one paid them any mind. Deputy Fulgham was scribbling so hard, Brando was sure he'd tear the paper.

24

Davey hated the way that his legs hung down in the water. He hated, hated, hated it. He wasn't sure if he should keep his feet moving or keep them still. Specifically, he wasn't sure which was more likely to get them bitten off. He thought about fishing, as if his legs were the line and his feet were the bait. Did people just leave the bait hanging there, or did they move it around?

They did both. That was no help. He decided to keep doing what he'd been doing before he saw the shark: pushing his feet slowly back and forth underneath him. The bottle was enough to keep him afloat without that, but he had to hold on tight and pull it down lower into the water. He didn't want to be any lower than he had to be, so he kept kicking.

He looked down through the bottle almost constantly now. There was another little fish. It was bright blue, like a piece of candy, and seemed to come and go. The four silver-gray fish — his little guppy guys — didn't pay it much mind. They'd settled into a patch of water between the bottle and Davey's slowly churning feet.

Davey looked down and waited for the little blue fish to come back. It reminded him of an aquarium. He really liked that idea, like this whole thing was just a show for his benefit. He'd been to two aquariums, the one in Cincinnati and the one in Cleveland. They were both pretty good. His favorite thing was that his parents would let him and Brando run around on their own. I guess they considered it safe, with all of the aquarium employees walking around in their rubber boots and short-sleeve shirts. It was probably his parents' favorite part, too, now that he thought about it.

This was back when he and Brando still did everything together — the lake, the aquarium, bikes. So they'd run all over the place, looking for the turtles. His little brother really liked turtles. He liked all kinds, but especially the big sea turtles. He'd wait by the glass until one came all the way around the tank. Then he'd just watch it, mesmerized. Sometimes it seemed like the turtle was watching him, too. At least that's what he said.

Brando and his turtles, thought Davey. He smiled, just a little. And then he remembered the hat. The last time they'd gone, Brando had spent all his money on a dumb foam hat that looked like a turtle. It had a little turtle head on the front and foam flippers sticking out from the sides. He'd worn it home, even outside the aquarium.

The smile fell away. It had been one of the first times he'd been really, truly embarrassed to be around his younger brother. How old had he been? He tried to remember. He'd probably just turned twelve, so Brando would've still been ten.

Absolutely alone and miles from shore, he thought about that. *A ten-year-old in a turtle hat . . . so what?* Davey remembered how he'd quietly but relentlessly made fun of his brother in the backseat until he took the hat off. *God, what was my problem?* If Brando showed up right now, he could be wearing a turtle hat and a turtle skirt, for all Davey cared. Just so long as there was a nice sturdy boat underneath him.

The little blue fish was back. It swam right through the other fish. They moved aside to let it pass and then regrouped. Below them, a shark cruised into view. It startled Davey, and his body jerked backward. He stopped kicking his legs. He was pretty sure it was the same one as before, but he wasn't 100 percent sure. It's not like they'd been introduced. He held his breath and stayed still. He sank down half a foot, pulling the bottle down with him.

The shark curved slowly off to the right. He followed it just with his eyes until it reached the edge of the bottle. Then he took a breath and moved the bottle with his arms, just enough so that he could still see it. At first he thought it was moving away, but as he kept moving the bottle it kept reappearing.

It was moving in a circle. Both of the aquariums he'd been to had sharks. They'd moved in circles, too, but they had no choice. That was the shape of the tanks. This one had a choice.

There's a shark in my aquarium, thought Davey, *and it's circling me.*

It came close enough for him to get a good look at it through the plastic even without his glasses. It was a blue shark, long and thin, like the kids on the junior high basketball team. It was a dark blue shape in clear blue water, hard to keep track of. Its head came almost to a point, like a shark pen you'd buy in an aquarium gift shop. As it circled, Davey could see the large eye on the right side of its head. It was wide open, unblinking and black, like a hole in the sea.

When it began its second time around — or at least the second one he was aware of — Davey began to churn his feet again. It made it easier to follow along and keep an eye on the thing. The little gray fish scattered and regrouped, scattered and regrouped, annoyed by the activity. The bright blue one skittered back down into the deep. Davey just looked past them.

He followed the shark twice more around, the circle getting wider, then tighter. When it got wider again, he gave up. The shark could keep this up a lot longer than he could. It was exhausting, and he was already spent. He'd begun to shudder now and then. It was less from fear than from his dropping body temperature. A deep, feverish chill passed through him.

He hugged the bottle and pulled his legs up so that his thighs pressed against the flat plastic bottom. He sank down again. He used his arm muscles to try to keep the top of the bottle pointed straight up and the back of his head pointed at the warm sun overhead.

But his arms and shoulders ached. He couldn't keep this up, either. He thought about the sharks at the aquarium, how they circled and circled. How there were other things in the tank with them: little fish, rays, and smaller sharks. They didn't even seem to notice. And a ray — how easy a meal would that be for a shark? They just glided by like floating pancakes, and still none of them got eaten.

Davey thought about the little fish, completely unconcerned with the shark and just waiting for him to get his stupid legs away from their beloved floating bottle. Maybe this shark was like the fish. Maybe it was just curious about this strange thing on the surface, this Unidentified Floating Object. That made him feel a little better. It even allowed him to breathe a little more normally and let his legs relax down away from the bottle.

He chose not to think about the other part of that: that the first thing the little fish had done to check him out was give him a good nibble. He was pretty sure that if the shark did the same, he was done for. There'd be blood in the water, and then they'd all come.

He looked down through the bottle often. Sometimes he could see the blue shark, sometimes he couldn't. He looked back over his shoulder, he worried, but he told himself the same thing over and over: *They've been looking for me for hours now back on the island. That's plenty of time to find my stuff. And now that they've done that,*

he told himself, *it'll be easy for them to figure out what happened.*
Maybe there's even a chart of the currents.

He took another long look below, waiting until the shark came into view. Then he forced himself to go back to his old routine: scanning the horizon and checking the sky before finally letting himself look back down into the water.

Maybe the planes are already in the air, he thought.

Maybe the boats are already out searching the water.

25

But back on land, they were still sitting around the pool and talking.

Still just talking.

"Did you get his name?" asked Deputy Fulgham.

"No, we didn't get his name," said Pamela. "He was a big, huge Englishman and he came up to us and said he saw a boy alone by the boat dock."

"But you didn't get his name?"

"How many gigantic Englishmen can there be on this island?" said Pamela.

"I remember him," said Marco. "Asked me what time the restaurant opened for breakfast. It's him and his wife and a daughter, I think. Suite on the fourth floor."

"Remember his name?" said the deputy. His pen was poised over his little notebook.

"I can get it," said Marco.

"Who cares about his name?" Pamela said loudly. Her frustration was quickly turning into anger.

Brando flinched, remembering the times she spoke to him that way. He watched the deputy, interested to see how he'd respond. Fulgham put his pen down on the table and looked at her. "I'd like to ask him some questions, that's all," he said. He had a little smile on his face, as if she'd just told him a mildly amusing joke.

Brando was impressed. He knew it probably made his mom even madder, but it gave her no good reason to show it. That was so much smarter than getting mad back, which was what he usually did. Maybe he'd underestimated this Cub Scout leader.

Tam had seen the whole thing, too. He knew his wife was getting angry and tried to step in. "It seems like the important thing is that Davey was by the docks early this morning," he said. "This guy — whatever his name is — told us that plain as day."

The deputy considered it. He had no reason to doubt him.

"All right," said Fulgham, "so you think he got on one of the boats and headed over?"

"Yes," said Pamela. She was calmer now, happier with where the conversation was headed.

"Why?"

"I don't know!" So much for her calmness. "He probably wanted to buy something else to read — he likes fantasy books and graphic novels. Or maybe he just wanted to take the boat back and forth. He probably just woke up early and was bored!"

"Okay, okay," said the deputy, putting his hand up in a stop sign. "I can see you've thought about this. And he's thirteen, right?

I know I did some crazy things when I was a teenager around here. Island life, man."

That last part didn't seem very helpful to Brando. And he didn't think his brother would do something like that, anyway. It's not that he hadn't changed now that he was a teenager; he just hadn't changed in that way. And he'd never been the hop-a-boat-to-party-city type. Brando decided to say something, but all he could come up with was: "He already has a book."

The deputy looked at him but didn't even write it down. He still had a far-off look on his face, thinking about that "island life." Finally, he snapped out of it. "Okay, okay," he said. "Hey, Marco, how much does Zeke charge for a ride these days?"

"Five dollars a head," said Marco. "But sometimes the kids slip on for free. He doesn't pay much attention."

"Well, there you go," said the deputy. "Did he have any money on him?"

"Yeah, sure," said Tam.

"He gets an allowance for his chores," said Pamela. "Extra for big ones."

"Not that much extra," said Brando. The deputy chuckled. Brando was starting to get as angry as his mom. They weren't listening to him. He wasn't complaining about his own allowance. He was saying that Davey wouldn't blow ten bucks for a round-trip boat ride.

And then Marco surprised everyone, himself included, by saying,

"I met the first boat when it came in." He was thinking it so hard that it just popped out of his mouth.

"Oh, yeah?" said the deputy, sitting up in his chair.

"What?" said Pamela.

"Yeah," said Marco, but what he was thinking was, *How am I going to dig myself out of this one?*

"Well," said the deputy, "did you see the kid?"

Marco let out a long breath. He picked one of the flyers up off of the table and looked at it. "I don't know," he said.

"What do you mean, you don't know?" said Pamela. "You either saw Davey or you didn't!"

Marco looked at her. He still didn't like her. "What I mean by 'I don't know' is I don't know, all right, lady? It was early, and there were definitely some boys there. Maybe a little younger, maybe a little older. I was looking at their hands more than their faces, just helping Zeke collect the fares."

"But you must've —" started Tam.

"Believe me, I've thought about it. I've looked at this picture about four hundred times now, and I want to say, yes, he was there. But I don't know if his face looks familiar because I saw it this morning or because it's been on every frickin' door I've walked through since you taped those things up."

"Unbelievable," said Pamela, waving her hand at him.

Marco shrugged. He was just telling the truth.

"Not very helpful, Marco, my man," said the deputy. "I'll tell you what, though. Why don't you run down there and tell Zeke I need a word with him. Next boat's got to be getting in soon. Maybe he's got a little better memory of things."

Marco doubted it. "Sure," he said, pushing out of his chair and standing up.

He headed toward the dock, but right away he ran into a little line of people heading up the walkway, luggage in hand. The boat was already here. Brando watched him break into a jog.

"Should we go with him?" said Tam. "It looks like the boat is already here."

"Well, hopefully Marco can lasso Zeke before it leaves," said the deputy. "Boat won't go anywhere without him. Meantime, let me just clear up a few other possibilities."

"What do you mean?" said Pamela.

"Just want to cross a few things off my list."

"Fire away," said Tam.

"All right, first of all, have you seen anyone weird hanging around since you've been here? Maybe someone Davey might've talked to?"

No one asked what he meant by *weird*. They all knew what he was getting at. Tam and Pamela looked at each other.

"No," said Pamela. "I keep an eye out for . . . people like that. We got in late: last boat. I don't even think it was this Zeke guy anymore, just some little boat. The lady checked us in, and we went straight to our room."

"We ordered room service," added Tam. "Guy didn't even come all the way into the room with the cart."

"Okay," said the deputy. "No red flags there. And this next one, it's not so much a vacation question, but it's standard. What do you do, you know, professionally?"

"We work together," said Pamela. "We run a business."

"What kind of business?"

"We import arts and crafts from Tibet," said Tam.

"Are you from there?"

"My family is," said Tam. "Originally."

"All right, so what kind of arts and crafts?"

"Handmade stuff," said Tam. "It's nice. A lot of religious-type stuff."

"How's business?"

Tam and Pamela both made faces.

"Not great," said Tam with a little shrug. "When we started out, we were just about the only people doing this. Now, well, we're not."

"So you have competitors."

"We do now," said Pamela.

"Any of them might have a grudge against you, anything like that?"

"I think most of them just . . . If anything, they probably feel a little sorry for us at the moment," said Tam.

Brando's mouth dropped open. He didn't know it was that bad.

"But you're here," said the deputy. "You can afford a nice vacation."

"We got a great deal," said Tam.

"And we needed a vacation," said Pamela. "The idea was some time with the family, some time to think about the business."

"Like how to fix it — the business, I mean," said the deputy.

Pamela looked at him, deciding how much to tell him. "Yes," she said. "I mean, like my husband said, a lot of what we sell is religious in nature, and we need to respect that. We can't just think of it as 'religious-type stuff.'"

"My bad," said Tam.

The deputy looked at him and then back at her. "So you think you're too, like, commercial?"

"And I think we're not commercial enough — it's still a business," said Tam. "She's the true believer. I'm the guy who left."

"Got it," said Fulgham. He paused to jot something down, and then looked up. "Ever argue about it?"

The table was quiet for a few moments. Finally, Pamela looked over toward the pool. "We just did, didn't we?"

The deputy looked over at Brando. Now he wanted his input. Brando gave him one small nod. The deputy nodded back and wrote a few quick words in his notebook.

"All right, that's enough of that," he said. "One last question."

"Yes?" said Pamela.

"I hate to even bring it up, but, well, we are on an island. . . ."

"What about it?" said Tam.

Now the deputy looked over toward the pool. Specifically, he looked at the little girl splashing around the shallow end in her water wings. "No chance your son would go swimming?"

"No!" said Pamela. "No, our boy, Davey, he's not a reckless . . ."

"He's not that outdoorsy these days," agreed Tam. "He used to go to the lake when he was younger, but not so much anymore."

"Okay, so you don't think he would, but he'd know how to swim if he did?"

"Yeah, sure," said Tam.

"Exactly," said Pamela. "So it's not that."

Brando thought about it. He remembered asking Davey to go to the lake so many times the summer before, and Davey saying no way. "I don't think he'd go in," he said. But then he remembered Davey before that, Davey diving off the big raft. "I don't think he'd go in far," he added.

The deputy nodded. Brando liked him better now that he was listening to him.

"I think I've heard enough," said the deputy. "I've seen this before. A kid, a teenager, gets to an island like this. Quiet little place. He's going to want some space, and he's going to want something to do. He's going to look to do something. What's he find?

Nothing. There's nothing to do here that early. But there's a boat, and he can get on it for five bucks."

That still didn't sound like Davey to Brando, but his parents were nodding and the deputy had just said he'd seen it before. And Brando liked the idea that Davey could just come back on his own, show up on the next boat. He'd be in some trouble, but he'd be safe.

Marco came pounding over from the walkway. His dress shoes slapped loudly against the concrete as he jogged past the pool.

"Missed it," he said in between huffs and puffs.

"Can you call him?" said Pamela.

"Not on the water. Left a message at the marina. Hopefully he'll get it. Otherwise" — he paused to get more air — "have to wait for the next boat."

"Forget it," said the deputy, standing up. "I'll go run him down."

Brando remembered the sight of the powerful police launch knifing through the water.

"We're going with you," said Pamela.

Tam nodded.

Fulgham considered it. This wasn't even an official missing person case yet. The boy had only been gone for half a day. But it was a good lead, and it didn't seem like there was much more they could do on the island. "Sure," he said. "Boat can take me plus four."

Four? thought Brando. *Sweet!*

"Marco, man, you stay here, all right?" said the deputy.

"No problem," said Marco. His relief at being let off the hook took the form of a dorky thumbs-up.

"Get me the room number of that English dude. You got my number. And have someone put together a list of this morning's checkouts."

"You need phone numbers for them?"

"If you got 'em."

"Sure."

"And Marco?"

"Yeah?"

"If the boy shows, don't let him go anywhere."

26

There were more sharks now. The blue, yes, but two more, as well. The newcomers cruised by in tandem, passing slowly underneath Davey's feet. He watched them closely and followed their progress.

Their fins had black edges and tips. They were blacktip sharks. Davey had seen the little blacktip reef sharks at the aquariums, but he could tell this was a different species, a whole different animal. Each one was as heavy and muscular as an NFL defensive back.

Davey examined their markings with a mix of fascination and horror. They were pure black — as black as their eyes — but uneven, as if each fin had been lightly dipped in ink. The blacktips passed no more than seven or eight feet beneath him. If he hadn't seen them and tucked his legs up, it would've been even closer. *Too close,* thought Davey. Another deep shudder ran through him.

And here came the blue. It hadn't adjusted its course enough, and now it was heading for the same patch of water as the blacktips. Davey watched, the sharks getting fuzzier with distance. He squinted and stared, coaxing his weak eyes to follow them.

Something was going to happen down there. Would they bump into one another? Would they fight?

At the last second, the blue veered off. It shot quickly away, vanishing into the distance. The blacktips continued on, crossing the empty patch of water unconcerned. Davey wasn't surprised. It was small, and they were big. It worked the same way on land. He hoped the blacktips would vanish now, too.

They didn't. They continued on for another dozen feet or so, until they were just a black-and-gray blob in his vision. Then they turned and slowly came back into focus. He pulled up his legs again. In a sense, they'd done him a favor with the blue: a circling shark is never a good sign. It was hard for him to feel too grateful, though, as they passed underneath him again. Closer this time. Not much closer, it's true, but they were in no hurry.

Twenty minutes later, the blue was back. It stayed down deeper, out of the way of the others. Davey could just make it out down there, its penknife body giving it away. It wasn't circling now, just lurking, waiting for the bigger sharks to do the work.

The blacktips passed by again. They were far enough to the side this time that he didn't pull up his feet. He was too tired anyway. The adrenaline that had flooded his system was mostly gone now, and he was crashing. It had been a fight-or-flight response, but he had no way to do either.

The blacktips headed away from him for now, and the blue was almost out of sight. Davey scanned the horizon and then the sky.

Still nothing. He wanted to believe they would find him. It was a bright and nearly cloudless day. The burn on his shoulders was plenty of proof of that. He was a dark dot on a clear sea. A boat wouldn't even have to be that close to see him. A plane wouldn't have to be close at all.

Yes, he told himself, *they'll find me.*

Six feet down, the blacktips arced gracefully and headed back his way.

If there's anything left to find.

27

Davey's aquarium was growing rapidly. The three sharks moved lazily around it, just like the ones back in Cincinnati. And now that Davey was mostly still, the four little fish barely budged from under the water bottle. Even the bright blue fish was back.

And now another one was headed his way. This one was bigger. If Davey had held his hand out flat, with all the fingers extended and together, it would have been the size, and almost the shape, of this new fish. But there was something wrong with it. It was just a few inches below the surface of the water, and Davey didn't even need to look through the water cooler bottle to see that it wasn't swimming right. It flicked its tail in spastic jerks that sent it almost as far sideways as forward.

As it got closer, Davey saw that it never fully straightened out. It always stayed a little curled up, like a dried-out flower petal on a windowsill. He couldn't tell if it was injured or sick or what, but he didn't want it near him.

"Get away," he said.

He didn't even know why at first, and then he did. The sharks . . . He looked at this new fish, struggling its way toward shelter, and all he saw was bait.

"Getawaygetawaygetaway!"

The injured fish kept coming, determined to reach the little island of shade and shelter. Davey scanned the water underneath him. He didn't see the sharks. Where were they? He leaned back, pulling the bottle with him. Slowly, he began to kick.

The other fish came with him. The new fish swam harder, flapping its tail, trying its hardest to go straight. Davey kicked harder. "No! Go away!"

And he was right to be worried. Davey felt the blacktip before he saw it.

A pressure wave of water pushed up against his feet and legs. The shark shot up out of the deep and bit the injured fish cleanly in half. Its momentum carried it up and out of the water, and for a split second Davey saw it there. Half of its thick body was above the water, its wet skin reflecting the sunlight. The rest was still below. Then it tipped and fell back. Water splashed across Davey's face, shoulders, and back.

He swore so loud that he owed the swear jar back in Ohio at least ten bucks.

As the surface of the water began to smooth out, Davey saw the tail of the little fish. Just the tail, still curled, leaking blood and little bits of flesh into the water. The muscles gave one last reflexive flick as it began to sink. Then a shadow, then a shape: The other blacktip surged to the surface. It snatched the scraps. The splash was smaller this time.

Davey kicked harder as the second shark disappeared from view. He hugged the bottle tight to his chest and backed away as fast as he could. He was twelve feet away by the time the blue shark arrived. He saw it thrash back and forth. Its fins broke the surface as it pushed through the bloody water, searching for food that wasn't there.

After a few more thrashes, it gave up. It had been right to stay near the blacktips, but it had been too slow to take advantage. It was too late to get its share. As it left the surface and descended, its primitive brain formed one simple thought.

It needed to be more aggressive.

28

Brando was enjoying the ride despite himself. Back on land, he'd felt angry and sad and guilty all at once. But out here, he could just watch the boat cut the water in half, leaving a wake of white spray.

As soon as the boat began slowing down, his thoughts crept back in. He looked up at row after row of boats tied to a network of floating docks. He'd overheard enough to know that this was the marina and that they were here to look for the captain of the boat that took people to and from Aszure Island. He'd overheard most of what was said on the trip, in fact, because everyone had been shouting over the noise of the engine.

Deputy Fulgham cut the engine and eased the police launch in toward an empty slip. As he did, Brando leaned over the edge and looked down into the vanishing sliver of water between boat and dock. He saw a flash of something on the bottom. It might have been a coin catching the light or a piece of metal that had snapped off the last boat to dock here. Brando would need a closer look to know for sure.

And just like that, he knew what Marco had meant when he

139

said, "No divers. Please. Not yet." It was so horrible, but so obvious. They would bring in divers to look for his brother's body on the bottom of the sea.

They were talking all around him. His parents were talking to each other. The deputy was talking to someone on the dock. The words were still loud enough for Brando to hear, but his head could no longer hold them. The five words he already had in there were taking up all the space. What did he mean, "not yet"?

Everyone got off the boat and headed down the dock, and he followed them. The concrete-topped dock floated serenely on the water, designed to rise and fall with the tide. They reached another dock that ran parallel to the shore and took a left. Brando finally looked up and saw Key West. The waterfront was bustling with activity. It was the early afternoon, and everyone was on the move.

Brando wasn't even really on Key West yet, but he could hear it clearly. A road ran along the shore. Cars and scooters honked, and bicyclists shouted. And behind that rose the muffled roar of thousands of people on vacation, drunk with sun and possibilities. A loud laugh cut through it all briefly, like a goose honking.

"No way," he said. No one heard him, but he knew it in his heart now. There was no way his older brother would want any part of this. He took a step toward his mom. She didn't have sleeves on, so he tapped her wrist. She turned toward him and leaned down.

"What is it, B?"

"Davey would hate this," he said.

"Okay," she said. "Now be quiet for a second. The policeman is talking."

The deputy was talking to a very short man in very long shorts. "Hey, Victor. You seen Zeke?"

"The Captain? Yeah, of course. He's made a few trips out to Aszure already."

"You been here all morning?"

"Yeah, and I'll be here all day, too."

The deputy took the flyer out of his pocket and unfolded it. "Seen this kid?"

Victor looked at the flyer carefully.

Tam and Pamela leaned in, waiting for his answer. Victor gave them a quick glance before answering. "Don't think so. Tough to say. Lot of kids running around the docks all day."

"Look again."

This time he took the flyer in his hands, but the answer was the same. "Don't think so. Something happen to him? He do something?"

"Just looking for him, that's all," said the deputy.

Victor glanced over at Tam and Pamela again and put it together. "Bad deal," he said to Fulgham. "Hope you find him."

Hope you find him "soon," thought Brando. *He should've said "soon."* But Victor had said what he said. It was another "not yet" for Brando's list.

"We will," said the deputy. Brando nodded in approval. "Where's Zeke now?"

"Probably still eating lunch."

"Yeah, you want to narrow that down for me a little?"

"Oh, sorry. He's at Mary's. Pretty sure, 'cause he asked me if I wanted anything from there."

"Okay, thanks, man."

"No problem. If you got another one of them flyers, I'll take it. Ask around for you, just the people who come and go, you know?"

"Yes, please," said Pamela, stepping forward and handing him a flyer. "We'd really appreciate it."

"No problem," said Victor, taking it in his child-sized hands. "It's a bad deal."

The Tserings followed the deputy to shore like a row of ducklings. He walked them straight off the docks and across the road. He even waved a car to a halt so they wouldn't have to wait for the light. He started up the walkway toward a small, one-story restaurant that seemed to be leaning ever so slightly to the left. The paint was weathered and peeling, hovering somewhere between the dark red it had once been and the washed-out red it was becoming.

"I thought it was Mary's?" said Tam, pointing to a sign that read BAIT 'N SWITCH in slightly fresher paint.

"Mary is the owner," said Fulgham.

Brando slipped by them, pulled open a battered screen door, and stepped inside.

"Hold on there, dude," he heard.

He felt a hand on his shoulder, but he couldn't see who it belonged to. Sunlight streamed in through the windows and door, but apart from that, the only light came from a few signs glowing behind the bar. A man's face emerged from the shadows by the door. What Brando thought at first was a lingering shadow near the man's left ear turned out to be a large tattoo.

"It's okay, Bacon, he's here on official business," said the deputy, stepping into the doorway.

Bacon? thought Brando. *Did I hear that right?* He had, and Bacon straightened up on his stool when he saw the deputy. He pushed a meaty hand through his greasy hair.

"Oh, hey, Deputy," said Bacon. "That's cool. Come on in."

"Glad to see you carding this time. Where's the Captain?"

Bacon let out a raspy laugh. "Gonna have to be more specific. This place is full of 'em."

"Zeke — never mind, I see him."

Brando did, too. He was sitting at a small table with the scattered remains of a BLT spread out in front of him. It was the hat that gave him away.

29

Zeke looked up from his ruined sandwich at the flock of newcomers headed his way. Brando saw his eyes flick across the whole group and then settle on Deputy Fulgham.

"Oh, boy, what'd I do now?" said Zeke. "If this is about last night, I'll tell you right now I don't remember it too clearly."

Brando was pretty sure he was joking.

"Nah, you're not in trouble, Zeke," said the deputy. "At least no more than usual. Wouldn't kill you to answer your phone, though."

"Well, that would be hard, considering there are about thirty feet of seawater over top of it at the moment."

"You drop it?"

"Something like that. How can I help you? Want the rest of my sandwich?"

"Just want to ask you a few questions about this morning."

"Have a seat," said Zeke. He looked around at the others. "You'll have to pull over an extra chair or two."

Tam and Pamela turned to look for empty chairs, but the deputy stopped them. "Why don't you all get some lunch?" he said. "I'll just talk to the captain by myself, if that's okay."

"I'm not hungry," said Pamela.

"Well, get the kid some fries, anyway. They make some mean curly fries here."

"Sure," said Tam, taking the hint. He leaned in and whispered something to Pamela. Brando couldn't hear what it was, but it worked.

"We'll be right over here," she said, pointing to a little square table nearby.

Fulgham nodded. "You can just order up at the bar."

"I'll save our seats," said Brando. He pulled out the chair closest to the other table and didn't knock himself out pushing it in.

The deputy was probably aware of what he was doing, but he didn't seem to care if Brando overheard. "Thought I'd spare you the full inquisition," he said to Zeke.

"I appreciate it. What's this about?"

"Well, that family there is one kid short right now. Thirteen-year-old boy, haven't seen him since last night."

Brando's back was to the deputy. He heard the sound of paper crinkling.

"Here's a picture. You see him this morning, maybe on the first or second boat?"

"Oh, jeez," said Zeke. "That's a tough one."

"Yeah, why's that?"

"Sundays are busy this time of year. Get a lot of checkouts, people who want to be home by Monday."

"Even that early?"

"Yeah, they got flights to catch, out of Miami and everywhere else. Busy on the way over, too. People spend the first night here and then head out to Aszure first thing. Adds up to a lot of people, lot of faces, on that little dock."

"So you don't remember him?"

"Lemme look again. . . . No, I don't think . . . Definitely not on the second boat. I'm a little fuzzier on the first. It was pretty early. Why don't you ask Mar—"

Brando missed the rest of the sentence. His parents had just shown up with a paper cone full of fries. He'd been leaning way back in his chair, and now the front legs clattered back to the ground. The talking behind him stopped.

"Hey," called the deputy. "Mind your own business over there."

Busted, thought Brando. But his parents barely said a word as they sat down, and the deputy didn't lower his voice. The family chewed silently on reheated curly fries and continued to eavesdrop.

"But come on," said Fulgham. "He's a teenage boy. You must keep an eye on 'em. I know I do."

"Yeah, but I don't know. This kid looks young."

"Yeah, his face does, but . . ." The deputy didn't even need to turn around to address the family. "Davey small for his age?"

There was no response.

"Come on, I know you're listening. The fries aren't that good."

"Yes, he's not that much bigger than Brando here," said Pamela finally.

Even with his back turned, Brando could tell they were looking at him. He sat up a little straighter.

"Okay, so he looks young."

"Yeah, well, there were definitely some kids on that first boat, but I honestly don't think he was one of them. And I know he wasn't on the second."

"Yeah, Marco doesn't remember seeing him down there, either."

"What makes you think he took my boat, anyway?"

"Some English guy said he saw him waiting by the dock, early."

"Oh, yeah, that guy. I just brought him back here this morning, him and his family."

"Oh, yeah?" said the deputy.

"Yeah," said Zeke. "Can't miss him. Nice guy, but he nearly sank my boat when he got in."

"They have luggage with them?"

"No, just day-tripping."

Brando and his parents weren't even pretending not to listen now. They'd turned in their chairs and were watching the whole thing.

"Okay, okay, want to do me a favor?" the deputy said to Zeke.

"Do I have a choice?"

"Not really."

"Then, yes, I'd love to."

"Take this flyer and show it to the big English guy when he shows up for the ride back. Ask him if he's absolutely sure this is the kid he saw. Just double-check, okay? And then give me a call. Or have someone whose phone is not currently at the bottom of the sea give me a call, okay?"

"He never saw the picture . . ." said Pamela, her words forming along with the thought.

"What?" said Fulgham. "I thought you said —"

"No," she said. "He just said he saw a boy. We assumed. . . ."

"Oh, great," said Fulgham. A shoot-me-now look flashed across his sunburned face as he stood up. "All right, thanks, Zeke."

"No problem. Say hi to the sheriff for me."

"Will do," said the deputy, already moving toward the door.

"We got these to go," said Tam, picking up the half-empty cone of fries.

"Good," said the deputy, "because we're going."

30

Drew looked around, unimpressed. She'd lobbied hard for this trip to Key West, but it wasn't the party she'd been looking for. Or maybe it was exactly what she'd expected, and she was just now realizing that she didn't much care for this sort of party. They were on Duval Street, the main drag. There were some nice shops, and the weather was lovely. But it was also the height of spring break, which meant that it was crowded, loud, and a little crazy around the edges.

"I heard Florida was full of old-timers," said Big Tony, "but this is just a bunch of rowdy yobs."

Drew agreed. They walked past a banner that read SPRING BREAK EXTREMEX. Inside the little building, she could see a bunch of those yobs getting even rowdier.

"What's the extra X for, then?" she called over the noise.

"That's extra extreme, isn't it?" said Big Tony.

Kate didn't answer. Her mouth was fighting a fierce battle against some salt water taffy she'd just bought. "Think I just swallowed half my fillings," she said once she'd finally chewed the piece to death. "Have some of this."

She extended the box to both of them. Drew passed, but Big Tony took two. He began unwrapping both at once. "Don't eat them both, dear," said Kate. "They're different flavors."

Tony looked down at them, one pink and the other light blue. He shrugged. "All ends up in the same place," he said, popping both into his mouth.

"Well that ought to keep him quiet for a while," Kate said to Drew. "What should we talk about then, just us girls?"

Drew smiled, but before she could answer, a group of college kids came barreling down the sidewalk at full speed. It wasn't clear if they were running from something or toward something. Big Tony stood his considerable ground, and the spring breakers either avoided him or bounced off. Kate and Drew shrieked and pressed themselves against the side of a building, narrowly avoiding a collision.

"GRRMMFERRLLS!" shouted Big Tony through the taffy.

"You tell 'em, Da," said Drew.

"What say we get back to our sleepy little island?" said Kate. "Just do some lying about and get some sun?"

That actually sounded really good to Drew. She was a little surprised at herself, but it did. When she got home and Becca asked her about "the party" on Key West, she'd just have to tell her it was a little too "extremex" for her.

She took her phone out of her pocket, just out of habit. The service was switched off — no calls or texts. She checked the time and pretended that's what she meant to do. It was already well into the afternoon.

"Hope that's switched off," said Big Tony, having finally defeated the taffy. "Those roaming charges are bigger 'n I am."

His own phone was back in their suite, switched off, but the hotel phone next to it had been ringing regularly with calls from the police.

Without another word, the Dobkins turned around. They walked slowly back toward the marina. They even crossed the street for some fresh window-shopping on that side of things.

They'd made it almost all the way back to the marina when Big Tony decided to duck into one final store. It was a liquor store, and Kate didn't approve. "They've got a bar on the beach and another one in the hotel," she said.

"Can only imagine what they charge," said Big Tony. "Captive audience and all that."

"Fine, but I'm going in with you," said Kate. "At least we can get something I like, too." She turned to Drew. "You stay out here."

"I'm not going to get legless just walking into the place," she protested. But it was no use. All she could do was post herself by the door as her parents disappeared inside. She watched the world go by, or at least the street. There were sunburned tourists and more college students.

She saw a young copper in shorts go by on the other side of the street. He was scanning the area. She stood up a little straighter as his eyes passed over her. She was standing outside of a liquor store, but there was nothing illegal about that.

She was about to forget the whole thing, but then she saw the family tagging along behind him. They looked familiar, but where had she seen them? It didn't take her long to come up with the answer; it had to be the hotel.

It was that family, that poor family from the lobby. She saw them following the young officer, scanning the street. *They're looking for that boy,* she thought. *But why do they think he's here?*

Tam and Pamela both looked in her general direction, but Duval Street was crowded and they were looking for a thirteen-year-old boy with glasses or a large man with a shaved head. She didn't fit either description, and they'd only seen her in passing at the hotel.

Their eyes washed over her in a big swoop, like the beam of a lighthouse. They kept going. They were past her, and that was just about that. But there was one other person with them, of course.

Brando was bringing up the rear in the search party. It wasn't a lack of enthusiasm; he had the shortest legs. He took one more quick look across the crowded street. A little red car sped by, and when it passed, he caught a quick glimpse of a girl. There was something familiar. . . . A stout cargo van passed, blocking his view. He stopped. He almost got run over by the man walking behind him, but he stayed put. The van rumbled by. It was the girl from the hotel, the daughter of the big British guy.

The guy they were looking for.

He looked more closely, just to make sure. She saw him now: the little boy, the brother. They made eye contact, and she smiled at him. Flustered, all Brando could think to do was wave.

Next to Drew, an elderly lady pushed her way out of the store. Drew helped her with the door and then ducked her head inside. She saw her parents waiting in line at the register.

"Mum, Da," she called.

She'd found something more important for them to check out.

31

Davey was wiped out. It was amazing that someone could be so drained and so waterlogged at the same time. He was cold, his shoulders and head still baking in the sun but his core temperature already down a few degrees from the long soak. He'd been in the water so long, he felt like cold spaghetti.

And he was tired. He'd been hugging the bottle to him since early that morning. Now he'd begun to let go a little. It wasn't going anywhere. He leaned forward onto it, one arm bent loosely around its thin plastic neck. They drifted in a lazy slow dance. Still, his shoulders and arms ached from the constant tension, and his chest was beginning to feel bruised.

But more than any of that, he was mentally exhausted. The sharks, the shocks, the situation, the endless squinting into the distance and listening for any sound . . . They had worn him down like a piece of driftwood. His mind was shutting down, partly to recover and partly to protect itself from the horror of it all.

It was bad timing, because the blue shark was agitated. It was no longer twenty or thirty feet down, avoiding the blacktips. Now it was cutting back and forth in sharp-edged zigzags in the warm band of water between the cruising blacktips and the surface.

It could still smell the injured fish it had missed out on. Traces of blood and the oils from its torn flesh still hung in the current. Now the blue shark was thinking about having a go at this big thing. The blue could sense the electrical charge coming from it and hear the occasional hollow thump of water on plastic. It was an unfamiliar mix. It wasn't a turtle, though it was big enough. The shark didn't know what it was, but it knew how to find out.

A quick bite and then retreat. If it was a tough thing, and dangerous, the other sharks would help tear it apart. The blue had learned that lesson early: There were always more than enough teeth out here. But with something this size, the blue would get its share.

It twitched erratically, making a few last adjustments to its course. The blacktips had seen this sort of thing before and cruised in close behind it. The blue shot toward Davey straight and fast, knifing up through the water at a forty-five-degree angle.

Davey was still leaning forward on the bottle, completely zoned out. Once again, the pressure wave of water arrived before the shark. Something inside Davey stirred. It was the base of his brain, the animal part that had kept him afloat when he was barely conscious that morning. *Danger,* it said. *Wake up.*

He lifted his head and pulled the bottle in a little closer to him. His eyes snapped fully open. There was no time for anything else. The shark was there. Its sleek, pointed nose cut through the last few feet of water. The black eyes rolled back in its head, and its permanent frown widened for the bite, revealing two rows of sharp, serrated teeth.

BONK!

It hit the water cooler bottle.

The impact carried through the plastic and knocked the air out of Davey's lungs. He bounced high enough that the top of his swim trunks broke the surface of the water. The cheap bottle, the plastic a little on the thin side, managed not to rupture. Instead, it bent all the way in and popped back out in midair. Davey held on tight to the top as he splashed back down.

The shark turned sharply to its right and then drifted there for a moment, confused and stunned. It shook its head violently from side to side, part surprise and part bite reflex. But there was nothing in its mouth. Something had gone wrong. It swam away quickly. It understood instinctively that if the other sharks realized it was stunned, they'd tear it apart. That's what it would've done.

The little fish had scattered. If fish could talk, these ones would say, "Ha ha ha! Hit your nose! Loser!"

But the news wasn't all good. The activity had agitated the blacktips, triggering their competitive instincts. And the impact on the empty bottle had created a big sound this time, like a bass drum beating underwater. And big sounds attract big things.

PART THREE

CATCHING HIS DRIFT

32

A misunderstanding that had endured for hours unraveled in a matter of seconds. Standing outside the liquor store on Duval Street, Deputy Fulgham showed Big Tony the flyer. "Is this the boy you saw by the docks this morning?"

"Nah, that's not him." He said it quickly and with a thick accent — *Nah-ats-not-ihm* — but just the initial *N* sound was enough.

Tam shook his head in disbelief, and Pamela dropped hers in defeat. The rest of the Dobkins crowded in for a look.

"No, the boy we saw was younger," said Kate.

"I saw him," said Drew. She reached out and touched the picture with her finger to leave no doubt which boy she meant.

"You did?" said Fulgham. "When?"

Everyone turned to look at her. She took a breath and told them what she knew. "Yeah, that other one, the little one, was just waiting for his family by the dock. I saw him. But this other one, this one here, he was farther on."

"Where was that?" said Fulgham. Everyone was leaning in now, even her own parents.

"Tell 'em, luv," said Kate.

"I was getting to it, wasn't I? He was by the little shed place, the little —"

"The bar stand?" said Fulgham.

"Yeah, that's it," she said. She hadn't wanted to say *boozer*. "It wasn't open yet, but he was sitting under a tree right next to it."

"On the path there?" said Fulgham.

"Little ways back."

Brando spoke up: "What was he doing?" No one else looked over at him or even acknowledged his question, but Drew did.

"He was reading."

I knew it, thought Brando.

Now that she'd answered him, the others started in: Where exactly, what kind of tree, when, and are you sure?

The deputy held up his hand to shush them. "Do you remember what time that was?"

"Quarter to eightish, your time. Maybe a little later, but I don't think it was quite eight."

She looked at her mom, who nodded.

"Yeah, that's about right," said Big Tony.

"Wait, did you see him, too?" said the deputy.

"No, but that's what time we were at that boozer."

Fulgham nodded and scratched another quick note in his little notebook.

"We were at that same place about an hour later, when we first went out to look for him," said Pamela.

The deputy wrote that down, too, before turning to face her. "And you didn't see him?"

"No, and we were there for a while. We definitely would —"

They were interrupted by a pair of middle-aged men wearing matching white hats. "You're blocking the sidewalk!" said the smaller of the two.

Big Tony turned and glared at them both. "I'll block your sidewalk!"

The men crossed the street so quickly that they almost walked into the door of a passing car.

Pamela continued: "And we talked to the guy inside, and he said he hadn't seen anyone."

Fulgham jotted down the new information. "All right, at least that's something," he said. "He was there when you walked by" — he pointed his pen at the Dobkins — "and gone before you got there." He pointed the pen at the Tserings. "Was it an old guy you talked to at the bar stand?"

Brando nodded.

"Old as dirt," said Tam.

"Okay, that's Morgan Bembe — Captain Morgan. I'll need to

talk to him." Fulgham looked around at the bustling street and shook his head. "And we need to stop burning time over here."

"Sorry for the confusion," said Big Tony. "Just trying to help, and I made a mess of it."

"Our fault as much as anyone's," said Pamela.

"Anything we can do to help," offered Kate.

"We may need to borrow your daughter," said Fulgham. "She's the last one to see the boy now."

Kate and Big Tony nodded.

"I'm in," said Drew. "Let's find him."

33

The police launch flew through the water, skimming over the surface and sawing off thick white plumes on either side. Fulgham was gunning the engine and shouting into his radio. The others were mostly just holding on tight. Tam and Pamela were closer to the cockpit, and Drew and Brando were squeezed in farther back.

Drew watched the docks disappear behind them. Her parents were still there, waiting for the next boat.

Brando tried to figure out what this meant. Davey hadn't taken the boat. No one had seen him there, not even its captain. That's what he'd thought all along, but he wished he'd been wrong. Because if he hadn't taken the boat, and he wasn't on the island, that only left —

Drew interrupted his thoughts. "That's your brother, then?" she shouted over the noise. "The one we're looking for?"

"Yeah, uh, Davey," he shouted back. "His name is Davey."

"He likes his books!" She formed her thumbs and fingers into circles and raised them to her eyes: glasses.

"Yeah!" called Brando. "He's really smart!"

"I'm Drew." She leaned over and extended her hand.

"I'm Brando." He leaned over and took it. It was bigger than his, and warm.

The boat bounced over a small wave and they both fell back into their spots. It was too loud to say much more, but Brando felt better now. It was true: Davey was really smart. Even if something bad had happened to him, he'd figure it out.

Drew was just glad Brando didn't look so sad anymore. She wasn't sure what help she could be. She didn't know much more than what she'd already told them. But she was determined to do what she could.

The next thing she knew, the boat was slowing down and pulling up to the little dock on Aszure Island. She braced herself as it bumped to a stop and the deputy threw off the line.

There was a man there to take it, but it wasn't who any of them were expecting. Brando looked around, but Marco was nowhere in sight. The man caught the line and fastened it with a few quick, strong tugs. He was dressed in a dark blue uniform, long pants and a short-sleeve shirt. Brando caught a quick flash of gold from his collar.

Brando thought the man looked like a superhero, and he was half right: He was an officer of the United States Coast Guard.

"That was fast," said Fulgham, hopping onto the dock.

The two men exchanged quick salutes.

"I'm coming from the same place you are," said the man. "At Station Key West all morning."

"Heading back to Marathon?" said the deputy.

"I was." A Coast Guard launch, a little bigger than the police one, was tied up on the other side of the dock.

"Well, I'm glad you're here, Beast."

Beast? thought Brando. Had he heard that right? He had. The man's name was Bautista, but people who could get away with it called him Beast.

Maybe he really is a superhero, thought Brando. Beast was one of the original X-Men, and he was blue, too. Brando didn't even realize he was staring until Bautista gave him a quick smile and snapped off a salute. Brando raised his hand slowly and saluted back.

"I'm Lieutenant Commander Daniel Bautista of the United States Coast Guard," he said to Tam and Pamela as he helped them onto the dock. "I'm here to help any way I can."

Bautista looked over at Brando, whom he'd been told about, and Drew, whom he had not. He didn't want to sugarcoat anything. The island was small and had been searched thoroughly. The boy had been missing for the entire day. That meant he was probably in the water, and that meant he was probably dead. Still, he tried to find something encouraging to say.

"I do have some experience with this sort of thing."

That was an understatement. He was the best they had.

34

Brando understood what had just happened better than his parents did. They'd just been sent away so the grown-ups could talk things over. It happened to him all the time, but it had probably been a while for Tam and Pamela. The "grown-ups" in this case were Bautista and Fulgham. They'd headed off with Drew, so she could show them exactly where she'd seen Davey. The Tserings weren't invited.

The deputy's mood had changed. He was very serious now, and so was the new man, Bautista. He was the one who'd sent them back to the hotel.

Brando broke into a little jog to keep up with his parents. They were headed for the office. People were making phone calls there. They were trying to reach the guests who'd left that morning, the ones who were up early and might've seen something. Bautista said they'd be a big help there. Brando had heard that one before.

They pushed through the back doors of the hotel. The flyers were still up on both sides of the double doors. Davey's face looked out of the paper, a small smile on his lips, oblivious. Tam paused to smooth out the tape on one of them.

"The office?" said Tam to the lady at the front desk. She pointed behind her and didn't protest as they walked around the counter. She knew who they were. There was a little doorway off to the side. It was open a crack, and the buzz of mismatched voices filtered out. The family walked through single file.

One quick look told Brando that they weren't needed. There were two desks, each with a blocky, old-fashioned phone. Marco was sitting at one desk, holding the phone between his ear and his shoulder. "Yes, this is a message for Delmar Granderson. I'm calling from the Aszure Island Inn. I hope you enjoyed your stay! I just wanted . . ."

A man in the same blue uniform as Bautista was at the other desk. Brando knew right away that this was Bautista's assistant, that when you have gold things on your collar, you don't drive your own boat. The man was sitting up very straight in his chair, holding the phone stiffly. He'd left his share of messages, too — many of the former guests were still on planes — but this time he was talking to an actual person. "I see. . . . Of course . . . So, nothing?"

Behind them, another employee was holding a piece of paper, probably waiting for her turn to dial. That made his parents second and third in line, if they even had enough numbers to call.

"I'm going to the room," said Brando.

No response, so he left. There were a few people in the lobby, and they all watched him as he emerged from behind the counter. Maybe they were wondering what he'd been doing back there, and maybe they thought he looked a lot like the boy on all of those flyers.

Brando didn't stop to ask. He went straight to the room. He fished the passkey out of his pocket and swiped it. He waited for the little light to turn green and went inside. The first thing he did was go to the little mini fridge and take out a brand-new five-dollar Coke. He dared them to bill him for it. He twisted the top off the cold plastic bottle and took a gulp so big it almost came out his nose. He wiped his mouth with his forearm and looked around the room.

The beds had both been newly made. The covers were tucked in as tight as ticks about to pop. He raised the Coke to his mouth again. Just before he took another sip, he saw the empty cot. The blanket had been folded into a square, and the pillow had been fluffed and left on top of it.

Brando stood there looking at it. The Coke bottle fizzed away a few inches from his mouth, but he'd forgotten all about it. He'd wanted his brother to get in trouble, to have to sleep on that thing all week. He'd seen it empty and said nothing.

"AAAAAAHHHH!" he yelled at the cot.

His body shook with the effort, and some Coke spilled out and ran down his hand. He looked down at lines of cold, brown liquid and then drew the bottle back like a baseball and threw it against the far wall. The room was still again after that. The only sounds were his breathing and the Coke glugging onto the carpet in the corner. He dared them to charge him for that, too.

He didn't want to be in the room anymore. He walked back to the door and turned the handle, but he let it go again. He walked over to the other side of the room. He pawed through his brother's little stack of books until he found the one he was looking for. *The Hobbit* — he was pretty sure that was the first one. It was the first one Davey had read, anyway. Suddenly, and for the first time, Brando wanted to read it, too.

He tossed it onto his bed, kicked over the cot, and walked straight back out of the room. He wasn't exactly sure where he was going, but he knew it wasn't back to that little office. He walked through the lobby quickly, trying not to look at the people who were looking at him.

"Hey there, hold on," someone said. He was going to ignore them, but something told him to stop and look over. It was probably the English accent.

"Hey, Drew," he said.

"Where you off to?" she asked. Having told them what she knew, she'd been sent to her room, too.

"Not sure," said Brando.

"Hey, let me ask you something," she said.

"Okay."

A couple came through the doors, and Drew motioned him off to the side.

"You're his brother." She was talking more quietly now.

"Yeah."

"So let me ask you: You have any idea where he might've gone?"

"Kind of," said Brando, thinking about it. "Maybe."

"And where's that, then?"

"Somewhere quiet. To read."

"Yeah, right! That's what I think, too. I mean, that's what he was doing when I saw him. Sitting under a tree and reading. Did you tell them that?"

"Yeah, but . . ."

"But what?"

"They didn't listen to me." What he didn't say: *Because I'm a kid, because they think they know better.*

"God, I hate that!" she said, and he could tell she knew what he meant.

A man walked up next to them and unfolded a brightly colored brochure. They took a few steps to the side and spoke even more quietly.

"Do you want to . . ." Drew continued. He could see she was thinking about something.

"Want to what? Go look for him? That's what I was going to do." He hadn't realized it, but as soon as he said it, he knew it was true.

"That's good, but I think we should go find those men."

He nodded.

"That big one, the Coastal Guard, he's . . . different. I don't know, but I think he might listen to you."

"And he's with the deputy," said Brando. The deputy had started to listen to him, at least a little. "Do you know where they are?"

"I know where they were."

"That's pretty good."

"You want to?" she asked again.

Brando had made up his mind. "Yeah," he said. "Definitely."

He started toward the front doors. "Out of our way!" he said to the man hovering with the brochure.

"Hmm?" said the man, still pretending he wasn't listening.

"Not that one," said Drew. She pointed toward the back doors, and they cut across the lobby. They pushed through the doors and past the flyers. They headed out into the light of the slowly setting sun, in search of someone who would listen.

35

Davey was wide-awake again. His nerves buzzed as his eyes scanned the water below him. He'd been riding the adrenaline-rush-to-crash wave all day, and what he had left filled his system. Both his body and his mind were starting to understand that he wouldn't have to do this much longer, one way or the other. If they didn't find him soon, there'd be nothing left to find.

The blacktips were up high now, their fins occasionally breaking the surface. Davey almost liked that. It made them easier to keep track of. With its old territory back, the blue had gone back to circling. The circle was tighter now. Everything was closer to the surface and closer to Davey. The blue's aggression and the blacktips' competitiveness had done that.

The little fish — the four silver-gray and the one bright blue — huddled tightly under the bottle now. Even they sensed the danger in the water.

Davey kicked his feet slowly underneath him. It helped keep him warm and alert. He was also using them as bait. He let them hang down into the water and moved them slowly back and forth.

They were the most obvious targets for the sharks, and he didn't try to fight that. He couldn't watch the whole ocean, but he could watch his feet.

He was so focused on them that a new arrival nearly bumped into him. It was a jellyfish. Its pulpy head pushed to within a few inches of Davey's left arm, which was wrapped around the bottle. He noticed it just in time and kicked himself a little off to the right.

He watched as the thing drifted past, its soft, ghostly head in front and the fine, stinging threads trailing behind. He'd never been stung by a jellyfish. He wondered if it would hurt more or less than a bee sting. But he didn't let himself wonder for very long.

He quickly looked back down at his feet. Nothing. He checked the surface for black-edged fins. Not there. He peered through the bottle again. After a long, bad minute, the blue circled back into view. He located the blacktips a moment later.

He let himself relax, just a little. He had no way of knowing that a much larger animal had slipped into a wider orbit around this little aquatic menagerie. He wanted another look at that jellyfish. It was such a weird creature. The light passed through it. The tentacles moved like curtains in a summer breeze. It could be a creature in *The Lord of the Rings*, straight out of the Sundering Seas. He wondered if J. R. R. Tolkien had ever seen one. Did they have them in England? Or maybe when he was in the army, in the First World War?

He reluctantly took his eyes off it and went back to his grim watch. Thinking about Tolkien had opened something up in him, though. He was looking down into the water, but his thoughts were a thousand miles away. He thought about home. He thought about seeing *The Hobbit* in the Cineplex and knowing before it was even over that he needed to read the books. All of them. He remembered his mom taking him to Joseph-Beth Booksellers and the haul of treasure he'd returned with.

And then he remembered taking that treasure and locking himself into his bedroom with it, as if he lived in the dark and doomed Mines of Moria. Why had he done that again? It seemed so dumb to him now. He had come to understand one thing very clearly during his time in the water: Being alone, truly alone — it sucked.

If I was home again, he thought, *I would take the first book to the living room table and read them all through right there. Mom and Dad would be just through the archway in their office, and Brando would be over on the —*

"Ow!" he said.

He felt a sharp pain on the back of his leg.

The first thing he thought was that he'd lost track of the jellyfish and it had stung him. He looked down into the water behind him. He was blinded by a momentary glare on the surface. When it cleared, he knew he was wrong.

He saw two things. The first: a shape disappearing down and away. The second: a little red cloud, wafting up through the clear water.

It was blood, his own this time.

36

It felt good to be running. Drew and Brando had been tagging along behind their parents all day: asking permission, moving at the speed of grown-ups. Now they were ready to get a move on.

"This way," said Drew, waving Brando over to the right.

"Where are we going?"

"The dock! That's the last place I saw them."

As soon as Brando knew where they were headed, he sped up. He passed Drew, but only for a moment.

"Oh no you don't," she called. She sped up and passed him back. She had longer legs, but was wearing flip-flops; he had shorter legs and sneakers. It was a pretty even race, and they were neck and neck when they reached the dock.

"Not here," huffed Brando.

"Doesn't look like it," puffed Drew. The two launches bobbed on the little waves on either side of the dock. The last time she'd been here, the two men were in the larger one, using the radio. Both of them were empty now. The dock was deserted except for a family of three, sitting on their suitcases, waiting for the next boat.

"Should we ask 'em?" she said.

"You do it," said Brando.

"You shy?" she said, and that did it. Brando marched right out onto the dock. She waited on the sand, catching her breath.

"They said they went that way," he said, pointing down the walkway that led toward the far side of the island.

Drew nodded and then reached down and slipped off her flip-flops. Brando knew he was in trouble now. He took off running. For a good ten seconds, all he could see was the open path in front of him. Then he saw Drew coming into view out of the corner of his eye. He leaned forward and ran even harder, but it was no use. Once he saw the soles of her feet, he knew he had no chance. On the plus side: It took them no time at all to catch up with Bautista and Fulgham.

"There they are," said Drew. She went from a run to a walk in the space of a few strides. Brando slammed on the brakes behind her and just avoided a collision.

Bautista and Fulgham were standing just off the walkway, looking out over the water. Now they looked over. Fulgham leaned in and whispered something to Bautista.

"Yes?" said Bautista.

After running flat out to find them, Drew and Brando suddenly realized that they had no idea what to say.

"Um," said Brando.

Drew gave them a weak wave with the hand that wasn't clutching her flip-flops. She felt a little dumb holding them, so she knelt down and put them back on.

"This isn't really a good time," said the deputy. That was putting it nicely. The island was too small and the boy had been gone for too long. The fact that they'd basically been chasing their own tails all day made it that much worse. "Do you have something to tell us?"

Drew pointed to Brando.

"Um," he repeated.

"Something besides 'um'?" said Fulgham.

Bautista was a little more patient. He'd just arrived, after all. "What's your name?"

"Brando."

"And you're Davey's brother?"

"Yeah."

"And is there something you'd like to tell us?" He wasn't, when it came right down to it, that much more patient.

"Um . . ."

Fulgham leaned over to say something else to Bautista. Before he could, Brando blurted out, "I knew Davey didn't take the boat!"

Fulgham gave him a look somewhere between *Now you tell me* and *Thanks for throwing me under the bus*. But Bautista was more curious. "And how did you know that?" he said.

"Because he's not like that."

"Like what?"

"Davey, he doesn't like, like, loud stuff."

"No?"

"No. He, um, reads a lot, up in his room. Like a not-normal amount. And he took his book with him. His favorite one."

"And he wouldn't go to a busy place like Key West to read a book," said Bautista.

It wasn't really a question, so Brando didn't answer. But Drew added, "And when I saw him, he was sitting under a tree and reading."

"So he found a quiet spot here," said Fulgham, the annoyance gone from his face.

"But then people start walking by," said Bautista.

"And it's not so quiet anymore," said Fulgham. "So . . ."

"He goes to find somewhere that is."

Bautista looked over at Brando and Drew. They both nodded: *Yes, exactly.*

"So, any ideas where he would find a place like that?" said Bautista.

"Whole island's pretty quiet, especially at that hour," said Fulgham.

"Yeah, but we're talking alone-in-his-room quiet," said Bautista. He turned to Brando. "You were all in the same room, right?"

"Yeah. He had the cot." He wasn't sure why he added that last part.

"Right, so he's thirteen, crammed into a room with his whole family, wants some me time . . ."

"There's a roof deck," said Fulgham.

"I was up there, right after we got back," said Drew. "He definitely wasn't there."

"Okay," said Bautista, looking out at the band of sand between the walkway and the water. "What about the beach?"

"People there, too," said Fulgham. "Morning walks on the beach . . . It's a thing."

"Right, right," said Bautista. He'd forgotten about that; it wasn't a thing in the Coast Guard.

Everyone was quiet for a few moments. The only sound came from the small waves and the gulls. Finally, Brando spoke up. "There's a little beach," he said.

"What do you mean?" said Bautista, but Fulgham already knew.

"Oooh yeah," he said. "But you went there, right? Marco said —"

"Yeah," admitted Brando. "We looked around a little."

"And?"

Brando just shrugged.

"What are you . . . ?" said Bautista.

"Little beach, at the end of the island, kind of cut off," Fulgham explained. "It's definitely secluded. People can get a little carried away out there because —"

"Carried away?" said Bautista.

"I didn't mean . . ."

Bautista looked over at Brando, then took another quick look over his shoulder at the water. "Think it's worth a second look?"

Fulgham thought about it. It was a small beach, and it had already been searched. But searched by whom? An upset, untrained family and the hotel manager.

"Might as well," he said.

Brando let out a long breath. Drew looked over at him. "I think this is good," he said.

"Aces," she replied.

They headed straight down the walkway. It wasn't far, and in just a few minutes they'd navigated the narrow path and arrived on the little beach.

"This is nice," said Drew.

Brando looked around. Everything was the same as this morning, except two ladies were sunbathing halfway down the sand. They looked up and saw two men in uniform and two kids in shorts.

"Is it okay to be here?" called one.

"There was no sign," called the other. "Except for that." She pointed to the sad little NO SW MM NG sign.

"No, no, you're fine," called the deputy.

The ladies dropped their heads and went back to catching rays. Bautista had missed the whole exchange. He was walking slowly across the sand and staring straight out at the water.

"Oh no," he said.

"What?" said Fulgham, but then he saw it, too. "Son of a . . ."

"What?" said Brando. He looked out at the water, but all he saw was, well, water.

"Please tell me that's not what I think it is," said Bautista.

"No, I think it might be."

Both men started jogging toward the water's edge. Then they started running.

"What are they after?" said Drew.

"I don't see anything," said Brando.

"It's not . . ." began Drew. She couldn't bring herself to say *a body*, but Brando read the word in her silence.

"I don't see anything!" he repeated.

They took off at a run, too. It was no race this time. There was a bad feeling in the air, like they'd already lost. They caught up with Bautista and Fulgham at the edge of the water.

"Well, I guess we know why that sign's there," said Bautista.

"It's completely inadequate," said Fulgham. "Gonna write about eight citations."

"Make it a dozen," said Bautista. Then he began to walk out into the breaking waves, shoes, long blue pants, and all.

"What's he doing?" said Drew.

Brando had no idea, and then he saw it. The water was higher and the waves were bigger than they'd been that morning. The larger ones tucked themselves into neat little barrels as they broke. They were bigger everywhere, except where they weren't. Where the rip current was cutting them down. Bautista waded diagonally into the stretch of flatter water off to their left. The waves hitting his knees there were little more than bumps on the surface.

Drew saw it now, too. She watched as he waded out a few more steps. He stood still there for a moment, then quickly turned and headed back toward shore. He was a big, strong man, but she could see he was working hard. He was powering his way to shore.

Fulgham saw it, too, and walked toward the water to give him a hand.

"Stay there!" Bautista said. He grimaced and pulled his legs forward through the shallow water.

"The sea is *pulling him*," said Brando.

Drew could hear the horror in his voice.

A few more powerful steps and Bautista broke free.

"Something must've shifted out there," said Fulgham. "Think there's a sandbar. If it'd been this bad for long, someone would've noticed."

"I'm afraid someone might've," said Bautista. He pulled a blocky device from a sheath on his belt. He pressed a button and got static back. "Akers, you copy?" he said. Brando remembered the Coast Guard man in the hotel office.

The big walkie-talkie crackled. "Yes, sir. This is Akers, over."

"Yeah, I need you to get down to the boat and patch me through to Marathon, ASAP."

"Now, sir?"

"Yes, now. Get it!"

"Roger that, sir. I'm gone!"

He turned to Brando and Drew. "Which one of you is the fastest runner?"

Brando pointed to Drew. It didn't hurt his feelings or wound his pride. He was glad she was so fast. Right now, he wished she had wings.

She reached down and slipped off her flip-flops.

"Get back to the hotel and get everyone off those phones and back here. Lead them straight here, to this beach, yourself. I don't want any more confusion today. I don't want any more wrong turns."

He cast his gaze around the edges of the beach. "We're going to turn this place upside down," he added, but Drew was already gone.

37

Davey had been bitten by a shark. It shouldn't have been that surprising; he'd been surrounded by the things. But it was. It honestly kind of blew his mind.

It was a treacherous little nip. The blue shark had tried the direct approach and failed. So it approached slowly and cautiously on the second attempt. It wormed its slender body up through the water behind Davey and gave the back of his right calf a quick bite, just to see what sort of thing this was. Sharks don't have hands, after all. If they want to know what something is, they bite it.

Two rows of sharp teeth punched through Davey's skin, creating connect-the-dot half-moons on either side of his lower leg. Then the blue let go and quickly swam off. It didn't clamp down hard and shake its head back and forth to tear off the meat. This was just a test. It knew there'd be plenty of time for feeding later.

That time had arrived. The blue cut in between the blacktips, emboldened by the blood in the water. The larger sharks swam farther apart and then back together, but they kept coming. They were all converging on Davey.

He pushed the mouth of the water cooler bottle below the surface, allowing some seawater to funnel in. The little fish that had been beneath it were long gone. They smelled the blood, too, and knew to get clear. The bottle sank lower as the sharks got closer. They were close enough to the surface that he didn't need the bottle to see them. Plus, it was his only weapon.

The reality was overwhelming, so he tried to frame it as fantasy. He pretended that the blue was an orc and the blacktips were trolls. The bottle was his wizard staff and sword both. The blue arrived first, and he pushed the bottle forward. It was heavier now that it was partially filled.

BLEHNNK.

It was a slow, glancing blow. The plastic brushed against the shark's gills. It recognized the thing from before, remembered the impact. It veered off to the side. The tip of its long, flat pectoral fin scraped the bottle as it went. And it didn't go far.

Davey located the two blacktips and tried to square the bottle up between them. If they split up, he wouldn't be able to block them both. He had to hope they wouldn't. As he watched the midnight tips of their fins slice through the surface toward him, a new fin rose into sight.

It was fifteen, maybe twenty, feet behind the blacktips. It rose up through the water and kept rising. It was six inches high, then a foot. Davey's eyes were weak, but a bat could've seen the massive shape moving toward him under that fin. This was no orc; the Uruk-hai had arrived.

The blacktips were almost on him. Reluctantly, he shifted his focus back to them. But they never arrived. They sensed the weight and power of the thing behind them. They were as big as pro athletes; the tiger shark was as big as a boat.

Davey wasn't even surprised when the blacktips veered off and dove down. He knew by now that blacktips were a timid, curious sort of shark. He knew just by the fact that he was still alive.

But they knew what they were doing. They would wait for the scraps.

38

They were spread out across the beach. Brando and Drew were working the tree line like monkeys. Pamela had walked all the way to the edge of the beach on one side, and Tam had made it all the way to the other. Marco was pulling a garden rake across the sand in long rows. It wasn't clear what he thought he'd find that way, but he was working hard at it. Sweat dripped from his forehead, and dark stains blossomed under the arms of his dress shirt.

The other hotel employee from the office was walking back and forth across the sand. Even the two sunbathers were doing their part, standing at the edge of the surf and looking out into the water. Deputy Fulgham stood nearby, shielding his eyes with his hand and scanning the horizon. "I should really go back to the launch and get my binoculars," he said to Bautista.

Bautista wasn't listening. He was talking to the Coast Guard station at Marathon. The one at Key West was closer, but he was stationed at Marathon. The radio in his hand had been patched through the more powerful one in his boat.

"I can't confirm anything right now," he was saying. "But that's what it's starting to look like."

And then someone started shouting and everything else stopped. It was Brando. He knew how his brother squirreled things away. He'd seen it many times: money and keys hidden under a hat under a shirt under a towel at the lake; his glasses tucked behind the ladder leading up to a waterslide.

By the time Fulgham and Bautista arrived, Brando was already walking back out from the scrub brush at the edge of the beach. He was crying softly. He had a book in one hand and a pair of glasses in the other.

Drew didn't know what to do and just stared at the glasses. Marco threw the rake down into the sand. Tam and Pamela converged from opposite sides of the beach at dead runs.

"Oh my God," said Pamela.

"No," said Tam. "No."

But there was no denying it anymore, and the two went to pieces after that. Bautista raised the radio back to his mouth. He spoke loudly and clearly so that he could be heard above the sound of it all.

"Station Marathon, this is Lieutenant Commander Bautista. You read me?"

There was a burst of static and then the response: "Roger that. This is Coast Guard Marathon. I got ya, Beast."

He took a deep breath in, pushed it out, and then pressed the button.

"What do we got in the air?"

*　　*　　*

Things happened fast after that. Above them, returning from an uneventful law enforcement patrol, an HC-144A Ocean Sentry radioed in. Lieutenant Commander Chris Abelson confirmed the surveillance plane's position and received his new orders.

"Search and rescue," he repeated. "Roger that."

Up at Air Station Clearwater, Lieutenant Amy Vandiemas had the rotors of her MH-60T turning. She shouted back at one of her airmen to stop moving around. Then, in a practiced, even tone into her headset: "Flight controls are checked. . . . Instruments are checked. . . . All checked." And the big helicopter lifted into the sky.

Back on the island, Fulgham was approaching the dock. His feet were as blurry as a hummingbird's wings as he pounded down the walkway. Behind him, Drew and Brando were doing their best to keep up. It was very clear that Fulgham didn't plan to wait.

Bautista was at the edge of the little beach, trying to reassure Tam and Pamela. "We'll do everything we can," he said.

His eyes scanned the water. Akers was bringing their boat around. Bautista could hear it coming now and waited impatiently for it to appear. Once it did, Bautista strode back out into the water. He grabbed the side and hauled himself aboard. Before his legs even cleared the gunwale, Akers pushed the throttle down.

39

The only reason Drew and Brando made it onto the police launch was that Deputy Fulgham had to navigate through the people waiting on the dock and then spend a few moments casting off the line. When Drew hopped aboard, he spent a few more moments telling her she really shouldn't be there. During that time, Brando hopped aboard, too. The boat was already drifting away from the dock, and Fulgham gave up.

"Fine," he said. "Just put those life jackets on and hold on tight!"

They snapped the vests on and hunkered down as he pegged the throttle. He honked his air horn twice as he zoomed past Captain Zeke's fat-bottomed boat. He carved a wide white semicircle in the water as he swung the launch around and headed toward the far end of the island.

Fulgham was pretty sure they were wasting their energy, but he had to try. If the kid was still alive, they didn't have much time. He'd been at sea far too long already. And if he wasn't, well . . . The body would either get hung up on the bottom and picked clean or would wash ashore on its own. Either way, he'd want to know — he'd *need* to know — that he'd tried his best.

Brando watched the shore until he saw the little beach come into view. He saw his parents' backs as they headed toward the path. Then he turned and began scanning the water. "I'll watch this side," he called over to Drew. "You watch that one!"

"Right!" she said, but she was already doing it.

Fulgham eased off on the throttle as they came up on Bautista's boat, which was floating almost motionless now. Brando looked over and saw Bautista throw something over the side. It was an orange ring with a blinking beacon attached. Drew watched it splash down. It caught the current immediately and began to drift away from the boat.

Fulgham cut his engine, and everything was suddenly quiet. For a few moments, everyone on the water was just watching the orange ring float away. Finally, Bautista broke the spell. "We're right on top of the sandbar," he shouted over. "You go on ahead! I'm just going to take it slow back here. Don't want to over-shoot him."

"Got it!" shouted Fulgham. Then he stepped back into the cockpit and hit the throttle.

Brando and Drew looked at each other as the spray kicked up around them. They knew what it meant. Fulgham had to risk zooming right past Davey. He had to take the chance to try to get there in time. Brando leaned out, his eyes open as wide as he could get them. They were covering water fast, just eating it up at this speed. He scanned the surface, looking for his brother, looking for anything.

Drew did the same, taking her eyes off the water just long enough to check the time on her phone. It was almost six.

Fulgham was thinking the same thing. "I don't like this," he was saying into his radio. "Too long to stay afloat without a life jacket. And that sun's going to go down. . . ."

Bautista was listening in on the other end. He knew what it meant. Once the sun went down, hypothermia would set in. And there was something else. Bautista lowered the binoculars from his eyes briefly and looked down under the surface of the water. *Dawn and dusk,* he thought. *That's when the sharks like to feed.*

But three miles away, the sharks weren't exactly watching the clock. The big tiger shark was bearing down on Davey. It was close enough now that he could see the faded stripes along its back. He had no idea what to do. This thing was blunt-nosed, thirteen feet long, and twelve hundred pounds. It was like a truck coming at him with bad intentions. He gripped the plastic water cooler bottle, but it just felt flimsy and pathetic in his hands.

For a moment, he thought maybe he could swim for it. The shark was moving slowly. But then he remembered: Swim where?

He had nowhere to go. And he was pretty sure the shark could move fast if it wanted to. He was right about that.

He watched, horrified. The thing was five feet away . . . four . . . three . . . He pushed the bottle forward and down. He wanted to get more water into it, to make it heavier.

BLUHMP BLUHMP

Water rushed in and fat air bubbles rushed out.

Two feet . . . one . . .

BLUHMP BLUHMP

This was it. He could see the shark's teeth now. He was close enough that he could see the serrations along their edges. He would be torn apart, mashed and sawed. He pushed the bottle forward at the thing. He was right, it was far too flimsy and light to stop so massive an animal. But the bubbles . . .

BLUHMP BLUHMP

They confused the shark. They hit its nose and slid across its skin. There was a faint, distasteful scent of sunbaked plastic and an odd gurgling sound. The big tiger veered past with a sudden burst of speed.

It brushed by the blue shark, which had slipped around behind Davey again. The smaller shark skittered away.

But once again, neither shark went far. Davey's leg continued to bleed, to bait the water, and they both circled back.

The bottle was heavy in his hands. He'd let too much water in.

Instead of lifting him up, it was dragging him down. The last few bubbles of air slipped out. He kicked hard and tried to lift it out of the water, to dump it out like he had before. But the strength he'd had then was gone now, all spent, and then some.

It slipped from his hands and disappeared. He honestly thought about following it down. It seemed so much more peaceful than being torn apart, eaten alive. But he didn't. He was a quiet kid, but no quitter.

He lifted his head out of the water and took a deep breath. The air seemed delicious to him, and he took another quick breath. He was greedy for it in the way you suddenly want something that's about to be taken away from you.

There was a droning in his ears now. He assumed it was his racing pulse, but his pulse couldn't get any faster and the droning was getting louder. He looked up just in time to see the HC-144A. The drone turned to a roar as it zoomed low overhead.

Treading water now, Davey turned and watched it go. A yellow flash caught his eye as something fell from the plane. Before it even hit the water, orange smoke began pouring from the little canister.

Like the sharks, the plane began to circle around. Unlike the sharks, though, it couldn't reach Davey. The Ocean Sentry is a surveillance aircraft, not a seaplane. Lieutenant Abelson did what he could: "Be advised, we have an update on person in the water." He read off the location, advised the other searchers of the smoke canister, and then added, "We need to hurry on this one. Looks like he's not alone down there."

The smoke signal landed fifty yards away, a good shot if you think about it. Davey swam for it, keeping his eyes on nothing but the billowing orange smoke. The tiger swam slowly after him, with the blue in its wake and the blacktips angling in from the other side.

Of the other searchers, Fulgham was closest. The deputy had overshot him, but not by much. He could just see the smoke now, like an orange cotton ball in the distance. The throttle was all the way down and Fulgham was stomping on the floor, kicking his launch like it was a lazy horse. Brando and Drew held on tight, trying not to get bounced out of the boat as it crashed through the late-day swells.

Davey didn't hear him coming. He barely had the energy to lift his mouth out of the water between strokes. His muscles ached from clutching the bottle all day. His lungs burned and his pulse pounded. Pain shot through his injured leg as he kicked it weakly through the water, but he kept going.

He was moving slowly and had made it a little more than half-way to the smoke by the time the police launch arrived on the scene. Deputy Fulgham saw the splashing first, and then the boy who was causing it. He was amazed that this kid was still on the surface, much less still swimming.

He aimed the boat right for him, but had to cut back on the throttle so he'd be able to stop in time. And then he saw the fins:

dorsal and caudal, and big, very big. He knew it was a sea tiger. It was right behind the boy.

"Oh no," whispered Fulgham.

His hand went to the gun on his hip, but he didn't draw it. He wasn't sure it would stop the thing, and they were a protected species anyway. Tiger sharks might attack a few people a year, but people had killed thousands of them in these waters, just for the sport and the fins. Instead, the deputy got back on the throttle and drove the launch right toward the thing's dorsal fin.

The shark heard the powerful engine getting closer and felt the vibrations shake the water. These were no little bubbles this time. It veered off and dove down. Fulgham let out a long breath.

Drew and Brando had spotted Davey now, too, and arrived at the cockpit.

"Was that a . . . ?" Brando began before swallowing his stupid question. Of course it was a shark.

"Get him quick! Get him quick!" said Drew. She grabbed the orange life ring hanging on the side of the cockpit, but it wouldn't come loose.

"Okay, okay," said Fulgham. He reached over and unclipped it. "I'm going to pull up alongside him, and you toss it to him. Throw it in front of him — don't hit him with it!"

Brando ran over to the side of the boat. "Davey!" he called. "Davey, we're here!"

Davey saw the boat now and changed course toward it. He saw his brother standing on it and waving, but he thought there was a good chance he was hallucinating that part. The boat cruised slowly toward him, and he swam for it. *Please don't let me die now,* he prayed, *not when I'm so close.* He saw the English girl he'd seen that morning, holding a big orange ring. *Yep,* he thought, *I'm hallucinating. Please at least let the boat be real.*

Fulgham edged it slowly forward. He flicked his eyes from Davey to the water around him, scanning for the tiger shark. He knew he'd shoot now if he had to. Drew did the same thing as she waited to toss the ring.

"Come on, Davey!" shouted Brando. "Get out of there, man! Get out of the water!"

What do you think I'm trying to do, Hallucination Brando? he thought.

The boat was close enough now. Fulgham cut the engine, and Drew tossed the life preserver. Davey took a few big swings at the ring and finally got his right arm over and through. Drew tugged him to the edge of the boat. Davey pushed the life preserver aside and grabbed on to the side of the boat with both hands.

Drew reached down and grabbed his right hand, and Fulgham hopped past her to get to his left. Everyone scanned the water. There was still no sign of the big tiger shark. But no one was looking for that sneaky little blue.

The smaller shark surged forward below the surface and clamped on to Davey's leg, harder this time. It swung its head to the side with surprising power and pulled Davey out of Drew's grasp and clean off the side of the boat. Davey's head dipped under the water, and a mouthful of seawater slipped into his lungs.

"Son of a . . ." said Fulgham. His hand was still extended, reaching for a hand that was no longer there. He could see the blue now, a few feet down and clamped on tight. He grabbed for the gun on his hip, but he never got the chance to use it.

Brando took two quick steps, jumped high up in the air, and then tucked himself into a tight ball. He plunged down into the warm, clear water and landed on the blue shark's back.

It was at exactly that point that he realized: *Holy cow, I just cannonballed a shark.*

The blue wasn't much happier about it than he was. This floating thing was a tough meal to get! Reluctantly, it let go. Brando felt its sandpaper skin scrape across his shins as it slipped away. He opened his eyes in time to see Davey pulled onto the boat. His legs disappeared, leaving only a red cloud in the water. A red cloud that Brando was now in the middle of.

As he bobbed back toward the surface, his eyes registered a huge darkness, approaching him like a thundercloud rolling in. He burst into the air, already grabbing for the side of the boat. Two arms reached for him, two hands just a little bigger than his own.

Drew pulled hard. She refused to let go and leaned back as far as she could. Brando's chest cleared the side, and then his hips. Only his legs were still in the water. He kicked frantically.

He looked into Drew's face. His eyes said *Please please please* and *Hurry!*

Drew gave one last tug and fell backward.

Drew's butt hit the deck, and Brando's legs cleared the water.

Fulgham saw that he was aboard, grabbed a towel, and turned back to Davey. The white towel turned red as the deputy pulled it tight around Davey's lower leg. Davey grimaced and then coughed up more seawater.

"Is he?" said Brando

"He'll be fine," said Fulgham, not looking up. "He's lost some blood. We just need to get him to shore."

Brando nodded. "He can have my bed," he said.

Fulgham had no idea what he was talking about. But Davey did. *That really is my brother,* he thought. Despite the pain and exhaustion, he smiled.

Drew heard a noise and looked up. Bautista's boat was easing up next to them. Overhead, she could just hear the first faint sounds of a helicopter's rotors. She looked back down at Davey and shook her head in wonder. *This boy was carried away by the sea,* she thought, *and the world has come to carry him back.*

40

The sun set over the ocean, and that was fine because Davey wasn't in it. He was lying in a clean white hospital bed with fifty-six fresh stitches in his leg. They'd done a lot of work in the little hospital on Key West. Cleaning the wound, cutting away the dead flesh, stitching him up. They'd knocked him out for it, but it was hardly necessary. After it was over, he slept straight on till morning.

For the second day in a row, he'd woken up to the sight of an unfamiliar ceiling. And now, a few hours later, he found himself once again crammed into a small room with his entire family. But they weren't snoring this time; they were talking.

"It's like a Bengals game out in the waiting room," said Tam.

"Browns!" said Brando. He had — in classic Brando fashion — chosen his own team. Two days ago, that was exactly the sort of thing that would've started an argument. Not now.

"It's like a Bengals-Browns game," said Pamela.

Tam and Brando smiled; those were always good games.

"Who's out there?" asked Davey. "Who's waiting?"

"Lots of people want to talk to you," said Tam.

"Like who?" said Davey. Images of state police, FBI agents, and possibly his school principal flooded his mind. He was still having a hard time believing that he wasn't in trouble for causing so much commotion.

"Reporters, for one," said Pamela. "You're big news."

No FBI agents, but that wasn't much of a relief. The thought of TV cameras and tape recorders — of having to explain himself — made him nervous. "Who else?" he said.

"Your aunt from Miami," said Pamela.

"I didn't know I had an aunt in Miami," said Davey. He looked over at Brando for confirmation. He shrugged.

"You *don't*," said his mom. She opened her eyes wide with fake fear.

Davey laughed. He must be big news to bring reporters and crazies to the same hospital.

"Yeah," said Tam. "We might keep that one waiting a while."

"How about forever?" said Brando.

Davey chuckled again. He looked down at the spot where his right arm emerged from under the hospital gown. It was badly burned from a full day of direct sun and devilish glare. He reached up with his right hand and poked a particularly wicked patch just below his shoulder. All he felt was a weird tingle. And now that he thought about it, why didn't his leg hurt more? He couldn't see what was going on beneath all that gauze, but they'd told him about the stitches.

"I'm pumped all full of painkillers, aren't I?" he said.

"Oh yeah," said his mom.

"Big-time," said his brother.

"What if I get addicted?"

"See, that question right there is why you won't," said his mom.

He looked over at the IV bag. It was hanging from a metal hook above his bed. A long plastic tube hung down, ending in a needle that disappeared under a strip of white tape on his left arm. "They're in there?" he said.

"Yep," said his dad.

"What else?"

"Just salt water and some antibiotics, I think."

"Salt water?" he said. "I think I've had enough of that already!"

It wasn't a great joke, but once they started laughing, they didn't stop for a long time. It was pure relief. When they finally stopped, Davey had something else to say. He almost chickened out, but he couldn't. Out on the water, he'd made a promise to himself: If he ever got the chance, he'd say it.

"I missed you guys."

The room was quiet now. It was his mom who spoke first. "It must've been so lonely out there."

He looked at her. They realized at the same moment that he didn't mean he'd missed them "out there," or not only that. He meant before that, too; he'd meant up in his room. Davey looked down, his blush hidden by his sunburn.

"We missed you, too." It was so quiet, barely a whisper, that Davey wasn't even sure who'd said it. It could have been any of them, and that was enough for him.

Someone knocked on the door: three firm raps. Tam straightened up and muscled a smile onto his face. "Ready for the first group of visitors?"

"Not the reporters!" said Davey.

"No," said Tam. "They can wait." He got up and went over to the door. When he opened it, one man filled the entire frame. Davey recognized him from the morning before: the big British guy.

"Thanks for coming," said Tam.

"Wouldn't miss it," said Big Tony. The room seemed smaller as soon as he entered. He was followed by the rest of the family.

"Hi, Drew!" said Brando.

"Hey, B-Boy," said Drew.

Just like that, Davey knew his little brother had a new nickname. Drew pushed Brando in the shoulder in place of a handshake. Then she turned toward the bed, where Davey had something else he'd been waiting to say.

"Thank you."

Drew had expected the words, but not the emotion behind them. All she could think to say was, "It was nothing."

All Davey could think to say was, "It wasn't."

Then suddenly the whole room was talking. Davey leaned back. Brando — or was it B-Boy? — started telling everyone about chasing after Deputy Fulgham and hopping into his boat. How Fulgham hadn't really wanted them there. How they weren't about to ask. After that, he did a spot-on impersonation of "the Beast." Everyone laughed. Davey lay back and listened. He felt lucky to have a brother like . . . well, like whatever his name was now.

And then, as if she was reading his mind, his mom said, "We were lucky."

"How's that, then?" said Big Tony.

"Lucky you were there on that street, that you took the boat you did."

"Oh, that was her idea," he said, hooking a thumb at his daughter.

Drew smiled shyly, slightly embarrassed by what she was about to say. "I thought this was where the party was."

"Yeah," said Brando. "The search party!"

The whole room laughed again, louder now, because there were more people. A few minutes later, a nurse came in with a fresh bag of IV fluid and the Dobkins were ushered out of the room. Brando walked Drew to the door. Big Tony, who'd been first in, was last out.

"I'll see you back on the wee island," he said before ducking out the door. "Business meeting and all that. Hope you don't mind I didn't bring a tie."

"Not one bit," said Pamela.

"I might make one out of a palm leaf," said Tam.

"What was that about?" said Davey once the room was quiet again.

"Oh," said his mom, "well."

Davey waited her out.

"All right, well, it turns out that he works in imports. . . ."

Davey turned to his dad for confirmation. "Thinks there might be a big market for Tibetan goods there in England. As long as they're authentic."

"And of the highest quality," added his mom.

Davey looked at them both. They were wearing cat-that-ate-the-canary smiles that made him smile, too.

"Ready for the next group?" said his dad.

"The reporters?" he said.

"Afraid so. Can't keep them out there forever."

Davey shrank a little further into his bed.

"Don't worry," said Brando, stepping forward. "I can be, like, your spokesman."

Davey sat back up. "Okay," he said. He couldn't think of a better guy for the job.

"Shake on it?" said Brando.

It didn't seem like the kind of thing that required a handshake, but Davey leaned forward anyway. And when Brando reached over and grasped his hand, he understood. His little brother held on tight.

They both did.

ABOUT THE AUTHOR

Michael Northrop has written short fiction for *Weird Tales*, the *Notre Dame Review*, and *McSweeney's*. His first novel, *Gentlemen*, earned him a *Publishers Weekly* Flying Start citation for a notable debut, and his second, *Trapped*, was an Indie Next List selection. NPR recently picked Michael's middle-grade novel *Plunked* for its Backseat Book Club. His latest title for young adults is *Rotten*. An editor at *Sports Illustrated Kids* for many years, Michael now writes full-time from his home in New York City. Visit him online at www.michaelnorthrop.net.

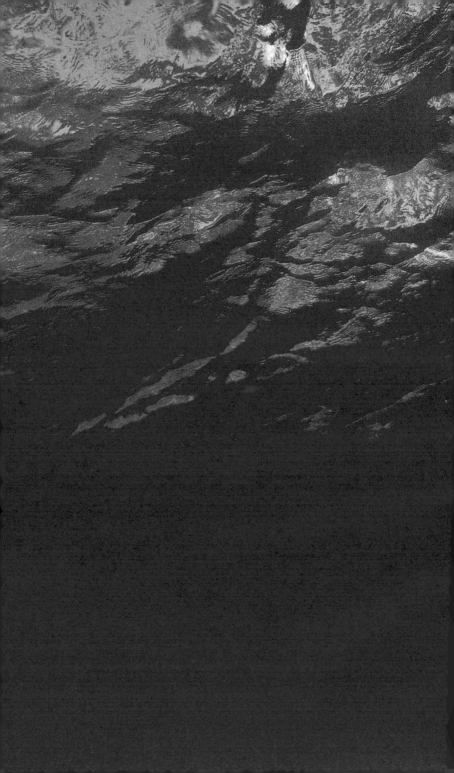

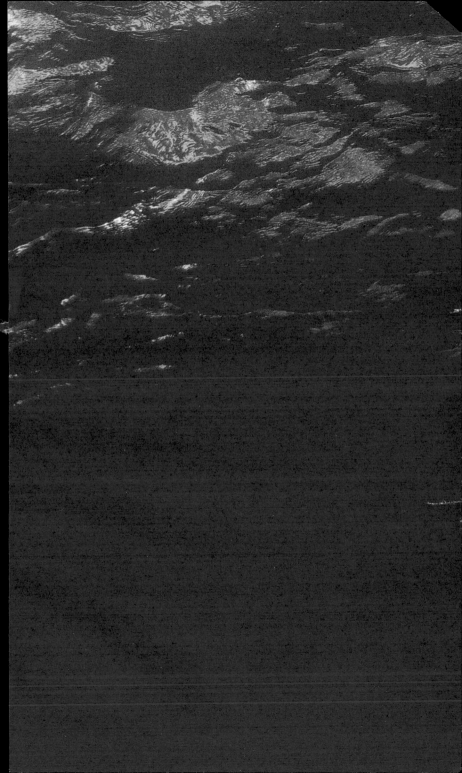